D0418729

THE CROOKED CROSS

THE CROOKED CROSS

Michael Dean

Book Guild Publishing

Sussex, England

First published in Great Britain in 2013 by
The Book Guild Ltd
Pavilion View
19 New Road
Brighton, BN1 1UF

Typesetting in Baskerville by
Norman Tilley Graphics Ltd, Northampton

Printed in Great Britain by
CPI Group (UK) Ltd, Croydon, CR0 4YY

A catalogue record for this book is available from
The British Library

ISBN 978 1 84624 818 4

For Judith

The course of history could have been altered in 1931 if Glaser had been able to insist on hlding an inquest ... [on Geli Raubal]

Ronald Hayman, *Hitler and Geli*

Contents

Part I
September 1931

1

There is no door between the cavernous dining room of Hitler's apartment and the sepulchral lounge. Geli Raubal walked through with a glass of wine. She settled in one of the low, Gerdy Troost-designed armchairs near the fire-place. In the dingy light from a red-fringed lamp-standard, she stared at an art book, open on the occasional table in front of her – *The History of Erotic Art*, by Edouard Fuchs. She knew what it was the prelude to.

On the wall, to her right, were two heavily varnished Romantic landscapes of the Bavarian Alps, by Loewith and Heinrich Zügel. To her left, was a brown Grüzner oil, showing monks tasting wine in a cellar.

One monk, who looked like Falstaff, beamingly held out a glass of white wine to the viewer. Geli hated the false hospitality of the painting. It was a trap – like this apartment where she lived with her Uncle Alf. With an ironic smile, she raised her glass, toasting the painted monk who was toasting her. She sipped her wine.

Hitler made his way toward her, along the massive oak table that dominated the dining room. Watching him draw nearer, she felt contempt for him – contempt laced with physical revulsion.

'I want to draw you,' he said, stopping in front of his half-niece. He had drawn her, naked, three times before. His eye dropped down to the *History of Erotic Art*.

Geli looked up at him from the armchair. 'I don't want

3

you to do that anymore.'

'I want to draw you,' he said again, in exactly the same tone.

'No! I can't.'

'Get ready.' He meant: 'Get undressed.' It was as if she hadn't spoken.

'I'm never going to let you draw me again. I'm leaving here.' She was pleased it had come to a head; she could not have waited much longer.

'Leaving? So you are leaving! You tell me just like that. Why didn't I know about this?'

'Because you would try to stop me.'

'And where do you intend to go, pray?'

She was silent, unmoving.

She had loved Emil from their first meeting in Landsberg Prison when she was a dewy sixteen. She was visiting her Uncle Adolf there, but her eyes had found those of Emil Maurice and never left them. They had expressed their love through music; she sang, he played guitar or accordion. They had written to each other every day.

When Hitler, Emil Maurice and the others were released from prison, his job as her uncle's chauffeur had been the perfect cover for their love. All the picnics he drove them to …

All was well until Emil had asked her uncle for her hand. It was at Hess's wedding. Hitler had gone berserk. Next day, no calmer, he had chased Emil from this apartment she had to share with him. He had brandished a pistol, threatening to kill Emil. And of course threatening to kill himself, as he did all the time.

Emil was Hitler's friend. He was not really a 'chauffeur'. He drove because Hitler couldn't drive. He had known Hitler since the early days, commanding his first bodyguard. He was one of only three people Hitler was on *du* terms with. But still Hitler sacked him – no references. She had begged Emil not to sue Hitler for unfair dismissal; it was too dangerous. But he did. And he won.

With the money he was awarded – a massive 800 marks – he had set himself up in a shop. He was a clock and watch maker and repairer – such sensitive hands, as well as a fighter's tough body and a rather sweet bandleader moustache. He had audaciously chosen a shop round the corner from Hitler's apartment, at the top of Schumannstrasse; number five it was. And there he plied his trade.

By turns appalled and excited by the risks they were taking, they made love at the shop whenever they could. By now, Hitler was having her followed whenever she left the apartment, often following her himself. But as she used to say, giggling, to her best friend, Ello von Hessert, love finds a way. It had become her favourite phrase. Well, love must find a way now.

The armchair was cutting into her legs. She felt heavy, lumpen. She pulled her beige dress down, as she felt him looking at her.

'You are in league with that deceiver,' he shouted. 'The one who betrayed me! The one you wanted to marry.'

She stood and walked off. 'I'm going to my room to pack,' she called over her shoulder. Her voice faltered, belying the confident words. She had made no plans with Emil. How would he receive her? She shook her head impatiently and went 'tsk, tsk' out loud. How could she doubt Emil, even for a second? She hurried to her room and locked the door.

Hitler followed her, his eyes fixed on her back all the way through the dining room. He went to his bedroom, separated from hers only by a bathroom and utility room. The pistol was on a shelf, above his bed. He picked it up, pausing with it in his hand. Facing him, on the wall, was a

Dürer copper engraving: *Knight, Death and Devil.* It showed an armoured knight riding through a forest, with a dog jumping up at his horse. A devil, a grinning death figure, threatened to pull the knight off, but he did not deviate from his goal.

With the pistol resting lightly in his hand, he walked out onto the balcony. The courtyard below was a blur in the wind and rain. Wind-driven spray hit him in the face. He made his way round to Geli's room and in through the unlocked French windows. Her suitcase was open on the bed; she was folding a dress into it. She looked up, slightly startled but no more than that, before resuming her packing.

He pointed the pistol at his head. 'If you leave, I will kill myself.'

She sighed, her eyes rolling in weariness at yet another of his threats of suicide. A reply was beneath her; she smoothed a blouse into the case.

'I will kill myself!' he said again.

She muttered under her breath, but it was audible to him. '*Du lächerlicher Zwerg*' – you ridiculous gnome.

He blinked, furiously. Rainwater dripped off his nose. The person of the Führer could not survive being called that. The Führer would no longer exist; there would be only Adolf Hitler. And that was intolerable to him. He pulled the trigger, to end his life. But somehow it was Geli who lay dead on the floor.

2

Hitler's Private Secretary, Rudolf Hess, was the epitome of The Following, as they were called. He had joyfully relinquished all autonomy as an individual, as if shrugging off a burden. Hess had come up with the *Führerprinzip* – unquestioning obedience to the leader. It was the externalisation of his own psyche. Hess always referred to himself as Hitler's harbinger, the bringer of the leader to his people. The first person ever to call Hitler 'Führer' was Hess.

So, early that Friday afternoon, when he answered a telephone call from Hitler's butler-cum-valet, Georg Winter, telling him Hitler had killed Geli Raubal, Hess was apotheosised, because he knew his service was needed.

His apartment in Löfftzstrasse was outside Munich proper, well into the outskirts, nearly halfway to Dachau. The harbinger drove himself. He didn't use a chauffeur; he was a rally-class driver, as well as a fighter pilot. To the end of his life he could remember every second of the twenty-minute drive to the Führer's apartment; he heard the trumpets of seraphim in his head all the way.

In answer to Hess's volley of knocks, the door to the Prinzregentenplatz apartment was opened by Anni Winter, Hitler's housekeeper. Dressed, as ever, in a floral garment that was as much housecoat as dress, her eyes were gleaming in her aquiline face in a way Hess knew all too well. Anni, too, lived to be of service.

Georg Winter, Anni's husband, appeared. His limp had got worse since Hess had last seen him. He absently saluted his commander, which is what Hess had been in the war. Georg Winter had continued to serve him when Hess had fought in a Freikorps band in the bloody battle against the Councils Republic communists – a civil war which had ripped Munich apart in 1919.

Unlike Anni, Georg Winter looked shaken. With his silver hair, he suddenly struck Hess for the first time as an old man. Hess instinctively turned to Anni for an account of what had happened.

'Well?'

'There was a shot from Raubal's room,' said Anni crisply. 'Herr Hitler has locked himself in his room. He won't answer us. The door to Raubal's room is locked, too. But we can see her through the keyhole. She's dead.'

Even in this desperate situation Anni managed to convey her contempt for Geli in the way she said her name. 'Raubal', in Anni's opinion, was a low-born Austrian slut who was distracting Herr Hitler from higher matters.

Hess went to Hitler's bedroom door and knocked twice, discreetly, with one knuckle. The three of them waited. Silence. Hess nodded to himself, then confirmed that Geli's room was also locked. He did that by gently turning the handle. He then looked through the keyhole, seeing Geli's body on the floor. He straightened up.

'Break it open.'

Old man Winter looked about to shoulder-charge the door.

'No, not like that. Use …' Hess looked round for inspiration. '… use a screwdriver.'

The old man limped his heavy way off in the direction of the quarters he shared with Anni. While he was gone the silence was tense. Anni's skinny figure did not seem

8

to be breathing. There was not a sound from Hitler's bedroom.

Georg Winter returned with a large screwdriver and a hammer. He hammered the screwdriver into the soft wood near the lock until enough of it had splintered for the door to yield to a strong shove by Hess and Herr Winter together.

Inside her bedroom, Geli's blood was darkening, congealing over the wound to her chest. Hitler's pistol lay abandoned on the sofa. A suitcase was half-full of clothes. Both the Winters looked at Hess for instruction.

'Put the clothes away,' Hess commanded Anni Winter. 'Put the suitcase under the bed. Otherwise leave everything as it is.'

'Everything' meant Geli Raubal.

Hess and Georg Winter watched Anni busying about for a moment or so, then Hess turned to the man who had served him for over twenty years.

'What are the Führer's plans? Do you know?'

'He has a Party meeting in Hamburg, sir,' Georg Winter said. 'Herr Schreck is to bring the car in ...' he consulted his watch, 'just over one hour's time. Hoffmann is accompanying Herr Hitler.'

Hess gave a thin-lipped smile at the lifelong servant's ability to convey his opinion of his masters by small signs:

Schreck was nominally a chauffeur, Emil Maurice's successor. But like Maurice and everybody else close to Hitler the menial job designation was misleading. Schreck was so senior in the SS his number was one. Though they hid it beneath a mantle of smooth servant behaviour, both the Winters were terrified of him.

Hoffmann, on the other hand, was regarded by the Winters as a bohemian drunkard and wastrel. They did not consider the way he earned his daily bread – photographer – as an occupation at all. Hess knew better; if asked which of the Führer's inner circle he could least afford to lose,

Hess would have unhesitatingly named Hoffmann.

Now, however, the Deputy Leader of the Nazi Party was mildly annoyed with himself for having forgotten his Führer's itinerary for a moment. Hamburg, addressing a Party rally, pushing Party influence into the north. Of course. Hess made a strange wincing grimace. For the first time he looked odd, even slightly mad. The Winters glanced at each other.

'Yes,' Hess said, speaking to himself. 'The Führer's entourage must break the journey in Nuremberg, as usual. Nuremberg is good. I will make some phone calls to the Party authorities there.'

Georg Winter nodded, showing mute support without understanding remotely what Hess was taking about.

Hess went on. 'But meanwhile we have more immediate tasks at hand. Where are the rest of the servants?'

'I sent them home.' This from Anni. She had finished putting Geli's clothes away.

'Get them back. I will speak to them here in forty minutes' time. I have instructions for them.'

Hess made to leave.

'Yes, sir. But … Herr Hess. I need to speak to you in private.' Anni was as flustered as Hess had ever seen her.

'Oh yes?'

Anni nodded to herself. 'Yes, sir. It's about Raubal. It's … it's important, sir.'

A few moments later Hess was making his way to Äussere Prinzregentenstrasse 10, the home of the Minister of Justice for Bavaria, Franz Gürtner. Handily enough, this was just a cat's jump away, round the corner.

Hess had calculated that there was no time to telephone the Minister's house to warn him of his arrival. And in any case it was more urgent that Anni use the telephone to recall the servants, so he could coach them in what to say. So when Hess rapped on the door of the Minister's first-floor apartment and presented his card to the maid, it was as a caller without an appointment.

Normally, such louche behaviour would be given short-shrift by the meticulously correct Dr Gürtner; the caller crisply dismissed by the staff. But Hess, even out of uniform and in a lounge suit, was an authoritative figure. And he was a senior political ally. He was therefore left waiting in the wood-panelled vestibule for less than five minutes.

During that time Hess planned his line for this coming conversation, on which the very future existence of the Nazi Party depended. He came to the typically shrewd conclusion that giving help can create as much of a debt as taking it, especially in politics. Gürtner had helped the Nazis before, so he must help them again.

Gürtner was a member of the German nationalist Mittelpartei – right-wing, nationalist, monarchist. But, to date, he had helped the Nazis more than anyone on earth, other than Hitler himself. Without Gürtner, Hitler would have been deported back to Austria after the failed Munich Putsch. Even if he had somehow stayed in Germany, he would not have been able to speak in public because there had been a ban on Nazi rallies until Gürtner had it lifted.

The returning maid ushered him into Gürtner's office. Hess had gambled heavily on Gürtner being at home so early on a Friday afternoon. But he knew his man. Most state officials took Friday afternoon off and Gürtner, beneath his stiff carapace of rectitude and correctness, was lazier than most.

'Herr Hess!' Gürtner stood in welcome, behind his desk. 'What an unexpected surprise.'

The tautology, reflected Hess, was typical of a mediocre mind. As Gürtner touched some papers to indicate work interrupted – a fiction Hess was sure – Hess sat down. And came straight to the point.

'Dr Gürtner, I have the sad duty to inform you that Herr Hitler's treasured half-niece, Angela Maria Raubal, has taken her own life. Unfortunately, this tragic event has taken place on Herr Hitler's premises, at his apartment.'

'Indeed? Please convey my deepest condolences to Herr Hitler.'

Hess nodded, only slightly impatiently. He was ready to spell out the implications. Gürtner was not exactly dim, but narrowly constrained, mentally.

'The socialist press would have a field day with this.' Hess meant the Social Democratic Party's newspaper, the *Münchener Post*, scourge of the Right since the Party's early days in the early 1920s. 'At this delicate time, the right-wing grouping could take a heavy blow from which it may not recover.'

Hess's phrase 'this delicate time' was code for the latest sex scandal involving the SA leader Ernst Röhm and large numbers of SA and boys.

'So ...?' Gürtner fiddled with a gold Parker pen, thoughts slowly gathering.

'It would be helpful if the processes involved following a death could be speeded up, so that too much fuss is avoided.'

'Speeded up ...?' The concept was clearly alien to Gürtner.

'A sympathetic coroner would help, greatly.'

Gürtner hesitated. Hess shut his eyes for a second. He simply could not fail, not now, not after the Party had come so far.

But Gürtner had made up his mind. 'All right. I'll make sure it's Müller. He's one of your people.'

He meant a Nazi Party member. Gürtner had nearly said 'your crowd'. He regarded the Nazis as a mob of wild youngsters whose hearts beat for Germany all right but who were a little uncouth, rough at the edges and in need of counsel from time to time from cooler, wiser heads, like his.

Hess nodded. 'Good! And the investigating authorities?'

Gürtner shrugged. 'Much more difficult to control.' His heavy, patrician-looking face creased with distaste at some of the independent spirits to be found both at the Prosecutor's Office, where the worst was Glaser, and the police.

'The best policeman for you is probably Forster, but with a case as important as this his superior, Sauer, would be involved. I could ring Forster. He's a keen enough chap.'

'No, don't. We'll report it in the usual way. Tomorrow morning.'

'Tomorrow? Er …' Gürtner's brow furrowed.

This was the difficult part. 'You see, Dr Gürtner, Herr Hitler was himself present when Fräulein Raubal committed this godless act.' Hess was pleased with 'godless'. Gürtner was a Catholic. 'The *Münchener Post* would make insinu-ations, as is the way with the gutter press. No doubt the Social Democrats will join in. Hoegner and his mob.'

That was clever. The SPD Deputy Wilhelm Hoegner had tried to have Gürtner removed as Minister of Justice. This was for suborning the judge, Georg Neithardt, at the Nazi trial after the Munich Putsch, over the issue of Hitler's deportation to Austria.

One more push: 'Quicker and cleaner to have Herr Hitler clear of the scene, the formalities with Raubal disposed of quickly. What do you think?'

It was masterful. Hess was playing Gürtner like a violin. That final phrase was designed to give the dim plodder the illusion that he was actually making the decision himself, that he had even thought of the plan himself.

Gürtner nodded. It was enough.

Back in the dining room of Hitler's apartment, at 1 Prinzre-gentenplatz, Hess drilled the servants in what they were to say to the police, when they were brought in tomorrow morning.

The only problem was Hitler himself. He had given curt replies to Hess's cajoling and wheedling through the bedroom door, but was showing no sign of unlocking the door, let alone coming out.

Fortunately, from Hess's point of view, Schreck and Hoffmann arrived early. The squarely built, stockily short photographer, red in the face from whisky even at this early hour, had Hitler out in minutes with that jocular tone to which he had a court jester's licence. He was another of the three Hitler intimates who used the familiar *du* form to him, as well as Emil Maurice. The third had been Geli.

Georg Winter, every inch the military man, had Hitler's case packed quickly, even helping the Führer to wash before the journey. Hitler, the while, was stone-faced. He answered one or two routine questions Hess put to him about the meeting in Hamburg, questions designed largely to make sure he had not lost his mind – always an issue. Neither Hitler nor anybody else mentioned the dead Geli Raubal.

As soon as Hitler and Hoffmann were safely on the road, with Schreck at the wheel of the Mercedes, Hess phoned Nazi Party headquarters in Nuremberg. Tomorrow morning, he explained, he intended to phone Hitler's hotel, the Deutscher Hof, with the terrible news that Fräulein Raubal had committed suicide. This news would reach the hotel after Hitler's party had left, to create the maximum fuss and to establish Hitler's whereabouts in another city unequivocally.

By now smiling, Hess asked for the name of any Nuremberg motor-police who were 'reliable' – he meant Nazi Party members – and would be on duty tomorrow. He was given the name of one *Hauptwachmeister* Probst and his telephone number in Nuremberg.

Hess's luck continued. Probst was in when he telephoned and was mightily honoured to receive a telephone call from the legendary Freikorps hero, Rudolf Hess. The next day, Saturday, he carried out his instructions to the letter.

And to the end of his days Hess was secretly amused that a speeding ticket issued by *Hauptwachmeister* Probst to chauffeur Julius Schreck at 1.37 p.m. on Saturday 19 September 1931, was held to provide the Führer with an alibi for the death of Geli Raubal, which had taken place around twenty-four hours earlier.

3

Inspector Forster was not a member of the Nazi Party, but its activities had given him a great deal of pleasure. His local branch, in the suburb of Schwabing, threw its social programme open to everyone. There were regular German Evenings. There was a fancy-dress parade, on Carnival Tuesday. There was a party for Hitler's birthday. Christa Forster hadn't joined any of the ladies groups, as she liked to spend her time with her husband. But the Forsters were in the choir, trained by Sepp Summer, the eminent composer and musician.

Only last week, the Schwabing Nazis put on a theatre performance entitled *Schlageter's Hero's Death*. In vivid tableaux, SA-men acted out the death of the martyr Leo Schlageter, killed by French troops during their wicked occupation of the Ruhr. The Forsters had taken the children along. Little Helga, aged nine, and little Erwin, six, had been saucer-eyed.

After the performance, the branch leader – the tall, scholarly-looking Karl Fiehler – took the Forsters aside. He invited Helga and Erwin to use the 1,000-book SA library, behind a cigar shop in Arcisstrasse, to help them with their schoolwork.

Herr Fiehler laid on fortnightly talks about the Jews, too, at the Blüte Inn. The last one, Forster recalled, was on why women giving birth should refuse to have Jewish medical students present. But dry subjects like that were not

16

Karl-Heinz Forster's idea of an evening's entertainment. He and Christa didn't go.

Early for his appointment, Forster sauntered along the elegant boulevard of Briennerstrasse. As the Brown House, the Nazi Party headquarters, appeared on his right, he glanced up at the Blood Flag on the roof, flapping stiffly over Munich in the autumn breeze. Opposite the house of the Papal Nuncio, the massive bronze doors came into view, topped by the Nazi slogan, 'Germany Awaken'. Forster's permanent smile widened.

He had been told to go in the west entrance, by the cafeteria. At the window of the guard station, he presented the pass, which had been hand-delivered to his apartment.

'*Heil Hitler!*' he said. Forster did not know himself why he said that. He usually said *Grüss Gott*. It just came out.

'*Heil Hitler!*' The brown-shirted guard studied the pass. He was armed with a gas pistol. The SA were not allowed weapons; yet another temporary ban by the Bavarian Parliament. Forster regarded them all as absurd.

'Inspector Forster to see Herr Hess.'

The guard nodded and waved him through. Forster smiled. He was proud to have an appointment with Herr Hess. Herr Hess was a hero of the Freikorps – wounded in the leg fighting Bolshevik criminals. Hess had been a vital adjutant to the revered Count von Epp, leader of the Freikorps group which bore his name – the Saviour of Munich, the Terror of the Reds.

Von Epp, Hess and the rest of the Freikorps heroes had marched on Munich, smashing the Rule of Horror – the Councils Republic, led by the Jew Eisner. Without them, Munich might be under the heel of Marxists, even now. Not to mention the Social Democrat fellow-travellers, who brought Germany the humiliations of the Weimar Republic. Democracy had been tried once and found wanting in

17

Germany. Never again!

Germany Awaken! – as it said on the doors to the Brown House.

Forster made his way into the vast rectangular Flag Hall. There, under four-man guard, lit from above, stood the holy relic of the tattered Blood Flag from the Beer Hall Putsch – Hitler's failed attempt to take Munich by force, eight years ago. The flag was said to be stained with the blood of Nazi martyrs, killed at the putsch, and riddled with police machine-gun bullets. Forster could see neither blood nor bullet holes, but his belief was undimmed.

Eventually, the inspector mounted the Grand Staircase and climbed to the second floor. The double-doors of the Meeting Chamber were open. Forster peered inside. The domed cavern was done out in rich red, with red leather armchairs at the front, like a Doge's Palace.

He walked on, finding himself treading gingerly on the gleaming parquet floor, as he made his way along the apparently endless corridor. The heavy doors had brass nameplates engraved in Gothic script. The corner office was inscribed simply *Adolf Hitler*. Forster stopped, suddenly breathless. An ecstatic feeling came over him, like taking communion in Memmingen church, as an altar boy. He felt purified and safe, deeply content.

This call to the Brown House, Forster thought, must have something to do with the Raubal case. Ribald rumours about Hitler and the delectable Geli Raubal, his half-niece, half his age, had entertained Munich for years.

On Saturday morning, a message had been delivered at Forster's home, from Chief Inspector Sauer. Forster was to meet Sauer at Hitler's apartment, immediately. Fräulein Raubal had been shot dead; it was supposed to be suicide. Forster's smile broadened at the thought, as he was shown into Hess's inner office, by his secretary.

Behind his desk, Rudolf Hess was in full-dress SA uniform, under his portrait by Walter Einbeck, a present from Hitler himself. His right leg was curled awkwardly round the leg of his chair.

'Sit down, Inspector,' he said absently, frowning as the policeman walked the length of the office, an intentionally enormous distance, to the chair drawn up facing him.

Forster sat. He waited.

Hess looked thoughtful. 'An opportunity has arisen, Inspector.' Hess tailed off into a silence so long Forster was apprehensive by the time he resumed. 'An opportunity to serve the Party.'

Forster found himself feeling pleased by that. He cleared his throat, hoping to bring Hess to the point. 'May I make notes?'

'Of course not!' Hess shouted. 'Suppose the *Münchener Post* got hold of them?' Hess's eyes glowed. 'Another sex scandal and we're finished,' he blurted out, with unusual directness and honesty, uncurling his leg from the chair, momentarily throwing his right arm to the back of his head, to regain balance.

There was a long silence. Hess stared at Forster.

'What would you like me to do?' Forster asked.

'Inspector, when your superior, Chief Inspector Sauer, was in the Führer's apartment, investigating the suicide of Fräulein Raubal, certain items were removed.'

Forster was amused, but not surprised. He smothered his smile.

'We need someone to keep an eye on Sauer.' Hess paused again. 'We've put him on the payroll, but we must be sure he does not dispose of the items. It is vital we do not lose track of them. Do you understand?'

'My task would be easier if I knew what these items were.'

'They are drawings. That is all you need to know. If Sauer

tries to sell them, you get in touch with one man and one man only.'

'Who?'

'You contact Georg Winter. He will contact me. You interviewed Herr Winter, did you not, over this unfortunate business with Fräulein Raubal?'

Forster nodded. 'Yes, indeed. I took a statement from him.'

Forster had also questioned Winter's wife, Anni, and one of the other servants. All three were obviously lying. Sauer, as the senior officer, had interviewed Hitler.

'On no account,' Hess continued, 'are you to contact me, ever again. And you are not to mention this discussion to anyone. You hear me?'

Forster nodded. 'Please do not concern yourself, Herr Hess. I will be proud to serve. I will have Sauer watched. I will inform Herr Winter if he sells the drawings.'

'Good.'

The day after his talk with Hess, Karl-Heinz Forster joined the Nazi Party. Christa Forster was delighted. So were little Helga and little Erwin.

4

Public Prosecutor Glaser, in the forty-third year of his life, sat puffing at his pipe at his desk. His tiny office was on the ground floor of the Ministry of Justice in Prielmayerstrasse. The windowless room, an old store cupboard, had been converted for him because of his artificial leg. All the other lawyers were on the third floor.

Glaser always started investigations by summoning every file which could conceivably be relevant. In the Raubal case, there was not much. There were three files on his desk, two buff, one blue. There was also a copy of the *Münchener Post*.

Glaser had put in a written request for another file – Hitler's police record. This was a courageous, or possibly rash, thing to do. However, the request had been ignored.

The thicker buff file was from Chief Inspector Sauer. It was labelled *Investigation into the Suicide of Geli Raubal*. In it were the witness statements, a Cause of Death Report by the police doctor, Dr Müller, and Sauer's own report as head of Munich Police Area Two.

According to Sauer's report, Munich police were notified of Geli's suicide on Saturday, September 19th. Sauer and Inspector Forster took statements from Hitler's staff: the butler-cum-valet, Georg Winter; Anni Winter, the house-keeper; the assistant housekeeper, Maria Reichert, and the maid, Anna Kirmair. They all testified that Geli's body was found in her bedroom at 10.15 a.m.

Dr Müller's report stated that Geli died of inner bleeding

from a gunshot wound to the lung. She had been dead seventeen or eighteen hours, at the time of his examination. So she died in the late afternoon or early evening of Friday 18th, while Hitler was in Nuremberg. On his return to Munich, on the Saturday, Hitler was interviewed by Chief Inspector Sauer, alone, at 15.30. Hitler could offer no reason why Geli would wish to commit suicide.

As ever, Glaser's first step was to separate the facts from surmise and hearsay. The attested facts in the case were as follows:

On Friday, September 18th, Adolf Hitler, the Party photographer Heinrich Hoffmann and the chauffeur Julius Schreck had spent the night at the hotel Deutscher Hof in Nuremberg. Next day, heading north, they were stopped by a car sent after them by the manager of the hotel, Herr Kramer. They were given the news that Hess had phoned the hotel because something had happened to Geli. Heading back to Munich to investigate, they were given a speeding ticket at Ebenhausen, near Ingolstadt, thereby completing a cast-iron alibi.

Glaser turned back to the witness statements. Incredibly, there was no statement from the chauffeur Julius Schreck at all. Glaser tamped down the burnt tobacco in his pipe and relit it.

He turned to Hoffmann's statement: It was two pages long, voluble and rich with extraneous detail. Glaser had known Hoffmann for years. He could hear the photographer's voice as he read. He was sure the statement was his own work.

Hoffmann's colourful description of events has the half-niece, very much alive, waving cheerily from the balcony as the party left: 'Goodbye, Uncle Alf,' she calls out. 'Goodbye, Herr Hoffmann! Have a good trip!'

As they drove away, according to Hoffmann, the Führer had a premonition that something bad was going to happen to Geli. Glaser laughed aloud. This was classic Hoffmann tosh – the Führer's otherworldly, uncanny prescience. They did not come more loyal than Hoffmann. Or more disingenuous.

Like Schreck, Hoffmann was far more important to the Party than his title implied – the title being Party Photographer. The Party's rooms in Schellingstrasse were owned by Hoffmann. They were behind his photographic studio. Two years ago, Hoffmann had become one of what was now eight Nazi Party City Councillors on Munich Council.

Glaser turned to Hitler's statement, given to Sauer, which, like Hoffmann's, did not mention what time he left the apartment. At one point Hitler referred to 'Friday afternoon' but Sauer had not thought to ask him for the exact time.

Glaser grunted, ran a hand over his neatly trimmed full beard and turned to the servants' statements. They were so similar there had obviously been collusion. They were also by far the briefest witness statements he had seen in fifteen years as a Public Prosecutor.

He re-read Georg Winter's statement – the longest of them – torn between rage and amusement: It was dated Saturday, September 19th, 1931.

First thing this morning, at nine-thirty, my wife informed me that something must have happened to Raubal, because nobody could get into her room and Hitler's pistol, which was kept in an unlocked cupboard next door, was no longer there. So I knocked on the door of her room again and again but got no answer. It was looking suspicious to me, so I forced the locked double-doors, at ten o'clock, with a screwdriver. When I opened the door, my wife, Frau Reichert and Anna Kirmair were there. As soon as I had got the door open, I went into the room and found Raubal lying on the floor dead. She had shot herself. I can give no reason why she should have shot herself.

Glaser turned to the blue file. According to his tax returns, Hitler had earned 1,232,335 marks in the last tax year from *Mein Kampf.* His industrialist friends, the von Hesserts, were paying the rent for Haus Wachenfeld, his country retreat in Bavaria, and for the Prinzregentenplatz apartment – the latter a massive 4,176 marks a year. More than twice, Glaser reflected, puffing at his pipe, what he paid for his pretty decent family apartment in Galeries-trasse. The NSDAP – the Nazi Party – paid for the Mercedes, 26,000 marks, and the salaries of the servants.

On to the next file, the thinner buff one: the police record of Julius Schreck. In his prison photograph, the chauffeur bore a strong resemblance to Hitler. He had several convictions for theft, deception, assault and affray.

A small-time crook, then, but he had co-founded Hitler's Personal Protection Guard, the *Stosstrupp-Hitler,* and ex-panded it to form the SS, which is why the first SS-brigade was named after him – *Standarte-I Julius Schreck.* Like all Nazi top brass, the Party paid him in inflation-proof Swiss francs.

Glaser turned to the report of Geli Raubal's death in the *Münchener Post.* He read it slowly, again smoothing his beard with his left hand – a sure sign he was worried.

As a lifelong social democrat, a card-carrying member of the SPD, Glaser knew all the *Post's* journalists well. He had warned the editor, Erhard Auer, to be careful about the Geli story, but Auer, a big bear of a man and too brave for his own good, had gone his own way, as ever.

The report on Geli's death carried Julius Zerfass's byline. Worse and worse, thought Glaser. He had known the cultured, elegant Zerfass for twenty years. He was the news-paper's articles editor. He knew nothing about crime.

Nevertheless, the *Post*'s coverage of Geli Raubal's death had certainly struck home. Glaser knew Hitler had sent his personal lawyer, Hans Frank, round to the newspaper's offices at Altheimer Eck with threats of a lawsuit. The night-time telephone threats to *Post* journalists had started. Whether or not they sent the SA in again remained to be seen.

The report was headlined 'A Mysterious Affair: Suicide of Hitler's Niece'. A wave of depression hit Glaser. He so much wanted the *Post* to be right, but he was more and more convinced they were not.

There was an allegation in the *Post* article that Geli's nose was broken and her body beaten. Glaser shrugged and shifted at his desk, easing his leg. He simply didn't believe it. He thought Hitler capable of shooting Geli; indeed, all his instincts were that he had. But beating her? It just didn't ring true.

Glaser leaned back in his chair, his eyes twinkling as he puffed his pipe, because what he was going to do defied procedure. He would speak to the police pathologist Katherina Bandl. He would ask her what she really thought, before she wrote a report, which she would have to sanitise if it incriminated Hitler.

And there was something else he would do: He was due to see his friend Ascher Weintraub this evening, at the gallery which bore the good old man's name. They would discuss art, as they always did. Glaser would then ask Ascher Weintraub what he thought of the *Münchener Post* report. This was a most irregular act for a public prosecutor; but Ascher Weintraub knew as much about Hitler as any man alive.

Glaser was looking forward to the discussion so much he pictured the old man in his mind and could almost taste the lemon tea they would drink together. But first there was Katherina Bandl.

25

5

Katherina Bandl had agreed to Glaser's request to examine Geli's body, as he knew she would. There was no question of discussing the death of Hitler's half-niece anywhere within the precincts of the Ministry of Justice. It would not have been safe. They arranged to meet for lunch at the Tiroler Bräu.

The Tiroler Bräu was packed. Prosecutor Glaser peered through the fug of smoke. The place had been designed in the early 1920s. It had high wooden banquettes with plush red seats and seat backs forming walls round three sides of every table. Many tables were in niches or on a dais or set at an angle.

He found Bandl in one of the many side-rooms. She was built to Bavarian proportions. Her cardigan stretched over bulging shoulders, her neck was thick, her round head large. She had managed to keep a table for six empty, except for herself.

Behind her, on a hook on the wall, hung her green felt hat with its jaunty feather and her green Loden coat. On the wooden table in front of her was a huge shank of roast pork on the bone, a side dish of potato salad and a litre mug of beer. At her feet lay her dachshund, Mitzi, its leather lead loose in her tweed-skirted lap.

'*Mahlzeit*, Frau Bandl,' said Glaser, touching his trilby to her. The 'Frau' was a courtesy title. Bandl was not married. She was ageless – anything from thirty-five to fifty; sexless –

Glaser had never heard her mention any emotional attach-ments; and, as far as Glaser knew, completely apolitical.

'*Servus*,' the pathologist replied, with the briefest of pauses in her chewing.

Glaser hung his hat and coat up next to hers and sat opposite her, easing the artificial left leg in under the table first. She broke off a piece of pork shank, so dark the inside was purple, then held it under the table. Mitzi lapped at it. A waitress started toward Glaser, but a dinner-jacketed head waiter, taking in Glaser's dark suit, wing collar and look of authority, waved her away and came himself.

Glaser chose baked trout with boiled potatoes, a tomato salad, and a dry Müller-Thürgau to wash it down. His round face beamed at Katherina Bandl. He was relaxed, or rela-tively so.

'I don't know whether I have good news or bad for you, Herr Glaser,' the pathologist began. 'But I agree with you about the *Münchener Post* report. It's wrong.'

'He didn't beat her up?'

'No, no, no. There is damage to the nose, as the report says, but it's more likely to be from a fall than a punch.' She looked at him piercingly, with shrewd small eyes. 'But as to the so-called bruising on the body, here, we can be one-hundred-per-cent sure.'

'And?'

'It isn't bruising. It's hypostasis.'

Glaser's wine arrived. He took a sip, nodding in reluctant appreciation. He had been born and brought up in wine country, Ludwigsburg, near Stuttgart, in Swabia, and made no secret of his disgust at the typical wine-offerings at the temple to beer that was Munich.

'Hypostasis,' Bandl continued, 'is also called post-mortem lividity. When the heart stops beating, the blood sinks to the lowest vessels in the body, causing livid patches on the surface. It looks like bruising, but it isn't.'

Glaser nodded. He knew all that, but excitement was pricking at him. 'Can you use it to determine time of death, in this case?'

Bandl smiled faintly, appreciating Glaser. She liked him and let it show. Mitzi snuffled in protest at the cessation of the food supply, forgotten during the account of hypostasis. A hunk of meat was dropped down to the dachshund. Frau Bandl was enjoying herself.

'Up to a point,' she said. 'The discoloration starts soon after death. The small patches fuse together and become distinct after twelve hours or so.'

'So had Geli been dead for more than twelve hours when Müller's examination was carried out?'

Glaser's food was put down in front of him. He realised he was hungry when he started eating. He hadn't eaten up to then. He had forgotten to.

'That is almost certain,' Bandl said. 'Rigor mortis takes from ten to twelve hours. The body loses eight degrees in the first four hours but only about one degree an hour after that. On occasion, that makes measurement tricky. But you are in luck.'

'I am?'

'Yes. I took blood and urine samples.'

Glaser looked at her, alarmed. This examination was off the record. Bandl had jumped the gun. He nearly said 'be careful' but realised it was a little late for that.

'And?' he said.

'She had had a drink before she died. White wine, like yours.' They both managed a grim smile.

'And that helps?' Glaser asked.

'Certainly! When you drink, the alcohol content in the blood and in the urine stay about the same. Maybe one to one point three at the most. But alcohol in the blood diminishes by oxidation after death; in the bladder it remains constant. It's a good indicator of time of death.'

Glaser nodded. 'And in Geli's case?'

'The deceased's urine had nearly five times as much alcohol as in the blood. The time of death was much earlier than Müller recorded. She had certainly been dead for at least eighteen hours, more likely as much as twenty or even twenty-four hours. I would testify to that. *If* I were testifying, which I won't be, of course.'

Glaser nodded. So now he knew. Geli had been shot some time during the Friday afternoon, probably early on the Friday afternoon. She had been shot before Hitler left for Nuremberg. His so-called alibi was nothing of the sort.

'Did she die quickly?' He asked that one for poor Geli.

'I'm sorry, Herr Glaser, anything but. A slow death, in pain.' She looked at him sympathetically and dropped Mitzi a huge chunk of meat. 'The deceased had leucocytes, white blood cells, round the area of bleeding. Lots of the little fellows. Very pretty under a microscope. That shows that life continued after the infliction of the injuries. As it would.'

'Would it?'

'Most certainly. The shot missed the heart completely. That's even in Müller's report, though damn all else is.' Frau Brandl took some vigorous gulps of beer. She banged the empty mug down, meaningfully.

'Would you like another one, Frau Bandl?'

'Thank you.'

Glaser waved a waitress over. She was balancing a flat board with six brimming mugs of beer above her shoulder. Glaser nodded at his own beer mat, to say he was paying. The waitress put a beer down. As she walked off, she scored his beermat with a stroke from a stubby pencil.

'Poor Geli!' he said, when the waitress was out of hearing.

'I don't know if our friend knew this,' Bandl said cautiously. She meant Hitler. 'But if a doctor had been called immediately, she could have been saved.'

Glaser was suddenly tired. 'I wish you hadn't said that.'

'You're not the only one who'd rather remain in ignorance these days,' Bandl said.

She gave a rare smile. She was a comrade-at-arms, Glaser thought warmly.

Bandl took a massive swig of beer.

'Anything else?'

'Plenty!' said the pathologist, with a hint of irony. 'The angle of entry of the bullet does not rule out suicide, but it makes it unlikely. It's something like this.'

Putting her stein of beer down, Bandl took her knife in her left hand and held the blade almost under her armpit, pointing steeply downwards. 'Damned uncomfortable,' she said. 'Very unlikely for self-inflicted. If you ask me, the deceased twisted her body sideways at the last moment, trying to get out of the way.'

Glaser nodded, leaving the rest of his food. 'Yes. I see.'

'And in any case,' Bandl said, warming to the theme, 'very few women shoot themselves. I can't think of any, in my experience. Can you?'

'Actually, no.'

'As you surely know, Herr Glaser, women are killing themselves in Munich every day. Mainly Jewesses. They all use Veronal. You can get it easily, at any apothecary. And it's painless. So why use a gun?'

'Why indeed?' Glaser sighed, the cares of the world on his shoulders. He was about to offer to drive Bandl home. He had a so-called Opel Frosch, converted so he could use his right leg only. He knew she didn't drive.

'There's one more thing. Of possible interest.'

'Go ahead.'

'Geli was pregnant. Just starting to show.'

6

The Weintraub Gallery, in Lenbachplatz, was Munich's leading gallery for Expressionist painting, but it was minute – one square whitewashed room. Ascher Weintraub unlocked the door to Glaser before he had time to knock, as he always did. Then he stood there, beaming, tiny, as he let his lawyer friend in.

The art dealer, when fully extended, reached the middle of the lawyer's sternum. As ever, he was wearing a dark suit, too small even for him. The sleeves left not only his wrists but half his skinny arms bare. As ever, the soft wing collar and once-white shirt managed to look ancient without being actually grubby. The habitual black tie was permanently at half mast.

And above that, the remarkable face Glaser never tired of gazing at, beamed up at him, in welcome. His head was long but the bottom part was entirely hidden by a thorn bush of a beard, brown with chestnut highlights, too thick to let the welcoming smile change its shape much. The smile splayed the spatulate nose a bit. Above that, surprisingly small dark eyes glowed.

'Gerhard! How are you?'

'Ah! Ascher! I'm fine. It's the world that's the problem.'

The old man laughed, waving vaguely with one hand which was too big for its skinny bare arm, partly in welcome but partly to indicate the latest selection of Expressionist paintings, leaping out from the whitewashed walls with their

31

glorious emotional colours.

'Thanks!' Glaser said heavily, as if the art dealer was actually giving him the paintings, which in a sense he was. 'I need this!'

And he was not disappointed.

'A Macke! An August Macke! An early work, surely?'

Glaser struggled out of his mac – it was warm in the gallery – as if about to perform some votive ceremony before the painting.

The art dealer's smile grew wider, slightly thinning the foliage of his beard. 'It's called *Anglers on the Rhine.*'

And there it was, all subdued blues and greens, reminding Glaser of another image in his heart – Ensor's *The Poachers.*

'How does he do it?' Glaser was speaking softly, his voice croaking slightly. He spoke like that to Lotte – his wife – before he made love to her. And that was not only out of love but because he still found Lotte naked movingly, unspeakably beautiful.

'Oh, he does it from love.' Ascher's voice was surprisingly light, even for a small man. Youthful. Glaser still hadn't got to the bottom of that accent. It might be Viennese.

But Ascher was speaking on: 'You see, he isn't painting anglers and he isn't painting the Rhine – at least not only anglers and not only the Rhine. He's painting the soul of the Rhine, the soul of the landscape. When he was painting, his darling Elisabeth was next to him. His soul is going out to her soul as he paints. So the colour of the anglers and the Rhine represents his love for Elisabeth, his soul and her soul in the shape of anglers and a river. He is painting love. He has unified the world he sees with the world he feels in one glorious loving pantheistic statement'

Glaser felt the feather touch of the old man's hand on his jacket sleeve, indicating they should go through to his office now. Weintraub knew better than to try to lead him. Any touch Glaser was not ready for could overbalance him, because of the leg business.

They found themselves on either side of Weintraub's desk, which, along with the large old-fashioned safe, took up most of his box-like office. Lemon tea was poured; a plate of *kichlach* stood ready to be nibbled but was being ignored.

'Tell me about Elisabeth,' Glaser said.

He knew Macke's childhood sweetheart was called Elisabeth, but he knew no more than that. But that was always the case, in his discussions with Ascher Weintraub. The old man always knew more, understood more. It was the understanding Glaser wanted, more than the knowledge. He imbibed wisdom from the frail old man. It was nourishment to his heart and soul.

Weintraub nodded absently, taking a minute bite from the outer edge of the sugared biscuits stuffed with fruit and a matching dolls'-house-sized sip of tea.

'They were so young. So young …'

Tears sprang to Glaser's eyes. August Macke was among the first casualties of the war, killed at Champagne seventeen years, almost to the day, before he and Ascher Weintraub sat discussing his amazing work.

'He was at one with the seasons; he saw everything as if it were a Japanese woodcut.' The old man was speaking as if intoning a prayer. Glaser was so rapt he was holding his breath. 'You see, he and Elisabeth wandered the Rhine; Lengsdorf, Ippendorf, their favourite one, Messdorf, Grau-Rheindorf on the lower Rhine. All day. Endless summer days of youth. And all that time their youthful beautiful souls entered the landscape he was painting. They were physically beautiful, as well, of course, both of them.'

Glaser joined in. It was like a catechism. 'So when Macke later came to paint masterpieces like *Girls under Trees*, it wasn't necessary to paint the faces of the girls …'

33

The old man was nodding. 'Exactly. Because their souls had entered the trees around them and the souls of the trees had entered them. One of the girls has a diagonal formed by her hair and part of her dress, down her back. Like the trunk of a tree. It's the most glorious pantheistic statement in all art.'

'All those curves!'

'Full of love and beauty and youth. Have you seen any of Macke's portraits of Elisabeth?'

'No, never, could you ...?'

The old man nodded absently. 'I'll see if I can get you copies from Hanfstaengl or somebody. One of them was called *Nude with a Coral Necklace*. Painted in 1910, it was. The year art died according to *Mein Kampf*. Elisabeth was a very beautiful woman and in this one we see her naked. We see her bare breasts. But, Gerhard, nothing could be less lascivious than that portrait. Yes, she is aesthetically beautiful but what we see through the beauty is love. A love that blazes with quiet but beautiful fire.'

There was silence between them for a while. Silence but no unease. Glaser's mind was spinning. Lotte. The children, Kaspar and Magda. Running through the maize fields in his boyhood in a little Swabian village.

'Do you still ...?' Glaser hesitated. It could have been a bright keen student asking a nervous question of his professor. 'Macke and Franz Marc ...?'

The two knew each other so well that their conversations frequently covered some of the same ground before pushing off into new aspects, insights or directions. One of the oldest of their old chestnuts was the comparison between two great Expressionists, close friends, both killed in the war – August Macke and Franz Marc.

Glaser was the champion of Marc, the painter of many studies of blue horses, mainly, but also yellow horses, pink horses – all glorious colour. For all the fabulous

Expressionist passion and sensitivity of Macke, Glaser saw Marc as harder, clearer, more masculine, if you will.

'My Munich man,' murmured Glaser with a smile. Marc had been born in Munich.

'Oh, August and Elisabeth loved Munich, too,' Weintraub said. 'Elisabeth had an uncle here. She loved the Englischer Garten. Not that I hold any brief for Munich. Not at the moment anyway.'

Glaser's mind raced. That was the nearest Weintraub had come to talking about the dire political situation. He could ask him about that. Or he could use the opening to probe, not for the first time, into where Weintraub was from and how he had ended up here.

But every moment with this man, with this wise magician from a fairy tale, was precious. Putting his forensic court-room training into play, Glaser led the old man back to the path they loved to walk together, the Expressionists.

'Marc's colour theory ...' Glaser began.

'Pah!' The old man did actually spit, though he had not intended to.

A flapping wave of a too large cuff and skinny arm brought Glaser to a halt. He would not have taken that from anybody else on earth. His colleagues at the Ministry of Justice, even Lotte, would have been amazed to see the splenetic, touchy, peppery Glaser behaving so meekly.

'Marc's colour theory!' repeated the old man, packing scorn accumulated over decades into the phrase. 'Yes, blue horses masculine, yellow horses feminine, pink ... It's rubbish. Absolute rubbish. Never trust an artist when he talks about his own work. They know less than the well-attuned viewer. A lot less. Marc wrote that in a letter. Maybe he was drunk ...' Glaser was laughing. 'Listen! Marc's horses are blue because blue horses are beautiful. And different. The unexpected is good art. The only thing you can say for Marc that is maybe above Macke is that he represented the beauty of the soul through shape as well as colour. But Marc is merely transformational. Macke is sublime.'

It was late in the evening before Glaser pulled the *Münchener Post* cutting from his pocket. As ever, or so it always appeared to him, Weintraub was ahead of him.

'What's that? The *Post*? Seen it.' Arm flap, hand wave like a dying kipper.

'And? What do you …?'

'Pah! S'rubbish!'

'Don't beat about the bush, Ascher, will you?'

'Rubbish is rubbish, Gerhard.'

'All right. Why?'

'Why? Why? Ever the bloody lawyer. What do you mean, why? Have they given you Geli's case?'

'Yes.'

'*Oy vay!*'

Glaser laughed. Weintraub had accompanied the Yiddish imprecation with a satirically Jewish shoulder shrug. All the Jews Glaser knew sent themselves up. It was one of the things Glaser liked about the Jews. One of the many things.

'About Hitler, Ascher. Tell me.' Glaser spoke softly, coaxingly. Now, nearer his own ground, they were public prosecutor and expert witness, no longer professor and student.

'You *are* worried, Gerhard, aren't you?' Small hand flap.

'Yes. How do you know?'

'You're breaking protocol. Stickler like you. Tut tut tut.'

Weintraub said the word, rather than tutting. Glaser laughed again.

'All right, Gerhard. The *Münchener Post* … It's totally wrong, sad to say.'

They were both silent a moment, as if in tribute to the brave fight the newspaper had put up against the Nazis since the early 1920s. Their offices and printing presses had been attacked, time after time, their journalists libelled, threatened and beaten up, and calumny after calumny had been thrown at them, often in the courts.

Glaser sighed. 'That was my impression, too. But go on.'

Ascher Weintraub suddenly looked tired, even a little afraid, his shoulders slumping.

'It is just – *just* – conceivable that Hitler got Geli to beat him. But him beating her? Bruising her nose? Never!'

'The pathologist said the same thing. But I'm curious, what makes you so sure?'

'Hitler's father beat his mother, the woman he loved above all others. Hitler identified with the mother, not the father.'

'And how do you know that?'

'It's in *Mein Kampf.* You read it?'

'No. Is it good?'

'Terrific. They should make a film of it. I'll be in touch with Sam Goldwyn in Hollywood.'

Glaser belly-laughed, big shoulders heaving.

Weintraub shook his head in mock sadness. 'Hitler is a sexual submissive.'

'Could he have shot Geli? Do you think?'

'Yes. That's conceivable. Provided it wasn't premeditated. Heat of the moment. Very powerful reason, maybe. Something that threatens him in a big way.'

Glaser was nodding. He packed and lit a pipe. 'Ascher, may I ask you something? How do you know so much about Hitler?'

'Oh … He used to be a client of mine.'

Glaser telephoned Lotte from Ascher's office, to say he would be home very late. An unsurprised Lotte said she would go to bed and asked him to be quiet when he came in, so as not to wake the children.

Glaser nodded into the telephone receiver. 'Lotte. I love you.'

There was a silence at the other end. Lotte Glaser knew that her husband loved her but it was first time he had said so since their courtship. The silence continued. Then: 'I love you, too, Gerhard.'

She rang off.

'Hitler …' Glaser prompted the witness.

'I knew him in Vienna,' Weintraub said flatly.

Glaser's mouth went dry. He hardly dared breathe. Ascher had never spoken about his private life before, despite frequent prompting. Glaser knew he was not married. He knew he had a sister, Professor Zipporah Ballat from Munich University. He thought Ascher lived with her, but he was not sure even of that.

'Go on.'

Glaser was afraid of breaking the spell but the art dealer was clearly in the mood to talk.

'This was the golden age in Vienna, Gerhard. The time of Klimt and Kokoschka. Hitler was selling his drawings. Making a good living at it, too. Earning 100 marks a month. And that's on top of his inheritance from his father and his orphan's pension. All that down-and-out stuff he wrote about in *Mein Kampf* is *laute Scheisse*.'

'And you …?'

'Yes, I bought his drawings and paintings. Most of the dealers who did were Jews. Maybe that's why he doesn't talk about it. And no we didn't do him down.'

'You don't have to say that to me, Ascher!' Glaser spoke hotly, almost yelling, the temper that flared with everyone but Weintraub now seen in this office for the first time.

Weintraub was surprised, even shrinking back for a second. He smiled faintly, moving the beard-bush. 'No. I know I don't. You see … Hitler imbibed the anti-Semitism from Schoenerer and the others on the streets of Vienna. It was all in pamphlet form. Ideal for him. He doesn't read too much. Gives him a headache. Where was I?'

'Tell me about Hitler's art.'

Weintraub shut his eyes, in for a long talk. 'Well, first of all he was unlucky not to get into the Academy. Very unlucky … He passed Part I, the first time. That was … 1907, I think. Yes. He failed Part II that year but so did some quite good people. You know Robin Christian Andersen?'

'Heard of him.'

'Well he failed Part II. Same year. And he ended up a teacher at the Academy.'

'So … this Part II is …'

'Part II is where the candidates present their own work. So Hitler works for the next year with a teacher. Good man. Name of Panholzer. A friend of mine found him for Hitler. And he worked hard for that whole year. I saw some of his portfolio.'

'And?'

'He's a good draughtsman. A very good draughtsman. He's got no depth and no soul, but he could easy make a living from architectural drawings, or technical drawings, maybe even landscapes. He does good competent work. Easy good enough to get in to *any* art academy.'

'So what happened?'

Weintraub shrugged. 'When he takes the examination again, next year he fails Part I, the set subjects. The part he passed the previous year. Just bad luck. They choose some terrible subjects, you know, the Academy. The Blinding of Samson. That kind of thing. So he never got a chance to show all the very good stuff he had done with Panholzer. The work which would have been submitted in Part II and got him in.'

'And if he had got into the Academy …?' Glaser mused.

'Aaagh, well! He would have had a career as an artist in Vienna. No doubt. He would never have come to Germany.'

39

Glaser put his pipe down on Weintraub's desk and put his head in his hands for a moment. Then: 'I wonder who chose the subjects that year. 1908? Yes? I wonder who did the judging. On such moments …'

'Yes. I tell you who chose the subjects. I tell you who did the judging. The devil, that's who.'

'Do you know, Ascher, the way things are going in Germany, I think you may be right.'

7

To Glaser's fury it was two days before the Minister of Justice, Franz Gürtner, agreed to see him to discuss a post-mortem on the body of Geli Raubal. Twice during those two days Lotte had asked him not to take his anger out on the children. This had been modified, during what amounted to a row, to a request not to let his anger show in front of the children.

Now, finally, Glaser was making his way to the rickety lift which Prielmayerstrasse thankfully possessed, in plenty of time for a two o'clock appointment at Gürtner's top-floor office.

The relationship between the two men, as Glaser acknowledged to himself, was dreadful. Glaser could not contemplate the man without the deepest indignation and disgust. Gürtner had excluded Glaser's friend and fellow Social Democrat, Philipp Loewenfeld, from Hitler's Beer Hall Putsch trial because he was Jewish. The grounds had been that his presence might have provoked a breach of the peace.

The courts under Franz Gürtner became places where Jewish lawyers were liable to face orchestrated low mutterings of 'Jew-Jew-Jew' as soon as they stood, continuing for as long as they spoke. Whenever a Nazi came before one of the Jewish judges, the judge would face a named attack in the Nazi press as part of the 'Jewish takeover' of German justice which was making it impossible for 'core Germans'

41

to get a fair trial. Any man of the law so named by the Nazis found advancement in Gürtner's justice system closed to him.

As the lift jerked its painful way upward, Glaser reviewed his attempt to finish Gürtner once and for all. In 1924, just after the scandalous Hitler Putsch trial, which had sent Glaser into a blinding rage, he had given every scrap of information he could about Gürtner to the only person of influence who would listen, the young SPD member of the Bavarian Parliament, Wilhelm Hoegner.

He and Hoegner had several meetings and became close. Hoegner had come to the Glaser apartment a couple of times. Glaser offered to testify against the Minister of Justice, accusing him of bias and exerting improper influence to prevent Hitler's deportation back to Austria.

As a state official, testifying against his superior would have ended his career as Public Prosecutor. Glaser said he didn't care, he would do it. Hoegner advised him to stay in the background. But he used the evidence Glaser assembled to make a brave and fiery speech to the Bavarian Parliament.

Glaser, against Hoegner's advice, listened from the public gallery and stood and applauded at the end. But the SPD were in a minority. Gürtner and the Far Right rode out the storm. Glaser was yet again left ruing Hitler's luck – Germany's misfortune.

He shook his head, literally shaking off the memory. He must get the Minister of Justice to agree to a post-mortem on Geli's body. To do that he had to establish at least some grounds for a formal indictment of Adolf Hitler for murder.

The two men of the law faced each other across the desk in the Minister's office. Out of the window, Public Prosecutor Glaser could just see the spire of the Lutheran Church in Arcisstrasse.

Dr Gürtner was seven years older than the Public Prosecutor, but the difference appeared far greater. His sleek grey hair was thinning; the moustache over his narrow upper lip was completely grey. His blue eyes stared dully through rimless spectacles. His head, thought Glaser, was as narrow and rigid as his principles. Even Hitler had referred to him as 'very correct'. A compliment, of sorts.

The antipathy between the two men was thickening by the second before either of them had even spoken. It was visceral. Gürtner's rigidity, in Glaser's view, hid deep insecurities. Franz Gürtner was a self-made man; his father had been a train driver. Glaser's father, Alois Glaser, was one of Stuttgart's leading jurists – little short of a legend in South Germany. In a people conscious of heredity and background, this mattered.

Also, despite his success in life, Gürtner was always intimidated by lawyers of greater sophistication; those with wider interests, greater depths of culture. Glaser fitted the bill nicely, with his passion for art, his expert knowledge of wine, a social ease which seemed practised to the Minister of Justice, though ironically Glaser thought of himself as clumsy and overly blunt, even maladroit, in company – a view shared by Lotte.

Nevertheless, when Gürtner looked at Glaser his nose filled with the stench of the railway yard which had permeated the shabby two-room *Sozialwohnung* he had grown up in. The Public Prosecutor attempted an affable smile; the Minister's barriers went up: The snob was patronising him.

'Herr Minister,' the Public Prosecutor began, aiming at brisk clarity. 'I wish to make an application for a post-mortem examination on the body of the late Fräulein Raubal.'

'Her mother wishes the body returned to Vienna,' said the Minister. 'She wishes it returned intact. They are Catholics.'

Gürtner did not move a muscle as he spoke, a tendency which always made the Prosecutor wish to fidget.

'The police pathologist Frau Bandl is prepared to act upon immediate authorisation,' Glaser said. 'The body of the deceased could be in Vienna by this evening, if a post-mortem is carried out immediately.'

The Minister raised an eyebrow. His mouth twitched down. He was signalling that he had received the implication that Glaser had contacted the pathologist and did not particularly like it. 'I have no doubt that Dr Bandl is prepared to carry out her duties,' he intoned. 'Nevertheless, there is no need for a post-mortem in a clear case of suicide. Dr Müller has established a cause of death. What more do we want?'

'A post-mortem would help us to establish a time of death more precisely, Herr Minister.'

Gürtner made a faint movement of his stiff shoulders, as if suffering from rheumatism. 'Up to a point, but only up to a point. And where would that get us, exactly?'

Glaser was only too aware that he could not use any of the knowledge he had gained from Katherina Bandl's unofficial examination of the body without ending the pathologist's career and probably his own with it.

'It would enable us to establish the background facts of the case.' Glaser hesitated. He took another route. 'And act as a check on the information given in the witness statements.'

'Do you have any reason to doubt the veracity of the witness statements?'

Glaser had expected this. His doubts were not evidence, not to a stickler like Gürtner.

'Not at this stage, Herr Minister. But that is precisely why I need further information from a post-mortem.'

The Minister blinked. 'Dr Glaser, I do not know if you have looked at the Suicide Register recently, but we are encountering a significant increase in numbers. We do not possess the resources to have a post-mortem for every Munich case, let alone those of foreigners. It is not possible, regrettably.'

The Minister looked down at the papers on his desk, signalling that the interview was over.

'I think Fräulein Raubal may have been murdered,' Glaser said.

The Minister looked up. 'Do you have any evidence for that?'

'The circumstances are suspicious. Certain alibis are suspect.'

'Any facts?'

'Not without a post-mortem. No.'

'A supposition, then? On your part.' Gürtner was scenting blood; Glaser was sounding woolly.

'One witness testified that the pistol was found on the sofa. You would expect it to be with the body. Dr Müller's report says the burn marks were on the deceased's skin, not on her dress, which is odd.'

'A post-mortem is irrelevant to the first of those points and is unlikely to clarify the second. Is that it?'

'Yes.'

'Then your request is declined. I'm afraid I have a rather heavy schedule today, Dr Glaser.'

Glaser rose. 'Thank you for your time, Herr Minister.'

'Not at all.'

As Glaser made his way laboriously to the door, Dr Franz Gürtner, Minister of Justice for the Free State of Bavaria, returned to the papers on his desk.

Glaser made his way to the rickety lift but stopped at the second floor. Most lawyers summoned a clerk when they wanted material, and had it brought to their desks. But Glaser frequently fetched files and the like himself – he

45

regarded such behaviour as egalitarian. For this reason, plus his larger reputation for decency, Glaser was greeted with genuine warmth when he entered the Clerks' Office.

The Suicide Register was kept on a shelf near the Senior Clerk's desk. Glaser took it down, as the clerks either got on with their work or pretended to and watched him. Small talk had ceased as he came in. These were cautious times.

They were also sad and fearful times. As the Minister had indicated, the suicide rates were soaring. The Suicide Register was a blue-green hardbacked legal ledger. Hand ruled lines spread across its double pages.

Glaser immediately found what he feared he would find. The last entry, numbered 193, was Fräulein Raubal. The spidery black handwriting in immaculate Gothic script was that of Minister Gürtner himself. The entry was dated Monday, 21 September. Geli had immediately been registered as a suicide to pre-empt any need for a post-mortem.

Glaser's face was a practised mask as he closed and replaced the book, wished the clerks a courteous 'Goodbye' as he left the room, and made his way back to the lift. He made one more call before returning to his own cubicle on the ground floor.

Katherina Bandl was at her desk. The dog, Mitzi, was at her habitual place at Bandl's feet. Glaser neutrally gave the information that Fräulein Raubal's death had been entered as a suicide. Frau Bandl equally neutrally added the information that, at the authorisation of the Minister of Justice, the body had already been returned to Vienna.

Glaser sat at his desk, staring at the near wall of his claustrophobic cupboard of an office. His body was rigid with rage; the white mist was clouding his mind. He never let his rages cloud his judgement; he kept telling Lotte that. He never let the anger affect his work. Not until now.

For a second he thought of summoning a clerk to dictate

this report, but rejected the idea as soon as it formed. He took the cover off the little used Adler typewriter, put paper in and started furiously banging away.

His report was headed 'The So-called Suicide of Fräulein Raubal, September 1931'.

In furiously bashed-out letters, words, sentences, Glaser outlined the suspicious circumstances of Geli Raubal's death. He stopped short of directly accusing Hitler of murdering her, but only just.

As a coda, he complained of the investigative procedures followed, criticising Chief Inspector Sauer, Dr Müller and for good measure the Minister of Justice for Bavaria, Dr Franz Gürtner.

Hardly pausing to read the finished document through, Glaser ripped it from the typewriter, fastened the pages together and made his laborious way to the cellar, where files on closed cases were stored.

There, he placed his report on file, with the other papers pertaining to the closed Raubal case. And there his report stayed, a secret he shared with nobody, not even Lotte, certainly not Lotte.

Now and again, not often, he thought about the report as the weeks and months went by, as the forces of democracy and decency grew weaker, as the Nazis grew stronger. Now and again, he even thought about the danger he had put himself in. But he always put the thought out of his mind.

So the report just stayed there, latent, like a quietly ticking bomb.

Part II
Winter 1933

1

Inspector Forster, newly transferred from the Criminal to the Political Police, was waiting in a doorway in a particularly run-down area of Milbertshofen – the most decayed and dilapidated section of Munich. With him, studiously avoiding his gaze and that terrifying smile, was a young detective constable, leaning against the door jamb.

Two more men were at the back door of the building. Even through the driving rain, in the stygian darkness, Forster had a good view of the place, almost directly opposite them. It used to be called The Milbertshofen Red Gymnastics Club, as a smashed sign above the door still testified. The word 'Red' had a hole in it, caused by a rifle butt.

The police watchers had only just arrived. They knew precisely what time the communists were coming – it wasn't necessary to get there early. And there they were! Forster's smile widened.

There were four of them. Pathetic! Four of them risking capture to deliver one bundle of newspapers. They had even forgotten to cover the bundle, which was getting soaked, despite their leader's attempts to tuck it under his jerkin. No coats, of course. Communists couldn't afford coats.

The leader was Franz-Xaver Schwarzmüller. They knew all about him. They could, of course, pull him in. But the point of operations like this one wasn't to catch the communists.

They could take them any time. It was the highly placed fellow-travellers who needed flushing out.

The young detective looked questioningly at Forster, straightening up off the wall, ready for action. Forster made an economical motion with his arm, waving him to watch and wait. Only Schwarzmüller went into the gloomily lit building – Schwarzmüller the whey-faced mummy's boy. He was almost beneath Forster's notice at all. No, the one the Inspector was watching, the only communist worthy of his enmity, was Sepp Kunde.

Even as he thought that, Kunde left the shelter of the doorway, peered round for a minute, then looked in the window of the building. Then he waited, out in the rain, small and compact, standing apart from the others.

Forster's hatred for him intensified, as his smile grew broader. He understood, now, why he hated Sepp Kunde so much: That sense of apartness, that aura of otherness. Unable to stand with the group, even for a few moments. Kunde always – always – appeared to be thinking.

One of the other communists was scratching at some-thing in the doorway of the building. Forster remembered a Social Democrat poster, stuck up there. The Inspector had seen it just after they parked the car. It was typical of the Social Democrats, a childish and pathetic insult to the Führer. As Forster recalled, it said something like 'Hitler has a house, a villa, two Mercedes cars and a rhino whip.'

As the communist – a lanky shit-Prussian called Paul Jahnke – clawed at the poster, Kunde stood watching him. You could read Kunde's derision all over his stiff little body.

'What are you thinking?' Forster murmured aloud, his gaze never leaving Kunde.

'Sorry, sir?'

'Nothing, Constable. Nothing for you to trouble yourself about.' Forster paused for a moment. 'What makes a Special Man, Constable. Eh? What do you think?'

The young policeman's face contorted with the effort of working out what was required of him. 'Er … Special ability, sir?'

Forster shook his head. 'No. Wrong my boy. The Special Ones are born not made. And to clear the way for this country to be great again, you know what we do, my boy? You know what our task is?' Forster did not wait for an answer. 'We eliminate the enemy's Special Men.'

'Yes, sir.'

I will get Kunde, Forster thought. I will have him. But not tonight. Not yet.

A pool of light briefly spilling onto the pavement showed Franz-Xaver Schwarzmüller emerging from the sometime Red Gymnastics Club. The fourth communist left the doorway and walked toward them, halfway across the road. He looked right at the vestibule where the two police were hiding. The light from the building showed his wall-eye.

'Idiot,' Forster said under his breath. He made a movement with his forearm, just as 'wall-eye' turned to leave with the others.

As the communists scurried off into the night, there was another questioning look from the young policeman.

'Watch and wait, my boy. Watch and wait.'

Two men emerged from the building, both in overalls. 'Don't bother,' Forster said.

Five minutes later a plump man in an expensive overcoat and homburg hat came out, a newspaper half under his coat. Forster grinned. 'That's more like it.'

They followed him to the end of the road, then Forster called out 'Stop, police.' The man actually screamed – a high-pitched noise, like a girl. Forster burst out laughing.

'What's that you've got there, chummy?' he said, reaching into the man's coat and pulling out a newspaper. Forster glanced at it. 'My my, subversive literature. O dear! O dear!'

The plump man shut his eyes. 'No … no please. I just …

I wanted to hand it in …'

Forster laughed again. The young policeman looked at him, holding the plump man's arm.

'What …?' the man said. 'What happens now?'

'Little trip to Ettstrasse,' Forster said.

The man whimpered. The street's name had a resonance far beyond the bland title of Main Police Station. They said there was blood soaked into the marble floors at Ettstrasse. Himmler himself had cut his teeth as Chief of Police there.

Forster spoke into his radio. Within minutes, the two policemen who had been at the back of the former Red Gymnastics Club drove up, with a prisoner in the back. Forster pushed his own prisoner in next to him, then he and the young constable walked away.

As the car with the prisoners reached the top of the street, Sepp Kunde watched it pass by from a shop doorway he had ducked into. He was alone. He had told the others to go on without him.

He thought back to the events of the night. They had delivered newspapers it had taken weeks to produce, to an address known to the Gestapo and the Political Police. One of the Comrades had scratched and defaced a Social Democrat poster, which the *Sozis* had stuck on one of their buildings.

Kunde shook his head at the childish futility of it all. And this at a time when working men were grubbing around for food to feed their families. One of Kunde's comrades, from his early days in the Ludwigsburg Communist Party, had been on the Hunger March at Darmstadt. When the march was attacked by the police, many of the Comrades were clubbed to the ground. And there they stayed, too weak from hunger to stand again. They lay where they had fallen until they died from starvation.

And still the Nazis successfully deceived the working man. Ordinary workers were flooding to join the SA. 'We have lost,' Kunde thought, there in the doorway. 'And what is our reaction to defeat? We produce windy newspapers and scratch the shit-bourgeois posters half off our own buildings.'

A certainty crystallised in him that night. It had been coming for some time: The head must be cut off the dragon, only then will the dragon die. Kunde saw the way forward, saw it with great clarity. He would take action, and he would do it alone – as he had always done, as he always needed to do.

He would kill the new Chancellor of Germany, Adolf Hitler.

2

When Hitler had been appointed Chancellor of Germany, the Nazis celebrated with a late-night torchlight procession through Munich. Glaser and his wife, Lotte, stood at the window of their flat in Galeriestrasse. The children, thankfully, were in bed.

You could hear the celebration coming for ages before you saw anything. There were shouts and whoops of jubilation from the crowds in the street and rhythmic, machine-like chanting: *Heil-Heil-Heil.* Then the local Nazis marched up Theatinerstrasse, on the far side of the Hof Garten, singing their Song of Triumph. They sang in that peculiar, jerky style the SA had adopted – tinny and robotic:

> And now comrades all, has come the time,
> That round the land, the bells of victory sound ...
> Chains of slaves that long our arms bound,
> Shatter under hammer blows around,
> And joy in all hearts rules, in this our time.

Glaser recognised some of the troopers, in their brown shirts, their faces shiny with triumph in the torchlight flames. Some were neighbours – Herr Göscherl, the butcher, for one. But he knew most of them from court. Petty criminals, extortionists, pimps and thugs were now bossing Germany. He and Lotte stood together, not quite touching, until the procession had stamped its way past, and the last of their burning wood torches were out of sight.

Glaser silently, bitterly, blamed himself for not 'nailing' Hitler while he had the chance, over the Geli murder. Lotte, knowing exactly what he was thinking, had silently squeezed his arm.

So what was to be done about it? The Munich Social Democrats were meeting at their *Stammtisch* at the Café Heck, a lively, spit-and-sawdust watering-hole in Galeriestrasse. The Heck was conveniently situated for Glaser, being just along the street from where he lived. But sometimes, Glaser thought, as he struggled through the slush on the pavement, close destinations were more of a problem than those more distant – when at least one could be dropped off at the door by a cab. Fortunately, Lotte had just bought him a new cane, ebony with a gold top – very stylish.

A wave of depression washed through him. This meeting he was struggling towards. It was all so futile. What could they do?

He knew there would be talk of a strike, this evening at the Heck. There were already protest strikes in Lübeck, up north, over the illegal arrest of their Jewish Social Democrat Deputy, Julius Leber. The massive Lübeck Machine Works was paralysed, although this had not brought about Leber's release. At least not yet.

In Berlin, the Social Democrats had organised a demonstration, in the Lustgarten.

The party leader, Otto Wels, had given an address. There had been quite a good turnout, by all accounts, despite the rain. The Nazis had let them go ahead. If it had been the communists, they would have smashed it. Does that mean the Nazis think the Social Democrats aren't even worth attacking?

Glaser arrived late at the *Stammtisch*. The other Social

Democrats were already seated on iron chairs round the rough wooden table, chatting, and drinking foaming steins of the sweet Paulaner beer. There were about a dozen of them. But a place had been kept for him, and Erich Rinner had waited for him before starting the business of the evening.

As an apologetic Glaser took his place, his cheeks burning in the sudden warmth of the café, Rinner rapped the table with his knuckles and began to make his case. He was one of the youngest men there, in his early thirties, but he spoke confidently, demanding attention.

'The communists have called for a general strike, to bring Hitler down,' Rinner told the Social Democrats. There was an expectant silence round the table. Rinner had a few communist posters, sent to him, he told the Social Democrats, by a local communist leader called Willi Bohn. They were passed round the table. Glaser ordered a glass of the Heck's mediocre Riesling, lit a pipe, and studied the communist offering:

MASS STRIKE!
HITLER IS CHANCELLOR OF THE REICH

The President of Germany, Hindenburg, the Social Democrat presidential candidate, the Reichsbanner and the Trade Union leaders have named their 'opponent' Adolf Hitler, as Federal Chancellor. Hitler has created a government of fascist counter-revolution …

There was a lot more of it, but Glaser stopped reading. The communists had lumped the Social Democrats in with everybody else responsible for Hitler becoming Chancellor. A murmur of anger round the table told him other Social Democrats had the same reaction. As he looked up, he was amazed to see Ascher Weintraub making his way toward him.

Glaser himself had mentioned this evening's meeting to the old art dealer, but he had not expected him to come. Weintraub was a rank-and-file Social Democrat. He had never turned up to a meeting of the leadership before – but then Adolf Hitler had not become Chancellor before.

As ever, Weintraub was dressed in the suit that was slightly too small for him, tie jauntily askew. He sat with an audible kvetch and ordered a beer and orange juice mix called a *Radlmas.*

When it came, he held Glaser's gaze, with that look of quizzical amusement of his, as if there was nothing he hadn't seen, and nothing he couldn't see through. Glaser shrugged. It was a gesture of helplessness. He felt a surge of love for the old man. And then a dreadful unease, which he did not understand.

Meanwhile, Erich Rinner was speaking again, raising his voice to cover the disquiet the communist poster had caused. 'The communists are on strike in a little place called Mössingen, in Swabia.' Rinner's voice rose even further against the roar of drinkers at other tables. He looked at Glaser, because he came from Swabia. 'Do you know it, Gerhard?'

'Mössingen? Yes, Erich,' he called up the table. 'I used to go there for summer holidays with my parents, as a boy.'

Rinner shot him an affectionate look, before turning back to the meeting. 'Their general strike has lasted for three days now,' he said. 'Amazingly for such a tiny place, they have no fewer than three textile factories – called …' he read from the handwritten sheet, 'Pausa, Merz and Burkhard.'

There was some laughter round the table, at the rustic-sounding names. Then Wilhelm Hoegner spoke. He had left the running to Rinner, but the strike was in his constituency. He took up the baton:

'Between them, these factories employ 1,200 people,'

Hoegner said. 'They are all solidly on strike. The farm co-operative is also on strike. If we give them support, others will join in. We can snuff out the Hitler Chancellorship before it gets going. There are only two Nazis in the Cabinet, after all, apart from Hitler. Just Frick and Göring.'

He looked hard at his colleagues. He did not have to tell them that Chancellors come and go – some had lasted a matter of weeks. 'Our chances of success are good. What do you think?'

Glaser had been shaking his head while Hoegner was speaking. He knew more about communist strikes in Swabia than he was prepared to let on. He had received a letter from his elderly mother that morning. Old Frau Glaser had watched, at daybreak, as Ludwigsburg's communists had tried to stop workers going into the Bleyle factory, on the main Hindenburgstrasse. Some workers had listened, and joined the communists at the factory gates, but most had pushed past and gone in to work. As soon as a worker joined the strike, one of the unemployed ran into the factory to take his place.

Glaser took his pipe from his mouth and poked it at Hoegner. 'Wilhelm, the communists read their policy off pastoral letters from Russia, which preach the destruction of social democracy. We must have no truck with them.' Glaser banged the table with his fist. And then, slowly, emphasising every word. 'They-do-not-support-the-law.'

Julius Zerfass was nodding agreement, a gesture which made his brown hair flop over his eyes: 'We Social Democrats embody democracy,' he said. 'We should oppose Hitler via our excellent deputies in Parliament, where we will undoubtedly win the argument.' Zerfass gave a nod and a flashing smile at Hoegner. 'All we have to do, is sit back and wait for Hitler to mess it up,' he went on. 'After Hitler, the next Chancellor will be a Social Democrat, you mark my words. Meanwhile, we don't come down to their level. I say no to strikes and no to the Reichsbanner.'

'Exactly,' Glaser said. He had always been against the Reichsbanner – the Social Democrat armed fighters.

'Sadly, we have been left no option but to defend ourselves, by any means available,' a *Post* reporter, Edmund Goldschlag, said. 'Even if that means supporting illegal strikes.'

'But Wilhelm Frick has assured us that all National Socialist measures will have their basis in legality,' said Zerfass

'Wilhelm Frick is a Nazi,' Ascher Weintraub murmured to himself.

The art dealer, his usually amiable face drawn and tense, glanced across at Hitler's *Stammtisch*. It was in the top right-hand corner of the narrow Café Heck, so the Führer could sit with his back to the wall – he was terrified of assassination. The table was empty now; the new Chancellor was back in Berlin. But the old Jew looked at him anyway, giving the merest shake of his head, and the smallest sigh, as if at the impossibility of explaining anything to anyone.

'Co-operation with communists doesn't work. Who should know that better than me?'

The baritone voice, from the bottom end of the *Stammtisch*, boomed off the walls and crashed off the low ceiling of the café. It belonged to the mouldering man-mountain that was Erhard Auer. Despite being a diabetic, Auer was drinking heavily. Glaser went misty-eyed as soon as the old volcano spoke.

Auer was a living history of the Social Democrat Party. He had been a Deputy during the Councils Republic. During the course of a long career, he had been shot, beaten up and had his home wrecked by both communists and Nazis. Only the Nazis had assaulted his wife, however. There was something typical about that.

Glaser sipped his warm Riesling – he was the only one round the table drinking wine. He ran his hand over his beard. It was obvious the Social Democrats were not going to back the communist call for a strike. Rinner and Hoegner, the main supporters of help for the communists, were now silent. Glaser had won the argument. He had got what he wanted, but he took no joy from it.

The politics was at an end; small talk bubbled forth. After all, it was Fasching – carnival time – the biggest, wildest celebration of the year. A roar of laughter burst out round the Social Democrat *Stammtisch*. The Tietz Department Store, opposite the Hauptbahnhof, was having a White Week; everything on sale was white. One of the *Münchener Post* reporters was joking about his impending white bankruptcy – his wife had been there so often.

Ascher Weintraub had had enough of the levity. He gave Glaser a sad smile. 'Goodnight, Gerhard,' he said, softly, and slid away unnoticed, like a shadow.

When Glaser thought back to that evening, he remembered only Weintraub. He pictured the cultured old gentleman as bordered in black, like the heavy black outlines round a Max Beckmann portrait. Glaser never saw him alive again.

Part III
Spring 1933

1

On his first return to Munich as Chancellor, Hitler was at a private Party entertainment called *At the Gallop*, at the theatre in Gärtnerplatz. He was in the stalls – middle seat, row six – the seat he always had. His companion, Ello von Hessert, was in the President's Box in the Upper Loge. Hitler could not be seen in public with a woman, because his bride was Germany and his exhausting work schedule was supposed to leave no time for a private life.

For the occasion, Ello had chosen a black dress, wide skirted, with two gold clasps on the pink shoulder straps, set off by a single string of pearls. Her long hair was pinned by a gold clip.

Flanking her, on the red-plush bench, were her friend, Henni, and Henni's father, the Party photographer, Heinrich Hoffmann. They had been deputed to take care of her until the evening was finished. Then she would be driven to Hitler's apartment, where she would be the only guest.

On the stage, a naked woman representing Diana the huntress was straddling a real shot deer. Earlier items had included a striptease artiste from Turkey, dancing the Dance of the Seven Veils, and Zeus as a swan circling a near-naked Leda.

Heinrich Hoffmann gallantly tried to distract Ello with pleasantries, as he had been doing all evening. Ignoring the photographer, she looked up at Eugen Neureuther's domed painted ceiling.

Henni Hoffmann, to Ello's left, had a new pageboy hair-cut. She wore a dark-blue jacket, to set off one of her daring short skirts, and red silk shoes. As usual, she wore hardly any jewellery – just a simple gold cross at her neck. The Hoffmann girl was being tediously waspish. There had been a series of digs about Ello's lack of make-up, though Henni knew perfectly well make-up antagonised Hitler.

It was not, Ello knew, that Henni wanted Hitler for herself – though God knows she told the story about Hitler trying to kiss her at the Hoffmann Christmas party often enough. It was just that she regarded Hitler as, in a general sense, hers: She had known him even longer than Ello had. She first met him when she was eight. He had bought her her first pair of skis. He had held her hand at her mother's funeral and told her she must learn how to hate.

Henni sensed she had gone too far; there was the usual quasi-apologetic retreat. She smilingly whispered a compliment in Ello's ear – something insincere about her Jean Desprez perfume. Meanwhile, the striptease music blared, the men roared and stamped in rhythm, the swan Zeus returned and had sex with Leda.

Ello looked away and glanced at Henni. She had a lovely heart-shaped face, Ello thought, but fretting about her bony, flat-chested figure drove her to flirt too much. There was that picnic at Lake Tegern, before Geli was killed – Henni insisting the girls undress behind a bush, where she knew perfectly well Hitler and the other men could still see them.

Ello remembered, too, the three girls sunbathing naked, when a cloud of white butterflies landed on Geli. It was as if they knew, and were trying to protect her. Ello blew her lost best-friend a kiss in her mind.

As the show was finishing, the chauffeur, Schreck, appeared in the box in his black leather coat with the collar turned up, looking, to Ello, like a larger, fiercer version of

Hitler. He had the same moustache, the same staring, deep-set eyes and small-lobed ears. Only the cleft in his chin was not shared with 'Uncle Dolf', as Ello called Hitler.

Schreck was carrying her silver-fox coat, passing it from one hand to the other, as he scratched his chilblains over it. Ello grimaced, snatched the coat from him and put it on, evading his attempt to help her on with it.

Then Schreck ushered her down flights of curving stone stairs, muttering to himself about how the Nazi Bonzen – big-wigs – in the audience were losing touch with ordinary people.

There was nothing of the servant about his manner. When the shrewder members of Hitler's entourage, like the architect Speer, wanted to put an idea into the Führer's ear, they whispered it first to Schreck – being careful to keep in the chauffeur's good books in order to do so.

Outside, Schreck strode ahead to the Mercedes, parked in the square. It was cold and damp; Ello could see her breath in front of her face. Schreck held the car door open for her. Sitting on the back seat was the huge figure of Hitler's adjutant, Wilhelm Brückner.

She got in beside him, blushing in the dark as her fur coat slid her toward him, on the leather of the seat. At private moments at the picnics at Lake Tegern, with Geli, Henni, Emil Maurice and Hitler, Brückner had kissed her, passionately, more than once. She had let him, every time. But he had not followed it up, in any way. Now, however, he was silent, bolt upright, not acknowledging her, as Schreck eased the heavy Mercedes out of the square.

The chauffeur drove fast through the darkness over freezing slush, parallel to the Isar.

They turned right and crossed the river at the Luitpold-brücke. Ello glimpsed Fischer's statues, allegories of the four Bavarian tribes, silhouetted in the darkness. Schreck then slowed, as the road narrowed at the Angel of Peace

67

monument, commemorating the victory over France at Sedan.

At the intersection with Ismaninger Strasse, the road was blocked off by concrete bollards, leaving a narrow gap patrolled by black-uniformed SD guards. From here, Prinzregentenstrasse was sealed off as far as the square – a new security measure since Hitler became Chancellor. The guards gave a Hitler salute when they read the number plate, and stepped aside. The Mercedes cruised silently in the darkness the rest of the way.

As Ello and Brückner got out of the car, a youth was pasting a Social Democrat poster on the brickwork, by the door to Hitler's apartment. Ello smothered a smile. Brückner reached inside his greatcoat for his radio.

Pretending to twist her ankle, Ello threw herself against him and screamed. The adjutant caught her in his arms and held her. His face lowered to hers. She shut her eyes, but he pushed her upright, then radioed Hitler's Personal Protection Guard, on the ground floor of the apartment building. They came running out of the guard room, one of them ripping the poster from the wall, but the youth had had time to make his escape.

Hitler met Ello at the foot of the polished wooden staircase to the apartment, flapping the escorting Brückner away. He was still wearing the brown uniform he had worn at the Party entertainment. He clicked his heels and bowed to her, then took her fox-fur stole from her shoulders. They walked up together, side-by-side, godfather and goddaughter, Ello and her Uncle Dolf, their footsteps clacking on the wood of the stairs.

Hitler's apartment was familiar to her from social occasions – as usual it was a good five degrees too cold – though she had never before been alone there with him at midnight. How was she going to get back? Presumably

Schreck slept some time.

Sheer annoyance quickened her stride to the seating area by the fireplace. She sat herself in one of the low armchairs, before he could lead her to the sofa. She looked away from him, up at the painting in front of her.

The triptych *The Four Elements* by Adolf Ziegler was above the fireplace. Stretching nearly to the coffered ceiling, it featured four soulless frontally nude females, two in the middle panel, one on each of the wings. More bastardised Greek mythology as an excuse for stripping women, she thought.

She knew Ziegler. He was a tall, handsome man who always eyed her at parties, with knowing arrogance. The Nazi pet artist, he taught over at the Academy of Fine Arts and had some administrative sinecure or other.

Hitler sat facing her. He reached across to her, took her hand, kissed it and murmured

'*Tschapperl.* Your eyes are like my mother's. Will you kiss me?'

Ello withdrew her hand and said, in a bored voice. 'Uncle Dolf, I'm tired. It's a little late for all this.'

He looked relieved.

There was a faint rustling noise as the tall, angular figure of the housekeeper, Anni Winter, bustled toward them. In a floral-patterned dress with puff sleeves, she exuded confident composure. Ello knew how much the housekeeper had despised Geli. But the aristocratic, ladylike Fräulein von Hessert was a much more suitable match. Anni's oily-skinned face, framed by a helmet of black hair, radiated approval, showing her views on the improvement only too clearly.

'Good evening, Fräulein von Hessert,' she said. 'How good to see you here with us again.' And then to Hitler. 'What may I prepare for you, sir?'

Hitler pouted at Ello, proud of his new girlfriend.

My God, she thought, this was like being on a first date with a teenager.

'Just coffee with chocolate for me,' he said to Anni Winter. 'And what would the lovely Fräulein like?' The pout deepened to a simper.

Ello groaned inwardly. Actually, the lovely Fräulein would like nothing better than to get out the hell out of this mausoleum and go home. She had lectures to go to tomorrow, at the university. She was qualifying as a psychologist soon; there was piles of work to do.

'Tea perhaps, Frau Winter,' she said. 'Chamomile, if you have it.'

'Of course, miss,' Anni Winter said. She gave a small bobbing curtsey, a sign of high favour. 'And if the Fräulein would like to tell me privately what is required from her room for the night?' She smiled, showing yellow teeth. 'Schreck will drive me to fetch it.'

Ello looked at Hitler, alarmed. 'What?' she said. 'I'm not staying ...'

'Nonsense, *mein Schatz*,' Hitler said. 'You shall stay in Geli's room. We've had it made ready for you.' Steel had entered his voice. The pout had gone. He looked at her for the first time that night – staring her in the eye. She dropped her gaze before he did.

Anni took her by the arm and led her gently to the far end of the room, so she could list her toiletry and nightwear requirements out of male hearing. Hitler was pouting again. At the end of it, the housekeeper nodded and gave Ello's arm a faint squeeze. They were under the arch that led to the dining room, private in the vastness of the apartment.

'I'll be back soon, *gnädiges Fräulein*,' she said. 'Herr Winter and I aren't returning to our little flat tonight. We'll be in our rooms here. We won't be far away.'

Never leaving the well-defined bounds of servanthood,

Anni gave her a quick complicitous look, woman to woman.
'Thank you!' Ello said.

Although she despised the fawning housekeeper, right
then she could have hugged her.

Anni bustled off. Ello walked back to the fireplace and sat
down again in the armchair. Hitler jumped up; the fart was
audible. He started pacing, a concentrated look on his face,
as if weighing weighty matters. Another volley of farts broke
from him. Half turning his back to her, he took something
from his jacket pocket and put his hand over his mouth.
Ello recognised the distinctive lozenge-shaped tin of Dr
Koester's Anti-Gas Pills. They contained strychnine and
atropine – one could but hope …

He began to pace in the vast room, until the nervous fart-
ing had stopped. The sleek, silver-haired figure of Georg
Winter appeared, in a plum-coloured velvet smoking jacket
and black trousers. He was carrying a silver tray with tea,
coffee and a two-layer silver cake-stand. The cake-stand
contained neatly-placed croissant-like *Wiener Kipfeln* (top
layer) and raspberry tartlets (bottom layer).

'Herr Winter!' Ello called out, relieved not to be alone
with her Uncle Dolf, however briefly. 'How are you? How is
your knee?'

The butler-cum-valet smiled as he laid out the delicacies
with soft hands. 'It's a little rheumaticky in cold weather,' he
said. 'But I don't complain, *gnädiges Fräulein*. Thank you
kindly.'

As the servant slowly made his way out, a shaft of intuition
ran through Ello, exciting and frightening at the same time.
Hitler wanted a second chance with Geli. He wanted to be
forgiven.

Her Uncle Dolf had sat down and was now looking at her
directly again. She told herself to note when these rare
occasions of eye contact occurred. It was when he wanted to
impose himself, she would take a wager on it.

71

Anni Winter came in, without knocking, with a portmanteau bag. She told Ello all her things would be laid out in Fräulein Raubal's room. There was another reassuring nod as she left, but Ello felt much stronger now.

She looked to her right and saw a drawing, framed, hanging low from a cord, between two paintings.

'I've seen that before!' she said. 'At the Hoffmanns'. It's City Hall. It's one of yours, isn't it?'

Hitler nodded. 'Yes. Do you like it?'

'Which one is the copy?' Ello asked. 'Herr Hoffmann's or this one?'

'Both. I did Hoffmann's for his birthday.'

'Both? What? Two copies?'

'Yes, I did these drawings all the time, when I first came to Munich. I can do them very quickly. I used to make a living from them. Do you know the Zehme Hat Shop, on Marienplatz?'

She was amused. 'Yes!'

Hitler sipped his drink, then spoke. 'I sold my first drawing of City Hall there. I got fifteen marks for it. It's actually called *The Old City Hall with View over Marienplatz*. I did another five or six the same day and sold them all. Do you know the baker's in Gabelsbergerstrasse?'

Ello smothered a giggle. 'Uh. No, I don't think I do.'

'It was run, in those days, by a chap called Franz Heilmann. This was just before the war. I used to go in there every evening to buy sweet bread for my supper. Anyway, this Heilmann bought my drawings – *The Old City Hall* and *The Residence*. He put them up in his shop window. Then all the shopkeepers started to buy them.'

'What else did you draw?'

Hitler shrugged. 'The Asam Church, the Deutsches Theater, the Hofbräuhaus – any interesting building. I would then go into the building, or wait outside, and sell them.'

'Always buildings?'
'Yes. I love buildings.'
'So you never draw people?'
'No, no. Except …'.
'Except?'
He shifted in his armchair. 'Two or three times … I did some drawings of Geli.'

Ello nodded. Geli had told her Hitler wanted to draw her naked – purely a device to see her undressed, Geli felt. He usually drew people as cartoons. Geli could draw well herself, and she had praised one of her uncle's cartoons to Ello. She said it had made her laugh. Drawn when Hitler was eleven, it showed one of his teachers holding an ice cream, looking like a child.

Ello thought back to the cartoon figures Hitler drew at the Ostaria Bavaria and the Café Heck. One, she remembered particularly, was the industrialist and politician Alfred von Hugenberg's face on the body of a cat. He had given the cat black riding boots and a dagger.

But his party piece, in company, was an architect's elevation, perfect in detail and proportion, of the Palace of Westminster. It was a copy of a picture in Spamer's encyclopaedia. Hitler dashed it off in seconds, to great applause from the hangers-on. He did it nearly every Wednesday at the Ostaria. She had had her suspicions since that time, but now she had a preliminary hypothesis, well, diagnosis. And she knew how to test it out.

'Tell me about the buildings you like best.'
'All right …' He was pleased. 'When I was in Vienna, I used to look at the buildings on the Ring for hours. There is everything there, you know. Some Classicism, some Renaissance, some baroque.'
'Go on.'

Rocking slightly in his chair, he dropped into the chanting rhythm he used when he was telling her things. She had

73

been familiar with it since childhood. 'There's the Votive Church – that's by Heinrich Ferstel. There's the Town Hall – that's by Friedrich Schmidt. There's the Parliament – that's by Theophil Hansen.'

'Go on.'

'Another one I love is the Opera. That's by van der Nuell. He put a bullet in his brain on the day it was opened. Because he thought it a failure. How glorious to die, just as one's work is complete!'

Ello remembered Hitler's frequent threats to commit suicide when thwarted. He had threatened to kill himself both during and after the Beer Hall Putsch, and at the Party's lowest political ebb, the November election last year, the first time the Nazi vote had declined from one election to the next. And she had been here, herself, in this apartment, when he threatened suicide after Geli died.

'Did you draw buildings in situ? When you first came to Munich, say?'

'No, no. I drew them back in my room. I was in the little room in Schleissheimerstrasse in those days. My real bestseller was the Registry Office. I used to sell that drawing to couples after they got married. I did a five or six of them a day sometimes, one after the other. I could draw it with my eyes shut.'

'So you could picture the building clearly in your mind?'

Hitler nodded vigorously. 'Yes, yes.'

Eidetic memory, then. Ello frowned, concentrating. 'How long did these drawings take you?'

He shrugged. 'About ten minutes.'

Ello took a deep breath. She pushed back a few strands of hair which were escaping from the gold clip. Hitler waited, not caring why she was asking these questions, content to follow her lead.

'Uncle Dolf, have you got any more of your drawings? Here?'

74

'Yes. A portfolio full. And there's a painting in Geli's room. It's …'

'Get the portfolio first, please. Show me.'

'Certainly.' He was on his feet before she had finished speaking.

While he was gone, crossing the huge room rapidly with his mincing gait, she reviewed the literature, her mind ice-clear. The Swiss psychiatrist Paul Bleuler had coined the term *Autismus*. But it was Dr J. Langdon Down who had first identified Savant Syndrome.

Savants have excessive ability at some aspects of one skill, occasionally art; other aspects of their mental make-up are impaired. An overlap with autism is proved; most savants are autistic but have normal or above-average intelligence.

A key case in the field is Clever Ludwig – an artistic savant, from Vienna. Clever Ludwig is obsessed by detail and order; any disruption of order disturbs him and makes him angry. When he was three, he would line up alphabet cards in the correct sequence on the floor, and if his parents moved any of the cards, he would become visibly upset.

Ello remembered a dinner at her home when, for some reason, she and Henni were there with Hitler before the guests arrived. A formal table had been laid. Hitler spent nearly twenty minutes tensely reordering the cutlery, napkins and tableware, until everything was lined up perfectly. Henni had made one of her waspish jokes – saying to Ello that Hitler was 'more Prussian than the Prussians'.

In her mind, Ello heard Hitler saying '*Ortnung*' in his Austrian accent, *Ordnung* – order. It was one of his key words. She thought of another occasion.

One of the regulars at the Ostaria Bavaria, his favourite restaurant, was Dr Manfred Curry – the man who classified human beings according to climate type. He always arrived for lunch in a flashy blue sports car. One day he parked it crooked – not obstructing anyone, just slightly crooked. Hitler arrived in the Mercedes and saw the car like that. He stormed into the restaurant and screamed at Curry to go back out into Schellingstrasse and repark the car straight – which the humiliated doctor duly did. *Ortnung* again.

Clever Ludwig had some repetitive motor mannerisms, like flapping his hands up and down. Ello pictured Hitler's flapping, fly-swatting version of the Nazi salute and his chopping motion while talking.

When Clever Ludwig was nine he was taken to the Prater – the funfair in Vienna. Some of what he drew there was like any other nine year old – the people were just stick figures – but the technical detail of the rides was extraordinary. The construction of the girders was rendered perfectly, every detail in place and in proportion. The drawings were completed in approximately ten minutes each.

There was something else, small in itself, but it confirmed the savant diagnosis: those closest to Hitler – Hoffmann, Bormann, Hess – all praised his memory, both his recall of past conversations and his grasp of the technical specifications of cars and ships. With cars, this extended to the exact weight, as well as the name, model and number of cylinders. Savants have good rote memory, especially of concrete information linked to specific contexts – corticostriatal memory – though nobody knows why.

Hitler returned with a portfolio of 35 × 45 cm drawings. The first one showed two sides of a nineteenth-century administrative building. He had titled it *Ratzenstadl, Wien*. Ello thought it showed multiple perspectives. Clever Ludwig's drawings of his day at the Prater showed multiple perspectives, inside and outside a ride-car. But she didn't know the building Hitler had drawn, which made it difficult to judge the drawing.

She pulled out a number of Hitler's early sketches of opera houses and the future Linz Art Gallery, but these were of imaginary buildings.

'Do you have any of the drawings you did of buildings in Munich? The ones you were telling me about?'

'Oh yes!' Hitler said. He smiled at her, showing a gold tooth on the right. His teeth at the front were yellow, which made his breath musty. 'Here's one of the Old Residence. I tinted it.'

The picture he pulled out was a yellow-tinted architectural pencil drawing. It showed the courtyard of the Old Residence, the medieval palace by the Hofgarten, in minute detail. There, foregrounded on the left, was the well of the Well Courtyard, there the mullioned tower, the steep tiled roof, the latticed windows. It was a perfect representation.

'It's good,' she said. It was very good, at least she thought so.

'My problem as an artist has always been with figures,' he said. 'That's why they refused me at the Vienna Academy. They told me to be an architect, but I wasn't qualified.'

She knew that. She was thinking rapidly. 'Uncle Dolf, will you draw something for me? Now?'

His surprise and pleasure were almost comic. 'Yes! I would be pleased to …'

She gave him a tight smile. 'Get paper and a pencil, please.'

He fetched his artist's materials from his room. He was wearing his glasses when he came back – the glasses he would never let Hoffmann photograph him wearing. On the way across the room, he switched on the overhead light and two more lamp-standards. He always drew sitting down, using an artist's block to rest the paper on. He settled back in the armchair with the block, paper and pencils now, blinking in the strong light.

'Uncle Dolf, I'd like you to draw a building you have not

77

seen for some time. Something from your Vienna days, perhaps. But not one that's already in the portfolio.'

Hitler nodded absently. The request aroused no curiosity in him. 'The Charles Church,' he murmured, and immediately began to draw, bent right over the paper, starting with the ornamental work on the campanile. He had small hands but large thumbs. His fingernails were bitten.

While he drew, Ello leaned back in the armchair and shut her eyes. Forcing herself to overcome growing exhaustion, she reviewed the behavioural characteristics of autistic artist savants. Savant artists spend between two and six hours a day compulsively drawing. They rarely draw people. Although they have difficulty drawing figures, they are good at cartoon renditions of people they have previously seen.

What else? They have a preoccupation with one subject, or type of subject, typically one offering strong linear perspective. They repeat this subject many times. Savants often draw from memory, with their faces close to the paper. They begin drawing a peripheral element of a scene, using colour only to fill in defined areas – like the yellow in Hitler's sketch of the Old Residence.

Hitler finished his drawing of the Charles Church in about fifteen minutes. Ello had been there once, with Geli. The detail, the proportion and the likeness were astonishing.

In particular, the proportions were perfect – autistics have superior ability to segment an image into parts.

'Will you sign it for me, Uncle Dolf?' she asked. 'And dedicate it?' Hitler pouted, delighted. 'Sign it to Ello and Rudi, please,' she added, wanting her brother included. Hitler nodded and complied.

Ello took her drawing and stood, a perfect excuse to end the evening. But as she did so, she noticed a pencil drawing half in and half out of the file. It showed a strange conic edifice, like a beehive on a hill.

'What's that?' she said, nodding at it.

Hitler was still pouting, expecting more praise. 'It's a mausoleum,' he said. 'A citadel for the dead.'

She held onto the back of her armchair, looking down at him as he put the drawings back in the folder. 'Which dead?' she asked.

'The dead in coming wars.'

'There … there will be wars?'

He shrugged. 'Naturally. The species is in danger. Sacrifices must be made today for the future.'

'But … why?' Her voice was thin, high and frightened. She thought she sounded silly, but he noticed nothing.

He looked at her, blinking behind his glasses. 'Because life has no other object but the preservation of the species. The life of an individual should not be given high value. The fly lays a million eggs; they all die. But flies survive. What remains alive beyond the individual is the race.'

Ello's voice was still thin and high. 'But don't the deaths … concern you?'

'No, no. Conscience is a Jewish invention. It's a blemish. Like circumcision.'

Ello turned on her heel and made her way to Geli's room, clutching her picture. She shut the door, but there was no key in the lock. It was freezing cold. The room was vividly familiar to her, with its light-green wallpaper and painted antique furniture from Salzburg. There was a thick smell of polish. A bunch of red chrysanthemums, Geli's favourite flower, were in a simple vase on the bureau.

Anni Winter had obviously been in. Ello's silver-fox coat was hanging on a hook on the back of the door. The day dress she had asked for from her room was folded on the sofa. Next to it, her silk brassiere and panties with the rose-bud pattern and her silk suspender belt were wrapped round her Jean Desprez perfume. Her nightdress had been laid out on the bed. Her toiletries were lined up in rows on top of the hand-painted chest of drawers. Nothing had been put away. Why not?

Ello opened the painted wardrobe. It was still full of Geli's clothes and shoes. The whiff of camphor was sickening. Ello hastily shut the door. On the painted antique bureau was a bronze bust of Geli.

Ello knew of this bust, though she had never seen it before. It was by the Munich sculptor Ferdinand Liebermann. Hitler had commissioned it after Geli's death. Geli was shown in profile, fixedly smiling, marcelled hair in a broad metal wave; her neck rising out of the plaster plinth which replaced her body.

And then Ello remembered. Geli's room was kept as a mausoleum to Hitler's dead niece. Nothing was ever changed: Geli's writing paper was still there, on the bureau, with the name Angela Raubal in black English script, at the top left. Next to it, the framed photo of Muck, Hitler's German shepherd dog. There was a photo of Ello herself, with Henni and Geli, taken on one of the picnics at Lake Tegern.

Ello shivered. No wonder the room was so cold, only Hitler and Anni Winter were ever allowed in, and neither of them stayed long. Frau Winter brought fresh chrysanthemums every day. And of course Geli herself was always there, fixed and unmoving, beautiful but lifeless, just as Hitler wanted her, dead for all time in Liebermann's bust.

The knock on the door was timid, more of a scrape. Ello assumed it was Frau Winter.

It was Hitler. He was carrying paper and pencil.

'Ellochen,' he said. 'My little Ello. I want to draw you.'

She backed away from him, one arm across her breasts. Frau Winter appeared in the doorway, her flat oily face wreathed in smiles.

'But, sir,' she said to Hitler, 'Can't you see how tired the

ɔoor girl is? Well, *mein Führer,* my husband has put a hot
drink in your room. It will help you sleep.'

She led him unprotestingly away, but quickly came back,
alone.

'My husband forgot to put the key in the lock,' she said,
in a businesslike way. 'Here it is.'

She inserted it and turned it, to make sure it was still
working. 'Excuse me, my dear Fräulein von Hessert. For this
oversight. I will see you in the morning. I have arranged
breakfast for seven, madam. And then Schreck will drive
you to the university. I don't imagine Herr Hitler will be up
by then.'

'Thank you, Anni.'

'Not at all, madam.' Anni Winter gave a bobbing curtsey
and was gone.

Ello strode across the room and locked the door as soon
as she left.

2

Rüdiger von Hessert was a probationer, the lowest rank on the legal ladder. He was doing the Criminal Law station, as they called it, of his three-year probationary period. Glaser was not one of his supervisors.

Every probationer required a satisfactory political report from each supervisor, before he could move to the next station. Glaser, while widely respected as a lawyer, would never have been entrusted with writing such a report, as he was himself not politically acceptable. It had therefore been easy enough for him to ignore the fresh-faced son of Cajetan von Hessert, Hitler's paymaster, when he first appeared at Prielmayerstrasse.

But Glaser gradually became intrigued by von Hessert's less than deferential public references to the Nazis, especially to the Nazi military camp which he had just attended. All law students now had to attend one of these camps for two months before they were admitted as probationers.

Von Hessert's clear-skinned, small-featured face creased in contempt as he described the lectures: Tactics at the Battle of Sedan, The Stab in the Back, The French Occupation of the Ruhr. 'So banal, I can't tell you.' The rest of the time had been spent on basic drill and competitive games: 'I have never experienced such utter tedium. And my uniform was of coarse cloth and didn't fit.'

At the end of his spell at camp, he had refused the

privilege of Nazi Party membership. News of that had done the rounds at Prielmayerstrasse pretty rapidly. Glaser reckoned only the family name had allowed von Hessert to pass to the probationer stage at all. He admired the young man for the courage of his stand. Then, for reasons known only to the probationer, frequent unannounced visits to Glaser's tiny office began.

Glaser's flinty exterior was resolutely battered by the von Hessert charm: 'Do call me Rudi, Dr Glaser. My father called me Rüdiger after the hero of the *Saga of the Nibelungen*. I never felt up to it. I told him I want to be called Hagen, the one who betrays and kills Siegfried. He was *so* much more interesting.'

Glaser had burst out laughing.

Out of the blue, von Hessert bounced into Glaser's office yet again in the late afternoon. His black silk lawyer's gown fluttered, fanning a smell of Yardley's lavender round the room.

'Hello, old man.' That with a cheeky grin. Without waiting for a reply, the imperturbable youth then invited Glaser to meet his older sister that evening: 'There's something we want to discuss with you, Dr Glaser.' It was arrogantly short notice.

There was no question of Glaser setting foot in the von Hessert villa in Karolinenplatz, with its Nazi associations. But he was intrigued by the chance to talk to Geli Raubal's closest friend. He agreed to after-dinner drinks at Ello's room, at the university.

In comfortable student quarters, Ello von Hessert was laid out on an expensive ottoman, presumably on loan from the family mansion. Her jet-black hair was loose down her back. She was wearing a sleeveless, tiger-stripe lime-and-black dress, cut away steeply at the shoulder. It was riding up her thigh, some way below which there were blue-and-black striped knee socks and red Turkish slippers.

Glaser's first impression was negative. When Ello finall deigned to look at him at all, she favoured him with languid blink, all the rage at the moment and known as the Bergner Look, after the film star Elisabeth Bergner. Glase was a plain man, physically. Under the close-shaven beard he had a face like a Dutch cheese. And for all his sophisti cation, he abhorred the stylish, especially in women. He wa deeply unimpressed.

'Wine for Dr Glaser,' Rüdiger murmured.

The von Hesserts served an outstanding Trollinger – delicate red. Another mistake. Glaser held it aloft, viewing i with suspicion, before taking a sip. It came from vineyard within walking distance of his family's home. The Glaser knew the owners of the wine company and the cellarman This far from Swabia, this particular Trollinger wa extremely rare. Had the wealthy von Hesserts done thi deliberately? Flashy. Too clever by half.

But, not least because of the mellow influence of the wine, he began to relax as the brother and sister told him tales of the Thursday soirées at the Karolinenplatz villa. The driving force was the mother, Elsa. The soirées were held a dusk because Elsa had once had smallpox and avoided bright lights, which showed the scars. The von Hessert parents had taken Hitler up; made him the centrepiece o their gatherings.

'That was when I first got interested in psychology,' Ello said, sipping wine, then giving herself a hefty top-up.

The psychologist Hans Prinzhorn had been among the guests. Ello described him, a little wistfully, Glaser thought, as a handsome and accomplished ladykiller. He got the impression Prinzhorn had been her first lover, young though she must have been, at the time.

Prinzhorn, Rüdiger said, taking up the story, compared the paintings and drawings of mental patients and those of artists. Glaser knew that, but he had not read Prinzhorn's book *Image Making by the Mentally Ill*. Both von Hesserts had.

Ello had by now abandoned the languid pose. She was sitting up properly – as Glaser thought of it – on the ottoman. Whether still in love with Prinzhorn or not, she was clearly still fascinated by his ideas. She added detail to Rudi's narrative with smiling charm and enthusiasm. Glaser was impressed – he was something of an intellectual snob. His conversion to admirer of the young von Hesserts was well under way.

So when Ello shyly said, 'Dr Glaser, Rudi tells me you worked on poor Geli's case. And that you're not convinced by Hitler's alibi,' he nodded, knocked back more wine and launched into the story of the shooting of Geli Raubal.

'Hitler's alibi depended on the time of Geli's death,' he said evenly. 'I suspected the police doctor, Müller, had recorded it as later than it really was. So I prevailed on our pathologist, Dr Bandl, to take some samples.'

Both von Hesserts were listening with total concentration. Glaser continued: 'Dr Bandl calculated that Geli died anything up to twenty-four hours earlier than the time on her death certificate. At that time, Hitler was still in the apartment. His alibi for the next day is an elaborate charade. And irrelevant.'

'So Hitler killed her?' Ello said.

Glaser ran a hand over his beard. 'I'd be amazed if he didn't,' he said.

'But why?' Rudi asked. 'Why would Hitler kill her?'

Glaser's face was neutral as he replied: 'Dr Bandl said Geli was pregnant. About two months. My guess is she wanted to leave, and there was a quarrel.'

'I tell you this, Dr Glaser,' Ello said. 'Geli would never, never have committed suicide.' Ello looked serious. 'She was such a fun-loving person, you see. Warm, funny. Full of life. And she was very much in love with Emil.'

Rudi shot her a questioning glance, eyebrows raised. 'You never told me that,' he said, very much the younger brother, sounding like a child.

'No. I'm sorry, darling. But it doesn't matter now, does it?'

It was after midnight when Rudi spoke deliberately, showing less effect from the wine than Glaser or Ello. He announced what Glaser felt had been the purpose of the evening all along:

'Dr Glaser, Hitler has become interested in Ello. He wants … The young probationer's face contorted oddly. 'He wants to defile her.'

Ello started to say something, but Rudi waved her to silence. 'Dr Glaser, Ello and I think Hitler is a dangerous lunatic. We think he must be stopped,' he said. 'We think he must be killed, if necessary. We would like your advice on how to achieve that.'

3

The chemistry laboratories at Munich University were five minutes' walk from the main building, where Ello's student room was situated. She arrived at five-thirty on a Wednesday, knowing that her contact there would be alone.

'*Grüss Gott*, Herr Fritsche.'

She held her hand out wordlessly. Fritsche, in a lab coat slightly too big for him, handed over that month's supply of ampoules in a brown paper bag. Ello snapped open her black patent-leather handbag, costing the equivalent of three months of Fritsche's salary, and popped the paper bag inside.

'I need to do some work here, for a while,' Ello said easily, as if this were a regular occurrence. It was not.

Fritsche sneered and waited. Ello fished in her handbag again and handed over an envelope. Fritsche opened it. Five twenty-Reichsmark notes. This must be important.

'Lock up, when you leave,' he said, handing over a key. 'I'll need that key back tomorrow.'

Ello nodded. She waited, concealing her impatience, as Fritsche, with a show of dumb insolence, slowly removed his lab coat and donned a grey jacket. He then languidly gathered his personal belongings – an apple, a novel, a Thermos flask – and put them into a navy duffel bag, which he slung over his shoulder, tightening the drawstring. When he finally strolled out, she let loose a sigh, revealing the tension she had tried so hard to keep from Fritsche's notice.

87

She set up the apparatus she needed on one of the wooden workbenches: a Bunsen burner, a retort, a condenser, some filters, a glass jar – not much, the operation was simple enough. She poured some water into a retort and heated it over a Bunsen. The resultant steam was led through the condenser. Just before it boiled, she dropped in greeny-purple deadly-nightshade leaves and roots, gathered from waste ground near the allotments out at Ramersdorf. She let the water reach boiling point, then moved the Bunsen away.

When the distillate had cooled, she filtered it into the glass jar to remove impurities, leaving atropine in what she hoped was reasonably pure state. Just to make sure, she added a few Dr Koester pills she had bought at the local pharmacy, and stirred them in. Not too many, or the strychnine in them would give the game away.

She stared at the result of her work, as a clock on the wall ticked, suddenly loud, in the silent laboratory. She intended to kill her Uncle Dolf, next time he came back to Munich. And with any luck it would look like a cumulative overdose of his regular anti-flatulence medication.

4

Hitler returned to Munich from Berlin for his birthday, planning to tour the art ateliers of his beloved City of Art. But before that there was a luncheon at the Prinzregenten-platz apartment. Ello was invited. She had chosen a dress with slit pockets, so she could keep the atropine capsules handy. The capsule form, she thought, would be easier to manipulate than powder.

She arrived at Prinzregentenplatz at noon, calculating, correctly, that Hitler would just have got up. She was concerned at her reception. Her Uncle Dolf had a remark-able facility for completely forgetting anybody who was not actually in his presence. That was why the house staff, people like Schreck and the Winters, who saw him daily, had such great influence, regardless of their function and station in society.

But she needn't have worried. Hitler's eyes lit up at the sight of her. She presented her birthday gift to him; a hand-rubbed, calfskin-leather belt, modelled on a British Sam Browne. When he had belted it above his wide hips, she helped him with the strap over the right shoulder of his brown uniform. The intimacy of this manoeuvre was having its effect on him, as she had intended. He was pouting and his mouth was dry.

They sat at the low nest of armchairs, where they had sat that last time, when she had got him to draw for her. And when he had tried to draw her.

'Shall we have coffee?' she said. Coffee before anybody else appeared would be perfect. She touched the atropine capsules in her pocket.

'No, we are eating soon,' he said absently.

He started to tell her of his routine in Berlin. How at the beginning they had piled files on his desk at the Chancellery for him to read. 'But I soon stopped that. I've trained them not to bring me every little thing.'

She smiled. 'Are you still drawing?'

'Oh yes, yes. Every afternoon.'

Then the luncheon guests started to arrive. To her disgust, the first of them was Adolf Ziegler, the President of the Munich Academy. Tall and classically handsome, he was everything she detested in a man. He never took his eyes off the most attractive woman at every gathering; his gaze implying that his selection could be his whenever he gave the word.

He painted female nudes, like the one in front of them in Hitler's apartment; large-busted, given spurious respectability by their subject – Classical myth. All the naked women appeared to have the same face, and wore expressions of uniform wooden deadness. They were in no way a renaissance of Greek culture, as the Nazis so often claimed. They were representatives of an anonymous, neutral, dead style created by National Socialism.

Ziegler gave a full salute to his Führer, acknowledged by a swatting flap through the air by Hitler. He then smoothly bent over the seated Ello, took her right hand, raised it and stared at it, as if appraising it for auction. He finally planted a lingering kiss in her palm. Ello gave him her sweetest smile, reserved for those males she especially loathed.

Ziegler presented his birthday gift, carried in by a minion. It was a painting, a seascape. Ziegler announced it as *Burning Sea by Capri*, by Karl Boehme. Hitler appeared pleased by it, leaving it balanced against the wall where he could see it. Ziegler then took over the conversation, discussing the arrangements for the afternoon's visit to the ateliers. Ello was ignored.

Other lunch guests began to arrive, ushered in by Anni Winter in one of her inevitable floral dresses. There was Hess and his wife, poor Ilse, for whom the word frumpy could have been coined. Her dress, Ello thought, appeared to be on loan from a folkloric museum. Hess, naturally, was in uniform, complete with holstered pistol. The Hesses greeted her cordially.

Next to turn up was the short, broad-shouldered figure of the Party photographer, Hoffmann. Hoffmann enthused over her warmly. As ever, it was impossible to resist his florid-faced bonhomous charm.

There were also two secretaries from the Berlin Chancellery, who Ello had never seen before. Hitler did not introduce them to her.

All these people, too, presented birthday gifts. Hoffmann's was an original, with negative, of one of his studio studies of Hitler. It showed his face only, boldly full-face, close-up, strikingly rearing out of a black background. Underneath, in stark white lettering, floated a single word – HITLER.

As ever with the Nazis, it was not an original idea. Ello was sure she had seen a face-only study of Hindenburg somewhere – with just one word under it. But it was stunningly powerful – just about the most effective photograph she had ever seen. She was pretty sure it had been used as a poster by the Nazi Party in one of the elections, last year.

The Hesses were now presenting their gift – a piece of Allach porcelain. It was specially commissioned, Hess informed his Führer, from the factory, up near Dachau. The Allach company had recently opened a branch in the camp itself, using captive labour. As Ello knew, they had already complained that outbreaks of typhoid among the prisoners were affecting production.

Hitler tore the wrapping paper from his gift, pouting the while. To gasps of appreciation from the onlookers, a panting porcelain Alsatian was revealed, modelled on Hitler's dog, Muck. It was, in Ello's view, the epitome of kitsch.

Anni had somehow summoned her husband, without appearing to move, to clear away wrapping paper initially, and finally the presents themselves, except Ziegler's offering.

Using the distraction, Ello rose with willowy grace, no mean feat from the low wide armchair, and with a murmur of excuse left the lounge. Hitler, his mind still on his gifts, hardly noticed her go.

She made her way out of the door, along the hall, past the library on her right, past the cloakroom, toward the kitchen. As she went, she thought of Rudi. She had told him she was away, visiting a girlfriend. The last time she had been in Hitler's company, he had been frantic with concern for her. It was weeks before he had simmered down and stopped twitching.

The kitchen was at the far end of the second floor, served by a staff stairway and external entrance. As Ello had hoped, the presiding cook was Therese Linke. She had been drafted in from Haus Wachenfeld, Hitler's country residence in the Bavarian Alps, to deal with the extra work in Munich, now that he was Chancellor. Frau Linke had known her since girlhood; she used to pat her on the head and call her *Mäuschen* – little mouse.

Now grey and much stouter, Linke was presiding over the loading of Hitler's tray. Hitler had a dish of poached eggs and creamed potatoes. Everybody else at luncheon was being served white sausages and sauerkraut, except Hess, whose spinach was being handwashed in mineral water by one of his own cooks.

'Frau Linke!'

For a second, the cook was annoyed at having her concentration broken, but only for a second: 'Fräulein Ello! I didn't recognise you! How long is it now? Oh, what a lovely young woman you have become!'

Ello smiled. 'Thank you, Frau Linke. I just came to say hello. But I can see how busy you are. May I take up the Führer's tray?'

Therese Linke's eyes widened at the request. Anni Winter would never have allowed this breach of protocol. And indeed Ello would not have tried it, if she hadn't known Anni was safely ensconced in the lounge. Ello waited, as two younger women cooks covered the food with silver chafing dishes to keep it warm, before its journey to the dining room.

As she expected, Frau Linke's surprise eventually turned to understanding. This happened slowly; the cook was not given to rapid thought. She saw that Ello wished to serve the Führer, in this most literal and feminine of ways, by bringing his food. She was delighted.

She took Hitler's tray and gave it to Ello. 'There, Fräulein Ello, and now if you'll excuse me ...'

'Of course, Frau Linke.'

Outside in the corridor, carrying the tray, Ello whimpered in frustration. The drink accompanying his meal was Fachinger mineral water. She should have known that, from the Wednesday lunches at the Ostaria. The gelatine round the atropine capsules would take minutes to dissolve in the cold water. Meanwhile, it would be clearly visible.

She had made a stupid mistake in not bringing the poison in powder form, in a twist of paper. If she had, Hitler would have been dead in hours. She considered trying to break one of the capsules, but rejected the idea. She might be seen, and anyway, the only way to break it would be to use her teeth. Suppose she swallowed some? The hallucinations accompanying mild atropine poisoning did not appeal.

The other guests were just taking their places in the dining room. There was a low hum of conversation, led by Hoffmann, who appeared drunk already. They all knew Hitler well enough not to wait for him to give a conversational lead.

Ello laid the tray on the edge of the table and served Hitler the first course of his luncheon, and his drink. His elaborate Viennese sweet would be brought up later. He beamed at her, as she took the place left empty at his right hand. She made up her mind to wait for the coffee at the end of the meal. The capsules dissolved in coffee almost instantly, she had tried it.

Georg Winter appeared again, bringing food. Hoffmann, purple in the face, was boomingly telling a string of Dachau jokes currently doing the rounds. Ziegler was smoothly paying court to the prettier of the two secretaries, with an occasional glance across at Ello.

Hess stared bug-eyed at Hitler, while mechanically munching food without tasting it. Hess had married poor plain Ilse Pröhl, now tucking into her sausages with gusto as Frau Hess, at Hitler's command. And then he had ordered the honeymoon postponed, so the long-suffering Ilse could chaperone Geli. Hess was a brilliant man – he had written all the difficult bits of *Mein Kampf*, in Landsberg. So why did he subsume himself in Hitler? What did he see in him? What did anybody see in him? Ello felt a wave of despair.

Hitler scoffed his sweet, then suddenly broke his self-imposed silence to hold forth on the subject of art. Perhaps he feared some of the ateliers they were to visit that afternoon would contain Expressionist or Cubist paintings. At any rate, a diatribe burst out of him, without warning or apparent prompting. Naturally, it was listened to in reverential silence by everybody around the table, although for reasons unclear to Ello, it was directed entirely at Hoffmann.

Hitler's unwavering gaze honed in on the photographer, ignoring everybody else. He chopped the air with his right forearm as he spoke:

'Art serves a social purpose, Hoffmann. It draws a true picture of life. It is clear and simple, in style and subject. It is healthy and beautiful. Solid and decent.' His voice was rising as he spoke. 'It is *German*,' he insisted, making an especially vigorous downward motion. 'And not international. Like the works of Böcklin. Like the works of von Schwind. Do you know the painting *A Symphony*, by Moritz von Schwind?'

'Er ...'

Ello smothered a giggle. This was one of Hitler's oft-repeated monologues. Another was how a premonition had helped him survive a gas attack in the war. The inner workings of his Selve car, the first he had ever had, was a third. At Haus Wachenfeld, the insomniac Hitler would summon Hoffmann or Hess or Bormann to hear these same stories over and over again, late at night, until they fell asleep – which Hitler fortunately took no offence at.

Without further ado, the Führer launched into his umpteenth exposition of von Schwind's painting. Everybody round the table had stopped eating.

'It was painted in 1852,' Hitler began. 'Oil on canvas. It measures 168.8 by 100 centimetres. It shows an orchestra playing a symphony to the court. But everything in the painting *has a purpose*. You see, Hoffmann?'

'Yes, indeed.'

'The parts of the picture represent the parts of the symphony: andante, scherzo, allegro and so on. Not only do we know which symphony they are playing – Beethoven, *Fantasie für Klavier, Orchester und Chor* – you can even see which *part* of it they are playing. You can *see* which *notes*.'

Hitler made chopping motions to emphasise his point. 'And we know who we are looking at. It is quite clear. In the choir we see Hofrat Spaun, in profile. Next to him, the singer Vogel, from Vienna. Then Franz Schubert and Franz Grillparzer. We *know* who the conductor is. We can *see* who the conductor is. He is recognisable as himself. He is *Kapellmeister* Franz Lachner. Clear and unmistakeable. He could be nobody else. In the wings, Maximiliana von Blittersdorf. The music was dedicated to her. How do we know it is Maximiliana von Blittersdorf, Hoffmann? Because it *looks like* Maximiliana von Blittersdorf. Hair, skin, eyes. It is Maximiliana von Blittersdorf, represented in *paint*. To be German, Hoffmann, *is to be clear*!'

There were vigorous nods and murmurs of agreement round the table – *Jawohl! Sicher! Richtig!* Only the Berlin secretaries looked down shyly at the napery – feeling a little out of their depth. When coffee came, Ello put her hand in her pocket, cradling the capsules. But Ziegler had grown bored with the prettier secretary and never took his eyes off her.

She hoped for another opportunity that afternoon.

5

To her surprise, Ello travelled in the lead Mercedes, with Hitler – acknowledged as his companion, at least among his intimates. Hitler shyly took her hand as they drove along, like an adolescent on his first date. But she was far more aware of the brooding presence of Schreck, at the wheel.

They drove to Paul Roloff's atelier in Odeonsplatz. As the second Mercedes disgorged Hoffmann, and then Herr and Frau Hess and Ziegler, Hitler's party were met on the pavement outside the atelier by Karl Caspar and his wife, Maria.

Karl Caspar was a Professor at the Munich Academy, mainly known for his altarpiece at Munich's Church of Our Lady. His work was being criticised by the Nazis. The *Völkischer Beobachter* had just devoted a full page to attacking him, describing his paintings as 'looking as if he had painted them with his elbows dipped in paint'. The Caspars had apparently been appointed as guides for the afternoon's tour of the ateliers.

Karl Caspar was a tiny man, a head shorter than his wife. He had a full beard, round glasses and a tight, turned-down mouth. He looked more like a passed-over bank-clerk than a professor of art. The wife, Maria Caspar-Filser – also a painter – looked tense and fearful at his side. She bobbed a curtsey to Hitler, who gave the couple a curt nod. Ziegler and Hoffmann treated them with disdain – a bad sign. The Hesses appeared not to have seen them at all.

Up in the atelier, the artist Paul Roloff turned out to be

young, skinny and painfully eager to please. His work was largely in the Old Master style. Hitler stopped in front of a portrait in oils of the architect Paul-Ludwig Troost.

Troost had converted the ancient Barlow Palace into the Brown House, following design sketches Hitler had scribbled on the back of menus at the Café Heck. Ello knew him well, from the soirées at her family's home. His wife, Gerdy, had designed the uncomfortable armchairs and the rest of the furniture at Hitler's apartment.

Roloff's portrait showed the bespectacled Troost full-length in a white coat, carrying a pencil, with an architectural model visible at a window to his right. Interestingly, to Ello at any rate, Troost was posed standing with his clenched left hand on his hip, elbow bent outwards. She had never once seen him stand like that – but the rather effeminate posture was characteristic of Hitler.

Hitler flapped a hand at Hess, who trotted to his side. 'This one,' he said, giving a jerky nod at the portrait of Troost. Hess nodded and spoke to the artist. A price would be fixed later. Hess would make all the arrangements.

Eventually, the Führer and his entourage decamped downstairs, and spilled onto the pavement. There was no question of the partially discredited Caspars travelling with the Führer, but nobody had given any thought as to how they were to get to the next atelier, as there was not enough room for them in the second car.

After some discussion, Hoffmann gave up his place; Hess radioed for a car to take him home. The Caspars squeezed into the second Mercedes, next to a disdainful Ziegler and Herr Hess, with Frau Hess perched primly on the jump seat.

The next stop was at the studio of the sculptor Ferdinand Liebermann – an official studio, paid for out of government funds. Because it was the atelier of a sculptor, it was massive, with a ceiling of skylights over twenty feet high. Hitler greeted Liebermann with a warm, self-consciously firm handshake.

Liebermann had made the bust of Geli, after her death; the one placed in the mausoleum that Geli's room had become. The sculptor had now created a bronze of Hitler, as a pendant companion-piece to the Geli bust.

As the group gathered round it, Liebermann, a portly figure who smoked incessantly, removed its covering cloth like a magician doing a party trick. In three-quarter profile, the Führer in bronze looked thoughtful, slightly frowning and, Ello thought, considerably more intelligent than he was. Geli, who had seen through her uncle around the time she went to university, would have laughed her head off at it.

'Excellent,' Hess murmured, giving voice to what he knew Hitler's reaction to be. For a second, Ello had an insane vision of Hitler actually pulling a string to make Hess speak. Ilse Hess nodded in silent support of Hitler, via her husband.

Hitler, too, was nodding to himself. 'Good work, Liebermann.' There was no need to tell Hess to arrange the purchase, it was understood.

Ello had hoped that refreshment would be offered at the ateliers, into which she could slip enough atropine to kill Hitler. But this was proving wide of the mark. It was *so* frustrating.

The next atelier was Max Rauh's, up near the university. Here, the atmosphere was very different to that in Liebermann's studio. Ziegler, Karl Caspar and Rauh were all colleagues at the Munich Academy, all of the same generation. But their situations under the Third Reich could not have been more different:

Ziegler, Hitler's pet artist – creator of the new dead style – was in receipt of commissions directly from the

Führer. Karl Caspar was a suspect figure. Rauh's position was somewhere between the two, though nearer to Karl Caspar's. In the public debate about art currently raging in Munich, the Nazis had praised some of Rauh's work – notably an autumn landscape. But when Hitler stopped in front of another of Rauh's paintings, there was a thickening silence in the atelier.

Ello wondered what Gerhard Glaser would have made of Rauh's *St Antony*. Her interest in art had deepened since her friendship with Glaser. She had asked him to take her to the Neue Pinakothek, and explain the paintings. The trip had not yet materialised, though Ello resolved to keep asking until it did.

Rauh had painted St Antony in a monk's cowl, holding a child. Both the forms and the colours were representational. Ello frowned, trying to master the new subject by sheer effort of will. The Nazis demanded a photographic norm in form and colour. They wanted a subject matter that celebrated some aspect of the Racial Community, usually what was commonly known as *Blu-Bo – Blut und Boden* – the mystical union of Blood and Soil.

Blond peasants tilling the soil with horses or oxen fitted the bill nicely, as did families of blond peasants eating, or blonde Germanic motherhood – preferably full-breasted. Brooding romantic German or Italian mountains in gloomy weather were also de rigueur – perhaps with a blasted tree. Seascapes in bad weather, like Ziegler's gift to Hitler of *Burning Sea by Capri*, were a permitted occasional variant.

Rauh's *St Antony* was a religious subject, which was bad, but not necessarily enough on its own to damn the artist. Nevertheless, Ello sensed that Rauh was doomed. The child the saint was holding was the main problem. There was something eldritch about him, reminiscent of the eerie children of Otto Dix – something otherworldly, something atypical. The saint himself looked, well, actually a bit

Jewish – much as Christ must have looked. Ello suppressed a giggle.

Hitler's face had turned thunderous. 'This won't do,' he said and stalked towards the stairs of the atelier. Taking his cue from Hitler, Ziegler nodded curtly at his colleague and said, 'We'll speak about this later, Rauh.' He followed his Führer toward the exit.

Karl Caspar was still standing, as if petrified, in front of Rauh's offending picture. He spread his hands helplessly, half-turning to Rauh in a timid gesture of support. At his side, Maria Kaspar-Filser was ivory-pale. She was a plain woman with hair scraped back off her face. Her mouth was working silently now, as if trying to make enough saliva to swallow. She knew what was next on the agenda. The visit to the atelier she shared with her husband.

The Caspars had a light, north-facing studio not far from the Neue Pinakothek. As they all filed in, Ello shot Maria Caspar-Filser a look of support, and gave her arm a brief squeeze.

Hitler and the entourage stopped in front of one of her pieces, entitled *Harvesting the Fruit*. The workers' joy at their labour in the sun had been conveyed by a blurring of colour and form; blending them into the landscape, making them one with it, after the style of August Macke. A clever composition showed a ladder against a tree, with another diagonal formed by a woman holding a basket aloft, all pointing the way to heaven. It was a celebration of fructitude – a celebration of life itself. Hitler glared at the hapless artist, who was close to tears.

At the far end of the atelier was Karl Caspar's *Easter*. Christ rose from a coffin, arms aloft and looked about to leap out at the viewer. His expression gave boundless love. Ello, who was not remotely religious, gasped at its audacious beauty. Tears sprang to her eyes.

101

'Men who are like wild beasts,' Hitler muttered to himself, 'children who, were they alive, must be regarded as the cursed of God.' Ello understood the reference to children to hark back to the Rauh painting.

The Caspars stood together in front of Karl's work. The little clerk-like figure drew himself up to his full height. 'Excellency,' he said, 'you don't understand anything about this.'

Ello thought it the bravest act she had ever witnessed.

There was silence for a second. Then Ziegler emitted an indignant coughing-gasp. Ilse Hess's mouth dropped open. Hess actually touched his gun. Hitler stared at Karl Caspar, his eyes flashing violet.

Ello stepped forward and took him by the arm. The contact startled him; he jumped slightly.

'*Mein Führer*,' she said respectfully, but firmly, unconsciously imitating the way Anni Winter handled him. 'Come, *mein Führer*. Why don't we go back to the apartment now? Hmm?' She stood close to him, letting her breast touch his arm.

Hitler looked at Carl Kaspar, then at her. 'Yes,' he said. 'Yes, very well.'

The others were dismissed; she and Hitler went back to the apartment alone. He acceded immediately to her request for a coffee. She shut her eyes for a second when he ordered one for himself, praying, finally, for some luck. But when it came, it was placed on the far side of her. He made no reference to the events of the afternoon. They sat in silence.

'*Ellochen*,' he said eventually. 'I want to draw you.'

His gaze met hers. She could leave now, but if she did, would there be another opportunity to kill him? She hesitated.

'I will fetch my materials,' he said, standing. 'Get undressed in Geli's room and then come back here. We shall not be disturbed.'

'All right.'

She walked with him toward the dining room, then turned back, telling him she was going to fetch her hand-bag. When he was out of sight, she tipped four atropine capsules into his half-drunk cup of coffee. Then she went to Geli's room. She undressed as quickly as possible, before she could start thinking about what she was doing.

When she walked back to him, naked, he had his drawing block and materials ready.

He started to draw her. The coffee was still there, cold and untouched, when he finished.

Part IV
Spring 1933

1

It was Glaser's first case from Chief Inspector Sauer since Geli Raubal. Ascher Weintraub had been murdered, shot dead at his gallery. Glaser sat in his office with his eyes shut, squeezing tears, picturing the old man in his mind. All the talks they had had echoed in his head, bringing the Expressionist painters they had talked about alive – Marc, Macke, Kokoschka, Beckmann, Kirchner, Gabriele Münter, Dix …

He even managed a wry smile as he heard the now dead old man testily say 'Dix was not an Expressionist, Gerhard, Dix was *Neue Sachlichkeit*. But colour! Ah colour … Dix could do colour, like you've never seen!'

Glaser sighed, running a hand over his beard. Sauer's report stated that Ascher Weintraub had three light bullet wounds in his head, but the shot that killed him went into his heart. His safe had been broken into. According to a statement from Weintraub's sister, Zipporah Ballat, a painting had been stolen from the safe – *Blue Horses*, by Franz Marc. Sauer's report gave the theft of the painting as the motive for the murder of the art dealer.

Glaser had known Ascher's sister was a partner in the gallery. He had not, however, known there was a third partner: Dr Johannes Lange. Lange's statement said he had employed the man charged with the murder – Sepp Kunde, the gallery's handyman.

The murder weapon, a Mauser 7.63mm pistol, had been abandoned at the scene of the crime. It had Kunde's

107

MICHAEL DEAN

fingerprints on it. Glaser's task was to establish whether there was sufficient evidence to warrant a prosecution of Sepp Kunde for the murder of Ascher Weintraub.

Anger and frustration overwhelmed Glaser's sadness. Glaser embraced them, hating the helplessness that sadness implied. On impulse, he left his office and went to see Sauer.

For eighteen months, the Chief Inspector had only sporadically put in an appearance at Ettstrasse. From the way he swaggered around, it was generally reckoned he had Party protection. As far as Glaser knew, he had no specific Party job, which made his untouchability even more intriguing.

Anyone wishing to see Sauer – even his superiors – had to visit him at home, where he held court in his villa, on the edge of the Englischer Garten. Nobody dared ask how he had paid for the place.

Glaser went there by tram. His motorcar, the adapted green Opel Frosch,was out of action at the moment – a nut in the radiator outlet had gone missing.

He had not given Sauer advance warning of his visit, to try and catch him unawares.

The lilac-washed villa was surrounded by chestnut trees. A tiny uniformed maid opened the door. Her petulant face, like a little Pekingese dog, tilted up at Glaser.

'Are you from Herr Forster? It's about time,' she spat out.

Glaser, taken by surprise, said 'No' and immediately regretted it. The maid bustled off, muttering something about money – *her* money. Glaser's mind was whirling, as he walked through the vestibule. The maid had said Herr Forster, not Inspector Forster. Forster is a common sort of name. Only this week he and Lotte had seen a tripey film about U-boats, starring Adolf Forster. But even so …

A door opened near the end of the hall and Sauer

108

appeared. The Chief Inspector was a huge man. He was carrying even more of a belly than the last time Glaser had seen him.

He had a widow's peak, walrus moustache and large, though heavily sloping, shoulders.

He reminded Glaser of Lovis Corinth's *Self-Portrait*, except that Corinth had painted a skeleton next to himself.

'Dr Glaser!' Sauer shouted. 'Here about the Jew from the art gallery, eh?'

Sauer's drawing room was sumptuous. The furniture was all strip-steel Bauhaus; new, but clashing with the older Regency-stripe wallpaper. Frau Sauer made a brief appearance, to ask if coffee was needed. Glaser had met her a couple of times. She was a downtrodden, long-defeated woman, with an air of ineffable tiredness. When coffee was ready, brought by the tiny maid, Frau Sauer did not join them – retreating from the fray, no doubt.

Glaser kept his questions bland. He had little hope of information about the case from the Chief Inspector; he merely hoped to get him relaxed and talking about himself, to see what would emerge.

'Three bullet wounds to the head; that's very strange,' Glaser mused. 'What do you make of that?'

Sauer shrugged his thick, low shoulders. He was wearing a check shirt and a brown tie with a huge knot. 'The Jew wouldn't tell Kunde where the painting was. So he was tortured.' Another shrug.

Glaser nodded, keeping his face neutral. Tortured to get a painting by Franz Marc? It made no sense. The prices for Expressionist paintings were plummeting, since the Nazis had declared them racially deviant. Although admittedly prices were down less for Marc than other Expressionists, because he was considered a war hero. But it still meant the killer wanted that specific painting, not any of the others in the gallery. Why?

109

'And the weapon being abandoned?'

Sauer looked impatient, then masked it with a smile so wide it could have been ironic.

'Kunde was disturbed,' he said with mock thoughtfulness.

'By …?'

Another huge shrug. 'Who knows? A visiting rabbi?' Sauer roared with laughter. 'Who visits art galleries? You maybe. Anyway, it's hardly worth coming all the way out here for, is it? Or did you just want to see my villa?' Sauer gave another bellow of laughter.

Glaser thought rapidly, deciding to chance it. 'Got it in one,' he smiled. 'Where did you get the money?'

Sauer's heavy mouth fell open, his eyes popped. There was a second of silence; Glaser thought the ploy had misfired. Then more laughter – more of a chuckle this time. Glaser understood – the Chief Inspector was bored out of his wits, and only too happy to talk about himself.

Sauer stood. 'Finish up your coffee. I'll show you something. You didn't come by car, did you?'

'No. How did you know?'

'I'd have heard it coming. We'll use mine.'

Sauer had a new cream-coloured limousine. It started to rain, as they drove into town. With the windscreen-wipers swishing, the Chief Inspector slowed past his recent acquisitions – proudly indicating the Peter Rath jeweller's shop in Theatinerstrasse, and the Gelateria Romana, an ice-cream parlour in nearby Löwengrube.

Glaser knew the ice-cream parlour well. He used to take Kaspar and Magda there when they were little. It was their big treat. He used to keep them out late, much to Lotte's annoyance. The place stayed open until midnight. It was closed now.

Both businesses, Sauer informed Glaser, had been Jewish-owned. The Chief Inspector talked enthusiastically about his plans for his new purchases. Then he headed the limousine back to Prielmayerstrasse, where he pulled up, grazing the white-walled front tyre on the curb.

'How long have you had the properties?' Glaser asked, as he got out of Sauer's car, outside the Ministry. The rain-sodden air stank of malt. Sauer shot him a suspicious glance, but wound down the window to answer.

'Not long,' he said. 'Now's the time to buy, I tell you. The Jews have got to sell up, and they know it. My advice to you, Glaser, is to liquidise your assets and buy Jewish property. That's what I did.'

'I'll bear it in mind,' Glaser said. 'Thanks for the advice.' But he was unable completely to hide his disgust at Sauer, and they parted coldly. He watched the limousine out of sight in the rain.

Back in his office, he reflected, puffing at his pipe. Buying two businesses in the centre of Munich meant a considerable outlay. Liquidise your assets, Sauer had said. Which asset had *he* liquidised?

2

'Hello, old man.' Without waiting for a response to the by now customary cheeky greeting, Rüdiger von Hessert perched casually on the edge of Glaser's desk, and flicked through Sauer's file on the Weintraub case.

'Weintraub. Wait a minute, you knew him, didn't you?'

'Yes.'

'Gerhard, I'm sorry!'

'Thank you.'

Rudi had his nose in the case file, reading and murmuring to himself at the same time. 'Start from the outside and work in. Interview the accused last,' he said. 'They're calling it the Glaser Method in law lectures now.'

Glaser tried not to let the younger man see that the compliment had pleased him. But Rüdiger spotted it and grinned.

'Hey!' Rüdiger dabbed at a name in the file. 'Johannes Lange. What's he got to do with it?'

'Apparently, he's a partner in the gallery. He hired the accused, Sepp Kunde.'

'Do you know Lange? Come to that, do you know Kunde?'

'I've never heard of Lange. I've seen Kunde once or twice, at the gallery, but never spoken to him.'

'Can I come with you? When you interview Lange? I know him.'

'You know everybody.'

'Then I'm in? On the Weintraub case?'

Glaser nodded. 'Yes, you're in, if you want to be. But let's look at the crime scene first, eh?'

Glaser was to meet von Hessert at the Weintraub Gallery. He went there by tram, as his motorcar was still out of action. He got off at Lenbachplatz, lowering himself gingerly from the high tram platform. His mood lightened as he took in the elegant open area of irregular shape, dominated by the Wittelsbach Fountain, with its massive limestone and marble statuary.

Aside from the Weintraub Gallery, three other art galleries and two of Munich's five art auction houses were here – Brüchwiller Brothers at number 78, and the Munich Art Dealing Company at 159.

On this chilly Friday morning, the square was bustling with shoppers and office workers. It had also lately become one of the gathering places for the unemployed. Sitting on the park benches, groups of them were talking in subdued voices. Two or three, near the fountain, were clearly newly unemployed. They were still clutching the dreaded Blue Letters, telling them they were out of a job.

A beanpole figure in a shabby jacket and plus-fours, who clearly knew the ropes, was addressing them:

'You can't have it any worse than me, lads. No benefit because I'm single, and got no kids. No work because I'm a communist. I pleaded with them at Thalkirchnerstrasse, but that bastard Wimmer's got a heart of flint. I tell you, when we come to power we'll string the *Sozis* up first. I will personally hang Wimmer by his moustache and bollocks from the nearest lamp-post.'

That got a laugh from the unemployed. Glaser was indignant. Thomas Wimmer, the newly arrested Chairman of the Munich Social Democrats, had a post at the Department of Works – a grandiose pile in Thalkirchnerstrasse. His life in

politics and the trade union movement had been dedicated
to improving the lot of the working man.

He was also, Glaser thought with rising anger, at least as
proletarian as his detractor – he was the illegitimate son of
a foundry worker. It occurred to Glaser to buttonhole bean
pole and tell him of Wimmer's imprisonment by the Nazis
but he thought better of it.

Beanpole noticed Glaser watching him, and balled his
fists aggressively. Glaser hastily walked on. On the grass, a
group of three, all in shabby suits, were playing *tarok* with a
pack of grubby cards. Glaser walked past them, intending to
cut across the square.

Ahead of him was an old war veteran with no legs, sitting
in the gutter, selling matches from a tray round his neck
His cry of 'Matches! Matches!' was ignored by the passers
by. A yellow mongrel appeared from nowhere, cocked it
leg and sprayed a few drops on the old man's tray. The old
man yelled at the dog, until it ran away.

A tinny grey van rattled past at walking pace, then
stopped with a jerk. Five SA got out of it, the folding seats in
the van springing back behind them. Their front-laced
boots thudded on the pavement, as they stopped to pu
their brown caps on. They were armed with belted daggers
and holstered pistols.

The Troop Leader wore gold-rimmed spectacles. From
his age, he could have been an Old Fighter, one of the beer
hall brawlers who had been with Hitler from the beginning
He fished a Blood Flag out of the van and planted it on the
pavement. Two SA flanked it, loudly and threateningly
rattling their collecting tins in the faces of passers-by.

'Winter Help! Support German workers,' they called
out aggressively. Occasionally they varied it, especially to
attractive women, with an ironic 'For the wicked Nazis!'

Everybody who walked past paid up, and paid up well
They were afraid not to. Two of the troop went up to the

114

unemployed men at the benches.

'Anybody here like a smoke?' one of the SA-men said. The men broke off their desultory conversation. True National Socialist cigarettes,' supplied the SA-man encouragingly. 'Smoke these and you'll be fighting bloated capitalists, not aiding them.'

Entire packets were offered round.

'These for free?' asked one of the men.

''Course they are,' the SA-man said. 'What's your favourite smoke? We've got Drummer, Alarm, Storm and New Front. The first packet's on us. After that you get them at the SA rate. Drummer's the cheapest. Three-and-a-half pfennigs. Come on!' The SA-man laughingly quoted the Drummer advertising slogan, on all the hoardings: '"Full of enjoyment to the last puff!"'

One of the unemployed took a packet of Drummer, took out a cigarette and let the SA-man light it for him. He drew on it luxuriously, then wordlessly led the way to the van, to sign up to the SA-man's troop. He changed into his new brown shirt there and then, on the pavement, showing his skinny body with its flabby grey skin.

The SA's brown shirts were originally bought up used from the Colonial Service, but now the Boss factory at Metzingen was making them: they were good shirts, thick and warm – stylish, too. The SA-man and his new recruit, in his new shirt, still smoking his first free cigarette, broke open a bottle of beer.

Glaser needed to pass the SA van to get to the Weintraub Gallery, on the far side of Lenbachplatz. Since the start of what the *Völkischer Beobachter* called the 'big clean-up' – the Nazi seizure of Munich by force a month ago – the SA had standing orders to beat up anybody who did not give a Hitler salute and say *Heil Hitler* to them.

Glaser had never used the Hitler salute, or the Hitler greeting. Would the fact that he was a public prosecutor save him from a beating? Glaser considered the matter. At the Ministry of Justice, it probably would. Out on the streets, after they'd had a few beers – no.

Now was not the time to take chances. The Nazis had smashed up the Social Democrat headquarters and the *Münchener Post* offices. Glaser knew who had done it, SA Storm 16/L led by Emil Maurice, Geli's former lover, now restored to Hitler's favour and a Munich City Councillor.

Unlike the many previous attacks on the offices, this time there were no SPD Reichsbanner fighters defending it. Those who, like Glaser, had argued for the winding down of the Reichsbanner had prevailed. After smashing the offices to splinters, the SA had left the wreckage all over the pavement, stopping anybody from cleaning it up, as a none too-subtle public reminder of what happened to their opponents.

As a further reminder, an SA troop had chosen the basement of the former trade union headquarters, in Pestalozzistrasse, for one of their torture cellars. It would be typical of the SA, if they found out Glaser was a Social Democrat, to take him there for a beating, or a whipping, or to have his stomach pumped over-full with water. It would make a point. That was how they thought.

He set off in the other direction, walking round three sides of a square. The Weintraub Gallery was closed. The sentry outside was Bavarian Police, green uniformed, not SA. This was pure luck, as the SA now had police status. Glaser identified himself, still without giving a Hitler salute, and was waved in.

The current selection was still on the walls. Glaser glimpsed the August Macke, *Anglers on the Rhine*, the painting he had discussed with the old art dealer. For some reason he mused that Elisabeth Gerhardt, Macke's beloved girlfriend, must have been the same age as his son Kaspar when Macke was killed in the war.

And then he remembered his discussion with Kaspar – was it a row? – about whether photography was or was not art. Kaspar, of course, took the modern line and said it was. The youth, sensitive for all his brawn, had got upset when Glaser called it 'the lying art'.

'The surface tells lies, boy,' he had said. 'Only the Expressionists have inner truth. They paint from inside, from the heart and soul.' Had he been too hard on Kaspar? Probably. Lotte was always telling him he was too hard on Kaspar.

Alone in the deep silence, in the tiny room that still smelled of the old man, with Expressionist paintings on the walls, Glaser thought of life as fragile and precious. For the first time since boyhood, he shut his eyes and prayed. He asked God for deliverance for Lotte, for Kaspar and Magda, and for Germany.

The Public Prosecutor walked through to the office where he had drunk lemon tea with Ascher Weintraub, and which was now the crime scene of the old man's death. He sat in Weintraub's swivel chair for a while, breathing deeply. Then he got down to business, checking the room, minutely examining the safe. While he was doing this, von Hessert arrived, all action, movement and smiles, flustering apologies for being late.

'Where do we start?' he said.

Glaser frowned. 'Herr Weintraub didn't co-operate,' he said, sitting down again and nodding backwards at the wall behind him.

The plaster had been blown away, exposing the stonework beneath. In the corner of the office there were still some shards of green safe.

'Safe blown with gelignite?' von Hessert said, peering at it.

Glaser swivelled in Weintraub's chair and nodded. 'Wad

117

of gelignite held in place by putty. Detonator with a fus
attached.'

'Noise?'

Glaser shrugged. 'Smother it with cushions.'

'Where from?'

'Brought them with him. Part of his kit. He meant t
blow the safe, not kill Herr Weintraub.'

'So, Weintraub disturbed him?'

Glaser nodded, filling and lighting his pipe. 'Probably
Six o'clock in the evening. Herr Weintraub maybe cam
back to the gallery for something. The murderer ties him
up, makes him play Russian roulette, because he won'
open the safe. Herr Weintraub holds out, the murdere
loses patience, kills him, blows the safe anyway.'

Von Hessert stared at the exposed stone, up close. H
touched it with his fingertips.

'Professional job?'

Glaser swivelled again in the chair, so he was lookin
at him. 'Shouldn't think so. The safe was a cheap one. Th
back was screwed on. You can still see some screws there
look. It was painted with green enamel to make it loo
welded. The murderer could have simply unscrewed it. A
real safe-cracker would have spotted that.'

'This stolen painting …?'

Glaser nodded again, puffing smoke. 'A real puzzle. Wh
blow a safe to steal a painting, when there are paintings a
round the walls?'

'And why would a handyman want a painting?'

Glaser laughed. 'That's your aristocratic snobbery, vo
Hessert. I checked Sepp Kunde. He's got a record. He ha
his own business once. No doubt, he worked as a handyma
because he's a convicted communist. It was the only job h
could get.'

Von Hessert strode athletically to the bits of green safe in th
corner and squatted down by them. 'So, why leave the gun?'

118

'Why not? If the murderer isn't Kunde. There are only Kunde's prints on it.'

'And why are Kunde's prints on it?'

'Because he moved it when he found the body.'

'OK. But if it wasn't Kunde, how did the murderer get in?'

'The door's been jemmied.'

Herr Weintraub's keys had not been found, Glaser recalled from Sauer's report. But such items often disappear in the aftermath of an investigation. He did not share that information with von Hessert.

Von Hessert frowned. 'You really don't think Sepp Kunde is our man, do you?'

Glaser blew another plume of smoke. 'I'd be surprised if he is.'

'So what's the next move?'

'We go and see your friend Johannes Lange.'

3

The distinguished doctor Johannes Lange was Departmental Director of the German Research Centre for Psychiatry. Tucked away discreetly in Munich's tree-lined northern suburbs, the Research Centre turned out to be a newish glass annexe to the much older, stone-built, Kaiser Wilhelm Institute.

When they arrived, Glaser and von Hessert were told at reception that Dr Lange had been delayed, but would be with them shortly. They were given directions to his office but not escorted there. The office turned out to be surprisingly small. Von Hessert took a seat. Glaser went to look at the books on Lange's bookcase.

On the bottom shelf were two heavy blue-bound volumes of *Studies on the Jewish Problem.* Next to them, stacks of bound and unbound copies of the popular magazines *People and Race* and *Magazine for Racial Hygiene.*

On the upper shelves were well-thumbed books in bright dust-jackets. Glaser ran his eye down them. There was Hans Günther's *Origins and Racial History of the Germans,* the garish yellow dust-jacket of Hermann Esser's *The Jewish World Plague,* and a disintegrating copy of Engelhardt's *The Jews and Us.*

At that moment, Lange swept in. He was immaculately besuited and suntanned, with swept-back greying hair. His appearance and manner were that of a middle-aged matinée idol. Without apology for keeping the lawyer

120

aiting, he greeted von Hessert effusively, pumping his
and, but nodded curtly at Glaser, as if at someone below
he salt.

'What can I do for you?' he enquired briskly, taking a seat
ehind his desk.

Glaser sat and began his questioning. 'You placed Sepp
unde as a handyman with the Weintraub Gallery, in which
ou are a partner,' he said. 'Why did you do that?'

Lange leaned back in his chair. 'Finding Sepp a job was
art of an arrangement I made with the Kunde twins.'

'Sepp Kunde has a twin?' Glaser failed to mask his
urprise. It wasn't in Sauer's report.

Lange gave the Public Prosecutor a pitying look. 'Yup. He
ertainly does. Sepp's twin, August, is in Stadelheim for
murder. In return for finding Sepp a job, Sepp and August
et us run some tests on them here.'

'What kind of tests?' von Hessert said.

Lange gave a small, impatient shrug. 'This Institute
tudies monozygotic twins – twins from the same egg. We
ompare their body hair patterns. We take semen samples
ver two days. We put tubes through the nose into the
ungs, then feed in coal gas, which makes them cough. We
ollect the sputum from the coughing and compare it.
Ve give them two-litre enemas, so their rectums are hyper-
istended ...'

Von Hessert had had enough of this. 'So that's what you
o here, Lange!' he blurted out.

After a short pause, Glaser asked 'What view did you form
f Sepp Kunde?'

Lange stood athletically and fetched a thick file from a
iling cabinet. It was marked '𝔎𝔲𝔫𝔡𝔢' in thick black Gothic
cript. He opened it on his desk, turning over papers, read-
ng aloud anything that caught his attention: 'Family from
wabia. Father was a smelter, died young of heart trouble.
Here they are, by the way, the twins ...'

121

Lange passed over prison photographs, showing the twins full-face and in profile. The resemblance was astonishing. Sepp had slightly less hair and a more sensitive face. He was wearing a tie and a wing collar. His twin was wearing a jacket with a round velvet collar. Von Hessert leaned close to Glaser to look at the photographs.

Lange continued to read snippets from the file. 'Sepp was once accused of receiving but it turned out August had done it. Sepp is more intelligent, knows poetry off by heart – Greif, Heine, Goethe. And understands it. Got through school easily, despite being lazy. He was a Red Guard in the Councils Republic – fought against the Freikorps von Epp.'

Glaser was impressed, though he tried not to show it. Like many sedentary men, he had a sneaking admiration for fighters, even fighters for a cause as repugnant as the Councils Republic – which he viewed as an anarchist – communist mob which had resisted the attempts of SPD men like Erhard Auer to civilise it.

'Became a clockmaker,' Lange went on, still describing Kunde's career, 'then a cabinetmaker. August was a vagrant for a while.'

Lange fell silent, turning over documents and carbon copies, some clipped together.

Then he read on: 'Their characters are identical. But Sepp blames his fate on problems with society, rather than his own innate criminality.' He looked up from the file. 'The point is, the Kunde twins are a classic example of how crime is in the blood. August is a born murderer; Sepp is a born murderer. Sepp committing his matching murder was completely predictable, from a study of August's criminal record.'

'Then why did you get him a job with Herr Weintraub?'

Lange lost his temper. 'Glaser, three to four births per thousand produce identical twins. We have waited a long, long time to find criminal twins, one of whom has committed a murder. Sepp committing his matching murder was a vital breakthrough. It validated the whole twin method. I have explained to you how important this work is. For heaven's sake, man!'

Again there was silence in the room. Von Hessert had a slight smile playing round his face.

'When did you become a partner in the Weintraub Gallery?' said Glaser.

'At the beginning of this year.'

'Just before you got Sepp Kunde a job there?'

Lange was still angry. For a moment Glaser thought he was going to refuse to answer, but finally he said 'Yes'.

'When did you last see Ascher Weintraub?'

'A couple of days before Sepp Kunde killed him.'

'What did you talk about?'

Lange expelled air in a kind of angry sigh. 'Weintraub was planning to emigrate to Palestine. I offered to buy him out.'

'Make him a good offer, did you?'

'Don't be impertinent, Glaser. I don't have to put up with this.'

Glaser stood. 'I think that is all for now, Dr Lange. Thank you for your time.'

Lange ignored him and spoke to von Hessert. 'I hope we meet again soon, von Hessert. Under more pleasant circumstances.' This with a glance at Glaser.

'By the way,' Glaser said, as they were leaving. 'There can be no sale of the Weintraub Gallery, or any part of it, until the criminal proceedings have run their course.'

Lange took a deep breath. 'We'll see about that. Don't try and obstruct me, Glaser. I warn you. I will be in touch with Dr Gürtner.'

'Oh, I've no doubt you will. We can see ourselves out.'

4

Glaser stood in front of the yellow villa where Ascher Weintraub had lived with his sister. It was on the edge of the
Englischer Garten. Visible through the chestnut trees was
the lilac end wall of Sauer's house. He had not realised,
from the address, that Herr Weintraub and the Chief
Inspector had lived so near each other.

All Glaser knew about the sister, Zipporah Ballat, was that
she was a partner in the art gallery, she had testified that a
painting in the safe called *Blue Horses* had been stolen, and
that she was a professor of history at Munich University. Or
rather she had been. All six Jewish professors had been
dismissed. Of the others, one had committed suicide, four
had emigrated.

Glaser spent some time beating at the door. Eventually a
young maid opened, looking furious, smoothing her black
skirt down over her petticoats.

'Yes!' she snapped impertinently.

'Public Prosecutor Glaser to see Frau Ballat. I am
expected,' Glaser said.

The maid tut-tutted in annoyance and wordlessly let him
in. As Glaser followed her along the brown linoleum
passageway, he looked up the stairs and saw a brawny youth,
dressed only in a pair of black trousers, looking down from
the top of the stairs.

The youth had the same sour expression as the maid. The
maid abandoned Glaser in front of a closed door and went

back upstairs to her paramour.

Glaser knocked and entered a large drawing room. The furniture was a mix of Second Empire and art nouveau. His eye settled first on a Mackintosh dresser, then a huge Manchu rococo vase, edged in brass. Directly ahead of him, on a shelf, was an old-fashioned clock. Above the face, it had a so-called God's Eye – a painted eye which moved every second, right to left and back again.

Books were scattered everywhere, some open face down. There were stacked copies of the Jewish newspaper, the *Jüdische Nachrichtenblatt*, on a pouffé. The only modern element was a gleaming metal-and-glass vitrine, running the length of the room. It was crammed full of porcelain and pottery ornaments, plates and dishes.

A remarkable figure sat at a round, walnut table in the bay window, overlooking the Englischer Garten. Frau Ballat was absorbedly playing Solitaire. In her late forties or early fifties, she had a long, sad face, narrow mouth and brown hair piled up elegantly, as if she were going to a ball. Despite her age, she wore a red-flounced velvet gown that showed one creamy shoulder completely, and barely covered her bosom. Despite himself, Glaser found the effect erotic, as he walked toward her.

'What happened to your leg?' called out a corncrake voice, as the cards snapped down.

Glaser was disappointed. In his baggy grey plus-fours and long thick socks, the artificial limb did not show. Indoors, over a short stretch, his gait was even and not noticeably slow. Outside was a different matter. Today was one of the days when he was not using his ebony cane.

'Riding accident,' he lied cheerfully.

As no invitation was forthcoming, he pulled up one of the walnut chairs with grey-blue cushions tied on, and sat opposite her. The slap of the cards going down did not slacken. She did not look at him.

'Public Prosecutor Glaser,' he murmured.

'I know.'

'I'm sorry about your brother. I will miss our friendship and the conversations I had with him.'

The former professor shrugged her shoulders. The telephone rang shrilly from the hall. She put the cards down and strode off to answer it. She was gone for a long time. Glaser could not hear her conversation. When she returned there was no apology, but she did not resume her card game.

'My friend Elsa Marx, from Franz-Josef Strasse,' she said, waving one arm in the direction of the telephone. The loose red dress slid off her shoulder, down to her elbow.

'What …? Marx, the banking family?'

She looked apprehensive for a moment, then decided she could trust him. 'Yes. She's married to Hugo Marx, of Heinrich and Hugo Marx, the bankers. Anyway, that didn't stop them taking three of her paintings. Right off the walls.'

'Taking? You mean stealing?'

'That's a difficult word to define, these days. They've given her about a third of their value. The Courbet was worth fifteen thousand. They gave her five, then took it away.'

'Who did?' Glaser said.

'The Political Police. Three of them. The leader called himself Inspector Forster. He kept smiling at her, Elsa said. I think she'd rather he hadn't.'

'The Political …'

'Well, they're just the muscle. The thugs. The one giving the orders is Buchner.'

'Buchner?'

'Who else?'

Glaser was confused. 'Excuse me, but who on earth …?'

'Ernst Buchner. Our new Director of Bavarian Art Galleries.'

Glaser started to reply when the door banged open. The youth who had been naked to the waist now had a white shirt on. The black trousers were those of a waiter, Glaser now realised. Without a word, the waiter walked over to the vitrine and tried to open it. It was locked. He gave the glass a thump with his fist.

'It's locked,' the waiter yelled at Zipporah Ballat, ignoring Glaser completely. His face was twisted with rage, veins standing out in his neck.

'I'll unlock it then,' she said.

'Who told you to lock it? You silly sow,' the waiter mumbled. He was drunk.

Zipporah Ballat approached the vitrine with a tiny key. Glaser did not see where she had produced it from. She fumbled while unlocking it, the waiter tut-tutting impatiently, in the same way as the maid had, when she let Glaser in. Eventually, Frau Ballat got the vitrine open and lifted the glass.

'What's worth most in here?' said the waiter, peering in.

Zipporah Ballat wordlessly lifted a white plate with a blue motif from its stand. Glaser thought for a second it was Delft, then realised it was from his own home town, Ludwigsburg. She handed the plate to the waiter.

'What's it worth?' he said.

'You should get two hundred for it.'

'What do I tell the Jew swindler, so he doesn't cheat me?'

'It's mid-eighteenth century. Ludwigsburg porcelain. Onion pattern. Painted by Leinfelder from a Chinese …'

'OK, Professor,' shouted the waiter. 'I didn't ask for a bleeding lecture.' He stalked off with the plate, but turned at the door. 'And next time, don't lock the glass cupboard. Or you'll get a clip round the ear.'

He slammed the door as he left. Glaser heard the maid's voice, talking to him, before the front door banged shut, presumably behind both of them.

'My dear Frau Professor ...' Glaser said. He stood and walked over to her at the vitrine. He was distraught.

'Don't worry about me,' she waved an arm at him. 'Sit down. Sit down. I'm OK.'

But she was white in the face, and she sat down heavily in front of her abandoned game of Solitaire.

Glaser resumed his seat opposite her. 'What on earth is going on?'

Zipporah Ballat shrugged. 'After six years in my employ, my maid has decided she's a Nazi.'

'And that entitles her ...'

'It's the villa they want,' Frau Ballat said, waving a hand round the room. 'My husband was killed in the war, you see. And now, with Ascher gone, there's only me. They are trying to find an excuse to report me to the Gestapo. Get me carted off.'

Glaser rubbed his beard. There was nothing he could do. Under the new Malicious Practices Act, anyone could be reported for insulting the Reich government, or any degradation of the National Revolution. Cases were heard in Special Courts for political crimes.

Glaser sighed and began his questioning, adopting a chatty, informal manner. 'Do you know Chief Inspector Sauer? He's a neighbour of yours, I see.'

She looked surprised, but answered readily enough. 'I know *her* – Frau Sauer. Some of the neighbours make a point of greeting me. They offer to get my shopping from shops that won't serve Jews, that sort of thing. Frau Sauer was one of them.'

'Was?'

Frau Ballat nodded. 'She stopped quite suddenly. I imagine he told her to.'

'The Chief Inspector, you mean?'

'Yes. Frau Sauer is completely dominated by her husband. He bullies her. I suspect he beats her. Mind you, it was a relief when she stopped talking to me.'

'Why? Don't you like her?'

'Not particularly. But that wasn't the reason. You end up feeling grateful for every kind word and glance. It's humiliating.'

'Did Chief Inspector Sauer have any contact with your late brother?'

She shook her head. 'Not that I know of. But Ascher didn't confide in me. We hated each other.'

'Oh, surely not …'

She grimaced impatiently. 'I'm not going to sanctify him because he's dead. Ascher was a Zionist.'

Glaser smiled. 'And you're not, presumably?'

'Huh! Listen! Can I tell you a story?'

'Please do!' He liked her enormously.

'My late husband was in a good regiment. The 120th – Bavarian Third Army. The only Jewish officer. He was wounded at Verdun. So they sent him back to the military hospital at Hagen. You follow?' Her heavily lined eyebrows went up.

'I do.'

'He had four operations to remove shrapnel from his skull. He couldn't wear a helmet after that, but he still insisted on returning to the front. You know what he wrote to me?: "Zipporah, if they see how we Jews fought for Germany, maybe they will finally accept us." The day after he wrote that he was hit in the head again, and killed. A helmet would have saved him. He died trying to be a German in Germany. No, Herr Glaser, I'm not a Zionist.'

'I'm sorry. About your husband,' Glaser said.

'Me, too. He was a clever man. Unlike Ascher, who was a *schmerul.* He believed in Fool's Gold.'

'Was he … planning to emigrate?'

'Sure!'

'How far had he got with this plan?'

'He had a place booked on a steamer, sailing from Marseille in three months' time – the *Mariette Pach*. But the British have decided you need five hundred pounds to get into Palestine. That was the problem.'

'Five hundred pounds is … a lot,' he mused.

Zipporah Weintraub nodded. 'They want lusty farmers out there,' she said. 'Not skinny old art dealers with lungs scarred from TB.'

Glaser fought down a smile. 'The painting that was stolen when Ascher was murdered, *Blue Horses*. Did it surprise you that it was in the safe? Not on display in the gallery?'

She frowned. 'Maybe Ascher hoped to take the painting with him. To Palestine. Sell it there. You'd get more for a Franz Marc outside Germany.'

Glaser nodded. It made sense. 'Blue horses were Marc's major theme, of course. But do you happen to know the provenance of the one actually entitled *Blue Horses* – the one that was stolen?'

'I've got the gallery papers upstairs,' said Zipporah Ballat. 'Do you want me to find the provenance note?'

'Please do!'

She strode out again. She walked quickly – a long-paced masculine walk. After the telephone call, Glaser was restless at the thought of another long wait. He pictured Franz Marc's handsome head, with its Roman nose and wavy mouth, in a brown cap, smiling through his yellow pipe, his eyes hooded. That was Macke's portrait of his friend, painted, so Ascher Weintraub had once told him, when Macke and Elisabeth stayed with the Marcs in Munich.

Frau Ballat was back quickly. 'Provenance note,' she said.

Glaser held out his hand for it, but she ignored him.

'Very interesting,' she said, reading the note at the table. 'Only two owners listed. The first is Maria Franck'

'That's …'

'Franz Marc's wife.'

'I don't think she's still in Munich, is she?'

'The Marcs had a studio in Schellingstrasse,' Zipporah Ballat said. 'Number thirty-three. But Maria's in Switzerland now. She had to get out in a hurry. Marc had a Jewish ancestor. It was the second owner who sold Ascher the painting. Heinrich Hoffmann.'

Glaser was amazed. 'Hoffmann?'

'Yes, why are you surprised? He came into the gallery all the time. You know Hoffmann?'

'I've known Hoffmann for twenty years. What's Hoffmann doing with …?'

'He advises Hitler on paintings. Not our sort of stuff, of course. But he knows a lot. Here!'

Zipporah Ballat handed the provenance note over.

'Look at the date it was painted,' she said, nodding at the note. The provenance note showed *Blue Horses* as dating from March 4th, 1916.

'Is there something significant about the date?'

'It was the day Franz Marc was killed.'

'Ah! I see! I didn't know he painted anything as late as 1916.'

'No, neither did anybody else.'

Glaser nodded. A previously unknown work by Franz Marc, painted perhaps hours before his death, made the painting much more valuable, especially if sold abroad. So murdering Herr Weintraub to get it was beginning to make sense.

He hit the provenance note with his hand. 'It doesn't say how much Hoffmann paid Maria Marc for it. That's strange.'

Frau Ballat shrugged. 'I hadn't noticed.'

'How well do you know Sepp Kunde?' Glaser asked.

'Not well. I didn't go into the gallery very often. Ascher didn't want him or need him. Lange brought him in.'

'Yes,' he frowned. 'How did Lange come to be a partner?'

'My brother was a weakling, that's how. Lange tried to muscle in on every Jewish art gallery in Munich. Ascher gave in first. Lange wants to buy us out, naturally. He's made me an offer.'

She looked tired, deep lines appeared at her mouth, around the gash of carmine lipstick.

'No good? Too low?'

She shrugged. 'About two-thirds of the value – for my villa, the gallery, the paintings. Everything I own.'

'Take it!' He hadn't meant to shout, but he did.

'I would if I could,' she shouted back. 'He's already threatened to lower the offer every day I delay.'

'So what's the problem?'

'The problem is – I have another suitor. I'm a popular lady.'

'What? Who?'

'Buchner.'

'Buchner's made an offer, too?'

She sighed. 'He wants to protect the gallery's Expressionist paintings from the Gestapo. Very kind of him. He says the Gestapo will destroy them.'

'There's something in that.'

'No doubt. He wants me to *give* him all the paintings, for the State Galleries. No doubt he'll send the nice Inspector to smile at me while he's taking them. That'll be something to look forward to.'

A grim smile broke from Glaser before he could stop it.

'And he wants my gallery, too, Buchner does. He'll pay for that, but not much. He's given me one week, before the Political Police seize everything and pay what they feel like. Probably nothing.'

Glaser groaned.

'Funnily enough, Lange has given me exactly the same amount of time. He says he will report me to the Gestapo for tax evasion. He tells me that always works.'

'Yes, that's what I've heard, too.' Glaser rubbed a hand over his beard.

'Being reported to the Political Police *and* the Gestapo on the same day would be quite an achievement, don't you think? We Jews always wish to excel.'

Glaser leaned forward. He put his head in his hands. Then came up again. 'Look ... do you want me to help you?'

He told himself it was for old man Weintraub. But he looked apprehensive at the possible astringent reaction – he even heard in his head the bitter jokes about the Aryan angel every Jew needs to get out.

'Yes, please,' she said immediately and humbly, looking at him with big brown eyes. 'I'd be grateful, if you would. I have absolutely no idea what to do.'

5

Late in the evening, in dim light in his poky office, Glaser sat staring at the wall and thinking of what Zipporah Ballat had said about Hoffmann's connection to the Weintraub case.

Along with Gürtner, Hoffmann was the man most responsible for Hitler's success. The first publicity brochure Hoffmann did for the Nazis – *Germany's Awakening in Pictures and Words* – came out at the time of the Putsch trial, but because it wasn't an official NSDAP publication, it wasn't banned when the Party and its newspaper were. It was vital in keeping the Nazi message alive during the ban, until Gürtner persuaded a reluctant Minister President Held to lift it.

Hoffmann more or less invented political photojournalism, and certainly invented the political photo-postcard. There were few citizens of Germany who didn't have a Hoffmann studio portrait of a uniformed Hitler on the wall of their home. Even the Hitler portraits on the cigarette cards children collected and pasted in albums were by Hoffmann. The Führer as soldier-statesman was a Hoffmann creation. All based on a photograph, a lying visual image.

On impulse, Glaser picked up the receiver on the telephone on his desk, phoned home and said he would be late for dinner. Lotte was displeased. Glaser banged the receiver down. He jammed his hat on, struggled into his mackintosh, seized his cane, and drove fast and dangerously through the twilight, heading for Schellingstrasse.

*

Schellingstrasse is at the heart of artistic Schwabing, and had been since before the war.

Then, Kandinsky and Klee had drawn and painted at the house next door to Hoffmann's. Knut Hamsun had written at the marble tables in the nearby Café Stefanie, in Amalienstrasse. The Stefanie was an artist's café; the waiters kept a notebook of unpaid debts. It was nicknamed the 'Café of Grand Illusions'.

As he drove past it, Glaser pictured Hamsun scribbling away in the May sunshine. He was the creator of the stage character Ivar Kareno – a believer in the Nietzschean born leader, the man who elects himself ruler of the masses.

Had Hamsun perhaps looked up from his writing and looked across at a nearby table? Had he noticed the nondescript individual, whose hips were nearly as wide as his shoulders, dandruff flaking the collar of his scruffy blue suit? He would have been browsing the café's free newspapers, making a single coffee last for hours. Even if he had, it is unlikely he would have identified this chap, with his strange moustache, as the natural despot his Ivar Kareno so craved.

Newly arrived from Vienna, Hitler had taken a room a few streets away in Schleissheimerstrasse. He was drawn to the Stefanie because that was the name of a girl he had worshipped from afar in his youth in Linz. He never spoke to her, but when she danced with officers at a military ball, she prompted his first ever romantic dream of suicide.

Glaser parked the motor car outside the photographer's studio. In the window, there were flower paintings by the German Romantics on the left, photographic studies of Hitler on the right. Hoffmann had started as a painter, a pupil at Professor Knirr's art academy.

Knirr was a respected establishment figure in Munich art. He had painted one of the very few portraits of Hitler not painted from photographs. Ascher Weintraub had told Glaser that Hitler had sat for it, so presumably it represented the man as he saw himself.

In it, the Führer was shown, three-quarter length, in a long, brown, single-breasted jacket, with swastika armband. His Iron Cross from the war was prominent on his breast pocket, as was his gold Party pin. One hand was cantilevered on his hip, the other gripped an *Alpenstock*, as if to help his progress through the pastoral German landscape behind him – the landscape so important to the fragile German identity. His expression was suitably severe, a balance between sound judgement and underlying bellicosity – ready to strike, and knowing when to strike.

Hoffmann could have ended up painting routine portraits at that level, but his father made him leave and go into the family photography business, which he regretted at first. His love of German Romantic painting – Hitler's favourites, von Schwind, Spitzweg and Gruetzner – was genuine enough, not at all put on to curry favour with the Führer.

He and Hitler had stood shoulder to shoulder, watching, united in grief, when the Glass Palace, home of Germany's biggest collection of Romantic painting, burned to the ground two years ago. It was the nearest Glaser had ever come to sharing an emotion with them.

Glaser made his way down an alley next to the studio, picking his way carefully across the cobbled courtyard, tapping with his cane to keep his balance. Lights were blazing in Hoffmann's small house. Muffled music was audible, but nobody answered the door. Glaser gave it a push and it opened.

The blaring music was *Carmina Burana*. Inside, there was a narrow passage. A door to the left was open. Glaser glanced into a room with a chimney breast covered by a Gobelin tapestry. In front of the chimney breast was Henni,

136

naked. Two SA men flanked her, one fully uniformed, one just taking his uniform off.

Tears sprang to Glaser's eyes. He thought of Henni as lost, fallen. He thought of his daughter, Magda, now fifteen years old, and the terrible things that could happen. Hoffmann had been a widower since his wife died in the flu epidemic of '28. No mother for Henni, and look what happens.

As Glaser was turning to go, Hoffmann's voice huskily called his name. The photographer was leaning down over the banisters, on the upstairs landing. He was wearing a white vest, knee-length white underpants, socks and suspenders. His hair was awry and he was red in the face, obviously drunk.

Glaser was embarrassed. Hoffmann, unabashed, gestured at him impatiently to come up. But before he could do so, a woman of the streets appeared at the top of the stairs. She was blonde, heavily powdered and rouged, in a tight black skirt and beaded waist-length jacket. She flounced down, holding onto her hat, pushing past Glaser in the hall, without a word or a glance, wafting sickly perfume. She slammed the outside door behind her.

Glaser felt he had little option than to do Hoffmann's bidding and join him. He made his way up to a landing bathed in rose light. The bare overhead bulb was mingling with red light from Hoffmann's laboratory, visible through an open door. Glaser glimpsed Hoffmann's Rolleiflex camera, on a bench, and large flat enamel baths full of developing fluid and fixer.

Almost against his will, Glaser had picked up quite a lot of information about photography from his discussions on the subject with Kaspar. So he also recognised the drying cabinet. Kaspar had told him Hoffmann's top-notch drying cabinet could dry film in twenty-five minutes. Kaspar thought Hoffmann the best photographer in Germany, by a

light year: 'Hoffmann is a master of the science as well as
the art of photography,' Kaspar had said, during their last
discussion, or quarrel, on the subject.

'Good evening, Dr Glaser,' said Hoffmann, peering up at
the taller man. His speech was slurred, but his practised
politeness was as polished as ever. 'Wait in there, would you,
while I get dressed.'

The room he indicated was a sparse office. Glaser put the
light on, from a naked overhead bulb. There was a dusty
rubber plant in the corner and, on the floor, untidy piles of
Illustrierte Beobachter – the Nazi news magazine. Hoffmann
was one of the founders of the magazine, which over the
years had been his main source of press photograph
commissions.

The only photograph in the room was on the desk.
Cheaply framed, it showed Hoffmann himself, immaculately clad, perched on some stone steps, photographing
Hitler in an adoring crowd. The Führer's only guard was
the gigantic figure of the adjutant, Wilhelm Brückner.
Although he didn't recognise the place, from the inform-
ality and lack of security Glaser guessed the photograph
had been taken in Munich, not Berlin.

It was freezing cold. Glaser sat down in a wing-armchair.
Hoffmann did not keep him waiting long. His hair was
now neatly slicked back and gleaming. His stocky, broad-
shouldered frame was encased in a heavy brown three-piece
suit, with the waistcoat neatly buttoned. He smelled of
lavender. He carried a bottle of Johnny Walker Red Label
in one hand and two glasses in the other. He plonked
them down on the desk and sat heavily at the office
chair.

'Drink?' He flashed his charming smile. It was suddenly
silent. The gramophone record of *Carmina Burana* had
come to an end.

'No, thanks.'

Hoffmann shrugged. 'Suit yourself. Don't mind if I do?'
The question was rhetorical.

Hoffmann poured himself a generous slug and knocked
it back. 'What can I do for you?'

'Excuse the intrusion,' Glaser said. Hoffmann nodded
impatiently. 'But did you sell a painting to Ascher Weintraub recently?'

'No.'

'*Blue Horses*? A Franz Marc?'

'Never heard of it.'

'Your signature is on the provenance note.'

'Forgery.'

Hoffmann took another slug of whisky. He liked and
respected Glaser. But, while never less than immaculately
courteous, he didn't give a damn if the Public Prosecutor
believed him or not, and it showed: Hoffmann represented
the Nazi Party on Munich City Council, he was the Party's
sole official photographer, and a close intimate of Adolf
Hitler. Since Hitler became Chancellor, he was beyond,
if not actually above, the law, and he knew it and Glaser
knew it.

'I see,' Glaser said. He sounded dispirited, even to his
own ears.

'Look, Dr Glaser,' said Hoffmann cheerily, 'it's sad poor
old Weintraub died that way. But I'm sure there's a decent
case against this handyman. What's ...?'

'Sepp Kunde.'

'Right. So, why don't you just rubber-stamp the document, and let it go to trial, eh? Why make life difficult for
yourself?'

Was that a threat? Hoffmann's reddening handsome face
was the picture of Bacchic innocence. He poured himself
another whisky and smiled. 'Here! Heard the latest one?
What's the Nordic ideal? Eh?'

'Don't know.' Glaser simulated polite interest.

'The Nordic ideal ... thin like Göring, tall like Goebbels, blond like Hitler.'

Hoffmann slapped his thigh, booming out laughter, checking Glaser was laughing with him. And he was. Hoffmann's ingratiation brooked no resistance. But a small alarm bell rang in Glaser's mind that he was quite so firmly identified as an anti-Nazi.

6

Ernst Buchner had art in his blood. He was the son of the painter Georg Buchner, one of the group known as the Munich Secession. He had studied art history at Munich's Ludwig Maximilian University.

At the age of forty-one, Dr Buchner realised his lifelong ambition and became Director of the Bavarian State Painting Collections. He was responsible for the art, not only of the three major galleries in Munich, but the 10,500 pictures in galleries all over Bavaria, from Aschaffenburg to Würzburg. His salary for this responsible position was a hefty 14,000 Reichsmarks a year. And yet he was not happy.

In fact, his wide-browed, intelligent face was contorted with fear above his red bow tie, and below a remarkable patina of hair. This hair rose not only above but also out to the side of his head, like the halo on a medieval saint – except that it was black, not gold.

Ernst Buchner had been in the dream job less than a month, and he was in danger of losing it. His world, he feared, was about to come to an end: The Restoration of the Professional Civil Service laws were naturally meant to get rid of Jews and socialists. But Hess was applying them so vigorously that any non-Party Member in a Civil Service job was under threat, especially in the arts. Twenty museum directors and curators had gone already.

Buchner had never used the Hitler greeting, well, not until recently, nor worn a Party pin. He was a natural conservative, deplored the Versailles Treaty, and believed in a Greater Germany and the superiority of German art. But he had expected a philosophy from the Nazis. What a disappointment. All there was, was gassy rhetoric about race, woolly anti-Marxism, and a jumble of pictorial projections and myths. Well, that's what he thought until this month.

To his horror, Buchner had been attacked in the *Völkischer Beobachter* for his friendship with a Jewish curator, August Levy Mayer – a friendship he now bitterly regretted. To counter the attack, he was trying to join the Party, only to find, horror of horrors, that he couldn't – or at least he might not be able to.

There was growing resentment among the Old Fighters about the March Violets – Johnny-Come-Lately opportunists who were trying to join the Party now, just as the Nazis were seizing total power. Party membership had been closed. Buchner's application to join might or might not get through. He twisted his red bow tie in anguish at the thought of what could happen if it didn't.

What more could he do? He had contacted his detested former wife, Hildegard, who he had not seen for two years, for the sole purpose of enrolling his two boys in the Hitler Youth and the girl in the BdM.

He had made a huge thing of taking race into consideration in promotions – writing to the Bavarian Ministry of Education that 'Dr Busch is of Ayran extraction and his orientation is national.'

He had revised his view of what is and what is not art. Art, he now understood, must reflect a world view embodied in the race. Works of art which did not reflect this world view, were *entartet* – a biological term meaning a plant or animal which had so changed it no longer belonged within its species. It was outside the race. Deviant, perhaps one could say. Racially deviant. Yes. Buchner was now quite clear there could be no racially deviant art.

But was it all too late? How unfair that would be. He had instigated the seizure of art from Jewish homes well before gallery directors in other cities. The Political Police – Section 4, responsible for cultural matters among other things – had allocated him half a dozen men under the command of Inspector Forster to help out. He would soon take over a private Jewish gallery – Weintraub – and add it to the list of state galleries.

But best of all, he had managed to establish contact, well, one brief meeting, with the Führer himself. Shortly after his appointment, he had been invited to the Führer's apartment in Prinzregentenplatz. There, sitting under Ziegler's modern altarpiece, he, Ernst Buchner, had purchased a painting from the Leader himself, on behalf of the Bavarian State Painting Collections. Surely this connection with the Führer would lead to Party membership, wouldn't it?

And then, out of the blue, there was this visit from the Justice Department. Two of them, here in his office, at the Pinakothek Galerie. The first a large, shapeless, serious-looking man with a close-cropped beard and piercing blue eyes. The other one a smooth-faced, pale young fellow with eyes like glowing coals, who was apparently the son of Cajetan von Hessert, no less. Buchner mopped beads of sweat from his brow with a red-spotted handkerchief, kept in the breast pocket of his jacket.

'Could you outline your dealings with the Weintraub Gallery?' the Public Prosecutor asked.

Buchner gulped, instinctively glancing at von Hessert. At this delicate time, it didn't matter how good or bad you were at your job. All that mattered was who you knew in the Party. A high-up enemy and you were finished; a high-up friend and you were made. He could do without his entire future hanging on this visit.

'I … er … was, am, in negotiation with the owner of the gallery, Frau Ballat, concerning the … er …' Oh God, where did the Public Prosecutor stand on Expressionist paintings? Did he want them saved or burned?

Goebbels had defended one Expressionist, Nolde, who was a Party supporter. He had a Nolde in his flat. But there was a rumour that the Director of the Berlin Galleries, Eberhard Hanfstaengl, cousin of the Munich Hanfstaengls, had selected it, and Goebbels didn't know it was racially deviant – or possibly what it was at all. There was another rumour that Hitler had been to Goebbels' flat, noticed the picture, and told Goebbels to get rid of it. It was all so complicated. Buchner decided to hedge his bets.

'Concerning the … er … repossession of artworks out of non-Aryan property …' Buchner stopped and smiled.

The Public Prosecutor gave a faint nod. 'Are you not trying to take over the Weintraub Gallery as well as the artworks?'

Buchner shrugged. 'Not "take over", no. I wouldn't say "take over."' He smiled at von Hessert. 'The Aryanisation of the gallery was mooted …'

'Mooted?'

'Floated. But … it was just a suggestion.'

'The owner intends to leave Germany,' the Public Prosecutor said. 'Arrangements have already been made for a sale. Your floated or mooted suggestion is interfering with that.'

'I had no idea!' Buchner expostulated, truthfully as it happened. 'Why on earth didn't Frau Ballat say anything?' He looked from Glaser to von Hessert, then back to Glaser.

'So would you withdraw from negotiations, to let the original sale proceed? Gallery and paintings?'

Buchner mopped his forehead with the handkerchief again. It was a damp ball in his fist. 'Yes! Yes!'

Buchner resolved to use his own trustees in future Aryanisations of Jewish galleries, not try to take them over direct. There were plenty of other Jewish galleries – he was already putting pressure on the Kunsthandlung Helbing on Wagmüllerstrasse. And the Fleischmann Galerie. So he could afford to write off Weintraub. Cajetan von Hessert's son! You don't cross men like that …

'Good,' said the Public Prosecutor.

Buchner again glanced at von Hessert, but the younger man was silent, staring straight ahead. Buchner sensed a tension between him and Glaser. It emboldened him, though he could not have said why.

'Do you know anything about a painting by Franz Marc, called *Blue Horses*,' the Public Prosecutor continued. It sounded like an afterthought.

'Why yes,' Buchner blurted out. 'I bought it last week.'

Von Hessert seemed to come to life at that. He met the Public Prosecutor's gaze, with a half-smile.

'Who did you buy it from?' Glaser asked.

Buchner spread his arms wide in an exculpatory gesture. 'Why from the Führer himself,' he said proudly. 'From Adolf Hitler. I made the purchase at his apartment. Herr Hess was there.'

7

'What's wrong?' Glaser said to Rudi von Hessert, back in his office, after the visit to Ernst Buchner.

Rudi had not slept properly for a month; his head was ringing. He sensed that, if he spoke now, a breach might open never to be closed. And in any case, they could no longer speak freely anywhere in the Ministry of Justice. So he did what he always did when faced with a problem, he introduced Ello into the equation. Another invitation to his sister's room was issued and accepted.

Ello had stained the floorboards green since Glaser's last visit. A white cat, introduced as Krafft, after Krafft-Ebing, was curled up on the ottoman. Rudi, in diamond-patterned sleeveless pullover and pale-blue open-necked shirt, looked a little more relaxed, though he was still hollow eyed and a cheesy colour.

'Look, I'm not getting into a tizz about this, Gerhard,' he blurted out as soon as Glaser had sat down, and been given wine. 'But I'm a bit miffed, frankly. I have no status on the Weintraub case, and I am considerably junior to you. I know all that. But if I am to be involved, you might at least let me know what's going on.'

Glaser nodded hard, understanding, agreeing he had behaved thoughtlessly. Lotte was always telling him he kept too much to himself, lived within himself too much, bottling up his feelings, not sharing. It went on and on. And

146

Glaser agreed. It was a fault in him, he acknowledged it, but he didn't see what he could do about it.

Rudi looked drawn and tense. 'I sat there in Buchner's office this morning,' the probationer went on, sounding really angry, 'not knowing whether I was coming or going. I had no idea why we were even interviewing the man. Because you haven't told me a ruddy thing '

Glaser held up a hand to stop him. Instinctively addressing both von Hesserts, he made a dignified but complete apology. He then told them what he had found out so far.

Zipporah Weintraub had been unable to sell up because threats from Lange and Buchner cancelled each other out. That at least was now solved, as Buchner had agreed to withdraw. The Marc picture had been sold to Weintraub by Heinrich Hoffmann, but Hoffmann had denied it when he visited. He recapitulated, as Rudi knew, that the Marc picture had ended up with Buchner, having been sold to him by Hitler.

'So we've lost the painting for good,' Glaser said. 'But I believe Hoffmann may hold the key. I believe he was lying, with his flat denial. But at the same time, I can't imagine how he could have got hold of a previously unknown picture by Franz Marc.'

To his amazement, the von Hesserts burst out laughing. The atmosphere in the room lightened. Rudi got up and topped up Glaser's quarter-litre glass, affectionately putting his arm round the older man while he did it.

'Shall I tell him, or will you?' Ello said to her younger brother.

'You.' Rudi beamed at her, sitting down and taking a large swallow of his wine.

'As you will see, Gerhard,' Ello began. 'It's best to keep us informed.' She softened the sentiment with a big smile. 'Gerhard, we've known the Hoffmanns since we were kids. They used to have an apartment in Schnorrstrasse. Then

147

Herr Hoffmann rented their present place in Schelling-strasse. Until last year, Franz Marc's letter box was still outside with his name on it ...'

Glaser groaned, holding his head in his hands. 'Schellingstrasse ...' he said. 'Frau Weintraub said Marc's studio was in Schellingstrasse, but I didn't make the connection.'

He thought bitterly, ironically, that Ascher Weintraub would have known that and could have told him, had he not needed the information to investigate the art dealer's own murder.

'Number thirty-three,' said Ello solemnly. 'When you went to see Hoffmann, you may well have been standing on the spot where Maria kept the painting. She left in a hurry, abandoning a lot of his work. Obviously, this *Blue Horses* was left behind. Hoffmann saw his chance to make some money and sold it.'

'Henni, by the way, loves Marc's work as much as you do, Gerhard,' Rudi added, smiling now. 'She was brought up with it.'

The mention of Henni's name brought back the image of her naked before two SA men, but Glaser would not have dreamed of telling the von Hesserts about that – regarding it as tittle-tattle.

But, anyway, Rudi was back on form, grinning at his big sister, the colour back in his face. 'Ello is a scientist, Gerhard, so she can't understand Franz Marc. No soul.'

Ello put her tongue out at him; Rudi blew her a kiss. Glaser wordlessly asked if he could open another bottle and, getting the nod, got up and did it himself.

They talked long into the night. There was yet another phone call home to Lotte, to say her husband would not be home for his dinner. Glaser asked the question he had been wanting to put to the von Hesserts for some time. Brought up surrounded by Nazis as they were, and having known

'Uncle Dolf' from such a tender age, was there ever a time …? He let the sentence hang there, unfinished.

Again, both of them laughed. 'Call it an Oedipal rebellion,' Ello said.

'No, not for a second, Gerhard,' Rudi said. 'We used to laugh at Adolf. But when the time for laughing stopped, we started to hate him. He's scum and his people are trash.'

'And your parents?' Glaser asked.

'Oh … Mother wants me to marry him,' Ello said. She tried a smile but it failed.

'Our father is no fool. And he didn't get where he is by being soft,' Rudi said. 'He knows our views, Ello's and mine, but if it came to it – he'd sacrifice us.'

Ello nodded. 'Oh, surely.' And then, with their friendship re-cemented, even firmer than before, Ello was the next one to broach something long on her mind.

'You think Hitler is involved in Herr Weintraub's murder, don't you, Gerhard?' she said.

She spoke guardedly, as if touching a sore point. It was obvious to everyone, except Glaser himself, that his desire not to let Hitler off the hook 'this time' was clouding his judgement.

'Yes!' said Glaser heatedly, as his trigger subject was touched on. 'After Buchner said he got the stolen painting from Hitler himself? Of course I do!'

'Maybe,' Ello said. And then, after a pause: 'I did a course in logic last year,' she added. She was lounging on the ottoman, now vacated by the cat, in the languid pose which had once annoyed Glaser, but certainly didn't now. 'A certain Professor Lachenmaier ran it. It trained you to look at the underlying assumptions being made in any procedure.'

'And?' Rudi said, smiling at her.

Ello looked questioningly at Glaser, who nodded to her to go on. 'It seems to me, Gerhard, that you are making two

149

assumptions in this investigation – one big, one small.'

Glaser smiled and poured more wine. This one was a Lemberger, dry as Glaser's wit. 'And what would these assumptions be?'

Ello concentrated for a second. 'OK,' she said and took a deep breath. 'The small assumption is that only one man was involved in the murder.' She waved an elegant arm. 'I'm not saying that's wrong, I'm just saying it's an assumption.'

Glaser nodded. 'True,' he said. 'Go on.'

She nodded to herself. 'The large assumption is that there was nothing else in the safe, apart from the Marc painting.'

Part V
Spring 1933

1

That evening at Ello's room at the university was the start of the Glaser family's friendship with Rüdiger and Ello von Hessert. It started with dinner at the Glaser flat, so Lotte could get to know these new friends of her husband's, which she did, instantly, as they talked long into the night. And she loved them, both of them.

After that, Rudi visited all the time. Ello popped in when her studies allowed. She never again came to a formal meal. Glaser suspected she would have felt trapped. She just telephoned when she needed a break, arrived and stayed as long as she wished. Sometimes she appeared every day, at other times not for a fortnight. This was a reflection of her mercurial temperament, the Glasers believed. Ello was as hard to pin down as sunshine.

How many cross-currents were there, in all the feelings between them, in what turned out to be the last weeks when happiness was possible? So many, all so complex.

There was Glaser's friendship with Rudi. He lost the last of his reserve; and that with a man half his age. They discussed the Nazis over and over again, in Ello's room or in the Glaser apartment – places where they were safe and private. They were the sort of discussions which needed no conclusion or outcome or justification. Sometimes analytical, sometimes anecdotal, often funny, they were a balm to both men.

And then there was Ello and Lotte. They formed a firm

alliance, becoming more like sisters than friends. Ello told Lotte about her studies, her suitors, love and sex, with no reserve or secrets. Lotte told Ello about her concerns for her family. Within the limits of loyalty she shared her fears for Kaspar and Magda and even for Glaser.

The last tangle of relationships was the most complex. The burly, sensitive, fundamentally shy, talented eighteen-year-old Kaspar developed a harmless crush on Ello, and Magda a consuming passion for Rudi.

The feelings were different in nature, as well as degree. Kaspar was well aware that a sophisticated and *soignée* young woman of twenty-five would not look at a schoolboy as a suitor. But he looked forward to seeing her, tried to find out everything he could about her, and nearly burst in the effort to impress her.

He had always worked hard and shone at school, but because Ello a psychologist he redoubled his efforts at science, not least because she sometimes helped him with biology. He started getting grade 1s in science class tests, something long achieved in history, English and German.

Ello behaved like a pal with Kaspar, with frequent punches on the arm and other horseplay. Kaspar genially worshipped the ground she walked on, which Ello let herself feel flattered by. The feelings on both sides were healthy, honest, open and positive. They were a gain for both of them, and that is how everybody perceived them.

Magda's feelings for Rudi, however, were altogether more turbulent, more troubled, and darker. She was a plain, stodgy, fifteen-year-old; no boy had ever shown the slightest interest in her. She was also not very bright. But she had been, until then, firmly grounded, content to be remorse-lessly quotidian, to plod along from day to day. Falling uncontrollably in love with Rudi cost her all perspective, all her balance and all her previous contentment. She cried

154

herself to sleep over him, and seriously hoped he would 'wait for her'.

Everybody behaved well: Lotte warned Kaspar not to tease Magda, and he didn't.

Glaser policed his tendency to the blunt remark. Rudi, the Glaser parents agreed, was 'superb'. He broached the problem to Lotte, when they were alone. He offered to take Magda and Kaspar out together, now and again. As Magda was by then starving herself in an attempt to lose weight to make herself more attractive to him, Lotte agreed. It was a masterstroke.

The three of them went to Munich Theatre's brave one-night revival of Krenek's jazz opera *Jonny spielt auf,* condemned by name in *Mein Kampf.* The Nazis had attacked the original production with stink-bombs. The powerfully-built Kaspar was half-hoping for a fight, so he could show off his boxing prowess, but keeping news of the performance quiet allowed it to pass off without incident.

They also went to see Erika Mann and Werner Fink in one of their last performances at the Pepper Mill – a political cabaret, just behind the Hofbräuhaus. Political cabaret was born in Schwabing; they at least saw it die there, thanks to Rudi.

They drank beer at the Turks Head, where the journalists from the satirical magazine *Simplicissimus* once had their *Stammtisch.* Rudi came to two SAJ – Young Social Democrat – musical evenings, with the Glaser parents, to hear Kaspar play the flute. They were the last performances before the Hitler Youth took over the SAJ.

On the second of them, Ello turned up, late, un-announced and without having bought a ticket in advance. Kaspar had never played so well. On that evening, all parties felt that the von Hesserts had become honorary members of the Glaser family.

2

With Buchner withdrawing from the sale, there was no obstacle to Lange buying Frau Ballat out. Rudi went to see him alone. The meeting was frosty, but Rudi persuaded Lange to revert to the original purchase price, with no punitive reductions for delay. Sale of the Weintraub Gallery, the paintings and the villa was agreed.

The money was paid into an account controlled by Glaser, at the main Dresdener Bank in Promenadeplatz. Glaser would send 200 marks a month – the maximum allowed – to England, as soon as Frau Ballat was settled. She intended to live in Middlesex, with a second cousin.

Frau Ballat's extensive porcelain collection was put in store in Glaser's name. Martin Brüchwiller, of Brüchwiller Brothers Auction House, advised him to offer it for sale piece by piece, in case it attracted attention as a Jewish collection. This Glaser did, paying the proceeds into Frau Ballat's account.

More time consuming were the emigration formalities. Glaser first established with the authorities that the Jewish emigrant was leaving for an approved destination. Next, he arranged for Frau Ballat's relative in Middlesex to provide an affidavit, confirming her intention to receive the emigrant. Frau Ballat then had to register with the police twice a day. Glaser arranged police registration at the Main Police Station, at Ettstrasse.

But the next steps in the procedure left him baffled and

156

splenetic with rage: 'I'm one of the leading lawyers in Munich,' he yelled at Lotte over the dinner table. 'And I'm damned if I can work out how she pays the Jewish Assets Levy, or gets a Clearance Certificate.'

The Clearance Certificate, confirming that Frau Ballat currently owed the authorities nothing in the way of state taxes, surcharges, fines, fees and expenses, was finally obtained after payment of a hefty bribe. Rudi paid it – Frau Ballat never knew. Reich Flight Tax of 20,259 Reichsmarks was paid, plus a Jewish Assets Levy of 26,738 Reichsmarks. Every item of value to be taken to England had to have a separate permit from the Foreign Exchange Office.

The police pathologist, Katherina Bandl, unexpectedly involved herself. She smoothed Frau Ballat's way at the initial police registration. It then emerged that, somehow or other, she knew the ropes on emigration procedure better than Glaser and von Hessert.

Her huge figure and air of authority cowed petty officials, who she did not hesitate to drop in on, unannounced, and then bawl at, until she got what she wanted. She even made a friend of Frau Ballat. When Lange lost patience and ejected the former professor from her villa, Bandl put her up in her flat, where she lived alone, except for the dachshund, Mitzi.

The very last delay was the Foreign Stamp, to be marked in Frau Ballat's passport. It was finally produced after another bribe, again paid without Frau Ballat's knowledge by Rudi.

One sticky airless day, the formalities were finally complete. Glaser, Rudi and Katherina Bandl saw Frau Ballat off at the Hauptbahnhof, along with her friend, Elsa Marx, from Franz-Josef Strasse. It was an emotional occasion. But there was a final hitch, after the train had pulled in, which threatened to stop Frau Ballat leaving. Noticing her Jewish appearance, a train official demanded to see her passport, as she was about to board. He saw the Foreign Stamp in it and summoned two policemen standing nearby.

'Emigrant's Passport,' the train official said, nodding at Frau Ballat.

The police searched some of her luggage and found items of jewellery.

'Jewish bitch!' One of the policemen yelled at Frau Ballat. 'Trying to smuggle out jewellery.'

Glaser politely pointed out that Frau Ballat had the necessary permit to take the jewellery out, arranged by the Foreign Exchange Office. Frau Ballat produced the permit.

'We'll have to check that with Berlin,' said one of the police, taking the document. 'Go home and we'll let you know.'

Any delay would mean the Foreign Stamp would expire, and they would have to start all over again. A heated discussion started up, on the platform, as Frau Ballat's train belched steam. Rudi evoked the von Hessert name, but even that failed to move the officials. Glaser then lost his temper, inveighing against bureaucracy and haranguing the two policemen. Frau Bandl pulled him away. Only Bandl's quick-thinking mention of Frau Ballat's status as a war widow stopped the former professor being ordered off the platform altogether.

Elsa Marx, white with fear at all the screaming and yelling, started to shake and then to cry. Rudi put a comforting arm round her, enveloping the tiny woman. Murmuring in her ear, he gently persuaded her to go home. After a tearful hug with Zipporah Ballat, she walked away, sobbing her heart out, finally breaking into a run as she left the platform.

The porters, who had waited until now, leaning on their trolleys, dispassionately watching events unfold, finally lost patience. They dumped Frau Ballat's luggage at the carriage steps, and walked off.

The police withdrew 'for consultation'. They came back with a typed form for Frau Ballat to sign. It was a prepared pro-forma with only the word jewels written in. It became clear that the whole charade had been put on solely to raise the sixty Reichsmark fine the policemen now demanded. This would be split three ways – the train official getting his share – as soon as Frau Ballat and her party were out of sight.

The form presented to Frau Ballat ran as follows:

I am a Jewish thief and have tried to rob Germany by taking German wealth out of the country. I hereby confess that the jewels found on me do not belong to me, and that in trying to take them out I wished to inflict injury on Germany. Furthermore, I promise not to try to re-enter Germany.

Frau Ballat signed. With Rudi, Frau Bandl and Glaser frantically helping her to load her luggage, she boarded the train with seconds to spare. Her last words on German soil, as she leaned out the carriage window were: 'Well, at least the train's heated.' And with that, Germany's foremost scholar of the Enlightenment left the country of her birth, never to return.

3

Glaser was waiting in his office in hat and mackintosh, carrying his cane and feeling foolish. He and Rudi were due at the new camp at Dachau, where Sepp Kunde had been transferred, because of his communist past. But Rudi had not appeared.

The probationer was becoming worryingly erratic and unreliable these days. He was late for court appearances and had even missed one or two altogether. He had received a formal warning as to his future behaviour from a judge. Glaser suspected him of being a secret drinker. Suppressing his anger, he telephoned the von Hessert villa. A maid told him that young Herr von Hessert was not available. He banged the receiver down and a call came through from Frau Sauer.

The Chief Inspector's wife was curiously insistent that Glaser visit her immediately. There was a note of crowing triumph in her voice. He told Frau Sauer he would be with her shortly. Then he telephoned the Dachau camp and left a message for the Commandant, Herr Wäckerle, rearranging their interview with Sepp Kunde for three o'clock that afternoon.

As he drove up to Sauer's lilac-washed villa, he hoped to speak to the maid – the one who had mentioned Forster so enigmatically last time. But when he knocked, the mistress of the house opened the door herself. Glaser remembered Frau Ballat's suspicion that the Chief Inspector beat her.

160

There was indeed an old bruise, faint and yellow, at the base of her neck.

'Come with me,' Frau Sauer said, and started to lead the way up the stairs.

'Frau Sauer!' said Glaser testily. 'I would greatly prefer to hear what you have to say down here.'

Frau Sauer stared at him. 'There's a good reason ... Oh! Can't you manage ...?' She stared at Glaser's cane.

Glaser, piqued, started to follow her. He assumed there was something upstairs she wanted to show him. 'Yes, I can manage. Thank you. But there had better be a good reason, as you say.'

He made his way up the stairs, then followed her along the landing, into the master bedroom. Sauer lay in bed, his huge upper body billowing in a white nightshirt above a quilt that covered him to his waist. His face was wrenched down to the right, one side of his walrus moustache almost under the other. The right side of his body was stiff.

'My dear Chief Inspector ...' Glaser said.

'He can't speak!' crowed Frau Sauer gleefully. 'He can't move either! If I didn't feed him ... he'd die!' She chortled to herself.

The Chief Inspector remained immobile.

'Shouldn't he be in hospital?' Glaser asked.

Frau Sauer shrugged. 'He'll be all right. More's the pity. I've got something to tell you,' she added, grinning at him.

Glaser hesitated. This ruse was clearly designed to torment her husband. But he remembered Sauer buying up Jewish property – that tour in the limousine. And anyway, he was too tired from the journey up the stairs to go down again immediately.

'Well?'

'I've got the information you want. You know. When you came here before? I can tell you what you want to know.'

'Go on,' Glaser said.

161

Frau Sauer pointed at her husband. 'He stole drawings, he did. Stole them from Hitler's place. They were dirty drawings. Three of them. Dirty. Hitler did them.' She sucked her cheeks in.

'Frau Sauer, I insist that we go downstairs.'

Glaser led the way back to the Sauer drawing room, with its Regency-stripe wallpaper and clashing Bauhaus furniture. He sat, uninvited, in what had clearly been Sauer's chair, still marked from the indentations of the heavy man's body. 'When did this alleged theft take place?' he grunted.

Frau Sauer sat opposite him, the unpleasant smile still in place but her back upright, as if she was not used to sitting in her own drawing room. Glaser realised that this was probably the case.

'A couple of years ago,' she replied to his question. 'When that girl died at Hitler's place. See … the evening after he was there,' Frau Sauer jerked a thumb upwards to indicate who was meant by 'he'. She dropped her voice dramatically. 'I saw him put drawings in our safe.'

'How do you know Hitler did them?'

'I asked my husband. I called him a dirty bugger for having the drawings. Of course he hit me. But I asked him again. Then he told me these drawings were worth a fortune because Hitler did them. Next day he put them in a vault in the bank. He said if anything happened to him, I was to go to a newspaper with them. I forget which one, now.'

'*Münchener Post*, by any chance?'

'Yes, that was it. He was ever so scared when he took the drawings out of the vault again. That was when he sold them to Herr Weintraub.'

'How do you know that?'

'I saw Herr Weintraub come round here late one night. I saw him come in, from the bedroom window. I asked my husband what was going on. I said he might as well tell me, in case I said the wrong thing. He said the old Jew was going out of the country, where he could sell the drawings on for even more. You know what Jews are like.'

Glaser gave her a withering look, then sighed. A man of Ascher Weintraub's sensibilities reduced to this tawdry trade – tears pricked his eyes. And the drawings had been in the same safe, in Ascher's office, as the Marc painting. Glaser felt that the Expressionist had been sullied by association, just as Ascher Weintraub had.

But at least there was now a motive for the murder that made sense. The motive, however, hardly matched the suspect arrested for the crime.

4

Glaser thought of Dachau as an idyllic artist colony with a castle, where they used to go for picnics when the kids were little. It was also the scene of one of his worst quarrels with the rest of the family.

Kaspar was eight, at the time, and Magda five. Glaser had abandoned a family picnic, to go off and visit one of his painter friends, Lovis Corinth. Corinth was an old man, he was ill, he was lonely. Glaser felt unable to cut the visit short, once the old painter had embarked on his stories.

When he finally returned, it was early evening. The family outing was ruined. Magda was howling, Kaspar shivering with cold and miserable. It was one of the few times Lotte had bawled Glaser out in front of the children. She had slapped him in the face. Kaspar had tried to hit him too, to protect his darling Mama from hurt or harm. *Plus ça change*, Glaser thought wryly.

He had no idea what to expect as he and von Hessert drove to the new camp at Dachau, a place he knew as the *Pumf* – a long-derelict powder and munitions factory. He knew the torture cellars, set up willy-nilly by individual SA-troops, were proving embarrassing to the Nazis, now Hitler was Chancellor. This new camp, people were saying, was a way of streamlining the terror.

They certainly shouted its existence from the rooftops. No doubt because there was little point having an instrument of terror nobody knew about. Indeed, on the very day the camp was opened, the *Münchner Neueste Nachrichten* joyfully reported that around sixty communists had been placed in custody there. Glaser promptly cancelled his subscription to the *MNN*, a one-time opposition newspaper, until its supervisory board had been taken over by the Nazis.

As they approached the entrance, Glaser slowed the green Opel-Frosch to walking pace. Some scruffy village children were giving each other a leg-up, to try to peer over the top of the concrete wall. The big wooden gates were open. The sentry peered at them as they drove up. Glaser slowed further, to a near stop, but the sentry waved them through.

They parked just inside the wall, on rough, unmade ground, and stepped out of the car.

It was a blustery spring afternoon. The wind was whipping noisily across the surrounding flat peat-bog into the exposed camp. Von Hessert shivered so violently, Glaser looked at him in alarm.

To their right, a group of ten or so prisoners, clearly just arrived, stood patiently near the lorry which had brought them. Two Bavarian police stood near them, looking bored. In front of the lawyers, a huge concrete parade ground was dotted with prisoners, standing to attention, out in the open. They had shaven heads and were wearing thin white linen shirts and trousers, flapping in the wind.

Glaser and von Hessert made their way into the camp. There were half-a-dozen or so white stone communal barracks, once storage warehouses for munitions – low buildings with steep, so-called saddle-roofs. Glaser peered through the windows of one, while von Hessert stared into the distance.

There were narrow two-tier rows of bunks inside, along with crudely made wooden tables and benches. On the wall was a fresco of the blue – white colours of Bavaria, with the

165

slogan Practise Comradeship scrawled in black underneath. Glaser looked at von Hessert, who was breathing heavily and would not meet his eye.

All the roads were still unmade, covered in pebbles and larger chunks of stone. To the lawyers' left, there was a company of prisoners harnessed to a massive roller, trying to pull it forward. As they strained against the leather harnesses, the roller inched forward over the road. Guards with whips drove the prisoners on.

The lawyers stopped a guard and asked the way to the Commandant's office. On the way, they passed the canteen. Glaser looked through the window. On the plaster walls were crude painted caricatures of Social Democrat and communist politicians. The ones facing Glaser were labelled Rathenau and Erzberger.

Matthias Erzberger was a Swabian politician who had been sent to sign the armistice marking the end of the war. Being the signatory of the German surrender had made him an object of hatred. A Freikorps band assassinated him in the Black Forest,the year before they killed Rathenau, the Jewish Foreign Minister.

The face on the wall labelled Rathenau had been given a Jewish skullcap and ringlets. The artist was clearly under the impression that Erzberger had been Jewish, too, as he had been adorned with the same crudely exaggerated Semitic features as Rathenau. Erzberger was a Protestant – co-founder of the Christian Trade Union in Mainz.

Outside the Administration Building, two bored-looking men in bits of brown and green uniform, with yellow armbands and black forage caps, were smoking and chatting. Both of them could do with a shave. It was not clear whether they were guarding the place or not.

Glaser identified himself. The men, without breaking off their conversation, nodded the lawyers through.

The Commandant's name, Hilmar Wäckerle, was painted

on the glass door of a breeze-block office. It was empty. Glaser looked at his watch. It was ten minutes after three o'clock. He sat heavily at Wäckerle's desk, while von Hessert went back outside and asked the guards to fetch Kunde.

'He's in the carpentry workshop,' von Hessert reported to Glaser. 'One of the guards has gone to get him.'

Kunde appeared quickly, flanked by the two guards, who dwarfed him. He was wearing the camp white linen jacket and trousers and his head was shaved.

'Wait outside, please,' Glaser said to the guards. To von Hessert's surprise, they obeyed.

'*Grüss Gott*, Herr Kunde,' said Glaser, from behind Wäckerle's desk. 'I am Public Prosecutor Glaser, attached to Munich Police District II. This gentlemen is Probationer von Hessert. We are here to assess whether there are grounds for a formal indictment against you, for the murder of Ascher Weintraub. Do you understand? Please sit down.'

'*Grüss Gott*,' Kunde replied, sitting. 'Yes, I understand. Are you Swabian?'

Glaser hesitated, but Kunde's confident charm won him over. 'Yes,' he said. Glaser's light Swabian accent was mainly noticeable by the shushing of the *s* sounds.

'I'm from Poppenweiler,' Kunde said with a grin, breaking into the broadest Swabian dialect. 'And where were you born?' This, still in thick, rural dialect, was cheekily in the *du* form – *Und wo bisht du gebore?*'

A smile broke from Glaser before he could stop it. As a boy, he used to run to Poppenweiler through the maize fields. He slept in a hayloft overnight, and got a hearty breakfast from Herr Ströhle, the farmer, before hurrying back next morning, in time for school.

'Not far away,' he said. 'Ludwigsburg.'

Kunde looked delighted. 'Fancy that! Small world, eh, comrade?'

Glaser absorbed the man. Sepp Kunde had remarkable fingers, thin and very long.

Apart from his thick moustache, he resembled Lenin. His small muscular body was in good condition. The compact, self-contained confidence he exuded was typical of a skilled craftsman. Glaser knew the type well. Swabia teemed with small backstreet workshops, run by independent-minded men like Kunde.

Kunde burst out coughing, doubling over in his chair.

'Are you all right?' Glaser said, concerned.

Kunde nodded through the coughing, then stopped as suddenly as he had started. 'Sorry, about that,' he said, on an in-breath, as he straightened up. 'It comes and goes. Souvenir of Dr Lange's coal gas experiments.'

Glaser shook his head, in angry disbelief at Lange. But it was time to start: 'You found Herr Weintraub's body?' he said conversationally.

'Yes.'

'Your fingerprints were on the gun.'

'I moved it. I wanted to put Herr Weintraub onto his back. See if I could save him. The gun was on the floor. In the way.'

'Do you remember how you moved it? Did you pick it up and put it down somewhere else, for example?'

'No.' Kunde thought for a moment. 'I lifted it by the barrel.'

Glaser nodded. Kunde's prints – fifteen points of resemblance found, just short of conclusive – were on the barrel, not the grip of the gun.

'Did you kill Herr Weintraub?'

'No.' Kunde sounded slightly impatient. His dark eyes never left Glaser's face. 'Why would I do that? His death cost me the only job I'm likely to get. My own business went bust. No employer will touch a communist.'

'You could have killed him to steal and sell *Blue Horses*.'

'Blue what?'

Glaser shot a look at von Hessert. There was nothing to connect Kunde with either the stolen Marc painting or Hitler's drawings of Geli.

'Did you see anybody near the Weintraub Gallery, about the time of the murder?'

'Yes.'

'Why did you answer no when Chief Inspector Sauer put the same question to you?'

'I didn't. I told him who I saw.'

Glaser shot another look at von Hessert. Both knew this wasn't in Sauer's report.

'Go over it again,' Glaser said. 'Start from the last time you saw Herr Weintraub alive.'

Kunde nodded. 'Herr Weintraub was working late. He sent me out to get some supper.'

'Where?'

'The Krone – Pacellisstrasse.'

'Go on.'

'I saw two men, coming towards me, outside the gallery. The first one was old. Grey hair, neat sort of chap. He had a limp. I saw him try the door of the gallery, but it was locked.'

'Who locked it, if you'd just left? You?'

'No. I didn't have a key. Herr Weintraub must have locked it behind me. As usual.'

'What did the second one look like?'

Kunde sighed. 'You're going to think I'm barmy.'

'I'll be the judge of that.'

Kunde shrugged his compact shoulders. 'OK. It was Hitler.'

Von Hessert laughed. Glaser shot him a furious glance. 'Hitler? Adolf Hitler?'

'Well, I don't mean his mother. I told you you'd say I was nuts.'

'Did you tell Chief Inspector Sauer this?'
'No. I just said I'd seen two men.'
'Why?'
'Instinct.' Kunde touched his fingertips together – meaning 'fingertip feeling'.
Glaser suppressed a smile. 'Go on.'
'He was carrying a bag.'
'Hitler was?'
'Yup. Workers' bag. Canvas with leather handles. He was passing it from one hand to the other, as he walked along.'
'Why?' von Hessert said incredulously.
Kunde shrugged. 'Not sure. I think he was scratching.'
'Scratching?' The probationer started to laugh, then suddenly stopped. He looked thoughtful.
'Scratching his hands.' Kunde spoke defiantly.
'How big was the bag?' Glaser asked.
'Big.' Kunde showed him, spreading his arms. It was big enough for safe blowing equipment and a cushion.
'What was he wearing?' Glaser asked. 'This second man.'
'Leather coat.'
'Brown?'
'Black. Collar turned up.'
There was silence in Wäckerle's office for a moment.
'So ...' Glaser said. 'The older of the two men tried the door ...'
'That's right. I stopped and watched. They both went in. I thought Herr Weintraub was expecting them and let them in. Didn't think much of it.'
'Go on.'
'I went to get Herr Weintraub his food. But as luck would have it they took a real long time making what he wanted.'
'Which was?'
'*Frickadellen* and French fries. They had to fry the meatballs fresh. They'd just run out. Then when I got back to the gallery the door was locked.'

170

'What did you do?'

'Banged and hollered. Nothing.'

'Nobody answered?'

'No. I didn't like the look of it. I couldn't see Herr Wein-traub sending me for food, then leaving the gallery. I thought maybe they'd taken him away. But anyway, the main thing was to get in.'

'So you jemmied the door?'

'Yeah, but I had to run back to my room for the jemmy.'

'What did you do with the food?' von Hessert asked.

'Left it in the doorway. Until I got back.'

'And when you got into the gallery ...?' Glaser said.

'Herr Weintraub was dead on the floor. The gun was half under him. The safe was blown.'

'And the two men?'

'Gone.'

'Is there a back entrance to the gallery?'

'No.'

'Windows?'

'Not big enough to climb out.'

'So how did they get out? If the door was locked?'

Kunde met his gaze. He paused, then defiantly em-phasised each word. 'I – don't – know,' he said.

But Glaser did. Herr Weintraub's keys were missing. The apparently irrelevant fact was crucial evidence in favour of Kunde's story. The two men had taken the keys from Ascher's pocket, as he lay dead on the floor, putting the gun down to do it.

They were amateurs, probably in a panic. They had blown the safe, taken the contents and forgotten the gun, half-hidden by Ascher's body. Either that or they didn't care about leaving it. They had locked the door after themselves, no doubt throwing away the keys, then fled. The workman, sitting compact and composed in front of him, was an innocent man.

171

Just as he thought that, Rudi asked to speak Glaser alone. They stepped outside. The two guards were nowhere to be seen.

'Those two men Kunde was describing,' Rudi said. 'I know who they both are. Kunde's innocent.'

5

Inspector Forster burst into Glaser's office, his brown mac flapping round his legs. He looked for a chair in front of Glaser's desk, in the cubicle. There wasn't one. He waved a carbon copy of a report at Glaser, from a standing position.

'Have you taken leave of your senses, Dr Glaser?'

'I beg your pardon?'

'You can't have Kunde released, he's a communist.'

'That's as may be, but there's not a shred of evidence that he killed Herr Weintraub.'

'What do you mean, "that's as may be"? Dr Glaser, were you perhaps on holiday during the revolution?'

'The revolution?' Glaser said. 'What revolution? Do you mean the day the Nazis seized all the ministries, after our esteemed Chief of Police, Herr Pöhner, withdrew the police guards the elected and now deposed Minister President had placed there? Are you perhaps referring to the day Mayor Scharnagl was thrown out of the Town Hall, and made to run an SA gauntlet, while that Nazi Fiehler was installed in his place? Then a Blood Flag was run up over the Town Hall, I do believe. To the great joy of a baying mob in Marienplatz, all singing the national anthem the while. And that would be the day, would it? that the Seventh Army sat on their collective backsides in their barracks, because the seizure of Munich was held in Berlin to be a local, Bavarian matter? That's what you call a revolution, is it? I'd call it a takeover by armed thugs.'

173

Forster looked stunned. 'I'll pretend I didn't hear all that. Dr Glaser, Kunde is an enemy of the Third Reich. Whether he did or did not kill some Jew art dealer is neither here nor there.'

Glaser stared at him. 'This is still the Ministry of Justice, Forster. Get out!'

'You can't order me out of ...'

'Oh, yes I can.'

Glaser stood at his desk. Forster started to leave, shaking his head. Glaser spoke again. 'No, wait. Listen a moment.' Forster turned at the door. Glaser was shaking with rage. 'My report, which I see you have in your hand, requested the resumption of the investigation into the death of Herr Weintraub. It requested that two men seen near the scene of the crime be sought. A detailed description of those two men was provided.'

Glaser drew a deep breath. This was the line ... but he had already crossed it. 'I will now tell you, although it is not in the report, who those two men are: I have reason to believe that they are Julius Schreck and Georg Winter.'

Forster was staring at him, his mouth open.

Glaser continued, jabbing a forefinger at Forster: 'I charge you, Inspector, with questioning Schreck and Winter at the earliest opportunity. You will report to me as to the result of this questioning. I will be awaiting your report, sooner rather than later.'

Forster started to say something, thought better of it, then left. As soon as he was out of the room, Glaser picked up the telephone. He asked the switchboard to connect him to the camp at Dachau. When he was put through to Wäckerle, he asked for confirmation that Sepp Kunde had been released from the camp. He was told that he had been.

6

That evening saw the last ever gathering at what had once been the Social Democrat *Stammtisch* at the Café Heck.

Glaser sat down next to Rinner, Hoegner and Auer. Edmund Goldschlag, the *Münchener Post* reporter, had disappeared. Such disappearances were common in Munich these days. Glaser glanced at the absent Führer's regular chair at the Heck, as Ascher Weintraub had once done. 'Down to business,' he said, with a touch of bitterness. He was addressing Rinner.

With Otto Wels and most of the Social Democrat leadership now in exile in Prague, Erich Rinner, despite his comparative youth, was in control of party affairs in South Germany. He had been given 30,000 Reichsmarks from the party's funds, with a brief to subvert the Third Reich from within.

Rinner told the others that some of the former *Münchener Post* employees had been taken into protective custody – the Nazi term for imprisonment in Dachau. Julius Zerfass, the *Post*'s former articles editor, was among them. Zerfass's wife had received a postcard from him, sent from the Dachau camp. Rinner wordlessly passed the postcard over.

Glaser examined it. Printed on the front, halving the space for the address, was Concentration Camp Dachau in Gothic script. Beneath were printed regulations about what could and could not be sent into and out of the camp, above the authority of the Camp Commandant. Glaser noticed that money could be sent in to the prisoners.

'Let's get that organised,' he said, bashing the postcard with the back of his hand. 'We'll take him some money and whatever he needs. As a public prosecutor, I have access to the camp. I shall visit Julius as soon as possible.'

'Good!' Rinner said. 'He also asks for cigarettes, note-paper, stamps and matches.'

He indicated Julius's two-line message to his wife on the postcard.

There was silence at the table. They all pictured the floppy-haired, handsome, cultured Julius Zerfass in their minds. There was nothing more to say on the subject.

'Thomas Wimmer's been arrested,' Hoegner said, in the manner of one giving an update on the football results.

Glaser nodded, puffing at his pipe. He already knew that.

'Dragged out of his bed in the early hours by the Political Police,' Hoegner continued in the same flat tone. 'They've taken him to Landsberg.'

There was a moment's silence, but they all knew there was nothing they could do to help the Chairman of the Munich Social Democrats.

'Apparently, they went to my place, too. Middle of the night,' Auer said, knocking back a good swallow of beer and some schnapps chaser. 'I've sent my wife to her brother's in Karlsruhe, so there was nobody there but the maid. They took her to the Brown House.'

'Any news of her?' asked Glaser.

'No.'

'Any damage?' Hoegner asked. 'To the flat, I mean.'

Auer shrugged. 'I put my head round the door before I came here. They've thrown my dirty washing all over the place. Taken a bust of me. The one the trade unions presented me with.' He hesitated. 'They've broken that old iron-bound chest of mine, and destroyed all the documents in it from the Councils Republic.'

There was silence for a moment. 'I'm sorry,' Glaser said flatly.

Auer shrugged again.

'They went to my old flat,' Hoegner said. 'Where I used to live, in Tengstrasse.'

Glaser knew that Hoegner had moved out of the family apartment, a common first step to protect loved ones.

'Heydrich has signed an arrest warrant for me,' Hoegner was saying. 'But, fortunately, their records don't seem to be up to date.'

Erich Rinner had some political news. Von Epp had been created the first holder of a newly invented post, *Reichstatthalter* of Bavaria. His first act had been to order the destruction of the SPD and *Münchener Post* offices, but now he was well into his stride: Jewish homes had been broken-into and robbed; the owners badly beaten up. There was a story that the SA had thrown a rabbi into a gravel pit at Oberwiesenfeld. Round the table, they received these stories in grim silence. Rinner was the only one not drinking heavily.

Glaser grimly quoted Kant: 'It is not worth living, if there is no more justice on earth.'

'They have made their revolution with the weapon of state violence,' Hoegner said. 'But they haven't won yet.'

'I've got a plan,' said Auer. Hoegner's bushy eyebrows went up in wry amusement. Auer always had a plan. 'Tomorrow we call a meeting of the Printers and Journalists Works Council,' the old volcano went on. 'The Nazis will see how many men they have made unemployed. And we keep calling these meetings. How are the Nazis going to deal with this unemployment? Eh? Eh?'

Glaser looked at Rinner, who motioned him to silence. Hoegner smiled faintly. He put his arm round Auer's still massive shoulder. 'Come old friend,' he said softly. 'The battle has been long, has it not? But now I think it may be over. You will stay at my flat. With any luck our friends will not have found it yet.'

He led the old man, unprotesting, out the back way of the Café Heck. There were no goodbyes. When one did know if every meeting with friends would be the last, one no longer bothered with goodbyes. Glaser and Rinner sat in silence for a while, Rinner finishing his beer, Glaser his wine. And then eventually they left, too.

Part VI
Summer 1933

1

Glaser crossed the pavement at Galeriestrasse, first thing in the morning. The green Opel Frosch was parked opposite the building. As he took his keys out to unlock its door, a man seized him under the arm.

'I've got a knife,' the man said, in a North German accent. 'Just get in and I'll tell you where to drive.'

His captor, a bony gangly figure, squeezed himself into the front seat. Glaser was made to drive to a one-family house in Rottenbucherstrasse, in Sendling. There, the captor indicated, with prods in the back, that he should go down the stairs to the cellar. A group of men were sitting round a table, evidently waiting for him. One of them was Sepp Kunde.

'*Grüss Gott*, Herr Glaser.' Kunde looked concerned. The fringe of black hair round his bald pate had started to grow back since their encounter at Dachau. 'Did these idiots bring you here by force?'

'They most certainly did!' Glaser shouted.

'We are the South Bavaria section of the Communist Party,' said a young man sitting in the middle of the group. 'Sit down, please.'

Glaser sat at a chair placed facing the men round the table. 'Thank you. That's very kind of you,' he said, with heavy sarcasm. He stared defiantly at the communists.

Kunde was sitting aside from three others, who were joined by the gangly one with the North German accent. 'I apologise most sincerely, Herr Glaser,' Kunde said. 'When I gave them your name, I made it clear you were to be treated with respect.'

'They didn't listen, did they?' Glaser shouted.

Sepp Kunde looked at the man who had spoken. 'Apologise, Schwarzmüller,' he said.

'What?'

'Apologise. Or I'm off. You can solder your own type-writer keys when they break. And fix your banda machine yourself, when it jams.'

Schwarzmüller shook his head, as if humouring a madman, softening the coming climb-down. 'Herr Glaser, we needed to talk to you,' he said. 'But, OK, I accept we could have done it a bit more ... nicely.' He looked at Kunde, who had started to rise from his chair. 'So I'm sorry,' he added hastily.

Kunde resumed his place, not bothering to hide his disdain. Glaser nodded, appeased. He looked round. The cellar was large and stank of damp, methanol, and the sweat of the men round the table. Most of the space was taken up by an ancient printing press and a banda machine. In front of him were shelves of the communist newspaper, *Neue Zeitung*, plus piles of grey copy-paper, spirit masters, com-positing equipment, lithographic plates and ink baths. There was no sign of the typewriter they needed Kunde to fix.

Glaser took a copy of *Neue Zeitung* at random off the shelves and sat down again.

Schwarzmüller seemed ill at ease, and far from in control of the group he was supposed to be leading. 'My name is Erwin,' he said in a conciliatory manner. Glaser realised this was a codename, not his first name. He had apparently forgotten Kunde had already betrayed his real name. 'This here is Paul.' Glaser's gangly captor nodded to him. 'This is Theo; this is Hugo.'

Hugo nodded and smiled. He needed a shave, his hair

was matted, his blue overalls were filthy, and he stank. Glaser thought he couldn't be more than about nineteen. Theo was older – mid-thirties. His clothes were neatly pressed, and could even be new. He had a battered face, with a broken nose and wall-eye. As Glaser looked at him, a pasted-on smile appeared.

'Very enlightening,' said Glaser, at the codenames. 'I suggest you tell me what you want.'

Schwarzmüller nodded. 'Our movement's funds have been seized. Unlike the Social Democrats, we did not have the resources to move large sums out of the country. We need money to continue to produce our newspaper.'

Glaser looked down at the copy of *Neue Zeitung* in his hands. There were seven double-sides of it. It was closely typed, obviously by a typewriter with broken keys, obviously reproduced on a worn stencil.

'How many of these do you run off?' Glaser barked out.

'About a thousand,' Schwarzmüller said.

'Distribution?'

Schwarzmüller shrugged. 'South Bavaria. Mainly Munich. Say, fifty to Augsburg, thirty to Rosenheim, twenty to Gröbenzell ... and so on.'

'Where, in Munich?'

Schwarzmüller hesitated, but finally answered. 'Two hundred to Westend, a hundred or so to Nordschwabing and Milbertshofen, sixty or so to Schlachthausviertel, then Sendling ...'

Glaser nodded impatiently. Predictably, the bulk were delivered to the industrial, working-class areas – preaching to the converted. 'How, exactly, do you distribute the copies?'

Schwarzmüller sounded and looked exhausted. He was a worn-looking, sad-eyed man – prematurely old. 'Mainly we leave them at factory gates. Or at the Red Sports Clubs and Red Gymnastics Clubs, which are defunct now, of course. But the Nazis know that. Distribution is our weak point.

That's where a lot of the comrades have been caught.'

'That and the Gestapo infiltrating your groups. Anybody here work for the Gestapo?' Glaser looked sardonically round the table at them all. Kunde laughed. Glaser found himself smiling when his eyes met his fellow Swabian's.

'We don't have to put up with this,' said the one introduced as Paul – the stringy fellow who had brought Glaser here. He leaned forward aggressively across the table.

'Shut up!' Glaser said. 'Just ... shut your mouth.'

'Do you want some broken teeth?' Paul said. 'I've always said it, the *Sozis* are the main enemy.'

'Oh ... just ... run off back to Russia,' Glaser yelled at him.

'I wish I could,' Paul yelled back, his mouth twisting to a snarl. 'I'd go to Russia like a shot, believe me.'

'Ladies! Ladies!' Kunde said, laughing.

To signal the end of the argument, Glaser put the communist newspaper in front of his face and ran his eye down the front page. A report on the banning of the Social Democrat Party was headed 'The Nazi Cat Plays with the Social Democrat Mouse'. The Social Democrats were referred to throughout the report as fascists, and the piece concluded with an appeal to Social Democrat party workers to defect and join the communists.

'And you want our help to print this piece of shit?' Glaser yelled, banging it. 'You've got a nerve.'

'I told you this was a waste of time,' Paul said.

'Come on, let's give this a chance, shall we?' said Theo, widening his phoney grin. 'I hear Otto Wels is in Prague now, Herr Glaser? Along with the rest of the Social Democrat big-wigs. Are they doing anything useful there?'

Glaser stared at him.

'Come on, comrade,' Theo said. 'What's the matter? Don't you trust us?'

'No.'

'Well, you should. We're on the same side. I've been in Dachau, chum.' Theo pointed at his battered face. 'I didn't get this walking into a door. Nazis did it.'

Kunde shook his head from side to side in mock weariness. 'You know, you shit-heads bore me,' he said conversationally, to nobody in particular. 'You bore me to tears. We going to work together, or not? We going to fight Adolf? If we are, let's get on with it. If we're not, let's all go home, eh?'

Glaser laughed. 'All right, Herr Kunde. Point taken.'

'Call me Sepp, my Swabian comrade. What's your first name?'

'What? You've got a nerve. All right, it's Gerhard.'

Glaser thought it over: Erich Rinner, still in Munich, had been given 30,000 Reichsmarks to subvert the Third Reich. Rinner, Glaser thought, should be told about this approach by the communists. He had, after all, wanted to back the communist call for a general strike, at that meeting at the Heck, back in February.

Glaser turned to Schwarzmüller. 'I agree with Herr Kunde that we should get on with it. And then perhaps I may be allowed to leave here? So ... I myself have no access to Social Democrat funds. But I am in contact with someone who has. I can arrange for you to put your case. I will establish a line of contact, but not with people who threaten me with knives.'

'Oh, stop whining. I didn't have a knife,' Paul said. 'I just told you I did.'

Glaser glared at him. 'I will work through Herr Kunde only.'

'OK,' Schwarzmüller said.

'What about this man with access to funds?' Theo asked. 'What's his name?'

Glaser was standing, preparing to leave. 'Erich Rinner.'

'You shouldn't have said that,' Kunde murmured.

2

Erich Rinner had heard of the Schwarzmüller Group, and was happy to meet them, to discuss financial help from Social Democrat funds. Meanwhile, he made a counter request of Glaser. Did Glaser know of anyone who would take material out to the Social Democrat resistance in Prague, and smuggle leaflets back into the Reich? Someone not known to the Gestapo and the Political Police was required; a person with no previous connection to the Social Democrats.

Glaser said he knew of no such person. Rinner suggested Rüdiger von Hessert, who he appeared to know all about. Privately, Glaser did not think Rudi was up to it. He was drinking heavily. Glaser feared he would soon make himself ill – if he hadn't already.

But he did not feel he could share these doubts about his friend with a mere acquaintance, like Erich Rinner.

When Glaser put Erich Rinner's offer to Rudi, he accepted immediately. He was delighted to go to Prague; he had friends there. The danger didn't worry him. Glaser said he would introduce him to Rinner.

Naturally, Rudi's meeting with Rinner would include Ello and, naturally, it would take place at the Glaser apartment, which had taken over from the *Stammtisch* at the Café Heck as the nearest thing the remaining Social Democrats had to a safe meeting place.

By now, Hoegner had left for Switzerland. Auer had

joined his wife in Karlsruhe, leaving Glaser himself and Erich Rinner as the only Social Democrat leaders still in Munich, apart from Zerfass, who was in Dachau. Glaser had been unable to visit him as Himmler had just issued a decree banning Ministry of Justice personnel from the concentration camps.

On the day of the meeting, young Kaspar was writing his homework, head down on the dining-room table, hoping his father would let him stay. Glaser had not sent him away. He was secretly proud that the boy was a Social Democrat, and had been since he was twelve. Lotte was off visiting her sister, Katya. Magda was in her room.

Glaser looked approvingly at Erich Rinner. He respected the young man greatly.

Rinner was an economist by training – he had been economic advisor to the trade union movement. There was a modesty about him, Glaser thought, and a precision which stopped short of pedantry. He had a quiet sense of certainty. He was sparing with words, compact of move- ment, but everything was made to count, nothing wasted.

He was drinking beer, as they exchanged small talk before the meeting. Everyone else had a glass of the fruity Pfalz wine the von Hesserts had brought. Glaser and Rudi were smoking, as was Ello. Her cigarette was clamped into an ebony cigarette-holder. This fascinated Kaspar, who was staring at her.

Glaser made a point of fetching an extra glass, and poured Kaspar's wine himself, publicly including him in the meeting. Kaspar looked away from Ello long enough to murmur 'Thank you, Papa.' His eyes shone as he looked at his father.

After the pause this created, with everybody expecting Rinner to open the meeting, Ello spoke. 'Herr Rinner, I know you have a request of my brother. But before you make it, may I make one of you?' She gave him her long-lashed, Elisabeth Bergner look.

Rinner was unmarried. Kaspar felt a pang of jealousy of him.

'Naturally, Fräulein von Hessert,' Rinner said. 'If I can meet your request, I shall.'

Ello gave him a bright smile. She spoke easily, masking the tension she felt. She had been ill immediately before the meeting, and had been prey to vomiting and stomach cramps since her unsuccessful attempt to kill Hitler. 'When you meet the communists, this Schwarzmüller Group, my brother and I would like to come with you.'

There was a silence. 'I don't wish to be rude, Fräulein von Hessert, but may I ask why?'

'I wish to suggest a way forward. A way of proceeding against our common enemy.'

'I am intrigued!'

'You were meant to be.' Rudi laughed rather wildly. The probationer was immaculate, his swept-back hair thick and glossy, his skin pellucidly clear, but he was already at the bottle. He knocked back the rest of his second glass and poured more.

Ello gave a tinkling, rather affected laugh. Much of her behaviour appeared to be for Rinner's benefit. She touched her top lip with the pink tip of her tongue. 'I think I'll leave it at that,' she said. 'When I've got you all together, I'll put forward a plan. I believe you will like it, Herr Rinner.' She put the ebony cigarette-holder in her mouth and took a deep puff, her eyes never leaving Rinner's face.

'I'd rather know in advance, if it's all the same to you.'

Ello shook her head. For a second she considered telling Rinner the truth - that she wanted help to kill Hitler, but she rejected the idea instantly. Rinner did not look like a desperate man, and taking a life was a desperate act – even taking Hitler's life. She hoped the communists would be desperate. 'And I would rather tell you all together,' she said. 'Then I need say it only once. You do want Rudi to go to Prague for you, don't you?'

Rinner clicked his tongue, trying, but failing, to hide his irritation. 'The Schwarzmüller Group might not react kindly to your family name,' he said.

Ello had thought of that. 'Then don't tell them we are coming, Herr Rinner. Say you are bringing colleagues – a delegation. Tell them to do the same. The more, the merrier.'

'All right. I agree to your conditions, Fräulein von Hessert.'

'Excellent!'

'I can't wait to hear what your idea is. When the time comes, of course ...'

Their eyes met.

'Shall we perhaps proceed, Erich?' Glaser said testily.

'By all means, Gerhard.' Rinner produced a bundle of closely typed material on green copy-paper, from an attaché case. It was tied with a piece of red twine. 'This is what I would like you to take to Herr Wels and the others in Prague, Herr von Hessert.'

He passed the bundle to Rudi, who left it on the table without glancing at it.

'What is it?' barked Glaser.

'I'm thinking of calling them Green Reports, for convenience,' Rinner said. 'Because of the green paper they are typed on. The one you have here is the first of what I hope will be regular situation reports on conditions and events in the Third Reich.'

Glaser nodded hard, puffing at his pipe. 'That's good.'

Rinner gave a thin smile, at Glaser's approval. 'These reports are based on witness interviews. They will be wide-ranging, but objective and neutral in tone. They are intended to bear witness. To keep the truth alive.'

'Good for you,' Ello said warmly.

Rinner was embarrassed. 'I have provided a rough summary in English, which my colleagues in Prague, with the aid of English sympathisers, can polish up. I shall have to leave the French version to them. My colleagues will send these foreign-language versions to newspapers abroad. First and foremost, to the *New York Times*, the London *Times* and the *Manchester Guardian*.'

Glaser took his pipe from his mouth and waved it enthusiastically. 'My dear Rinner! This … This is a magnificent contribution. Let me shake you by the hand.'

Glaser leaned over the table and pumped Rinner's hand, leaving him even more embarrassed. 'This is exactly what is required at this present point,' Glaser went on. 'Rüdiger, we should be proud to be associated with this work.'

Rudi gave a glassy grin, knocked back more wine and gave the bundle of papers a quick pat with the flat of his hand. 'Where are you staying, Herr Rinner?' he asked. 'They will be giving me material in Prague, to give to you, will they not?'

'Indeed they will. I have a room at the Bayerischer Hof,' Rinner said, standing, preparing to leave. 'You know it? It's in Tal, near the Isar Gate.'

Rudi nodded, then stared blankly past Rinner. There was a second's silence as everybody else followed the direction of his gaze. Magda was in the doorway. Her muddy-brown hair had been scraped back and forced into plaits, even though it wasn't quite long enough. She was wearing the blue skirt, white blouse and loose blue toggle-tie of the BdM. There was a swastika pin on the button-down breast pocket of the blouse.

Before anybody could react, the key turned in the lock and Lotte came in. She had her black coat on, and her best hat: black straw wound with grey ostrich feathers.

Glaser put his pipe down on the table, something Lotte hated, and stood. He pointed at Magda. 'Go back to your room and get that Nazi uniform off. Now!' he bellowed.

Magda shrugged. 'Why?'

'Because I just told you to,' Glaser roared. 'Lotte, did you know she had that damned uniform?'

Magda started to cry. Lotte walked over to her and put her arm round her. Magda cuddled into her, like a child.

'Yes, I knew,' Lotte said. 'She needs it for camp.'

'Camp? What camp?'

'BdM camp. Two weeks under canvas at Waldkirchen. She's going next week.'

'What! Not while I live and breathe she's not.'

Lotte shook her head. Her eyes were blazing with anger. 'We have no choice,' she ground out. 'The BdM have made it a class trip. If we refuse, she would be at school for two weeks, in a classroom on her own.'

'Except for the Jewish girls,' Kaspar said.

'Correct, Kaspar,' said Lotte. 'But at the moment, that is not helpful.'

'Sorry.'

Glaser shook his head, as if trying to clear it of fumes. 'But surely she doesn't have to wear that uniform? Take it off! It's got a bloody swastika on it. In my house ...'

Magda stepped to the side of her mother, like a sniper leaving cover to return fire.

'What do you expect me to wear for camp, then?' she screamed. 'Do you want me spend two weeks in my knickers?' There was spittle running down her chin.

Glaser lumbered unevenly towards her round the table. Magda screamed and tried to hide behind her mother again, but Glaser caught her by the wrist, pulled her half off-balance and slapped her round the face.

'Wash your mouth out,' he yelled. 'You dirty girl!'

Magda screamed, cried and buried her head in her mother's coat. Kaspar looked bewildered. They all knew Magda went to BdM meetings, but he hadn't seen the uniform before, either. His reaction was much the same as Glaser's. Lotte was breathing heavily. She glanced furiously at the onlookers – Rinner was still standing, as if part of a tableau, the von Hesserts were looking at the ceiling.

She turned to her husband. 'Gerhard,' she said, 'as God is my judge, I swear, if you hit one of the children ever again, I will leave this home and take them with me.'

Glaser made a guttural noise, something between a grunt and a croak. He looked at his hand, as if it had acted independently of him. The only sound in the room was Magda sobbing into her mother's coat.

'I … perhaps I … acted in haste …' Glaser said finally. 'But why wasn't I told about this camp?'

Lotte's eyes, usually soft, were still burning. 'Gerhard, for heaven's sake. The girl has been talking about nothing else for weeks. Listen to the children, once in a while. Hmmm?'

'He does listen,' Kaspar said. 'Sometimes. If he likes the subject.'

Everybody ignored him.

'You're not going to stop me,' Magda shouted at Glaser. 'We've got a tennis competition, movement to music, military nursing, air-raid protection. And we've got wood craft and drill, just like the boys. For the first time, in the Third Reich, girls too are being given equal freedom to their male compter … counterparts and an equal chance to have fun.'

Glaser looked stunned. 'Where is she getting this stuff?' he said, appealing to Lotte, in genuine bewilderment.

Rinner finally broke in. 'Look I … I really must be off. Goodbye, Gerhard, Herr von Hessert, Fräulein von Hessert,' he said hastily. On the way out he murmured 'Goodbye, Frau Glaser' to Lotte. She ignored him.

'We're leaving, too,' Ello said.

'No, wait …' Rudi looked at Magda with open sympathy. He was perturbed, even distraught, on her behalf. 'Magda …'

'Did you not hear me? I said … Come along, Rudi.' Very much the older sister, she seized him by the arm and hauled him to his feet. Rudi took his bundle of papers; the von Hesserts made to leave.

And then Kaspar blurted out what came into his head, without thinking: 'Magda,' he said. 'Did you hear Herr Rinner say where he was staying? And, in fact, how much of the conversation *did* you hear?'

3

At a booth at Prague Main Station, Rüdiger von Hessert pointed to and purchased a bottle of the local hooch. He read the name on the label – Borovichka – then stuck it in the top of his leather travelling bag. Outside it was cold, damp and blustery. He took a taxi to the Hotel Julis, where he was paying his own bill.

The Julis turned out to be a pseudo art deco wedding cake of a place. But he was welcomed effusively enough. A blond flunkey, blue-uniformed as a boy hussar, carried his bag up to his suite. This was a gloomy and chilly tomb, even when he finally managed to turn the wheel which clankingly activated the huge radiators.

In the bathroom, he poured himself half a tooth-mug full of the hooch, then went back to the lounge and flopped out in a floral armchair. The drink had the colour and consistency of loose phlegm, but tasted marvellous and warmed him through. What was that taste? Juniper? He took a couple more slugs. As he drank, he defiantly rubbed his brilliantined hair all over the antimacassar. How bizarre to be here. He owed it all to his Uncle Dolf.

When he was still in short trousers, he and Ello had unearthed a copy of Spamer's *Encyclopaedia*, in a forgotten corner of the library at home. They bore it off excitedly to the nursery. Sitting cross-legged on the floor, under the shadow of the huge rocking horse, they flipped over the pages. Within half an hour they had located around half of everything Uncle Dolf had ever told them. They howled with laughter as each fresh item of his information was tracked down to its source. Rudi had nearly made himself sick, laughing. Ello had held his head.

The hooch was kicking in. At the thought of Ello, Rudi grew rigid with tension. When Ello had gone off to the theatre in Gärtnerplatz with Hitler, then back to his apartment, Rudi had been up all night, pacing around frantically. Eventually, he swallowed everything in the bathroom cabinet and passed out on the floor. If that vile creature has his way with her, Rudi thought, taking a huge gulp of the Czech drink, he would kill himself or kill Hitler, or both.

He was shivering; his arms and legs had pins and needles and ached. Jumping up, he made his way back into the bathroom. The bath was the size, shape and colour of a horse trough. The water was yellow and tepid, but he felt better once he had wallowed in it for a while.

A languorous dressing followed – in fresh silk underwear, crisp pale-blue shirt, lemon tie. Plenty of eau de Cologne was applied. His blue blazer and grey flannels were irretrievably creased from the journey, but never mind. These people were socialists, weren't they? They shouldn't mind a few creases.

He threw everything out of the travelling bag onto the bed, except Rinner's manuscript. Winding a scarf round his throat, he gathered himself, standing stock still, eyes closed. Downstairs, he got the frock-coated concierge to call him a taxi. He had the address on a piece of paper, though he needn't have worried. The driver spoke German, as everybody here seemed to. It was early evening by the time the taxi drew up at the address.

A matronly female intercepted him in the wood-panelled vestibule of the building, while he was still working out where to go. Indeed, he was wondering if these people had perhaps gone home, it was so late.

'Would you, by any chance, be Herr von Hessert?' asked the matron. Her German was faultless, but heavily accented.

'Indeed, I am.'

The matron smiled. 'I am Mrs Lukacskova. I am the Senior Secretary to Herr Wels. You are very welcome. I saw you out of the window, arriving by taxi. We have been waiting for you.' There was just a hint of reproach.

Rudi pulled a boyish face of apology. She laughed.

Mrs Lukacskova led him into an ancient lift, barely big enough for the two of them. She shut two lots of gates and it jerked and rumbled its way up to the second floor. She led him to a ribbed-glass door, marked *Verlagshaus Graphia* in black lettering. In the cluttered outer office, to his utter amazement, there was a burst of applause from half a dozen people, as he came in.

'Here he is!' cried the delighted Mrs Lukacskova, holding tightly to Rudi's arm, as if to prevent a last-minute escape.

She steered him to the tiny, grey-faced figure of Otto Wels. Rudi recognised the Social Democrat leader from newspaper photographs.

'You are our first guest from Germany, Herr von Hessert,' a beaming Wels told him, taking the travelling bag, pumping his hand. 'Welcome, welcome. What can I get you? Coffee? Beer is good here, though not as good as your Bavarian beer, naturally.'

This standard joke from a Berliner brought a dutiful laugh from the two typists and the rest of the Social Democrats, all excitedly gathered round him. Mrs Lukacskova pulled Rudi round until he was facing her. She had grey hair in a bun. When Rudi was a child, he and Ello had played a card game called Happy Families. You had to collect a family of various animals. Mrs Lukacskova was like the mother in all of them.

She looked hard into his eyes. He knew what she had spotted. A shrewdness came into her face. 'I'll make him some tea,' she said. 'That's as good as anything for him.'

Everyone introduced themselves in a frantic rush, with complete disregard for rank and standing. One of the typists was called Martina. She gave him a sweet smile, which he gallantly returned. The grey-haired, intellectual, Jewish-looking fellow turned out to be Friedrich Stampfer, who he had vaguely heard of as a figure on the Left. There were two other old boys whose names he didn't catch. The only one obviously under forty, a tubby little chap with round, tortoiseshell glasses, introduced himself as Erich Ollenhauer.

They went off to one of the two offices, which had decent Adler typewriters, a small printing press and a banda machine. There were papers all over the place. He was steered to a chair and served chamomile tea. The typists disappeared. The Social Democrats were drinking Pilsner beer, except Ollenhauer, who had a coffee.

Wels sat behind his desk, the others drew up chairs or perched themselves on desktops. They were all casually dressed – open-neck shirts, pullovers, plus-fours. One of the old boys was even wearing a pair of spectacularly vulgar two-tone salesman's shoes, in cream and tan.

'Excuse me a moment,' Wels said abstractedly, and looked at Rinner's Green Report, which they had fished out of his travelling bag without asking him. Wels turned the pages rapidly, head down, a smile slowly spreading across his face. 'Our friend Rinner has excelled himself, Friedrich,' he murmured to Stampfer. He looked up. 'Herr von Hessert, please give our warmest greetings and our congratulations to Rinner, on your return.'

'Happy to,' Rudi said, appreciating the sobering effects of the chamomile tea, while at the same time wishing he could have had some champagne.

'What did you make of Rinner's report?' Stampfer asked him, his eyes boring at Rudi.

197

They all looked at him, wide-eyed with interest at his reaction. Rudi had meant to read it on the train, but had fallen asleep. 'Very good,' he said.

'Let us quickly show you what we have for you, to take back to what used to be Germany,' said Wels.

Mrs Lukacskova appeared on cue, carrying a plastic workers' suitcase. As she put it down next to Rudi, the contrast between the case and Rudi's expensive clothes was obvious to everybody. Mrs Lukacskova looked questioningly at Wels.

'You won't be carrying the case for long,' Wels said. 'When you travel back tomorrow, you will give it to a contact. We'll give you the details later.' His manner was becoming brusque, because of the mistake with the suitcase.

Stampfer, however, was still smiling. 'Soon, we will be producing a newspaper here,' he told Rudi. 'It will be called *Neue Vorwärts*. As the name implies, it will carry on where our old newspaper, *Vorwärts*, left off.' Stampfer beamed proudly; the newspaper clearly very much his baby. 'We're not quite ready yet. Perhaps you will come and visit us again, Herr von Hessert?'

Rudi smiled warmly at Stampfer. These brave old boys. They had been hounded out of their homes and their country. Yet here they were, burning with enthusiasm, making plans, for all the world as if they were students running some club or society back in Munich – the Chess Club, say, or the Chamber Music Society. Rudi couldn't give a damn about politics, Social Democrat or any other flavour, but he could cheerfully have hugged the lot of them.

'Yes, Herr Stampfer,' he said. 'If I can be of service, I will be most happy to come here again.'

Stampfer beamed. So did Wels. He unlocked the workers' case and pulled out sample leaflets. Rudi looked at one. Wels was certainly right to be proud of it. It was well-produced and in a small format, so it could be smuggled

into the Reich more easily. The heading wrung a smile from
him. It was 'Germany Awaken' – the Social Democrats had
pinched the Nazi slogan.

Rudi read on:

Wilhelm II once said, there is only one ruler in the kingdom, and that is me. And the whole world laughed. Now
Adolf Hitler says there is only one ruler in the kingdom,
and that is me. And nobody laughs any more. Adolf
Hitler now possesses a power which no German king, or
even a Russian czar, has ever possessed. Germany is now
the most complete despotism in the world.

'Bravo!' Rudi said.

'Your train leaves at 8.55 tomorrow morning, Herr von
Hessert,' Ollenhauer chipped in. His buttoned-up jacket
was gaping, as it stretched tight over his tummy. He looked
less at ease than the others. 'When you board, please walk
through until you find the Mitropa restaurant car. An atten-
dant in the car will be on the lookout for the case. He will
approach you when he sees it. Give the case to him. He will
keep it safe, and return it to you, when you reach Munich
Hauptbahnhof.'

Rudi nodded. 'Sounds pretty straightforward to me, Herr
Ollenhauer.'

'As you leave the platform,' Wels took over. 'Rinner will
meet you. He will relieve you of the case. You won't have it
for long. No, no.'

'Say hello to Munich for me,' Stampfer said, without a
trace of self-pity.

Rudi nodded again. Then came the invitation he had
been dreading.

'My wife, Toni, and I will be delighted to welcome you
to our necessarily modest home this evening, Herr von
Hessert,' Wels announced. 'Toni has killed the fatted calf,

so please let nothing pass your lips from now until then. The others have promised to put in an appearance …' He smiled at Stampfer, who smiled back. They were all beaming. 'I hope it is not ungallant of me to reveal that one of our young helpers, Martina, has been preparing herself for this evening for some time …' All the Social Democrats laughed. 'In fact,' Wels added, with heavy roguishness, 'when she finally saw you, I believe preparations intensified.'

'Enough!' Stampfer laughed. 'That really is ungallant, Otto!'

Rudi took a deep breath, hating himself. 'I would love to, normally,' he said firmly. 'But I'm afraid I have taken a chill, from draughts on the train. I really must rest in the hotel this evening. These things can pass to the lungs, you know.'

There was a silence. Then Wels said. 'Never mind. Never mind. That is your final decision, is it?'

'I'm afraid so.'

'Yes. Well, never mind.' Wels nodded to himself. 'We are truly grateful, Herr von Hessert. More than words can say.'

'Herr Wels, let me tell you this,' Rudi said, looking the frail figure in the eye, 'I hate Adolf Hitler with every fibre of my being. It is *I* who should thank *you*, for giving me this opportunity.'

To Rudi's mortification, this brought another round of applause, and some knuckle-banging on the desks, led by Wels. One of the old boys hugged him, bending over him awkwardly, smelling of old man. Somebody else shook his hand. Stampfer was close to tears. Even Ollenhauer looked moved.

That evening, as the Social Democrats began their festivities at Wels' flat without him, Rudi took a taxi to an address he had been given before he left. It turned out to be a converted warehouse in a dock area, right on the Voltava.

He paid at the door and went in. Raucous jazz music boomed out, played by a quintet of negroes on a makeshift stage. Couples were dancing on the small dance floor, or kissing in corners – some wore dresses and make-up, some evening clothes, some workers' overalls. There was an MC in a smoking jacket, just preparing to make an announcement. Rudi made his way to the bar. A blond came up to him. He said something in Czech.

'You speak German?' Rudi said.

'Sure. You new here, darling?'

Rudi gave him the once-over. He was a worker; smelled of oil. But not bad – not bad at all. 'You got a place we can go?'

'Sure. You want to tell me your name?'

'Not particularly.'

4

There was, Inspector Forster reflected sourly, nothing English about the Englischer Garten. His jaundiced eye took in the steep slopes of unkempt parkland; his face falling into the sneer which was all that was left of his smile these days. And he doubted there was anything Chinese about the Chinese Tower. His eye traversed six tapering tiers of pagoda-shaped roofing. But at least they had put a beer garden at the foot of it – a decent authentically German beer garden.

Forster sipped his beer, shutting out the cries of the children at the tables around him. He turned his face into the wind as it whistled across the open parkland, ruffling the overlong grass. This was one of Hitler's favourite views; from the Chinese Tower looking toward the Monopteros. He had ordered the trees blocking the sweep of the view to be chopped down.

Forster thought back to his early view of the Nazis. He had seen von Epp in the flesh, in the spring of 1928. He had revisited the family farm in Memmingen, on holiday. With his parents and sisters, all in their Sunday best, he had gone along to an open-air election rally addressed by the Count. There must have been three thousand people there – a festive atmosphere. Before the meeting began, a stunt pilot from Munich looped the loop, then dropped Nazi leaflets from the air, to the amused delight of the crowd.

202

Von Epp was a good speaker. He had a microphone – you could hear him perfectly even in the far corners of the field. The neighbours Forster had grown up with, small-holders and shopkeepers, loved it, cheering and clapping him. Von Epp said he was the son of a painter. He had joined the Nazis because he was attracted to their idea of the Racial Community, a homogeneous group of racially pure people. It would restore national unity, destroyed by class hatred and class struggle.

Also, the Nazis represented the fighting spirit of the German front, applied to politics. That got a roar of delight. The Nazis had the firmest will, he said, the greatest awareness of the danger Germany faced. And their rough elements were understandable because they had youth-fulness.

He received an ovation at the end. Ursula, the younger of the Forster sisters, threw May flowers up to him. Forster cheered with all the others. After the von Epp rally, he began to take the Nazis seriously. And now? Now he was not so sure.

The sun went in, dipping behind the Chinese Tower. Elsperger was late. Forster's sour mood curdled further. SS-Captain Anton Elsperger appeared just as Forster tilted his head back to drain the last quarter of his beer. He was hurrying from the direction of the Monopteros – a temple-building which wasn't Greek, in the same way the Chinese Tower wasn't Chinese, and the whole park wasn't English. He was in uniform. Forster had made it clear that he should come in civvies.

A slightly flustered Elsperger was full of apologies. He sat down opposite Forster. A waitress appeared immediately; Elsperger ordered a coffee. Forster eyed him, with the same jaundiced gaze he had run over the Englischer Garten and its buildings.

The captain, he thought, was a beneficiary of Himmler's

policy of surrounding himself with the blond and the blue-eyed. This applied not only to his SS soldiery. Any dark-haired typists, filing-clerks or chauffeurs in Himmler's ambit were being ruthlessly weeded out, in the hope of eventual replacement by blonds. The immediate impact of this boost to racial purity had been a chronic shortage of typists and filing clerks.

Forster, who, like most South Germans, was short and dark, saw himself as a professional among amateurs – albeit racially pure amateurs. He realised he was becoming dis-illusioned with the Nazis, but put the thought out of his mind.

'Something came up,' Elsperger said, still apologising for his lateness. 'We got a tip-off about some communists.'

'Not Kunde, by any chance?'

Elsperger shook his head. 'Afraid not. Still no trace of him.' His coffee arrived. He sipped at it, looking curiously at Forster.

Forster, as he tended to, came straight to the point. 'I have just found a reference to Rüdiger von Hessert, in a report from a plain clothes officer at the Hauptbahnhof. The officer had been watching the arrival of a Moscow train, which stopped in Prague. He saw von Hessert on the concourse, just after the train arrived. He was carrying a workers' suitcase, as well as his own travelling bag.'

'Handover?' Elsperger asked.

'Probably, but our man lost von Hessert in the crowd.'

'The idiot,' Elsperger muttered, meaning von Hessert, not the policeman.

'You were at school with him, weren't you?' Forster said. There was an edge in his voice. Farm boys from Memmingen do not attend the sort of schools the von Hesserts and Elspergers of this world go to.

'He was a few years younger,' Elsperger said. 'But, yes, I knew him from school.'

Forster swigged the last of his beer. 'We need to know what he's up to. We need quality intelligence,' he paused, 'from the inside.'

Elsperger nodded again. 'What do you want from me?'

'I want you to get close to von Hessert.'

'Can't you just have him followed?'

Forster gave a thin-lipped version of his smile. 'Cajetan von Hessert's son? I think not. No, Captain, something more … intimate is required.'

Elsperger's thick-lipped face hardened. 'What do you mean?'

'I'm sure you can pick up the threads from your school days, Herr Elsperger.'

'What? How do you …? Oh, never mind. Is this an order?' He glanced sceptically round the beer garden and up at the Chinese Tower.

'Would you like your early association with von Hessert, and others, to be more widely known, Captain? We don't want your little wife upset, now do we?'

Elsperger swore under his breath. 'All right, I'll do it.'

'Damn right you will. And you'll need these. Tell him you can get as many as he needs.' Forster dug into his mackintosh pocket, pulled out a flat black box and passed it to Anton Elsperger.

Elsperger knew what it was, but opened the box anyway. Nestling in tiny red-plush compartments, there were a dozen clear-glass ampoules of morphine.

5

Rüdiger von Hessert was slumped in an armchair in his room at the family villa in Karolinenplatz. The tallowy light of a single lamp-standard with a heavy flower-patterned fringed shade cast his face in half-shadow. He was staring into space. There was a bottle of vintage French champagne on the floor, half empty, and he had swallowed a few – maybe more than a few – amphetamines. And none of it was working.

He was, he reflected, two people: He was Rudi-alone and he was Rudi-in-company. Rudi-in-company was, he had to admit, damned amusing – much sought after and understandably so. Invitations rained down like confetti. He sometimes thought there was nobody in Munich, at any rate nobody in Munich society, who he did not know. Rudi-alone, however, was a pretty desperate case. How, oh how, did other people fill in all that time? It hung so heavy on him, Rudi-alone could scream.

There were those, Rudi knew, who worked in the evenings. But unfortunately he was easily bright enough to absorb gigantic amounts of material at first reading, and so didn't really need to. The law bored him, but he had a facility for it. One could say the same for games and pastimes. He was one of the best tennis players at his club, but the game was so irksome he could hardly be bothered to turn up to play. He hadn't read a book for pleasure since he was ten. Ennui was more than a mood; it was a state-of-being.

Anyone would think that being in love would be a release from this. If you were in love, so went the common wisdom, you were lifted from the confines of the self. You were no longer alone. But Rudi-alone was in love, for the first time ever, and he was so lonely he could slit his throat.

He splashed more champagne, now warm, into a Bohemian crystal goblet, tried to shed a few tears for himself, and failed. He had had crushes on Normals before, of course, but nothing like this. Not that the love-object was a bona-fide Normal, not from the way he took him – Rudi – but he had a family he was unlikely to leave, so he might just as well be a Normal.

Rudi-alone put the goblet down and faced being in love. What it amounted to was that the other person was always inside you. He giggled at the double entendre. Sometimes that was rather pleasant. He treated himself to saying the love-object's name aloud: 'Anton,' he said. It was pleasurable, but it didn't take long, even if he said his second name, as well – 'Anton Elsperger.' He could hardly sit there all evening saying 'Anton Elsperger' to himself.

So, what now? What to do? Aaah! A thought. A happy thought. Go and see him. Just be with him. Rudi's entire being lifted. He knew only too well where the love-object was. His family were with him, but so what? Just engineer a meeting. The love-object didn't know he knew; a mutual friend had mentioned the arrangement for this evening. He could make it look like chance.

Happiness flooded Rudi-alone's being. Just a moment ago, he could not imagine a Rudi, of any sort, at the end of this painful stretch of time that was the evening. But now … He absently popped another amphetamine, showered, changed into something sporty – light flannels, linen jacket, open-necked shirt and cravat – and set off in his papa's Horch.

*

The SS Club was at 19 Altheimer Eck, previously the site of the Social Democrat headquarters and *Münchener Post* editorial offices. It had been converted, using money paid out by the *Sozis'* insurers, after the place had been trashed when the Nazis took over Munich. Only SS and guests were permitted, but friends fought to sign Rudi in.

The *Kegelbahn* was in the cellar, where the *Münchener Post*'s printing presses had been. The clatter of the *Kegel* skittles going down as the wooden balls hit them made Rudi feel cheerful again. There were three lanes, making it one of the biggest skittle-alleys in South Germany. Some tasteful pine cladding round the walls and a bar in the corner made it all nice and homely.

Barbara – Bärbel – Elsperger saw him first and waved. He had known her long before she married Anton. At the age of eighteen, they had done their *Abitur* exam together, then been in the same year at university. Anton was a few years older, so ahead of both of them. He and Anton had had it off a few times both at school and university, but the feeling, this overwhelming love and passion, had only come upon him when Anton had started everything up again.

Bärbel told their two boys to stop the game, as soon as she saw Rudi coming over to them. SS-Captain Anton Elsperger gave one of his fleshy-lipped smiles. Rudi thought his saxe-blue pullover and powder-blue shirt set off his blond colouring perfectly.

'Rudi!' Bärbel, who was gamine and pretty, in a pert sort of way, flung her arms round his neck. She was wearing a wide-skirted dress, not entirely suitable for skittles.

'Rüdiger!' Anton Elsperger boomed.

To his relief, Rudi could see he did not suspect this was anything other than a chance meeting. And, naturally, Anton had no idea of the depths of his feelings. Rudi would have died rather than tell him.

'Anton!' Rudi was poised and suave. 'What a surprise ...'

'What are you doing here?' The thick-lipped SS-Captain was smiling.

'Oh, you know. Loose end.'

'Papa!' The older boy was fractious at the interruption to the game. Rudi put him at about seven, and the other one perhaps two years younger.

'Well, I won't disturb you any further.'

'Nonsense.' Bärbel said. 'I haven't seen you for ages. Come and join us.'

Rudi looked at the boys. He was completely at ease with children. 'What do you two think? May I join you?'

'Are you any good?' said the older one.

'Wolfgang!' rebuked Bärbel, smiling.

Rudi looked the boy in the eye, his face a picture of earnestness. 'Wolfgang, I have the official designation of *Kegelmeister*. Do you know what that means? It means I am one of Germany's leading experts at skittles.'

'Good. You can be on my team,' Wolfgang said. He blinked owlishly behind his spectacles. 'It's me and Mama against Papa and my brother, here. His name is Gero. But we're losing.'

'Not for much longer, you're not,' said Rudi.

With Bärbel's fond laughter ringing in his ears, and feeling Anton's smile washing over him, Rudi-in-company loudly demanded paper and pencil. Wolfgang produced one of his school exercise books from a leather satchel. To screams of glee from the children, Rudi proceeded to tear a blank page from the back. Checking that Anton and Bärbel were laughing, too – they were – Rudi sketched two diagrams:

He was good at drawing – it would be difficult to come up with anything he wasn't good at. The first diagram showed what happened if you threw straight down the lane and hit the head-skittle head on. Five, possibly six, of the nine skittles would go over. Rudi showed the direction of force by

MICHAEL DEAN

means of skilfully sketched arrows.

A second diagram showed what happened if you threw slightly to the right, catching the vee of the lead and right-hand skittle – all nine would go down. Rudi then gave a demonstration, hitting the skittles head on, standing the prophesied five felled skittles, then throwing all nine over with a consummate throw into the vee.

The boys hooted with laughter. It was like being one of the family. Rudi-in-company was exhilarated. It was one of the happiest evenings of his life. When the *Kegel* game was over, Anton casually asked him to keep an eye on Gerhard Glaser, in case he did something stupid. It would be in Glaser's own interest, the SS-Captain said, putting a hand on Rudi's shoulder, to keep the foolish old boy out of trouble.

Rudi agreed immediately, unhesitatingly. He suggested a meeting with Anton, somewhere private, the very next day, so they could talk about it. He said he would tell Anton all about Glaser then.

He would be counting the hours. There was nothing he wouldn't do for the love-object.

6

Karl-Heinz Forster, newly promoted to Chief Inspector, had been put in charge of an expanded Political Police, transferred from Ettstrasse to the former Wittelsbach Palace, just down the road from the Brown House. He reported to Reinhard Heydrich, who reported directly to Himmler.

His new chief, Heydrich, had been the most spectacular gainer from Himmler's policy of promoting blonds. He was a disgraced naval Signals officer, not even a Party member, originally, and not yet thirty. He had been chosen to head the Political Police solely because of his lank dark-blond hair. This after a ten-minute interview at Himmler's chicken farm, set up by his mother's personal contacts.

Heydrich sat, stiff and blond, behind his massive desk, in his full-dress, black SS uniform – swastika armband over the left sleeve, yellow braid on both shoulders, oak leaf cluster on the lapel. On the index finger of his right hand he wore a Death's Head Ring, a gift from Heinrich Himmler.

He was sitting beneath a portrait of himself as a fencer – perhaps considered more virile than his other hobby, playing the violin. The painter was Josef Vietz. Vietz had copied the portrait from the porcelain figurine of Heydrich, mass-produced by the Allach company in Dachau, and now widely available.

Heydrich was chairing a meeting. Present were Chief Inspector Forster and the wall-eyed Max Troll, code-named Theo by the communists.

Forster was still in his mac from outside. At the age of thirty-nine, the Chief Inspector was at the height of his powers, and he knew it. His demeanour, while never less than respectful, was far more secure than the edgy figure overawed in Hess's office, just over eighteen months ago. He sat on one of the red plush gilt chairs lined up along the wall, not bothering to move it opposite Heydrich's desk. His leonine face bore a pasted-on smile. He was here to give advice, not commands, but advice based on considerable expertise. Advice likely to be listened to, and then followed.

Max Troll, by contrast, was perched on the edge of a chair, set an awkward angle. His bearing was tense and defensive.

Heydrich leaned back and stapled his fingers. 'How,' he asked, in his high-pitched voice, 'did the Schwarzmüller Group manage to base themselves at the Asam Church?'

Troll answered eagerly. 'One of the group, Georg Limmer, the one code-named Hugo, was a congregationalist at the church, *Herr Oberführer*. He was once a stage-manager for a theatre company, which put on plays for the congregation at the church. They let the company use a room in the Asam House to rehearse. The Asam House is next to the church ...'

'I know where the Asam House is,' Heydrich said petulantly, his voice rising to a squeak. As one of only a handful of non-Bavarians in the Nazi hierarchy, he was sensitive to any imputed lack of local knowledge.

Troll licked his lips. 'Anyway, Limmer kept the key. Later he told the priest he wanted to write ... a play or something. So they made a room in the Asam House available to him. The communists brought in a typewriter quite openly.'

'What do we know about Limmer?' Heydrich asked.

'Age nineteen. Parents are communists of the old school,' Forster supplied. 'Limmer used to live with them. Walked to Austria on the first day of the revolution. The

212

Austrians threw him out – no papers – so he walked back to Munich.'

'Why haven't we picked him up?'

Forster shrugged, keeping his voice even, not letting his low opinion of Heydrich show. 'We could if we wanted to, but it would take time. He sleeps on the floor of a different Marxist sympathiser every night. He never goes back to his parents' place. Known address.'

'And is he involved with this subversive newspaper they produce?'

'Sometimes. But only in the distribution. Paul Jahnke and Schwarzmüller put it together in the Asam House. Then the spirit masters are smuggled out to the banda machine in Rottenbucherstrasse. The newspaper is copied and distributed from there. They also possess a printing press. But it doesn't work.'

'So what are we doing about it?'

Forster waited a moment before answering. 'We traced the serial number of their banda machine, and closed the company that sold it to them. Kunde is patching the machine up. When he can longer do that ...' Forster shrugged, '... they're finished.'

'We haven't moved against them?' Heydrich asked.

'No. Except for Kunde, who's a real danger to the Reich. He was released from Dachau by Glaser, before I could stop it. I've issued an arrest warrant. We're looking for him.'

'Why not the others?'

Forster raised his eyes heavenwards, but Heydrich missed it. 'They are quite useful to us,' he began carefully. 'We seize the newspapers after they distribute them. In that way, we flush out sympathisers we may not know about. We've caught some pretty big fish that way, in the past.'

'I see,' Heydrich said. 'But you haven't managed to apprehend this Kunde yet?'

'No,' said Forster. 'But we will. We'll give it priority. This link with the Social Democrats changes everything.' The Chief Inspector nodded approvingly at Troll. 'I mean Troll's information that Rinner is still in Munich and will be at this meeting.'

Heydrich nodded. 'Certainly. Our main priority is Rinner. But what about Glaser? This lawyer who was at the meeting with Schwarzmüller and the rest of them. And you say he's the one who had Kunde released?'

Forster started to speak, but Troll, anxious to make an impression, cut across him.

'Glaser was brought there by force,' Troll said. 'Paul Jahnke brought him at knifepoint.'

Forster noted the point in his notebook. 'Glaser's an obsessive,' he said to Heydrich. 'He keeps sending me memos about the murder of a Jew art dealer called Weintraub. Kunde was accused of the murder. Glaser keeps asking for a progress report.'

Heydrich knew enough about the Weintraub case to avoid the subject – the word was, the Party Bonzen were involved, perhaps even Hitler himself. He ignored the remark.

'Two things,' Heydrich said. 'Is this Glaser against the revolution? And is he dangerous?'

'Against the revolution, certainly,' said Forster 'He opposes the Third Reich and all we stand for. Dangerous? A one-legged idealist?' Forster's old smile reappeared. 'I think not.'

Heydrich tilted his chair back. 'So …' he said, 'do we find Rinner and pull him in, or …?'

Troll shook his head. 'Pull him in now and they'll call off the meeting. I've got the date, the time and the place. Just turn up in force.' He enumerated on his fingers. 'You get Rinner. You get Kunde. You get Schwarzmüller, Limmer and Jahnke. You get Glaser, if you want him. And – now here's something – you get people from the Social Democrat side we don't even know about. I know they're bringing more people. A delegation. But I don't know who.'

Heydrich nodded judiciously. 'Chief Inspector?'

'Troll's right. He's done well.'

The informer licked his lips.

'You're sure they don't suspect you?' Heydrich said to Troll.

'Quite sure.' Heydrich gave him a stern look and Troll added, '*Herr Oberführer.*'

'All right,' Heydrich said. 'The Asam House meeting it is. And we'll see who else we fish up in the net.'

7

Sepp Kunde's father pulled buckets of ore up and down by rope in a factory, from morning to evening. That was his life. On his way to work, he used to see the local landowner's carriage pulled by four grey horses, when only two were needed. What he told his twin sons, Sepp and August, was this: 'Character is determined neither by wealth nor by position; devotion to duty alone is the mark of true nobility.' The young Sepp grew up with a holy respect for the vast, silent heroism of the labourer.

When Sepp was twelve years old, he developed blood poisoning in his left arm, after falling on a bottle while he was playing. He was confined to bed for almost two years. The solitude helped him break the shackles of being a twin. After that, he felt August could go his own way, the more so when that way involved a life of crime. When August attacked a woman, Sepp told him he no longer considered him a brother.

Women were Sepp's only companions. From the age of fifteen, he asked any woman he desired to make love with him. Many agreed to do so. He never made promises in order to have his way. He held fast to the belief that to tell a woman you love her, when you do not, is low and despicable. But afterwards, he would thank her for the bounty of her beauty and her body. He would kiss her hand. Then he would say goodbye.

As he grew to maturity, Sepp came to believe in the

brotherhood of all men across the artificial boundaries of nation. When war came, he refused to fight against working men from other countries. But the parish council put up a poster with the names of three boys from his village who they would send in his place if he refused. So he had to go. After the war, he went to Munich to find work. He also hoped to escape August, but his twin had made the same decision.

In Munich, August continued a life of crime. Sepp fought for the Councils Republic. After their defeat, he worked as a clockmaker and a cabinetmaker, then opened his own locksmith shop. Working alone best suited his temperament. But he kept certain papers, including forged identity documents, to help the communists. The Nazis found them, closed his shop down, and sent him to prison – to Stadelheim.

He was in Stadelheim, for a while, at the same time as August, who had murdered a man in the course of a theft. Shortly after his release, Lange had found him a job at the Weintraub Gallery, in return for agreeing to undergo tests at his hospital.

When Herr Weintraub was murdered, Sepp was briefly returned to Stadelheim, then Dachau. When they released him from Dachau, he got sucked back into the Schwarzmüller Group, because they needed him so badly, though he had intended to leave. When the idiots kidnapped Glaser, he would have welcomed the chance to walk out, when he threatened to.

He was still convinced that the only way to stop the Nazis was to kill Hitler, and he had been thinking about ways to do it. A bomb was the answer, he believed. He had been planning its construction, but he lacked information about where to plant it. So for now he continued to work with the Schwarzmüller Group. But he intended to go it alone soon.

*

217

Kunde hurried from the Sendlinger Tor along Sendlinger-strasse. It was raining in sheets; he was soaked to the skin. He remembered another occasion in the rain. Max Troll standing staring into a doorway, while newspapers were delivered to the old Red Gymnastics Club. And men leaving that club being arrested, and driven away by the Political Police, who must have been waiting.

He had suspected Troll for a long time, but he had no proof. A just man did not pass on suspicions when he had no proof. But he intended to check out this meeting in advance, to see if Max Troll was betraying them.

He believed he had plenty of time. His watch showed just after one-thirty. The meeting had been fixed for three o'clock. If, as he suspected, this was a trap, he reckoned the Gestapo would take up position from two o'clock, or so.

He ducked into the Asam Church, intending to go out the back, into the cloistered gardens, then through to the Asam House. The church was exceptionally narrow, dimly lit and layered with what Kunde regarded as obscene luxury. There was a white marble balustrade, then salmon-pink pillars flanking encrusted gold starbursts over not just one altar, but two. For above the first altar was another balustrade, then the second altar, above which was a round yellow window, like an artificial mockery of the natural sun.

Kunde wondered how much blood and sweat of decent working men had gone into the construction of this elaborate hall, whose very purpose was to cow and deceive the workers into giving yet more docile labour for the benefit of the rich. Then he heard a noise.

The heavy wooden door near the altar, which led to a passageway through to the Asam House, opened. He ducked down into the choir stalls, just as Forster came in.

Butcher Forster, they called him. The man who had hunted down the original leaders of the communist resistance in Munich, leaving them with that useless mummy's boy of a plasterer, Franz-Xaver Schwarzmüller, in charge.

Kunde crouched, tucking himself behind a carved wood misericord. His jerkin and shirt were steaming from the rain in the sudden warmth. He could hear Forster walking up and down, and he cursed himself for a fool, trapped and unable to warn Schwarzmüller and Glaser. Then he nearly betrayed himself by laughing aloud – Forster started praying.

Kunde put his head round the side of the choir stall to see the broad back of Forster, encased in a mackintosh, kneeling before the altar, praying for the successful outcome of his afternoon's work: the arrest of the communists and Social Democrats. Forster then prayed for his family; for his wife, Christa, and his children, Helga and Erwin. He finished with a prayer for the safety of his Führer, Adolf Hitler. Then he stood up and crossed himself.

Kunde put his head down again and heard Forster barking instructions. An SS guard appeared at the door leading to the Asam House. Another guard stood at the main church entrance, the one Kunde had just come through – leading back into Sendlingerstrasse. Forster left. Kunde was trapped.

He settled down in his hiding place and glanced at his watch. It was twenty minutes to two. He curled into a ball and waited. Eventually he heard the door to the Asam House slam. The guard had gone into the passageway, probably for a cigarette. This was the guard who would certainly have seen him, if he had moved from his hiding place. The other one did not have the same direct line of vision.

Kunde took a chance that this other guard was not looking along the nave towards the altar at this precise moment. He straightened up, left his hiding place and walked toward the guard, as if he had just come from the Asam House. His luck held. As he swaggered down the nave, the guard noticed him for the first time.

'Herr Forster wants you,' called out Kunde, his voice echoing to the high ceiling.

The SS guard gazed blankly at the communist. He was a callow, swarthy youth, with fruity spots dotted on chin and cheeks. 'OK,' he said uncertainly. He started to move away, down toward the altar, then stopped. 'Who are you?' he said.

'Max Troll,' Kunde said, without breaking step.

He kept walking. The guard hesitated again, then nodded and walked off. Outside, the rain had stopped. Kunde checked his watch. Two-thirty. If Forster had his wits about him, he would realise his operation was compromised, as soon as the guard reached him. Would he move to arrest everybody now? Or would he still wait at the Asam House?

A little way down Sendlingerstrasse, there was a bicycle leaning against the facade of a building. Kunde took it, and set off fast to Haidhausen, where Schwarzmüller lived. He was afraid Lange's coal gas experiments may have damaged his lungs, but the deep breathing seemed to be restoring them. Kunde had been a member of a Red Cycling Club in his youth; he made good time.

Schwarzmüller was just setting off for the Asam House. Kunde caught him in the street, outside the front door of his building.

'Schwarzmüller!' Kunde called to him, breathless. 'It's a trap. Warn the others.'

Franz-Xaver Schwarzmüller looked startled. 'It's too late,' he said.

'Warn as many as you can,' Kunde shouted. He turned the bicycle round.

It was the last time anybody saw Schwarzmüller alive. The plasterer left Germany for Moscow that evening. As soon as he arrived, he was arrested and sent to a labour camp, along with every other German communist who made the same journey.

8

Kunde crouched low over the handlebars, racing style, and pedalled for all he was worth to Glaser's address in Galeriestrasse. There, he threw the bicycle down in the gutter, and furiously rang Glaser's bell. Nothing. He tried the outside door of the block of flats. It was locked. He cursed and railed against the fates. Then he rang Glaser's bell again, out of sheer defiance. As he was turning to leave, a big, red-faced, jolly-looking youth opened the door.

'Gerhard Glaser!' Kunde shouted, breathless from the ride. 'Is he still there?'

'Yes, he is,' the youth said. 'Would you be Herr Kunde?'

'Yes, I would,' Kunde said, gasping.

'Come in, sir, please,' said the youth. 'You're in luck. Herr Rinner was late, or we would have set off by now. My name is Kaspar, by the way.'

Kunde ignored the hand he offered. He followed Kaspar into the Glaser family flat, on the ground floor. Kaspar had a rolling gait, like a boxer, but he moved clumsily. There was something of his father's forthright, almost naive, decency about him. But even at this early stage, Kunde discerned a buffoonish quality, too, absent in the father.

In Glaser's drawing room there were two women: Frau Glaser was statuesque, with green-grey eyes, auburn hair and full breasts. The other woman, the one seated at the table, was a sensual creature, with hennaed hair. As Kunde came in, she looked wide-eyed at him, then looked away, with a half-smile. He knew she would make love with him, if he could create the opportunity.

Next to her, von Hessert looked much the worse for wear, since Kunde had last seen him at Dachau – nervous and strained, with much of his composure gone. 'Hello, Kunde,' he said, in that aristocratic drawl of his.

Kunde did not trouble to reply. He sat down at the table. 'The meeting is a trap,' he said without preamble. 'One of the communists is an informer.'

There was a murmur of consternation. Kunde lay his head down on his arms on the table and rested. Exhausted from the bicycle riding, he dozed for a few seconds. When he looked up again, the brunette was looking at him, highly amused. She was obviously intelligent, which is neither here nor there as far as love-making is concerned. Her dark good looks reminded him of a Vicki Baum heroine. He was aroused by her – tumescent.

Introductions were made, round the table, after the bourgeois manner. The girl was introduced as Fräulein von Hessert. Kunde asked her first name straight off, looking her in the eye. She laughingly said he could call her Ello, immediately using the *du* form. So far so good, thought Kunde. The one with the attaché case was introduced as Herr Rinner.

'I'd better go,' Rinner murmured.

He was distracted, but not, Kunde thought, afraid. He had an air about him. Kunde began, reluctantly, to respect him.

'You should not go back to your lodgings, Herr Rinner,' Kunde said. 'Or any address connected to the Social Democrats that they might know about.'

'I know,' Rinner replied. 'The Gestapo came for me at the Bayerischer Hof yesterday.'

Kunde frowned. 'Are you sure they were Gestapo?'

'Quite sure.'

'Not Political Police?'

'No. They introduced themselves as Gestapo. Our people stalled them long enough for me to make my escape. But it was close. I could take nothing with me.'

Kunde nodded. 'That's interesting. It's not Troll's doing, then. Our communist informer.'

'How do you know?' Glaser asked.

'Forster was running the Asam House operation,' Kunde said. 'Forster is Political Police, not Gestapo. And, anyway, if Rinner had been arrested yesterday, it would have wrecked the Political Police operation today.'

'So who betrayed Herr Rinner?' said Kaspar. Everyone ignored him.

Glaser went white. 'Was there much of value in your room, Erich?' he asked. It was obvious to everyone in the room that he was changing the subject.

Rinner shook his head. 'No. I had hardly started on the next Green Report. And there are no names there for them to find. I know better than that.' This last was said with a glance at Kunde, the amateur to the professional. Kunde's opinion of Rinner continued to rise.

'Do you have anywhere to stay tonight, Herr Rinner?' asked Frau Glaser.

'He can't stay here, sad to say,' said Kaspar. 'Magda is out at the moment, but she'll be back soon.'

'Who is Magda?' Kunde asked him.

Kaspar grinned. 'My sister,' he said. 'But then we all have our cross to bear.' He laughed at his own joke.

Kunde frowned, disliking him even more. He thought him a clown.

'Kas-par!' Frau Glaser said. She smiled at her son and he smiled back. Kunde thought she had a truly lovely smile.

'I wouldn't dream of imposing, in any case,' Rinner said.

Frau Glaser stood. 'I'm phoning my sister.'

Glaser started to protest, but she ignored him. The Glaser telephone was on a telephone table in the corner of the room. The company were silent, with everybody listening to the telephone call.

'Hello. It's me. How's things?' Frau Glaser was silent, nodding as she listened to the answer. Then she said, 'How are you placed for an overnight guest? ... Yes. Thank you. One coming soon, then. Goodbye. And take care.'

She rang off, having mentioned no names. Kunde approved. There was a rumour that the Gestapo were bugging all the telephones, and it was probably true.

Frau Glaser turned to Rinner. 'Herr Rinner, you can stay with my sister, Katya. Katya Bachhuber. She is not known to the authorities. You should be safe there for a while.' She smiled at Rinner, then gave him her sister's address.

'My thanks to you, Frau Glaser,' Rinner said. He left, with ornate goodbyes and handshakes, which sent Kunde's opinion of him down again.

As soon as he was gone, Ello spoke. 'I know we must leave soon,' she said. 'But there was something I wished to put to the people at this meeting, which will not now take place.' She was speaking directly to Kunde.

'And that was?'

Ello looked serious. 'I know Hitler quite well. In a manner of speaking, I am his lady friend.'

'Are you now?'

'Yes.'

There was silence in the room. Von Hessert favoured everyone with a cheesy grin. Kaspar was gazing at Ello. Only Frau Glaser looked a little cool. Ello was obviously weighing up Kunde's reaction to her news. His reaction was that the day was looking up, in more ways than one. Ello continued, but only when she was good and ready. Kunde raised an eyebrow. She was a woman of true independence; one could respect such a woman.

'I am also a psychology student, Herr Kunde,' she said.

'Call me Sepp.'

'Very well. Sepp. And I've known Hitler since girlhood. So I'll tell you what makes him tick, shall I?'

'Please do.'

'Right. Well. To keep it simple ...'

'You don't need to keep it simple, Ello. Working men aren't necessarily stupid.'

There was an uneasy silence. Kunde didn't take his eyes off her. Getting her into bed depended on winning this.

She dropped her eyes. 'That's not what I meant.'

'Good.'

The briefest of pauses. 'I'm sorry.'

'Apology accepted. Please continue.'

She nodded. 'As well as being a psychopath, Hitler is an artist-savant ...'

Kunde interrupted. 'How do you know what he is?'

'I got him to draw,' Ello said. 'The key is his architectural drawings, not the watercolours. They are done using eidetic memory, and at speed. They are perfectly in proportion. He draws the same subject again and again, starting with small detail and working outward. The buildings he draws have strong linear perspective, often multiple perspective, using colour to fill in defined areas only, like the yellow on his drawing of the Old Residence. All this is typical of autistic artist-savants.'

'Can you be sure?' Glaser said.

'I'm ... reasonably sure of the diagnosis.'

'But if he's autistic, wouldn't he be ... I don't know, stupid?' Kaspar asked.

Ello shook her head. 'Not at all. Most autistic savants have average or above-average intelligence.'

Kunde stared at her, fascinated. 'So, how did he get like that?'

'I can't be completely certain. But probably when his

father beat his mother while she was pregnant with him, it caused circulating testosterone to become neurotoxic. That's also what made him a psychopath. We can't know the exact nature of what has been destroyed in him. He is a severely damaged being, but it is more a question of what is missing than what is wrong. Much, perhaps everything, that makes us human is simply not there. He is not, in the fullest sense of the word, a human being at all.'

There was complete silence in the room.

'Can a person not be human?' Kaspar asked.

'I think so. Yes.'

'Then what future is there for Germany?' Glaser said.

Ello shrugged her narrow shoulders. 'Hitler over-evaluates his short-term goal, the achievement of power, to such an extent that nothing else is left for him, or of him. If he does not achieve total power, he will commit suicide, as he keeps threatening to do. But we cannot rely on that. He craves his own death, but also the deaths of others. And this will not change. He is at the extreme end of the changeable – unchangeable axis.'

Kunde spoke softly, with great respect. 'So what do we do?'

'We kill him.'

Glaser took his pipe from his mouth, shocked. 'Ello! No!'

Von Hessert laughed, a little shrilly.

'Bravo, Ello!' Kaspar said. 'Is there any wine?'

'I ... thought of poison,' Ello said, 'but it's so difficult to get him alone and ...'

'A bomb would be better,' Kunde said.

'Really? Oh, what a relief! Will you ...?'

'Yes,' Kunde said. 'I'll do it for you. The communists are finished and the *Sozis* are useless. So I'll do it alone. It's always better that way.'

Ello felt a rush of happiness. 'Oh, but I can help you. I can tell you about his plans; tell you where he will be. He still goes to the Ostaria without his bodyguards, for example. I can tell you when he'll be there.'

'And what about the other people in the Ostaria?' Glaser said. 'Do they not matter? Are innocents to die, too?'

'You are putting my family at risk even discussing this here,' Lotte Glaser said angrily, to Ello. 'Kaspar, you must not breathe a …'

'For heaven's sake, Mama,' Kaspar interrupted her. 'Herr Kunde, Ello. Please let me help. I can run messages. I can find out information.'

Ello smiled at him. 'Thank you, Kaspar,' she said, her eyes wide. She touched her top lip with the tip of her tongue.

'Ello, that's enough!' Lotte Glaser said, really angry now.

'I'm sorry, Lotte,' Ello said, standing. 'As Sepp said, we really should be leaving.'

'Yes,' Kunde said, standing, too. 'Forster and his men will be here soon.' He turned to Glaser. 'They will ask you about your meeting with Schwarzmüller. Max Troll, the one they called Theo, will have told them everything.'

'I know,' Glaser said.

Kunde walked round the table and clapped his fellow Swabian on the shoulder. Glaser smiled at him. Kunde turned to Ello. 'We should continue this discussion,' he said. 'But I dare not go back to the room I was staying in.'

'I have a room at the university,' Ello said. 'Let's talk there.' She turned to her brother. 'And you are going back to Prielmayerstrasse,' she told him. Then she took Kunde by the arm. 'Come on. Get a move on.'

9

After the von Hesserts and Sepp Kunde left, Gerhard, Lotte and Kaspar Glaser sat in silence round the table. So much had happened … Glaser was thankful that for once Kaspar did not chatter. Then Magda arrived back from a BdM tennis tournament. She was wearing her uniform. As she busied about the room, she affectedly and tunelessly sang a BdM song under her breath:

> Youth, we are the future soldiers.
> Youth, we do the future deeds.

'Herr Rinner has narrowly escaped arrest by the Gestapo,' Glaser said. 'Did you by any chance betray his whereabouts to anybody at your Nazi club?'

Magda stopped singing and stood there, feet planted apart, with her tennis racquet in its green cover across her body, as if she was about to defend herself with it.

'Gerhard, is it worth it?' Lotte said wearily. She looked exhausted. 'Frankly, I'd rather not know.'

'Well, excuse me!' Glaser yelled. 'But if my own flesh and blood has betrayed one of the bravest men in Germany, and jeopardised the only chance we may ever have to record what that lunatic Hitler is doing, then I *would* like to know. Is that too much to ask?'

'Go and have a shower, dear,' Lotte murmured to Magda.

'You did tell someone at the BdM, didn't you?' Glaser

said, ominously quietly.

'Yes, I did. So what?' Magda said, staring at him.

'Oh, Magda!' Lotte put her head in her hands. She looked about to cry, but didn't.

Kaspar strode over to his sister and made to hit her, with the flat of his hand, but couldn't. Lotte did not try to stop him.

Glaser's face was blank. 'You are too young, at the moment, to look after yourself, Magda,' he said. 'But as soon as possible, I want you out of my house.'

'Your house?' Lotte said. 'And do I have a say in who lives here and who doesn't?'

They stared at each other.

'You're wrecking this family, you ... you ...' Kaspar shook his head, unable to finish his insult.

Lotte waved an arm at him. 'Kaspar. You're not helping, darling. I know you mean to, but ...'

'Why is she so stupid?' Kaspar yelled at his mother, waving at Magda, red in the face.

'We are really clever people – Papa, you, me. How did this cretin become part of this family? Was she an accident?' Kaspar turned back to his sister, still seeing his mother's horrified face, but unable to stop himself. 'I wish you had never been born.'

Magda screamed and ran into her bedroom. Kaspar burst into tears. 'Midge,' he said softly, using her baby name. He stared after her. 'Midge, I didn't mean it.'

There was silence. Glaser expected Lotte to go after Magda, but she didn't. 'I can't believe she did it,' Glaser muttered.

Lotte gave a deep sigh.

There was a thunderous banging on the door of the flat. They had got into the building without using the bell, to give Glaser as little warning as possible. Kaspar let them in.

*

Six armed, uniformed SS and two plain-clothes Political Police were led by Chief Inspector Forster.

'Not interrupting anything, am I?' Forster said with a sneer, looking from Glaser to his wife and son.

Magda's screaming sobs were clearly audible from her room.

Forster faced Glaser. '*Heil Hitler*, Dr Glaser,' he said, giving a Hitler salute. 'We need to search your flat. I think you know why.'

'*Heil Hitler*,' Glaser muttered, avoiding his gaze.

The SS and Political Police scattered and started searching the place. The search was deliberately destructive. Papers in the bureau were screwed into a ball and thrown on the floor. Lotte's harmonium was tilted on its side and banged. Lotte got up and went into Magda's room without a word. One of the Political Police followed her.

Kaspar moved to an armchair to watch them. He remembered a thriller he had read: when the police are searching a room, they always look at the suspects, who cannot help glancing at the place where the money, or the jewels, or whatever, has been hidden.

Kaspar stared with fixed intensity at Kokoschka's *The Emigrants*, facing him on the wall. Like all Glaser's paintings, it was an expert reproduction, from the Hanfstaengl Art Company. Forster ordered it taken down. There was nothing behind it.

Kaspar repeated his performance with the reproduction on the right-hand wall: Kirchner's portrait of a young girl, *Marzella*. When two SS had taken that down, too, and found nothing, Forster glared at Kaspar, his face contorted with fury. Glaser looked almost as angry, at the provoked manhandling of his paintings. The youth, slopping in his armchair, met Forster's gaze with a practised look of innocence.

Magda screamed piercingly from her room. Kaspar sat up

in his chair, his fists clenched, and got a warning wave to stay put from Forster. Lotte's voice came through from the open door of Magda's room: 'You can leave that alone. It's private.'

An SS-man came into the drawing-room with a battered school exercise book. He handed it to Forster. 'Looks like some sort of diary, sir,' he said.

Forster sat in an armchair and opened it. Lotte and Magda came back into the drawing-room. Magda was streaming tears; her mother had her arm round her. Magda's BdM uniform, Glaser noticed, wasn't impressing the SS.

'It's a young girl's private diary,' Lotte said evenly to Forster. 'When you have satisfied yourself of that, perhaps we can have it back.'

Forster ignored her. He settled to read, with a twisted grin, while the search of the flat continued around him. 'I love him so totally,' Forster read aloud from Magda's diary, to guffaws from the SS, as they continued rummaging and throwing things about. Magda, to their great delight, howled in her mother's arms. Kaspar clenched his fists again, but Glaser motioned him to be still.

'I count the hours until I see him,' Forster's mocking reading continued. 'It's only then that I truly come alive. He is so handsome, but it is more than that. He is kind and funny and a genuinely good person.' Forster waved the exercise book in the air. 'Who is this marvel?' he asked Magda.

'Have you got a daughter, Chief Inspector?' Lotte asked him.

'Yes,' Forster said. 'She's a good National Socialist.'

'Actually, so is Magda.'

'Who is it?' Forster repeated to Magda, who still sobbing. 'What's his name?'

'It's a boy at school,' Lotte said. 'It's a harmless crush, as most teenage girls go through. You are doing your cause no good by humiliating a fifteen-year-old child. Have you nothing better to do with your time?'

Forster widened his twisted grin and looked into Magda's diary again. Kaspar thought and spoke instantaneously. What he said cost him his sister's friendship for ever, and saved his father's life. Magda never believed it was not said in revenge for her betrayal of Herr Rinner, but in fact the quick-thinking youth had realised Lotte's deception would not last much more of Forster reading the diary. He had also correctly calculated the effect of the von Hessert name. He spoke solely to stop Forster tormenting his sister any further.

'My sister is writing about Rüdiger von Hessert,' Kaspar said to Forster. 'You know? Cajetan von Hessert's son? She is very attached to Rüdiger, who is a family friend, as well as a close colleague of my father's.'

Magda's howls redoubled. Forster shot Kaspar a shrewd look. He knew Rüdiger von Hessert was at the Ministry of Justice, but not that he and Glaser had any particular connection. As Kaspar had intended, Forster was more circumspect now he knew about the von Hessert connection: the search was conducted with greater care and Glaser was treated courteously when they took him away for interrogation.

But the main effect of Kaspar's revelation was to connect Glaser to a known suspect, who was already under surveillance – Rüdiger von Hessert. Forster now believed he had underestimated Glaser. Glaser, he thought to himself as they headed for the Wittelsbach Palace in a police car, was far more dangerous than he had once supposed.

The second Chief Inspector Forster and his men were out of the door with her husband, Lotte sprang to the telephone. Her voice was strained but steady. Ignoring the probable bugging of the phone, she telephoned the Ministry of Justice at Prielmayerstrasse, asked for Rudi, and told him what had happened. She told him to tell Ello.

Magda returned from her room, while her mother was still on the telephone.

'How are you?' Kaspar asked his sister.

She ignored him, curling up in one of the chintz armchairs, almost in a foetal position, sucking her thumb. The front of her BdM uniform was damp from spittle and tears. When the call to Rudi was finished, Lotte perched on the wide arm of the armchair. She put her arm round Magda.

'You see the sort of people they are, darling?' Lotte said, stroking Magda's plaited hair.

Magda took her wet softened white thumb from her mouth. 'If the Führer knew what they just did in his name, those people would be in disgrace.'

She shook herself free of her mother's embrace, stalked back to her bedroom and slammed the door.

Then, in the silence, breathing deeply, she reaffirmed her faith by repeating the BdM oath – which she knew by heart:

> You Führer are our commander,
> We stand in your name.
> The Reich is the object of our struggle.
> It is the beginning and the Amen.
> Your word is the heartbeat of our deeds,
> Your faith builds cathedrals for us.
> And even when death reaps the last harvest,
> The crown of the Reich never falls.

10

Glaser sat facing Heydrich, who was behind his desk, beneath the Vietz portrait of himself as a fencer. Forster was perched on one of the plush chairs, sideways-on to Glaser. There were no guards. They were not felt necessary.

'Who was at the meeting you had with the communists at Rottenbucherstrasse?' Heydrich asked.

'I don't know; they used codenames.'

'You didn't recognise anybody?'

'No.'

Forster spoke. 'So, you didn't recognise Sepp Kunde, despite having interviewed him at Dachau?'

'Yes. Kunde but nobody else.'

'Please don't lie, Dr Glaser,' Heydrich said. 'You, of all people, should co-operate with an investigation by the legitimate authorities. You are a man of the law, are you not?'

Glaser nodded. 'Yes,' he said, 'I am.'

'But you made common cause with a felon,' Forster said. 'That's what Kunde is.'

Glaser half turned in his seat, so he was facing the Chief Inspector. 'What do you mean by common cause?'

'Who do you think gave the communists your name?'

'No doubt, Herr Kunde did. But without my permission. Have you asked Herr Kunde if he was responsible?'

'We will,' Heydrich said, 'when we catch up with him.'

Forster winced. Glaser gave the faintest of smiles.

234

Heydrich had just told him Sepp Kunde was still free. This was vital. They would have tortured Kunde; he would have talked; they would know everything. But with Kunde free, Glaser thought he could see a way out.

'What did the communists want?' Heydrich asked.

'Money.'

'And what did you say?'

Glaser was mindful that they already knew what had been said at the meeting, from the spy Troll: 'I told them I had no access to money. I gave them the name of someone who had. Erich Rinner. I said a meeting could be arranged.'

'So you co-operated with them completely?' Forster said.

'No, I deceived them completely. I am a lifelong anti-communist. I was brought to that place against my will, at knifepoint. Having been kidnapped, I simply strung them along, in order to get out of there as quickly as possible. Erich Rinner is in Prague.'

Glaser tensed, but it was quickly obvious, as he had gambled, that the Gestapo had not shared Magda's information with the Political Police, so they had only Troll's word – from him – that Rinner was in Munich.

'Did you report your contact with these traitors to the authorities?' Heydrich asked.

'You know I didn't.'

'Why not?'

'Because they threatened to kill me if I did.'

Forster shot him a look of amused admiration. 'So you were not just about to go to the Asam House, when Kunde warned you?' he said.

'The Asam House?' Glaser's look was one of pure incomprehension. ' I know nothing about the Asam House.'

'When was the last time you saw Kunde?' Forster asked.

'At the meeting at Rottenbucherstrasse.'

Forster looked at Heydrich, shrugging, meaning there was nothing else to ask. He didn't believe a word Glaser had said. Kunde had warned him away from the Asam House meeting; Forster would have staked his children's lives on it. But he had no evidence, and without evidence he was not going to arrest a man he had found out, just in time, was close to the von Hesserts. After the fiasco at the Asam Church, things were going badly enough for him as it was.

'Herr Glaser,' Heydrich said, leaning back in his chair, his squeaky voice rising. 'Are you aware of the deliberations of the Reich Commission for Population Questions?'

Glaser stiffened. 'No.'

'Under the chairmanship of Dr Lange, the commission is preparing a Law for the Prevention of Genetically Diseased Offspring, which will come into force soon. It will be enforced by the new Hereditary Health Courts. I think you may be able to see how this may concern you?'

Forster laughed unpleasantly, and stared with mockingly exaggerated attention at Glaser's artificial leg, stretched out in front of him. Glaser went pale but said nothing.

'As I say,' Heydrich went on, 'nothing has been published yet, but I do know from Dr Lange what the provisions will be. The forced sterilisation of a variety of categories will be enacted. Let me see …'

Heydrich checked that Forster was watching him. Forster gave a sycophantic leer of support. 'The feeble-minded will be forcibly sterilised. Schizophrenics, too. And manic depressives. Those with Huntington's chorea. Those with genetic blindness, deafness or alcoholism. And … I know there's something here that affects you, Glaser. What is it now? Oh yes, the mentally and *physically* handicapped.'

Forster snorted a sardonic laugh.

Heydrich let loose a few goat-like brays, then continued. 'You see, the care of the handicapped already costs the Reich one billion Reichsmarks per year. And they and the inferior races are breeding faster than those of pure blood. A situation which cannot be allowed to go on indefinitely, without damage to the racial stock. Do you not agree?'

Glaser thought of Hitler's family: The word was that his sister Ida was an imbecile. Another sister, Paula, was simple-minded. She had a job licking envelopes all day. His aunt, Johanna Pölzl, was a hunchback, and schizophrenic.

But even as he thought these things, Glaser knew he was being brought down to their level. He was seeing Hitler's family the way Heydrich was seeing him. And that was wrong. Wasn't it?

'Nothing to say, Glaser?' Heydrich said.

Forster gave another burst of sycophantic laughter. Heydrich joined in, braying away. Then he suddenly stopped. He leaned forward over the desk.

'Can you have sex, Glaser?'

'I'm not answering that.'

'Glaser, there is a button on my desk here. I am about to ring for troopers who will lower your trousers and we will answer the question for ourselves.'

'Yes, I can.'

'Thank you. What happened to your leg?'

'I had a riding accident.'

'Do you agree that the state cannot be expected to maintain any children of yours who may be hopping around, at its expense?'

Glaser took a deep breath. 'As I think you know, Herr Heydrich, the children of partial amputees do not inherit any ... deficiency. Otherwise you would have to sterilise a good proportion of the troops returned from the front, including the man Hitler has put in charge of Munich, Gauleiter Wagner, who has had his lower leg amputated, as I have.'

Heydrich looked furious. 'Nevertheless,' he shouted, 'if you have any further contact with enemies of the Reich, at knifepoint or not, I will have you forcibly sterilised under the laws I have quoted.' He paused, then went on more quietly. 'Do you agree that that would be perfectly legal?'

'Once these laws have come into force, yes, it would be.'

'Thank you. Now you may hop off home.'

'I have a question,' Glaser said.

Heydrich and Forster looked amazed. 'Go on,' Heydrich said.

Glaser turned to face Forster. 'My question is to Chief Inspector Forster,' he said. 'Chief Inspector, I have on several occasions sent you memoranda enquiring about the progress of the investigation into the murder of Ascher Weintraub. I have received no reply. Would you please now inform me of the progress of the search for two men seen near the scene of the crime? As I told you, I have reason to believe that the men are Julius Schreck and Georg Winter.'

Heydrich looked at Forster, amazed. 'What?' he said. 'What's he talking about? You didn't tell me that.'

'Get out, Glaser,' Forster yelled, all trace of his smile gone. 'Get out while you still can.'

'Very well,' Glaser said, standing. 'But let me formally give you notice, Chief Inspector, that if you do not interview these two suspects, I shall do so myself.'

Glaser left the room, limping heavily, before either Forster or Heydrich could react.

11

The Saturday after his interrogation by Heydrich and Forster, Glaser parked the Opel and crossed Prielmayer-strasse. His head ached in the fresh air. Last night, alone in his study, he had got drunk for the first time since his student days. He had swigged the best part of a bottle of *Korn*. Then Lotte refused to let him into bed with her. He went back to the study, finished off the bottle, and passed out. He had slept with the artificial leg on all night. His stump was sore.

It was eight o'clock in the morning. The street was deserted, eerily silent and chilly. Glaser was casually dressed in weekend attire. Although he hated deceiving her, he had told Lotte he was taking the motorcar to the mechanic for a bit of tinkering.

He stared up at the Ministry of Justice; the step-gables, the figure of Roland atop the south tower, the garish murals on the facade – as if seeing it for the first time. The place had become strange to him. Never having been here at the weekend before, he had no idea if he could even get in.

As he approached, Glaser wondered if the back entrance, in Elisenstrasse, might not have been a better bet. But even as he thought that, he noticed one of the heavy wooden double-doors of the main entrance was slightly open. He pushed it and crossed the threshold.

Across the vestibule, he could see a notice tacked to the inner door. It was handwritten in crude block capitals:

In order to maintain the undisturbed and orderly trans-action of legal business, and to protect the reputation of German justice, Jewish lawyers are forbidden, until further notice, to enter the Courts.

In the same block capitals, the notice announced itself as being from the *Administration*. Glaser felt sure the caretaker, Herr Vollmer, had put it up, probably on his own initiative.

The Ministry of Justice is built round two inner court-yards, side by side. Glaser turned left along the first of them, making his way along the outer colonnade, to the back entrance to the courts. The back door to Court One was locked, but Glaser peered in at the window. It looked the same as it had always looked. But it wasn't. The Special Courts for political cases had virtually taken over the prosecution of justice.

He entered the building through a side door. As he approached the stairs, the strutting figure of Herr Vollmer came toward him, in brown SA uniform, with swastika armband.

Herr Vollmer was an Old Fighter, given this job as a sinecure reward. He had been one of Hitler's original Hall Guard, smashing communist skulls with chair legs and clay beer mugs, under the command of Emil Maurice. His curriculum vitae also included wrecking the *Münchener Post* offices on the night of the Beer Hall Putsch, as one of the SA troop lead by Karl Fiehler, the man who was now Mayor of Munich.

'Oy! You! Where d'you think you're going?'

Glaser turned. A few months ago, there would have been a cold stare, a demand to be addressed by his title, *Herr Staatsanwalt*, or at least as Dr Glaser. But not now.

'I need a document,' he said. 'I'm working at home. Rush for Monday,' he smiled, a placatory gesture he immediately regretted.

'Oh yes? What's this document, then?'

Vollmer, a squat, damply oleaginous figure, puffed himself up like a frog. Glaser felt a rush of hot blood, but fought it down. Suppose the caretaker actually ejected him? Took him by the collar? Word would spread round the Ministry like wildfire. He would be a laughing-stock.

'I'll show it to you on the way out, Herr Vollmer,' said Glaser jocularly. 'Then you can make sure nothing improper is taking place.'

The caretaker hesitated. He had already asserted his authority. Back in his room, a cosy armchair and the latest edition of the SA magazine, *The Flamethrower*, awaited him. Not to mention a second breakfast of buttered rolls and ham, washed down by the first schnapps of the day.

'Bring the document to my room before you leave the building,' the caretaker commanded. He knew perfectly well Glaser would do no such thing, but honour had been satisfied.

Glaser nodded agreement, his face blank. The caretaker nodded back; one short nod, simultaneously dismissing Glaser and giving him permission to fetch the document. As soon as Glaser had turned away, the caretaker strutted back the way he had come, swinging his arms as he walked, moving his head from side to side, inspecting, as he went, for any possible breaches of order. The Guardian of the Revolution.

The lift was not working. Glaser made his way laboriously up the stone stairs to the second floor. His stump was so sore he would have to bandage it, unless generous applications of cold cream did the trick. Fighting down pangs of self-pity, his mood improved when he found the Clerks' Room open. It was being cleaned.

The cleaning women continued as if he wasn't there. There were multiple copies of the key to the cellar hanging on a board at the back of the room. Glaser took one and made his way all the way down, hoping against hope he didn't have another run-in with Herr Vollmer. Thankfully, however, there was no sign of the caretaker.

In the cellar, the documents were classified by year in gunmetal filing cabinets. He opened one of the drawers for the year 1931. After a short search, he found the Geli Raubal file. He looked through it. He remembered exactly where he had put the report he had written, accusing Gürtner of a cover-up and pretty much accusing Hitler of murdering Geli.

It was not there. Somebody had removed it.

12

Early on the following Monday morning, Glaser requested files on Georg Winter and Julius Schreck. Most of the Old Fighters had criminal records, but many files had mysteriously disappeared since the Nazis seized power, along with Hitler's, with its details of his conviction for assault and his two-month jail sentence.

Georg Winter's file, he was told by a clerk, was among the missing. This was a pity because Glaser would have started with Winter, as the softer and more malleable of the two. But to do that he needed his address. Even Glaser was not prepared to turn up at Hitler's apartment, braving a detachment of armed SD, to interview Herr Winter at work.

Schreck's file, however, which Glaser had last seen in 1931, after Geli was murdered, was still available. It was dropped on his desk, as if it were electrified, by a young clerk, who then dived for the door. In the last two years nothing had been added to the pages of the chauffeur's many convictions. All this, however, was of less interest to Glaser than where he lived.

To his surprise, the file informed him that Schreck lived in one of the concrete-fronted, monolithic blocks of flats out at Milbertshofen. Thrown up quickly for the BMW car workers, each of these monstrosities contained over seven hundred identical flats.

As he drove up to the block listed as containing Schreck's flat, Glaser doubted the chauffeur would still be living there. He surely did not need to live in a place like this. But he did. At least, his name was among the hundreds hand-written next to the push-button bells in the vestibule.

Glaser stared at his name for a long time. Then he went back to the Opel Frosch and sat at the wheel. Schreck would deny any involvement with Herr Weintraub. To mention Sepp Kunde's statement would be to sign his death warrant – a known communist was in no position to make accusations.

And what about his own safety? Schreck was a dangerous man. He would not be Schreck's first murder victim. Or he could call the SS or the SD – have Glaser tortured in the cellars of the Wittelsbach Palace, or the Brown House. Or he could have him sent to Dachau. He could be pulling a heavy roller by nightfall.

It was dusk. A pale moon rose over the looming chevrons of blocks of flats. Glaser slowly accepted that the writ of the law no longer ran. But to turn the car and drive home was to collude in this surrender to brute force. He just could not do it. So he sat there, in the driving seat, as dusk turned to dark. He felt endlessly desolate, worse than worthless. First Geli Raubal, then Ascher Weintraub – he had failed them both.

Glaser did not hear the quiet purr of the Horch, as it parked behind his car. He was unaware of the footsteps coming toward him, on the pavement. He did not even react when the door of his Opel was opened. He just stared straight ahead, through the windscreen, into the darkness.

'Hello, old man. Doing a bit of sightseeing, are we? Munich by night, and all that. I say, Gerhard, are you all right?'

Glaser sighed, not turning his head to look at Rudi.

'Lotte's just a little bit worried.' Rudi laid a hand gently on Glaser's shoulder, as if waking Rip van Winkel. 'Well, actually, she's frantic. She's got it into her head that you might have been arrested. But don't worry, Ello's with her.'

Glaser nodded. Rudi kept talking. 'So, anyway, Ello sent me to the Palace of Fun – Prielmayerstrasse – to see if I could pick up any clues as to where you were. And, what-do-you-know, open on your desk, was the lovely Julius's file. Complete with his address. "Pretty good clue, there, Rudi," I thought to myself. Gumshoe manqué that I am. And so I drove here.'

Glaser was still, immobile. But finally a smile broke from him. Rudi had always been able to make him laugh.

'That's better,' Rudi said. 'Gerhard, look, I think it might be best to pass on the lovely Julius. I mean, Schreck's a terrific conversationalist. Known for it. And I hear he plays a mean game of backgammon. What better companion for a lonely evening? In a way. But all the same … um … I mean …'

It was working. Glaser shifted in his seat, as if waking up. 'All right, Rudi. Shut up, there's a good boy. Drive back to my place. I'll see you there.'

Rudi blew out his cheeks in a sigh of relief. 'Good. Yes. See you back at Galeriestrasse then, Gerhard.'

Part VII
Summer 1933

1

Ello and Hitler sat facing each other in the Prinzregenten-platz apartment.

'The first building of the new Reich,' Hitler was saying, 'will be a temple – a temple to art.'

'An art gallery?'

'Yes, an art gallery. It has always been my dream to build one. I will not live to see all the buildings I shall plan for the new Reich. But I shall live to see the first one.'

'Why, won't you live …?'

'Ah, *Ellochen*, I do not expect to reach old age. Great men rarely do. The buildings will be my monuments.'

Ello nodded. 'Tell me about the art gallery,' she said.

'Yes, yes. It will be called the House of German Art. It will be near this place, which will always be my home.' He waved a hand round the apartment.

'When will it be ready?'

'In October. There will be a Great Exhibition of German Art to mark the opening.'

'October? So soon?' October was five months away.

'Yes, yes. Troost and I have already done the plans.'

'May I see them?'

'Wait there, *Ellochen*,' he said playfully.

Ello's forced smile faded as soon as he left her alone. That evening they were going to the birthday reception for her mother, at the von Hessert villa. Before that, she was to spend the day with him. So far, she had evaded his attempts to draw her again, though the strain of doing so made her tense and tired. She felt sick the whole time, these days.

Just after she had arrived, on the pretext of going to the bathroom, she had got away from him from a few minutes, and looked round his bedroom. It was as sparse and spare as the German people had been told: A military-style campbed, a chest of drawers, a bureau, a Regina typewriter. And a pistol on the shelf above his bed.

It must have been the pistol he had used to kill Geli. He *had* killed Geli – she was more and more sure of that. She stared at the pistol, breathing hard, wondering. But she had never fired a gun in her life. Suppose she just wounded him? And even if she killed him, his guards would be there in seconds. Was she ready to die, almost certainly under torture?

As she stood there, the sleek figure of Herr Winter came in, behind her. She had not heard him coming; he was suddenly there. His habitual servant's pleasant half-smile was gone. He was cold and sinister. She wondered why she had not realised that before.

'Oh, Herr Winter! You made me jump. I was just … The Führer has a kind of aura, don't you think? It's strong in places where he is often there.' She chattered on for a while longer with this rubbish. It was enough. Just. Herr Winter turned and wordlessly left the room, limping slightly. It would not be a good idea to be caught in Hitler's bedroom again, though.

However, the news of this new building was transforming her mood, offering, she thought, real hope. It was the obvious place for Sepp to plant a bomb. She could leave killing him to Sepp. It was the first time in her life she could leave anything to a man – the first time she could lean on a man. Just for once, she was not the strong one. She thought of Sepp's skilled and practised love-making, then put it out of her mind.

*

Hitler came back with some sketches and an architectural drawing. He laid them all out on the massive dining-room table, weighted down with encyclopedias and books. Then he bent over them, staring down at them concentratedly, one hand cupped under his chin. Ello looked down at the plan, trying to memorise it.

'The building will be 160 metres long and 60 metres wide,' Hitler intoned. 'With entrances from all four sides. The main entrance, at the top of Prinzregentenstrasse, is behind an eleven-metre-high colonnade. At the north side, a four-metre drop with stairs to the Englischer Garten. There, there will be restaurants, a café and a small beer tavern. The centrepiece is the Hall of Honour, twenty-four by thirty-six metres, lit by natural light through the glass roof. Eleven exhibition halls, placed symmetrically off this main hall, will celebrate Aryan creative genius. Some halls are rectangular, ten metres by sixteen. Some are square, ten by ten.'

'With pillars?' said Ello faintly.

Sepp had told her a bomb could be built into a pillar. He had explained to her the rudiments of bomb-making, so she would know which questions to ask.

'Yes, yes. Eleven metres high. Yellow. Jura marble.'

'What's that?' she said, pointing to a shaded section along the bottom of the plan.

'The air-raid shelter,' he said. 'And I have planned the motto to stand in stone over the threshold: *Art is an Ennobling Mission Demanding Fanaticism.*'

'Demanding fanaticism?'

'Yes, yes. Art is far more important than politics or economics.'

'I see,' she said.

She felt a wave of disgust at him. But at least she had no need to hide her feelings. He noticed nothing. She needed a break from his suffocating presence; from his insane, banal opinions; from the stink of his breath, and from his flatulence.

'I won't be a moment,' she murmured, heading, again, for the bathroom next to Geli's room. On impulse she tried Geli's door. It was unlocked. The tall, angular figure of Anni Winter was inside, in a floral dress. Ello jumped. 'Oh, I …' She stopped just inside the door.

The housekeeper was placing the vase of red chrysanthemums, put there fresh every day, in memory of Geli. 'That's all right, *gnädiges Fräulein*,' Anni smiled. 'You can go where you want. If I may say so, madam, we all hope to see you as mistress of this house one day soon.'

The shift to addressing her as 'madam' signalled that Anni was openly treating Ello as her employer. Ello knew Anni was her champion, so to speak. She was giving Hitler's other girlfriend, Eva Braun, Hoffmann's photographic assistant, an even harder time than she had given poor Geli.

Ello was about to leave when she noticed a grave urn on the dresser. She felt sick.

'What's …? Is that …?'

Anni looked worried for a second, then her brow cleared. 'Nobody is to know, really. But, well, seeing as it's you, madam. Best not tell Herr Hitler you know, though.'

'It's Geli?'

'Yes, madam.'

'How?'

'The day after Fräulein Raubal's funeral, Herr Hitler, Schreck and my husband visited the cemetery, in Vienna. That night, Herr Hitler instructed Schreck and my husband to exhume the deceased. The empty grave was closed again. Schreck arranged the cremation. They brought the ashes back with them.' Anni Winter crossed herself. 'It was kept secret.' Her voice dropped to a conspiratorial whisper. 'Nobody knows. Except us.'

'What's it doing there?'

Anni hesitated, then smiled at Ello. 'Well, madam, Herr Hitler has ordered it opened. He did some drawings of Fräulein Raubal. They are to be placed in with her mortal remains.' Anni crossed herself again.

'I see,' Ello said.

2

Ello said she had to prepare herself for the reception this evening. She knew this would get her away from her Uncle Dolf more effectively than a need to study. But after Schreck had driven her from Hitler's apartment to the university, she thankfully crammed in some reading, before heading to the Glaser flat by taxi.

As usual, she arrived unannounced. Magda was away, at a BdM gymnastics display, so Ello could speak freely: 'I need to borrow your camera, Kaspar, if you don't mind?'

'Of course.'

'And could you get the film developed for me? Nobody else must see it.'

'Yes!' the youth said, shouting in his enthusiasm. 'There's a darkroom at school. I have a key. I can go in whenever I like. Nobody else would see the film.'

'I think you'd better tell us what's going on,' Glaser said.

Lotte looked up from her sewing, measuring Ello with an appraising gaze. She had been noticeably cooler with the younger woman lately.

Ello explained the opportunity presented by the House of German Art. 'I've seen the plans,' she said. 'But I need to photograph them. I don't think I can describe them well enough to Sepp.'

Glaser puffed at his pipe. 'Kunde plants a bomb,' he said. 'Let's say you kill Hitler. You also kill others. You injure more. You destroy paintings. Are we so sure of our cause?'

'Yes,' Kaspar said.

Ello shrugged. 'Most of the people round him will be Nazis.'

'Most?'

'Suppose your father attends the opening?' Lotte said, without raising her head from her sewing.

Ello looked hurt. She shrugged her slender shoulders. 'Lotte …'

'Look ! We have to do this,' Kaspar said.

There were tears in Ello's eyes. She made to leave. 'I'm sorry,' she said. 'There must be a camera at home some-where. It's just … I thought you were with us, Gerhard.'

'I am,' Glaser said. 'Sad to say. Sit down, Ello. You don't have to leave. You may use Kaspar's camera. You and Kunde can meet here, if you wish. You can't keep smuggling him into the university, he'll be seen and reported.'

'Thank you.'

'But that is where I draw the line. I shan't watch your murder, or play any active part. I am still a lawyer. I still believe in the law.'

Lotte shook her head angrily. She said nothing.

'I understand,' Ello said softly. 'In view of that, I don't suppose you'll want to come to the reception this evening, for my mother's birthday. I could give the camera back to you there. It would give you a chance to see Hitler in the flesh. I'll introduce you, if you like.'

Lotte looked up, her eyes flashing. 'Is it too much trouble for you to bring the camera back here?' she said.

Ello ignored her, waiting for Glaser.

Glaser pretended to think about it, but he had already decided. His curiosity was aroused by the chance to observe Hitler. 'I'll need my dinner suit, then,' he said. 'Won't I? Are you coming, Lotte?'

'I've got work to do.' Lotte stared at Ello. 'You are very clever,' she said, matter-of-factly. It didn't sound like a compliment.

255

'I'll fetch the Leica,' Kaspar said. 'I'll show you how to use it.'

Ello asked if she could use the Glaser telephone. She telephoned her mother. The Glasers heard her say she would be late for the reception this evening. The furious reaction was audible from the other side of the room. Ello rang off hastily.

She sat quietly in an armchair until she knew Hitler would have left for the reception, then telephoned the Prinzregentenplatz apartment. When she was put through, she asked for Anni Winter. She told Anni she had left something personal in the apartment, and needed to get it herself. She brushed aside Anni's offer to fetch it, whatever it was, and have it sent on. She told the housekeeper she would be there shortly, then replaced the receiver in its cradle, before Anni could argue any more.

Ello's next move was a taxi back to her room at the university. There, she put her evening dress in a small valise, along with Kaspar's camera. She had kept the taxi, and went on to Hitler's apartment. Georg Winter opened the door to her, as sleek as ever. Was the greeting slightly cooler than it used to be? Or was she imagining that?

The most difficult part was coming now. The tall figure of Anni appeared – welcoming, concerned, shrewd. Her gaze was bright in her sallow face, never leaving Ello's eyes.

'Anni, you're going to think I'm mad,' Ello said.

The housekeeper smiled. 'I doubt that, madam.'

'Anni, the thing is … Herr Hitler has asked me a certain question. And I think he expects an answer this evening.'

Anni beamed. But then looked puzzled, her head on one side.

'I'm going to the reception soon,' Ello went on. 'In fact I'd better change here. I've brought my clothes,' she indicated the valise. 'Anni, I want to change in Geli's room.

Sometimes, when I have a big decision, I can hear Geli's voice, telling me what to do. I want to be close to her now.'

To Ello's relief, Anni nodded hard. 'I know exactly what you mean, madam. My former mistress, Countess Törring, often used to ask for advice from the other side.'

'Did she now?'

Anni paused. 'So ... you didn't really leave anything here, then, madam?'

'No, Anni. I didn't want to say ... what I just said ... on the telephone. Oh, Anni, do you think I'm a little fool?'

The housekeeper beamed. 'Not at all, madam. I'll leave you to it. Unless you need any help dressing?'

'No, Anni. Thank you. I'll be fine.'

As soon as Anni was out of sight, Ello went into Hitler's bedroom. The various plans and sketches for the House of German Art were still half rolled-up on the bed, where he had tossed them, after he had shown them to her.

She chose the architect's elevation, which showed the placing of the pillars. Sepp had told her that to be sure of killing Hitler, they had to bring the roof down on top of him. So it was important to be sure where the load-bearing pillars were. In a neoclassical design like this, some of the pillars could be purely decorative.

Carrying the rolled architect's elevation and her valise, she went into Geli's room and locked the door. At least the grave urn with Geli's remains was not around – in the wardrobe, probably. She shuddered. She unrolled the elevation on Geli's bureau. It was too long. She tried weighing it down on the bed, but it kept curling up. She whimpered in frustration. Then she laid the elevation on the floor, weighted down at the corners with Geli's books and records.

She took the Leica out of her valise and took photographs, as Kaspar had shown her. She realised the Hall of Honour was all that was needed, but she took some of the frontage, too. When she had finished, she put the elevation back in Hitler's room. Then she showered, dabbed on some of Geli's perfume, did her hair and put on her white evening gown. On the way out, she told Anni that Geli wanted her to wait. But the answer would be 'Yes' in the end.

Anni beamed. 'Madam, the Führer has a saying: There are two ways of judging a man: by the woman he marries, and by the way he dies.'

3

The von Hessert drawing room, designed by Paul Troost, was pleasantly proportioned, with sea-blue walls and panelling picked out in gold leaf. The vaulted ceiling was painted with tumbling sea nymphs, tritons and an emerging Venus.

Along one wall was an extensive buffet, where Cajetan von Hessert had placed himself, with a plate of foie gras he had no intention of eating. Later on, he intended to slip away down to the kitchen, cut himself a chunk of Bavarian *Leberkäs* and some black bread, pour himself a beer, and get some peace.

The hostess, Carola von Hessert, by birth a Romanian princess, was at the other end of the crowded room. She was glowing with happiness. Herr Hitler had sent her a telegram, on the morning of her birthday. He had arrived carrying the whip she had given him as a present, not the one Frau Bechstein had given him. A birthday gift from him was to be presented to her, at some point during the reception. It would be the high-point of her life.

The only blot on this otherwise blissful day was Eva Braun, who she always referred to as 'that Hoffmann fellow's assistant'. Carola regarded the photographer as a tradesman. She regarded Eva Braun's aspirations to rival her daughter in Hitler's affections as the grossest impertinence. Eva's attempted suicide with a pistol, in imitation of Geli Raubal, had left Carola gibbering with rage – especially as the transparent tactic appeared to be working. Hitler felt sorry for Eva; he had visited her.

It was important to Carola that her daughter make up any lost ground this evening. Arriving at the reception late was hardly the way to do that. For that reason, Carola's carefully cultivated Latin passion had ignited with rage at her daughter, on the telephone, earlier. Her dark eyes kept flickering at the door, impatient for Ello's arrival, even as she chatted with Herr Hitler.

Glaser, feeling clumsy in black-tie, watched Hitler curiously, through the crowd of guests. He edged closer, to hear what he was saying to Carola von Hessert:

'I hope one day the furniture in my apartment will become the uniform standard for all furniture: What's the point of having a hundred different models for washbasins? Why these different dimensions for windows and doors? For my car, I can find spare parts everywhere, but not for my apartment.'

Glaser thought him an ordinary little man. He thought of what the political satirist Kurt Tucholsky had once said of him: 'The man doesn't exist, he is only the noise he makes.'

He had studied Hitler's social performance. Early in the evening, Carola von Hessert had got him to eat a bowl of caviar. Apart from that, he had eaten nothing, and drunk nothing. He had been circulating the whole time, his mouth a rictus of cordiality.

To Glaser's surprise, he was still deferential to industrialists, military men and foreigners, even now, when he was Chancellor. He was elaborately gallant with women, kissing their hand, in the Austrian manner: 'May I have the pleasure of bidding you good evening, *gnädige Frau*?' That sort of thing.

Particularly in motion, Glaser thought, there was something faintly ridiculous about him – not least because the brown batwing trousers of his latest uniform were too baggy.

A couple of young diplomats from the Italian embassy were laughing behind their hands at him. Glaser caught himself feeling indignant at that.

Across the room, he saw Rudi, deep in conversation with a fair-haired, thick-lipped man in SS uniform. Glaser caught his eye and smiled. Rudi – who had definitely seen him – snubbed him completely. He turned his back.

A remark surfaced in Glaser's mind: It was something Ello had said to him after he had been interrogated at the Wittelsbach Palace. It was along the lines of 'if only I had known', or something like that. But Lotte said she had telephoned Rudi at Prielmayerstrasse. She had told him her husband had been taken, and told him to tell Ello. Rudi had not only never mentioned telephoning Ello, he hadn't said a word about the interrogation and Glaser's release.

Glaser thought of the joke Rudi had made, not long after he started at the Ministry – about wanting to be called Hagen, the one who betrays and kills Siegfried. Was Rudi betraying them now? He was still with his thick-lipped SS friend, deep in conversation.

But even as the suspicion formed, Glaser rejected it. It would be remarkable if Rudi did not have friends in the SS and other Nazi organisations. And as to him telephoning Ello, Ello's room at the university did not have a telephone. There may or may not be one in the corridor, Glaser couldn't remember. Suppose Rudi had simply been unable to get hold of Ello on the telephone? The explanation could be as prosaic as that.

Glaser's debate with himself was broken by the late arrival of Ello, floating in with her white dress swathed over her slender top. Glaser thought she looked like a film star. He beamed at her. She spotted him immediately and headed straight for him, breaking into a sparkling smile.

'Gerhard! All alone in the crowd?'

'I'm fine, Ello. Thank you.' He raised his flute of champagne to her. 'I'm relieved to see you.'

Ello laughed. 'I'm rather relieved, myself! I'll tell you about it later. Let me take you off somewhere private, so I can give Kaspar's camera back to you.'

'Ello ...' Glaser hesitated. 'Does Rudi know you've taken these photographs?' He spoke softly, trying to make sure nobody in the crowd overheard.

Ello shook her head. 'No, he doesn't. Best not to mention it to him.'

Was Ello just trying to protect her younger brother, as ever? Or didn't she fully trust him, either? He was about to ask her if she knew the SS-Officer Rudi was with. Or even to bluntly ask whose side Rudi was on these days. But at that moment Carola von Hessert called for quiet and asked Hitler to say a few words.

The Führer shyly refused: 'I must have a crowd when I speak. In a small circle, I never know what to say.'

But he summoned Hess, who passed him a small water-colour painting. Hitler presented it to his ecstatic hostess. As he handed it over, he muttered the title: '*Haubourdin, The Seminar Church*. I painted it during the war.'

Glaser had a good view of it. Although emotionally empty, it was technically accomplished, just as poor dead Ascher Weintraub had said about Hitler's watercolours.

Certainly, Carola von Hessert was delighted with her watercolour, whatever its objective merits. Clutching it to her bosom with one hand, she waved at her daughter to come and join them with the other. She flamboyantly motioned her to stand at Hitler's side. But Ello ignored her.

'Come on, Gerhard,' she said, taking his arm. 'Let's go to the telephone room. It's private there. I'll give you the camera. The sooner Kaspar gets these photographs developed, the better.'

As Ello bustled ahead of him along a corridor off the

main drawingroom, her bottom wiggled busily in the tight white dress. Glaser, making his way laboriously along behind her, felt a wave of irritation. Ello was spoilt, he thought, and more than a little bossy.

Lotte had not mentioned her to him, either positively or negatively, but her antipathy for the young woman these days was plain enough. Glaser was beginning to wonder if she had a point.

Ello led him to a small, oddly shaped room smelling of sandalwood furniture polish. Cups, shields and other athletic trophies were dotted on occasional tables, covered by fringed silk tablecloths. A stag's head with resplendent antlers stared down at them, glassy-eyed, from one wall.

'The telephone room,' she announced grandly, waving Glaser to be seated. There was indeed an old-fashioned telephone, screwed to the longest wall. 'Would you wait here a while, Gerhard, while I go and fetch the camera? It's in my room.'

Glaser settled into a capacious armchair, with a floral-patterned covering draped over it. He shut his eyes, cherishing the silence. It was broken, soon enough, by Ello's bustling return.

'Here we are, Gerhard,' she said, handing over Kaspar's Leica wrapped in a brown paper bag. 'If Kaspar can get the film developed quickly, that would be wonderful.'

'I'll see what I can do,' Glaser said, dryly.

'Excellent! Give him a big hug and a kiss from me, won't you?' Ello turned to the door. 'I must rush now. Fences to repair with Mama. And I suppose I'd better keep Hitler sweet, at least for now.'

She swept out in a cloud of white, like a Greek hetaera going off to entertain the company. She was, Glaser reflected sourly, loving every minute of this. Well, he damn well wasn't. But then he reproached himself for his grumpiness, and consciously summoned the memory of that first evening in

Ello's room, when he had so taken to the von Hesserts.

He started to get up to leave, but heard a commotion outside the door and recognised Rudi's voice. The fringes at the bottom of the armchair's covering hid a gap between its wooden frame and the floor. Glaser slid the paper bag containing the Leica along the floor, through the fringes, and under the armchair before Rudi saw it.

'Thought he'd be in here, when saw Ello leading … away,' Rudi's speech was badly slurred. He was rolling, paralytically drunk.

The fair-haired, fleshy-lipped SS-man followed him into the telephone room. Rudi slumped into the other armchair the small room boasted, ignoring Glaser, as he had all evening. He shut his eyes, chin on chest.

This left the SS-Officer to introduce himself. 'My name is Elsperger, Dr Glaser. Captain Anton Elsperger. *Heil Hitler.*'

'*Heil Hitler.*'

Elsperger drew up the room's remaining chair, mahogany with a red cushion on it, used for sitting on while talking on the telephone. 'Rudi has told me about you. I've been wanting to meet you.'

'You appear to have achieved that.'

'So I have. You're an individualist, aren't you, Glaser?'

'Am I?'

'I think so. It's out of date, you know. The individual is merely a cell in a biological organism – the Racial Community. He has significance only for his function within the organism, and can be replaced by another cell with the same function. All that matters is the survival of the race.'

'I will never, ever believe that.'

Elsperger stared at him, his watery blue eyes steady. 'Then your future in the Third Reich will be a short one. A new type of person will be created, Glaser, to replace the likes of you.'

Glaser's head cleared. He felt suddenly more alert. 'What

do you mean, "a new type of person"? Are you saying the Nazis intend to redesign people? Like Hitler redesigns buildings? Like converting the Barlow Palace to the Brown House?'

'Exactly. People more adapted to what the Racial Community requires of them.'

Glaser suddenly understood: The Nazi programme was nothing less than the forced excision of the human soul. 'You won't get away with it,' he said.

Elsperger spread his fleshy lips. 'Yes, we will. Glaser, we have been indulgent with you so far, not least because you know Rudi here. But this is your final warning. Take it. Or you're finished.' SS-Captain Elsperger stood. 'Come on, Rüdiger. Let's get you tucked up in bed.'

Rudi didn't move. His eyes were shut. There were small blue – white bubbles at the corners of his mouth. Elsperger made an impatient noise. Then he stalked out of the room.

As soon as he had gone, Rudi opened one eye, then the other. 'Have a little faith, old man,' he said. 'Have a little trust, why don't you? Oh, my bloody head!'

Glaser kicked the Leica further under the armchair with his right heel. 'Why don't you go back to the party, Rudi,' he said. 'I'll see you there.'

But he didn't. Once Rudi had staggered off to find his friend, Glaser retrieved the camera. He used the telephone room's telephone to call a taxi to take him home.

4

SS-Captain Anton Elsperger was reporting to Heydrich and Forster, in Heydrich's office.

'With von Hessert's help,' Elsperger was saying. 'I have now made contact with Glaser and spoken to him. I have no doubt that he is an enemy of the Third Reich, involved in treasonable activity. This may be the dissemination of subversive material, printed abroad.'

'Does von Hessert suspect you?' Heydrich asked.

'No, *Herr Oberführer.*' Elsperger said. 'He values our ... contacts.'

Forster leered. Elsperger licked his thick lips and ignored him.

'Your views on how we should proceed: You first, Chief Inspector.'

'Pull Glaser in,' Forster said. 'Take him to the cells downstairs. Beat out of him what he knows. I'll do it myself, if you like. Pompous, smug bastard.'

'Glaser was at Frau von Hessert's birthday celebration,' Heydrich said. 'Along with the Führer. We must proceed with caution where the von Hesserts are concerned. Your view, Elsperger?'

'I have two recommendations, *Herr Oberführer*: The first is to have Glaser followed at all times. Put men outside his residence. Plain clothes, but make the surveillance obvious.'

'Why?' asked Forster.

'In my view,' Elsperger said, 'both Glaser and von Hessert are close to cracking. The more pressure we put them under, the better.'

Heydrich nodded. 'Good,' he said. 'That's what we'll do, then.'

He started to rise, signalling the meeting was over. Forster sneered. 'You said you had two recommendations,' he said to Elsperger. 'What's the second one?'

Heydrich sat again.

'My second recommendation,' Elsperger said, 'is that we find out where Fräulein von Hessert is getting Rüdiger's morphine from. We then arrest the source. It's obviously coming from the university chemistry laboratories, so this should not be difficult. Rüdiger has started to accept his morphine from me. I wish to be his only source of supply. Then, gentlemen, I am confident of telling you anything you wish to know about these traitors.'

Just as the meeting finished, in Heydrich's office, Sepp Kunde and Ello joined Glaser and Kaspar round the table at the Glaser flat. Lotte and Magda were away at Lotte's sister, Katya Bachhuber's, house. They were spending more and more of the summer there, including frequent overnight stays.

Kaspar fetched the photographs of the plans for the House of German Art. He had enlarged them. They had come out gratifyingly well.

'And Hitler reckons this will ready by October?' Kunde asked Ello, looking at the photographs.

'Yes,' she said. 'He keeps telling Troost how quickly Speer built the Propaganda Ministry in Berlin. He's really saying, if Troost can't finish it, he'll bring Speer in. He told me the renderings, ground plans, cross-sections and a first model are ready now.'

Kunde whistled, reluctantly impressed.

Ello looked at him. 'Sepp, are you sure you don't want me to try and get hold of the model?'

Kunde and Ello had obviously been discussing all this before they arrived.

'No,' Kunde said. 'I've got all I need. I know where to put the dynamite. You did well.'

They looked at each other. They hardly took their eyes off each other.

'So what's your next move?' Glaser asked Kunde gruffly, puffing at his pipe.

'Get a job in a quarry. Back in Swabia. The one near Königsbronn. Know it?'

Glaser nodded. 'Heard of it, at any rate.'

'I can steal all the dynamite I need. I'll stay there over the summer and on until the art gallery is ready.'

Glaser nodded, puffing smoke.

'Gerhard,' Ello said, 'Sepp feels it will be dangerous to try and bring the dynamite back by train.'

'They'll be watching for anybody with a suitcase of any sort,' Kunde said. 'Checking for leaflets.' His tone made it clear how lowly he regarded leaflets, as a form of protest.

'So, when we're ready,' Ello continued. 'Rudi will drive up to Königsbronn, pick up the dynamite, and take it back in the Horch.' She smiled. 'My daddy's favourite car.'

Glaser puffed a plume of smoke. 'Is it wise to involve Rudi?'

'Why not?' Ello said.

'This friendship with the SS-Officer. The one at your mother's reception. Elsperger.'

'Anton? We've both known him for years. He's a pussy-cat.' She smiled. 'You worry too much, Gerhard. Rudi strings all his Nazi friends along. It could be useful. He picks up a lot of information. '

Glaser shrugged. 'Sounds as if you've got it all worked out,' he said.

'Good luck, with everything, Herr Kunde,' Kaspar shouted.

Kunde ignored him, as usual. 'There is just one problem,' he said.

'And that is?' said Glaser.

'I need a new identity card, in another name. But the people I know who can do that are all in Dachau.'

'Leave it to me,' Glaser said.

'I was hoping you'd say that.'

'Gerhard, are you sure?' Ello said, remembering Glaser's reservations from their previous conversation. 'Lotte doesn't seem to want you involved. What will she ...?'

Glaser took his pipe from his mouth to interrupt, unwilling to have his wife discussed behind her back. 'I shall speak to Edgar Hanfstaengl.'

'Hanfstaengl! Are you mad?' Kunde was thinking of Ernst Hanfstaengl, known as Putzi, Hitler's Foreign Press Chief.

Glaser laughed. 'Edgar's Putzi's older brother,' he said. 'He's a good friend. He runs the family art reproduction business, where I get all my paintings. Edgar knows a lot of artists who could do this sort of thing. He would help us, I'm sure of it.'

'You'll need a photograph, for the identity card, Herr Kunde,' Kaspar said. 'Perhaps I can help there.'

Kunde finally acknowledged Kaspar's existence. 'Yes,' he said.

Kaspar took two photographs of Kunde, head and shoulders, suitable for an identity card. He grinned all the way through it, remembering his father calling photography the lying art. The grin antagonised Kunde all over again.

Half an hour after Kunde and Ello left, Kaspar looked out the window and noticed a watcher opposite the Glaser block of flats, sitting on the low wall round the Hof Garten.

Kaspar gave him, and all the subsequent watchers nicknames. This first one, a nondescript middle-aged man he called Joppe after the brown jerkin-style jacket he was wearing.

'Let me go to Herr Hanfstaengl for you, Papa,' Kaspar said, looking out the window at Joppe. 'I'll go on my bicycle. They won't follow a schoolboy. When the identity card is ready, I'll give it to Ello at the university. She can pass it on to Herr Kunde.'

Glaser nodded. 'Yes,' he said. 'Thank you, son.'

It was the first time he had ever called Kaspar that.

It was the summer holidays, but Kaspar had managed to sneak back into his school, to get the photographs of Kunde developed in the darkroom. The photographs were now in a leather pouch, which he tied to the handlebars of his bicycle, in the vestibule of the block of the flats.

Outside, he glanced back at the watchers as he stood on the pedals, pulling away from the building. As he had forecast to his father, he was not followed. He cycled to the Hanfstaengl Art Company, in Widenmayerstrasse.

The tall, stooped figure of Edgar Hanfstaengl, formal in frock coat and pince-nez, received Glaser's son cordially. He readily agreed to provide a forged identity card, using a photograph of Kunde. The artist he had in mind for the job, Max Rauh, had just been dismissed from the Munich Academy. His paintings had been declared Racially Deviant; some had been destroyed. Hanfstaengl asked for fifty Reichsmarks payment for Rauh, taking nothing for himself.

Kaspar asked his father if he would get the money from the wealthy von Hesserts, possibly Rudi. Glaser told him he would pay it himself, preferring to keep Rudi out of it. He had not seen the probationer for a while. They both went into the Ministry as infrequently as possible.

Rudi's visits to the Glaser flat had stopped. Glaser would

not have had it any other way, now the flat was being watched. In fact, no visitors braved the ostentatious observation, word of which had quickly spread. The Glasers also stopped visiting anybody else, to avoid putting them at risk. Their social life was at an end.

When the forged document was ready, five days later, Kaspar cycled to the former artist's atelier, not far from the university. As soon as the youth came in the door, Herr Rauh handed over the card and took the fifty Reichsmarks, saying nothing.

Kaspar looked at the forgery. The identity card was in the name of Kurt Engel. The name was written in heavy Gothic script, and a signature had been forged. Obviously, it was a signature Kunde would be unable to replicate. One of the photographs Kaspar had taken of Kunde stared up at him. It now had a purple eagle and swastika half over the face, and half on the grey card.

Kaspar whistled. 'That's very good.'

Max Rauh glanced over his shoulder, as if afraid of some hidden eavesdropper in the atelier. 'Tell your friend not to take it out in the rain. Also, I haven't got the correct tool to close the eyelets. You see, there, at the corners of the photograph? I had to use pliers. I hope it holds.'

Kaspar nodded. 'How are you, sir?' he blurted out. He laughed at his own clumsy gaucheness.

'I'm not allowed to paint,' Rauh said, like a child who had been forbidden a treat. His voice sounded cracked, as if he hadn't spoken to anyone in a long time. 'I'm forbidden to buy paint. The Gestapo come and search the atelier. They make sure there's no paint here. Do you want something to drink? Or eat?'

'No, thanks.'

'Just as well. I haven't got much. You'd better go now.'

Kaspar wondered whether to give him more money. He

decided to. He searched through his pockets and handed over every pfennig he had on him. Rauh took it without a word.

The youth cycled to the university with the forged identity card, and waited in Ello's room until her lecture was finished. Ello greeted him warmly, giving him a long hug and a peck on the cheek. She told him she would meet Sepp in the Englischer Garten, to hand the document over. As he left the university, cycling home, Kaspar was followed. A black Opel with two men in it, in trilby hats and leather coats, kept just behind his bicycle all the way to Galeries trasse.

Back at the flat, when Kaspar looked out of the window, the Opel had disappeared, but the regular watchers, Joppe and another, younger, man were still there.

'Do you think the ones who followed me are watching Ello?' Kaspar asked his father.

His usually beaming, ruddy face was drawn.

Glaser shrugged. 'I hope not. But to try to warn her would only make matters worse.'

Father and son were silent, both thinking of what would happen if Ello were picked up with the forged card on her. Even the von Hessert name would not be enough to save her. At that moment Magda and Lotte came in. They had been sunbathing in the Hof Garten.

'What's going on?' Lotte said, looking at the tense faces of her husband and her son.

But she realised, even as she spoke, that she could not be told what was going on, because Magda was there. Glaser and Kaspar looked at each other. Neither replied.

'Oh, that's the last straw,' Lotte murmured.

Forster, on his own initiative, had had the surveillance extended to Lotte. A man had just followed them into the Hof Garten and watched her and her daughter sunbathe. The surveillance stopped only when they stayed at the

Bachhuber place, with Lotte's sister.

Lotte knew nothing of the forged identity card. The knowledge would have endangered her. But as she saw her husband and son standing there, in conspiratorial silence, it was clear to her that Kaspar, too, had become involved in some sort of dangerous activity. That is what she had meant by 'the last straw'.

'Ello is behind this, isn't she?'

'Behind what?' Kaspar said, with a touch of his old facetiousness.

Magda shot him a look of hatred. Despite pleas from both parents, and an apology, given under duress by Kaspar, she had refused to address a word to her brother since Forster's search of the apartment.

'I don't know you any more, Gerhard,' Lotte said. 'And I'm not sure this convoluted, secretive person you have become is someone I care for.'

'Lotte, I don't think that's entirely fair,' Glaser said, but his heart wasn't in it. He sounded feeble, even to himself. He knew what was coming next. And it came.

'It's time to go and stay with Katya,' she said. 'Just … for a while.'

Glaser nodded. He had nearly suggested it himself. She would be safer there. And she would be happy enough, back at the family home she had grown up in, with Katya, the unmarried older sister she had always been close to. He tried to speak lightly, despite a heavy heart. 'Yes. All right. Stay with Katya, for a while …'

'Good,' said Magda. 'It'll be good to get out of here. I'll go and pack.'

She stalked off to her room.

'Kaspar, put some things in a bag, darling,' Lotte said. 'You don't have to take everything.'

Kaspar shook his head. 'I'm staying here,' he said, 'with Papa.'

Part VIII
Autumn 1933

1

Sepp Kunde, now known as Kurt Engel, had found a room in Königsbronn, a pretty Swabian small-town, the nearest to the quarry. He lodged with a retired miner, Arnold Weitig, and his wife.

The Weitig home was a modest two-family house. Herr and Frau Weitig lived in the upper half. The red-tile roof was steep-pitched. Kunde's tiny room was under the eaves, which sloped so much he could not sit up in bed without hitting his head on the plasterboard. The Weitigs had put a hotplate and an old kettle in the room, as well as an absolute minimum of battered, second-hand furniture.

Arnold Weitig was in his sixties and an invalid. He spent most of his time neatly dressed in collar and tie, lying on the sofa in semi-darkness, covered by a blanket. His wife, Erna, was a handsome, buxom woman in her late forties.

The chalk mine was reachable by bicycle. Once there, Kurt Engel proved adept at drilling blast holes for the dynamite, loading the charge at the base of the chalk benches, and, after the shoot, helping to fill the shuttle cars with the blasted rock. He kept himself to himself, but he was a good worker, and a Swabian, so the other miners accepted him in days.

The dynamite was kept in a padlocked shed behind the administration building, on the edge of the mine. Since the Nazi takeover, dynamite stores were carefully monitored. Party headquarters in Ulm sent out two officials, in SA uniform, every Wednesday. Arriving during the afternoon, they watched carefully while the Mine Director, Herr Schröder, unlocked the shed. Then they all went in together, and the sticks of dynamite were counted and the total recorded. If more dynamite had been used than usual, Herr Schröder would have to justify the increase.

Kunde realised that stealing even one stick of dynamite was not possible. It would be noticed – no doubt of that. But there was another way. He waited for the next moonless night, then tiptoed down the stairs and out of the Weitig house at midnight. Cycling in complete darkness, surrounded by heavy silence, was a sensual delight to him – motion without thought, almost without consciousness. When he reached the administration building at the mine, he took an S-hook from his light rucksack, and made short work of the lock on the door.

As he padded lightly through the outer office, the stillness and solitude were exhilarating. He had never been truly happy in the presence of another human being. But, as if to challenge all his certainties, a picture of Ello, naked, formed in his mind. He wanted to make love to her. He smiled at her and told her that he had work to do. For now.

Walking on the balls of his feet, silently through to Herr Schröder's office, he wondered if the keys to the shed would be in the safe. He might be able to crack the safe, without it showing – or he might not. He could not risk attracting attention. Attention was the last thing he wanted, as a criminal with an identity card which would not stand up to careful scrutiny.

The safe was in the corner. It was a massive, keyless British Chubb. There was one more possibility: Kunde tried the drawers of Herr Schröder's desk. They were locked, but a couple of flicks of the S-hook opened them. In the top left-hand drawer, were two copies of the all-purpose skeleton-key known as a Dietrich. They would open anything – locks or padlocks –

in the entire mine area. He pocketed one of them. Schröder wouldn't miss it; if he did he'd think he'd lost it. Like most people these days, all Schröder wanted was a quiet life.

Kunde took the first sticks of dynamite the following Wednesday night, and worked on them in his room. The twenty-centimetre-long sticks, bound tight in layers of thick brown paper, stuck out of the kettle. But once heated on the hotplate, the water eventually softened the immersed end. The mix of nitroglycerine and kieselguhr in each stick skimmed out easily enough. Kunde poured the colourless oily goo into a ewer he had bought in town.

In a real stroke of luck, he discovered that a home-made hatch under the eave, by his bed, led all the way under the roof. He kept the ewer with the dynamite under the main roof joist, where it was cool and dark.

Once the sticks of dynamite had dried out, they showed no sign of having been tampered with. But to be on the safe side, Kunde placed them at the back of the stock in the shed the following Tuesday night. Fresh sticks were always removed from the front of the supply the next night, after the Nazi stock-check.

Erna Weitig came into his room to clean, so he made sure none of the nitroglycerine mixture adhered to the kettle, and kept the window open, to clear what little smell there was, after the boiling. At the end of his first week, after a vigorous bout of cleaning, Erna fell into bed with him. They made love every Saturday after that – just before Erna's weekly bath. Kunde believed Herr Weitig knew.

The other regular occurrence in Kunde's life was the arrival of letters from Ello. She wrote twice a week. To his own surprise, Kunde replied – not as often as she wrote, but whenever the mood took him. Slowly, he came to realise that this time in Königsbronn was the happiest of his life. The realisation puzzled him greatly.

2

Rüdiger von Hessert and Anton Elsperger were in a comfortable three-room flat in the prosperous suburb of Bogenhausen. It belonged to an SS colleague of Elsperger's, who let them use it for trysts. On this occasion, von Hessert was kneeling at Elsperger's feet, naked, weeping and kissing his hands.

'Please, Anton, please. I love you so much. Please don't make me suffer any more.'

'You say you love me, Rudi. But you don't mean it. You just lie to me.'

Von Hessert screamed, redoubling his kisses of Elsperger's hands. 'No, no, no. I'll do anything you want. I'll tell you everything ...'

The fleshy-lipped SS-man kicked him in the face with the point of his boot. 'Oh, don't say it again. You *say* you will help me. You *say* you are my friend. And then you just lie and lie and lie.' He took a morphine ampoule from out of his pocket. 'You don't deserve my help.'

'Give me it,' Rudi said. 'I'll tell you what you want to know.'

He was calmer. Elsperger sensed a breakthrough. 'Come on,' he said. 'Come and sit next to me on the sofa, baby-boy. There there. To live is to suffer, as Goethe said.' He took von Hessert by the hand, pulled him up and led him to the sofa, where he put an arm round him. 'Now tell me everything. And if you lie, or leave anything out, I will know. I *will* know.' Elsperger tilted von Hessert's chin up and looked into his eyes. 'You have one chance and one chance only. If you try to deceive me, I walk out of that door, never to return. Speak now.'

Von Hessert nodded. He was thin and unshaven, spittle was running down his chin.

'He is planning to kill Hitler.'

Elsperger was amazed, but didn't show it. 'Who is?'

'Kunde.'

'Just Kunde? Rudi, tell me everything. What about Glaser?'

'Glaser doesn't want anything to do with it.'

'But he knows about it?'

'Not the details. Only that Kunde wants to kill Hitler.'

'What's Kunde planning?'

'I don't know, Anton, and that's the truth. Kunde told us at Dachau. He wants to use a bomb to kill Hitler, and he wants to do it in Munich. Maybe it's a communist plot. Glaser told me he doesn't want anything to do with it, because it's murder. And that is all I know. I swear it. Why would Kunde tell me his plans?'

'Because he wants your help?'

Von Hessert gave a yelping laugh. 'What use would I be?'

'Good point. Rudi, if I find you've withheld anything ...'

Von Hessert screamed. 'I haven't, Anton! I haven't!'

He began to cry. Elsperger threw some morphine ampoules on the floor. Von Hessert flung himself down after them and scrambled around on all fours, picking them up.

'When they are finished, come and see me,' Elsperger said. 'If you try and get a supply anywhere else, I'll have you flogged, understand?'

'Yes, Anton. Thank you.'

Neither Elsperger nor Heydrich wanted to pull Glaser in.

281

They had been watching him anyway, and they believed he did not know where Kunde was. Glaser's fervent anti-communism, they knew, was genuine. Forster, however, had developed a consuming hatred for Glaser, and again asked Heydrich to have him arrested and tortured, to find out what he knew.

'No,' Heydrich said. 'We continue to keep tabs on Glaser. And we turn Munich upside down until we find Kunde.'

Himmler was notified, as was Hess, but news of a plot against the Führer's life was not shared with the Gestapo or the SD – the Reich Security Service. Forster was put in charge of finding Kunde. He interviewed Kunde's twin, August, in Stadelheim Prison. August cut a deal readily enough, but the names and addresses he gave were either hopelessly out of date or false. The Kunde farmhouse in Poppenweiler was raided by the local SS, but Sepp had not been there, or been in touch, for years.

The communist political apparatus in Munich, as well as their sports and gymnastics clubs and their charitable organisation, the Rote Hilfe, had been smashed between January and March. But local informal splinter groups had evolved to replace them. With the help of Max Troll and other informers, anybody in these groups who was known to the Political Police was arrested and tortured for informa-tion about Kunde. Nobody knew where he was, and those who died under torture died cursing his name. These included Paul Jahnke, the North German who had brought Glaser to his meeting with the communists.

When SS-soldiers, led by Elsperger, arrived at the house of Georg Limmer, the nineteen-year-old, code-named Hugo, he was not there. Limmer's elderly parents, the old com-munists, were beaten up. They said their son had gone back to Austria. They also said, convincingly enough, that they had never heard of anybody called Sepp Kunde.

3

With Ello walking slowly behind him, Hitler took the stairs two at a time to the architect Troost's atelier, in Theresien-strasse. Under his arm he carried rolled sketches of his latest design ideas for the House of German Art.

'Herr Professor! I have some drawings to show to you.'

Troost appeared at the top of the stairs. Exceptionally tall, with a serious manner, he looked a lot older than his fifty-five years, and heavier and balder than Roloff's portrait of him. Many in Munich shared Hitler's opinion that Troost was the best German architect since Schinkel. His style was as spare, as solid, as unfussy and unadorned as his speech. Hitler gave him a firm handshake. Ello nodded in greeting.

Up in the atelier, there was a model of the House of German Art, on a long table down the middle of the room. As Hitler began to unroll his architectural drawings, Troost spoke bluntly, with no trace of sycophancy. His clipped Westphalian accent always made him sound authoritative, but now he spoke as if stating a fact, not an opinion.

'Herr Hitler, the House of German Art cannot be ready for 15 October. Not even if we use labour from the Dachau camp. I am unwilling to compromise the standards expected of me by trying.'

Ello gasped at Troost's audacity. But he was getting away with it; a sideways glance at Hitler told her that. She under-stood the relationship: Here, in his atelier, Troost was the master builder. Hitler had returned to what he had been in his youth – a skilful, though unoriginal draughtsman, hoping to realise his boyhood ambition of working in an architect's office.

Ello willed Hitler to countermand Troost, but he nodded, wordlessly accepting what the architect said. Plans for the building would be put on hold, perhaps for years. And that meant the end of the bomb plot. She would have to get a message to Sepp.

Ello escaped from Troost's atelier as soon as she could, looking cow-eyed at Hitler, telling him she felt faint. She packed an overnight bag at her room at the university, and began the journey to Sepp. On the way – two train journeys and a taxi from Königsbronn Station – she felt elated at seeing him again.

It was dark by the time she reached his address. She rang the bell marked 'Weitig' and a handsome middle-aged woman came down in answer. Unable to keep the smile off her face, she asked for Kurt Engel. Frau Weitig gave her a sharp, appraising look and nodded in the direction of her lodger's room.

Sepp opened the door – he had heard her coming. They fell into each other's arms.

'I've got news,' she said breathlessly. Through his kisses she said, 'It's bad news.'

Sepp had already guessed why she was here, but would not be denied making love to her. Lying in bed, later, by the wan light of moonlight coming in the dormer window, she asked what he would do now.

'Destroy the dynamite,' he said. 'Get to France, while I still can.' His forged papers, as he knew perfectly well, would not pass the kind of check he would get at the border, where they would ask him to replicate the signature. 'I can cross over at night. They can't watch the whole border,' he added.

'Will you go tomorrow?' she said.

He smiled, knowing the answer she wanted.

She kissed him on the nose and said, 'There's no hurry. Why don't you show me your childhood home?'

'Poppenweiler? There's nothing there except cow-shit. And I'm not going back to my family's place.'

'OK, then show me Ludwigsburg. You went to school there, didn't you?'

'All right.' He kissed her and they started to make love again.

She slipped out of his room early in the morning, holding her overnight case in front of her as she tiptoed down the stairs. He had given her directions to the local inn, the Linde. He told her to book a room there, and he would meet her later.

She beat at the door until the innkeeper came, took a room, then paid him an exorbitant amount to make her a breakfast of cheese, ham, black bread, butter and coffee. She ate it at a table downstairs. There was a telephone behind the bar. She booked a long-distance call to Rudi.

Her brother was deeply asleep, so early in the morning, but he was happy to hear her voice. She told him she would be away for a couple of days. She told him where she was, as she always did. As an afterthought, she gave him Sepp's address at the Weitigs', too, carefully spelling it out, in case there was a slip-up and he needed to contact her via Sepp.

'Plans have changed,' she said. 'It's all off. The building won't be finished in time. The ...' she hesitated, wanting to avoid the word 'dynamite' on the telephone. 'The stuff will have to be destroyed.'

When she rang off, Rudi recalled something he had heard about the House of German Art. It was only a rumour, but it was worth checking. He telephoned Anton Elsperger and arranged to meet him for lunch.

285

4

Anton Elsperger was delighted to get Rüdiger's call, in his office at the Wittelsbach Palace. He nominated the Ratskeller for lunch – nice and central. He licked his thick lips as he replaced the receiver. Calling his adjutant, he rearranged his schedule, leaving himself free for the entire day.

'Everything comes to he who waits,' he quoted to himself. Von Hessert, bright boy though he was, had always been transparent. He, Elsperger, to vary the metaphor, could read him like a book.

The Ratskeller was an ancient, stone-walled catacomb beneath Munich's Town Hall. Colourful armorial shields of medieval South German knights hung on iron brackets on the walls, at an angle over the diners. The place seated over three hundred for lunch and dinner, but still felt intimate, as it consisted largely of a maze of private rooms, ante-rooms, intimate corners, and even corridors with tables along them.

Elsperger, however, reserved something even more private: a *Priokl*. This booth carved in a niche in the thick stone walls had wooden shutter-doors, like a saloon in the Wild West. They close off the diners, once food has been brought. Ideal for lovers, Elsperger thought, as he slid onto the *Priokl*'s polished wooden bench seat. Ideal for spies. So doubly ideal for lovers who were also spies.

Rüdiger was late. When was the dear boy ever anything

else? But this, Elsperger thought, would be worth waiting for. Knowing that a bomb was planned, somewhere in Munich, limited the possibilities to a few: There was the opening of the House of German Art, in October. There was the annual commemoration and re-enactment of the Beer Hall Putsch, in November. Plus, it was common knowledge that Hitler returned to his beloved adopted city as often as he could, and still drank with the Old Fighters. So known Munich haunts like the Heck, the Ostaria Bavaria, the Café Neumayr at the Viktualienmarkt, or the Sternackerbraü in Tal were also possible.

Elsperger accepted a menu and ordered his favourite beer – Augustiner Pils. When it arrived, he waved the waitress – in her low-cut Bavarian dirndl – away. She reappeared when von Hessert finally turned up.

Rüdiger, all smooth bonhomie, ordered seasonal asparagus with hollandaise sauce and a *Viertl* of Alsace wine. Elsperger himself ordered a more manly dish of braised steak with onions and a second Pils. When his beer came, he licked the foam off it with his tongue, smacking his thick lips: he felt a wave of lust for Rudi.

Rüdiger stroked Elsperger's hand behind the closed *Priokl* doors. 'I've missed you,' he said.

'I've missed you, too.' Elsperger's pale-blue eyes blinked hard. He meant it.

When the food arrived, and the doors were once more closed, Rüdiger got down to business, with what he fondly imagined was subtlety: 'A little bird told me the plans for the new art gallery have been postponed, which would be sad. Another little bird told me they haven't. Do you know what's going on?'

Elsperger was delighted. The art gallery was the most likely site for the bomb. He had already worked out what he would tell Rudi. Everything.

'Troost said it couldn't be done in time,' said the

SS-Captain, his moist mouth full of the Austrian-style dumpling that accompanied the braised steak. 'But I believe the Führer had anticipated that. He is usually two or three steps ahead. That is why he is the Führer.'

'So what did he do?' Rudi said.

'According to Himmler, a contingency plan was already in place, involving Speer. The Führer simply contacted Speer, in Berlin, and activated it.'

'Don't tell me. Speer can't stand Troost. He saw his opportunity; he's taken it over. It's all going ahead as planned.' Rudi was smiling, delighted, already imagining himself telling Ello the good news. He realised he would have to contact her quickly, before she and Sepp destroyed the dynamite.

'Not exactly. Actually, baby-boy, Speer has more respect for old Troost than many people think. But, leaving that aside, he is ever the pragmatist is Speer. His plan was to go ahead with the ceremony, and just lay the foundation-stone.'

Rudi dabbed at herb-filled butter on his chin with his napkin, unsure whether this was good or bad. 'So …'

Elsperger fought down a smile as he put him out of his misery. 'Apparently, this foundation-stone is a block of white granite,' he said, 'about waist high.' He watched, with some amusement, while Rudi registered that this was big enough to put a bomb in.

'The top will be hollowed out,' Elsperger added casually. 'The Führer will place a scroll in it, commemorating it as the First Stone of the New Reich.'

Rudi nodded, simulating the mildest of interest. He asked about Bärbel and the kids. Elpserger said, truthfully, how much they had enjoyed their skittles evening with Rudi. While he was speaking, he touched the morphine ampoules in his pocket. He had originally intended to give Rudi some at the end of the meal, but changed his mind.

Suppose Rudi went home and swallowed them now, rather than leading him to the rest of the plotters?

Pleading an appointment, Elsperger hurried their meal to an end, opened the *Priokl* doors and paid. They parted outside the Ratskeller, in the sunshine, making plans to meet up again soon. As Rudi strolled off, Elsperger watched as a plain-clothes follower tailed him. Then he turned off the square and radioed for his car. It was there in seconds. It drove him to the von Hessert villa in Karolinen Platz, where Elsperger jumped out and sat in the back of a souped-up BMW, with an SS driver in civilian clothes. Elsperger had ordered it parked there immediately after Rudi phoned.

He should let someone else follow von Hessert, Elsperger realised that. But frankly he couldn't resist it. He slid down low in the back. His radio crackled. The man he had put to follow von Hessert from the Ratskeller reported that he was on his way home.

Rudi went into the von Hessert villa, but emerged minutes later driving a brown Horch. Ever one to look the part, he had put on a white silk scarf and a pair of motoring goggles. He set off in the Horch so fast the engine screamed. Elsperger nodded to his driver to follow. The plotters would be rounded up, that very afternoon, he thought. Glory beckoned. The first thing he would do, when he received his massive promotion, was sideline that moaning hayseed Forster.

He wondered what line would be taken with Rudi. One way or another, the young fool would be looked after. He rather hoped so. It was difficult not to … Elsperger bit his lower lip hard, to make himself concentrate on the issue at hand.

The Horch was heading north out of Munich. Elsperger was puzzled.

'Keep him in sight,' the SS-Captain called to the driver, suddenly alarmed.

But it was too late. Ahead of them were three hired open trucks, full of prisoners heading towards Dachau. Rudi threw the Horch into the convoy, then out, accelerating suddenly. The souped-up BMW got stuck behind one of the trucks, the driver hooting furiously. Then it couldn't catch the Horch. It was out of sight. Von Hessert could have been heading anywhere – Augsburg, Ulm, even Stuttgart.

Elsperger furiously yelled at the driver to stop. At the side of the road, he pulled the man from his seat, slapped him round the face, then landed three heavy punches into his stomach. He couldn't mention this debacle to anybody now, and he would make damn sure the driver didn't either.

And as to von Hessert … Elsperger stopped hitting the driver and licked his fleshy lips. Little Rudi was going to suffer.

5

As Sepp Kunde was leaving the house to meet up with Ello at the Linde, he was stopped by Frau Weitig.

'My husband would like a word with you, Herr Engel.'

'I'm just on the way out. Can't it wait?'

'No, it cannot.' Frau Weitig looked ready to bar Kunde's exit, if necessary. Her full-bosomed body was rigid with anger.

Kunde went into the Weitig livingroom. Herr Weitig, pale and formally dressed, was sitting up on his sickbed, in semi-darkness.

'Please take a seat, Herr Engel.'

'No, thanks.'

'Very well. Herr Engel, as you must know, we are tenants here, ourselves. We are subletting to you. *Damenbesuch* – visits by ladies – is not permitted. We, too, could be asked to leave, as well as you.'

Kunde shrugged. 'My friend was just visiting.'

Weitig's face twitched in spasm. He had a coughing fit, but mastered it. 'Herr Engel, do you take me for a fool? You have made a pigsty of our bed. We intend to inform your employer. You must leave immediately.'

Kunde did not react. They might well sack him from the mine, though that hardly mattered now, with the bomb plot called off. The priority was getting the dynamite out of the bedroom and disposing of it. He thought of calling off his day in Ludwigsburg with Ello, but realised he was looking forward to it.

'Herr Weitig, I am surely entitled to a day's grace, to put my affairs in order and find somewhere to lay my head. I will leave tomorrow.'

'Very well. Tomorrow it is, then. Goodbye, Herr Engel.'

Herr Weitig lay down again on his sickbed. Kunde looked for Frau Weitig as he left the house, but there was no sign of her.

On the train to Stuttgart, where they would change for Ludwigsburg, Ello was concerned that she had been the cause of Sepp's eviction. Kunde, however, was unruffled, and amusingly spiky at the petit-bourgeois morality of the Weitigs: 'Must have been the first time anybody's fucked in that house since the war.'

Ello's laughter pealed round the train compartment. It was cut short by the appearance of two Gestapo, bracing themselves with difficulty against the swaying of the train as they made their way down the aisle. She tried to look relaxed, but decided against smiling at them.

'Identity cards, please.'

The one who took their identity cards was a short man with a huge belly and receding hair. He was sweating profusely in the stuffy train. He opened the cards, looked at the photographs, gave Ello a quick glance and stared at Kunde. He moved Kunde's photograph with his thumb. The eyelet at the top-left corner was coming loose.

'That needs to be fixed on properly,' he said. The podgy Gestapo man pressed it down more firmly, with thumb and forefinger.

Kunde nodded. 'I know.'

'Get it done, then. Otherwise you'll lose your photograph.'

'I will.'

The Gestapo man handed both cards back. He gave Kunde a lascivious look, then continued down the aisle.

*

The sun broke through the clouds in the afternoon. Ello was pleased with her choice of a sleeveless, yellow dress. Her lover was in shirtsleeves and plus-fours, with his tweed jacket slung over his shoulder. They strolled together in Marktplatz, a lovely colonnaded eighteenth-century square. It reminded her of girlhood holidays in France and Belgium. They stopped at Carlo Ferretti's statue of Ludwigsburg's founder, Count Eberhard Ludwig, in the middle of the square.

'Small, wasn't he?' Kunde said.

'Look who's talking. Oy!' She squealed as he seized her wrist, bending her arm behind her back and kissing her. Passers-by crossing the square stopped to look at them, some smiling, some – war widows armoured in black bombazine – scowling ferociously.

'Let's go in there,' she said, waving at the towered church which forms one flank of the square.

'Where?' Kunde blinked in the sunshine.

'Over there! Look, it's a church, isn't it?

'No idea.'

'No idea? You're supposed to be my tour guide. Don't you have childhood memories of this place?'

'Not of the bloody church, no. The brothel's down there, Seestrasse.'

'You're disgusting!' She took his arm. 'We're going in the church.'

Frisoni's neo-baroque interior drew a coo of admiration from Ello. 'It's beautiful.'

'It's beautiful for the few,' Kunde said.

'Rubbish. It's beautiful for whoever looks at it.'

'It's part of the same con trick as that aristo outside in the square. Noblemen and God, artificial hierarchy. It must all be swept away. One day we shall create an equal society, instead of all this.' He waved an arm round the church. 'I'd tear it all down, if I could. I'd tear it down tomorrow.'

'Are all communists as miserable as you?'

'Yes. I'm normally the life and soul of the party.' He tried to kiss her again, but she insisted on admiring the font.

The sun was even brighter when they emerged from the church. 'What do you want to do now?' she asked.

'Undress you and fuck your beautiful arse.'

'Yes, but apart from that.'

He flatly refused to take her round the palace, Ludwigsburg's main tourist attraction. It occurred to her, as they stood there in the brilliant sunshine in Marktplatz, that this was Life in a Day, all the time they may ever have together. It was as if the war Hitler needed so badly had already started.

Sepp was a warrior, Sepp was a soldier; he was going away soon. He would fight against evil, she knew he would, but he might be killed. She felt melancholy, a wave of sadness she knew could turn to depression any minute. She took his arm.

A brigade of uniformed SA marched into the square, then diagonally across it. There were about thirty of them in rows of three. The lead man in the middle carried the standard with *Germany Awaken* emblazoned on it, topped by a circled swastika and a gold eagle. The next three had rifles over their shoulders, the three after that carried huge Blood Flags, aloft. Their boots stamped on the cobbles of the beautiful square.

'SA Brigade 123,' Kunde said laconically. 'Or part of it. I know some of them. This isn't safe. Oh, what the hell.'

'Should we go?' Ello said. She was frightened – as frightened as she had ever been.

'No, I'm damned if we will. Come on, I'll show you where I went to school.'

'I'd like that.'

The Mörike Gymnasium was just off the centre of town. Its heavy, lichen-encrusted stone exuded Wilhelmine confidence and stolidity, a promise to the future that nothing would change – a promise about to be broken. They looked through the paling-fence at the school building.

'Which subjects did you like best?'

'Everything. Until I started to think for myself. Then they cut up rough. I wrote an essay on Internationalism. It wasn't the title I'd been given; I just did it. The German teacher, Herr Knaus his name was, threw it at my feet in front of the whole class. I refused to pick it up. So he went to visit my parents, to complain about me. My father gave him a beer in the kitchen. He said he was proud of me. My grades plummeted after that.'

She touched his face. 'How old were you? Then?'

'Fourteen. I left soon after.' He looked into her eyes. 'I remember this though:

> This was the last time
> I went with you, O Klara.
> Yes, the last time
> that we were happy, like children.
> When one day we hurried
> through the wide sun-bright rainy streets,
> hidden under one umbrella, running.
> Both secretly wrapped
> like in a fairy mushroom,
> finally arm in arm.'

'That was lovely.' She paused. 'Who wrote it?'

'Mörike.' He waved at the building. 'The one my school is named for. Swabia's great poet – a Ludwigsburg man. He was at school with Klara, the one he wrote the poem to. She was his first girlfriend.'

'That is really sweet. You're full of surprises, aren't you?'

'You mean, how come a low-born peasant knows poetry?'

'Precisely. Hold me. Just put your arms round me.

295

Please.' She thought if he put his arms around her, and did not try to kiss her, she would marry him, if he asked.

He put his arms round her. He did not try to kiss her. She stayed there for a long time, with him, but it still wasn't long enough. Eventually they meandered back, their arms round each other's waists, to the town centre. They had no idea where they were heading for. The first shades of dusk were creeping over the pretty town, outlining the towers of the church as fingers over Marktplatz. A carillon pealed out a quarter-hour.

'Do you need food?' he said.

She smiled because he made it sound so functional, not a matter for pleasure. 'Yes. But I'm not leaving it to you. We'll end up with a boiled sausage with mustard, eaten on the pavement.'

'I'm not going into a fancy restaurant. I'll tell you that for nothing.'

They compromised. The Post-Canz served Swabian specialties, but it was not intimidatingly formal. It was understood that Ello would pay the bill. As they sat at a wooden booth, the owner, Herr Buhl, greeted Sepp in a delighted roar: '*Grüss Gott*, Herr Kunde.' It echoed round the restaurant; all the diners looked up.

For a moment, Ello was alarmed, peering round the wood-panelled, cheery place, fearing the consequences of the blowing of Sepp's cover. Would he always be a wanted man? But as the bubbly Swabian conversation went on – Ello thought Swabian dialect sounded like water gurgling out of a bath – she relaxed, smiled, and finally joined in. She interrupted their reminiscences of mutual friends to ask Herr Buhl what Sepp had been like as a boy.

The innkeeper made a lugubrious face, pretending to think. 'As a boy? Much the same as now, except perhaps a little bigger.'

Sepp grinned. He ordered a plate of lentils, with a slab

of belly-pork and two red boiled sausages. Conscious that Ello was paying, he demanded a *Halbe* of the higher-price Pils beer to wash it down. At Herr Buhl's recommendation, Ello had Swabian *Maultaschen* – minced pork and spinach in pastry envelopes – served in a bowl of bouillon. Herr Buhl personally selected her a *Viertle* of 1932 Obertürkheimer Spätlese from a local vineyard, served in a white-stemmed Römer glass.

They were silent as they ate. Sepp could be silent and at ease. She liked that.

6

Stiff from all that rally-style driving, but proud to have outsmarted Anton and shaken him off, Rudi drove into Königsbronn. He found the Linde by asking passers-by. The innkeeper told him his sister had indeed taken a room, but she was out at the moment. Rudi asked directions to the Weitig address, assuming Ello would be there, with Sepp.

A well-preserved older woman, presumably Frau Weitig, looked angry when she opened the door, in response to his overlong pull at the doorbell. It was late in the evening, after all. But her expression softened when she looked at him.

'Yes?' She leaned against the door jamb coquettishly.

'Excuse the disturbance, *gnädige Frau*. My name is von Hessert,' Rudi said. 'My sister should be here, somewhere. She is visiting a friend of ours who lodges at this address.'

'You mean Herr Engel?'

'No, his name is Sepp Kunde.'

'There's nobody here of that name.'

'No? Little chap? Not much hair?'

But Frau Weitig had already closed the door. Rudi blinked a couple of times. He made his way back to the Linde, but Ello still had not returned. Washed up by fate at an inn, he let himself be carried by the current of events, and went to the bar. He ordered a *Viertle* of the famous Swabian wine and started chatting to the locals. They were welcoming to the stranger, plying him with more wine, until pretty soon he was pleasantly sozzled.

After the meal, Sepp and Ello made their way back to Stuttgart, and then Königsbronn, by train. Ello fell into a deep sleep on Sepp's shoulder. Sepp saw her back to the Linde, then strolled to the Weitig house. Up in his room, he got the ewer with the dynamite out of its hiding place, put the dynamite in a canvas bag, and left with it, intending to bury it in the woods.

Ello walked into the Linde and saw her younger brother at the bar. He was standing, obviously drunk, holding a furled umbrella in the 'On Guard' position. She listened as he gave a comprehensive explanation of the etiquette of duelling, as practised at the universities of Tübingen and Heidelberg. The fascinated Swabian farmers were hanging on his every word.

'Rudi!'

As soon as he saw Ello, Rudi dropped the umbrella, staggered over to her, hugged her, and managed to convey, very loudly, that their plan, which fortunately he did not describe in detail, could go ahead after all.

'There's goin' be a stone foundation-stone,' he blubbered. 'Granite! Waist high. Bloody great big thing. You can stick it in there!'

Knowing she could hardly knock on the Weitigs' door herself, having just been the cause of Sepp's eviction, Ello told Rudi he must come with her, to tell Sepp the news. Getting Rudi out of the bar, however, was unexpectedly problematic: Rudi did not want to go, and the Swabian farmers were reluctant to see their evening's entertainment disappear into the night, at least before the finer points of the honour duel were completely clear to them.

But eventually Ello managed to half-walk, half-drag Rudi as far as the Weitig house.

She got him to ring the doorbell, while she hid. At the last moment, she remembered Sepp's false identity and called out to Rudi that Sepp was known as Herr Engel here. Herr Engel, Rudi was told by a now-seething Frau Weitig, had just left. Ello hauled Rudi back to the Linde, where the Horch was parked. Not for the first time, she cursed her father for not letting her learn to drive – Cajetan von Hessert regarded driving as an unsuitable activity for a female of rank.

The drunken Rudi installed himself at the wheel of the Horch, sending it skidding into the middle of the dark street, before pointing it forward and on its way in a series of jerks. Ello tried to imagine where Sepp would go. He would surely try to bury the dynamite.

She concentrated hard and conjured up a patch of woods in her mind. She had seen it on the way in to Königsbronn in the taxi, when she first arrived. But where, exactly? She got Rudi to stop the car, ran back to the Linde, and asked if anybody had a map of the town.

The innkeeper went up to his room, at the top of the inn, and reappeared with a battered and much-folded map which looked as if it might be pre-war. She unfolded it with difficulty and, with the help of Rudi's new friends, the Swabian farmers, found the nearest woodland. Then she ran back to the car.

Rudi had fallen asleep at the wheel. Ello half-steered, while at the same time trying to give Rudi directions. As they found the woods, they came across Sepp, walking along, carrying a canvas bag. Ello gave him the good news in a rapid whisper.

Sepp, it transpired, could not drive either, so he sat in the back of the Horch while a sobering Rudi got them back to the Weitig place. Ello handed Sepp enough money to pay the rent for his room, until the end of the month. She told him to mollify the Weitigs, if at all possible. Sepp left the dynamite in the car and went back in, on his diplomatic mission.

Sitting in the car, the von Hesserts could see the light come on in his room, as he cleared the rest of his belongings. Sepp reappeared. Frau Weitig's parting shot, he told the von Hesserts, was to ask whether Engel was his real name.

Sepp had told them, as convincingly as he could, that it was. He had showed them his identity card. He told them the young man who visited them, earlier this evening, was an unreliable drunk, who always got names wrong. They would just have to hope the Weitigs' suspicions were allayed, and they would not go to the police.

Back at the Linde, the von Hesserts financed a room and living expenses for Sepp, until the granite foundation-stone was placed at the site of the future House of German Art. Ello was to telephone him at the inn as soon as the stone was in place. Rudi went off to Ello's room, and fell fast asleep, fully clothed, on her bed.

As Ello fell asleep in Sepp's arms, in the room they had just taken for him, she felt sure the bomb plot would succeed. Evil would not prevail – they would kill Hitler soon.

7

At one of his infrequent visits to the Ministry of Justice Glaser asked for Rudi to assist him with a prosecution. He was told the probationer had resigned.

The Opel Frosch was outside the Prielmayerstrasse entrance, watched by two Political Police. They had followed him there in a sporty, open-topped DKW, presumably the personal property of one of the policemen. They had then parked behind Glaser's car, and waited for him to return. Glaser left the building by the Elisenstrasse entrance. He caught a tram to the university.

Ello was in her room, sitting on the ottoman. She looked tense and hollow-eyed, and had lost a lot of weight. The door through to her bedroom was open. Glaser could see Rudi in her bed. He appeared to be asleep, or unconscious. His face was badly bruised and swollen. What Glaser could see of his upper body was a mass of livid contusions, and what looked like whip or lash marks.

'My dear Ello …'

Ello put her fingers to her lips, then closed the bedroom door. 'He was dumped in my room like that. I found …'

Before she could go on, there was a banging at the door and two women of about Ello's age burst in. One of them was in a brown-gold uniform, with red epaulettes on the shoulders, the other wore a traditional Bavarian dirndl dress. Neither wore make-up. Both had their brown hair in plaits.

'Get out,' Ello spat at them.

'You are not to have any more visits from men. How many more times do we have to tell you?' said the one in uniform.

'Whore!' the woman in the dirndl said. 'Slut! Painted Jezebel!'

Glaser looked astonished, but Ello spoke before he could. 'My guest and I will find somewhere else to talk,' Ello said. 'Be quiet or you'll wake my brother.'

'He can't stay here,' the one in uniform said.

'I know. He's being moved later today.'

'I'll make sure it really is the brother,' said dirndl. She looked into the bedroom at the still-sleeping Rudi.

'Come on, Gerhard,' Ello said. 'We can talk outside.'

Gerhard and Ello left the room first, followed by the two women. The women watched them out of sight down the corridor.

'So you have block wardens at the university, too?' Glaser said, with a nod back at the woman in uniform. He sighed. 'We have one for our block of flats. She reports on everything.'

Ello did not reply. She and Glaser walked out to the scrap of grass at the front of the building, facing Ludwigstrasse. 'I wanted to keep Rudi here,' she said. 'But he'll have to go to my parents' now.'

'Who did that to him?' Glaser looked sad rather than surprised.

'Elsperger. I've had the emergency doctor here. Aside from the beating, he's taken an overdose of pills. Morphine.'

'Deliberately?'

'Yes, I think so. Gerhard, I went through his things. He's … he's joined the Party.'

She started to cry. He took a step toward her, hesitated, then held her against his chest.

Some passing students glanced at them curiously. Glaser

glared back, and they looked away and hurried on.

Ello disengaged herself. 'Sorry about that. I'm a bit low at the moment. They caught my cat, Krafft. I found him strangled and hanging from the light in my room.'

'Oh, Ello!'

Ello shrugged, pulling herself together. 'Rudi was due to collect the dynamite, in the Horch. But I don't think he could face it. I'll get word to Sepp. We'll have to call it off. He can't carry the dynamite back himself. They're looking for him everywhere.'

Glaser looked round. The university's autumn term had just started. Crowds of students were rushing past them, more were coming towards them along the wide boulevard of Ludwigstrasse, from the direction of the Victory Gate. But there was nobody close enough to hear what they were saying.

'Ello. Forgive me, but do you think Rudi told Elsperger anything? Perhaps under duress?'

'I don't think so,' Ello said. 'If he had, I would have been picked up by now.'

Glaser nodded. 'I'll do it,' he said. 'I'll collect the dynamite and bring it back by train.'

'Gerhard …' She glanced down at his leg. 'Are you sure?'

Glaser smiled. 'No time like the present. Our friends are still watching my car, parked outside the Ministry. I'll get a tram to the station and catch a train to my mother's house, in Ludwigsburg. Where is Sepp staying?'

Ello thought for a second. 'Give me your mother's address. Sepp can contact you there.'

Glaser told Ello the address. She did not write it down.

'How will Sepp get back to Munich?'

'He was planning to walk back, at night. Once he's planted the bomb, and set the timer, he'll make for Austria, again walking at night.'

Glaser nodded. 'Right, then. I'll be off. Tell Rudi … Tell

him I wish him well.'

Ello nodded absently. She turned and walked back into the university.

8

The two Political Police following Glaser sat in their open-topped car, chatting and watching Glaser's green Opel, until late afternoon. Then they went into the Ministry of Justice to check up on him. They discovered he had gone.

Chief Inspector Forster had given standing instructions that, if information emerged about Glaser, he was to be contacted at any time of the day or night. As the two police watchers returned to the Wittelsbach Palace to report their quarry's absence, Forster was watching the late-afternoon showing of a Mickey Mouse film, with his children, Helga and Erwin.

Christa Forster had not been happy when two uniformed SS on motorcycles arrived at her home, asking for her husband. But when his instructions about Glaser had been quoted to her, she reluctantly told them where he was.

With the film well under way, the two SS walked down the centre aisle of the cinema, shining torches at the hundred and fifty or so adults and children, peering at faces, looking for the Chief Inspector. They couldn't find him.

They tried both side-aisles. Nothing. They discussed having the film stopped, before one of them remembered the balconies. They made their way up the vast curved stairs. There were another fifty or so people up there.

Eventually they found Forster, chuckling away, next to his children. Mickey had been leading the mice in the defence of their homes against an invading army of cats. Just as the

306

SS spotted Forster, Mickey had become a soldier, been given a machine gun and sent into battle. No wonder the Führer himself was said to be among the rodent's admirers.

Forster left the SS-men in no doubt that they had done the right thing by coming to find him. He left one of them with the children and set off with the other to Glaser's flat. As luck would have it, the film had been showing at the Hofgarten Lichtspiele, five minutes from Galeriestrasse.

'Where is he?' Forster said to Kaspar in the Glaser drawing room. 'Where is your father?'

Sprawled in his father's armchair, unwashed and sporting three days' growth of fluffy ginger beard, Kaspar smiled. Glaser had phoned him from the Hauptbahnhof, just before he left. He wanted to say goodbye, he had said, before his holiday in Switzerland. Kaspar had understood perfectly.

'He's on holiday,' the youth said.

'Where?'

'Switzerland.'

'Address?'

'Don't know.'

'Does he usually leave without telling you where he's going?'

'No. But this is the first holiday he's taken without Mama. I think he's a bit fed up, you know. He's a bit low. Yes. Not on top form at all. He's been snappy to be quite honest with you. Ill-tempered. He ...'

'All right, all right. Where's his car?'

'Isn't it parked outside?'

The SS-man had briefed Forster as they had crossed the Hof Garten to the apartment.

'No, it is not. It's outside the Ministry of Justice. If he was going on holiday, why would he leave it there?'

'It's probably broken down again. Look, you couldn't get some of your people to get it started and bring it round here, could you?'

Forster glared at him. He held up thumb and forefinger close together. 'Sonny-boy, you are *that* close to a cell at the Wittelsbach Palace.'

Kaspar shrugged. '*Sancta simplicitas.*'

'What?'

'O the glory of simple things.'

Forster shot a glance at the SS-man. He was pleased there was only one there to hear such defiance. He addressed his subordinate – to regain face as much as anything. 'Did Glaser have any luggage with him?' As soon as the question was out of his mouth, Forster realised he shouldn't have asked it in front of Kaspar. He was rushing, and he was making mistakes.

'I'm not sure, sir. I don't think so.'

'He tends to travel light,' Kaspar said, in the same irritating tone he had adopted since Forster came in. 'For one thing he can't carry much. It unbalances him. His leg, you know.'

Forster and the SS-man made a quick search of the flat. It was impossible to tell whether anything was missing or not. The place was in a disgusting state – untidy and filthy. In the bathroom, there was toothpaste all over the sink.

Forster and the SS-man came back into the drawingroom where Kaspar appeared to be dozing. 'You're living like swine here, you and your father,' Forster said to him.

Kaspar shrugged.

'If your father contacts you,' Forster continued, 'you are to tell me immediately. Do you understand?'

'Naturally, Chief Inspector.'

'It'll be the worse for you if you don't.'

Kaspar grinned. The second the Chief Inspector left the apartment, he jumped up and telephoned Katya

Bachhuber's house. His Aunt Katya answered. He asked to speak to his mother.

'Hello, darling,' he said, booming cheerfully and very slowly down the telephone, which they now knew for certain was bugged – they could hear a click after the other person rang off. 'Chief Inspector Forster was here. He asked some questions about Papa. I thought he phrased them very well. The man is a fine state official – a credit to the Third Reich. I hope they promote him. He does so deserve it.'

His mother laughed and said 'Kas-par!' in that mock-exasperated way she had used with him since he was five. He loved it to distraction.

Glaser had phoned Lotte, too, from the Hauptbahnhof, before he left for Ludwigsburg. It had left her feeling strangely happy. She told Kaspar she hoped his papa was having a good time on holiday. She then issued yet another invitation for him to join her, at Aunt Katya's. Kaspar again turned it down. Lotte rang off before her son could say anything else that would get him into trouble.

Kaspar went back to his father's armchair and reflected on the toothpaste. It had swastikas running through it. When he and his father had first seen it on sale, Glaser had said 'We're not buying that. The bastards may have invaded everything else, but at least we can keep them out of the bathroom.'

But the second his father had rung off, after his call from the Hauptbahnhof, Kaspar had gone down to the chemist's shop and bought a tube of swastika toothpaste. He had given his teeth a vigorous brushing with it, then squeezed the rest all over the sink. He had no idea himself why he had done that.

'Herr Glaser is wanted by the authorities. Where is he?' Forster asked Lotte, Magda and Katya Bachhuber, at the imposing Bachhuber family home overlooking the Isar.

The tall, willowy Katya looked enquiringly at her younge sister.

'He's on holiday in Switzerland,' Lotte said.

Forster stared her in the eye. 'Frau Glaser, you know and I know that that is not true. May I remind you that with holding information from the Reich authorities is a seriou matter. Misleading the Reich authorities is a crimina offence. So I ask you again, Frau Glaser. Please tell me the truth this time. Where is your husband?'

Lotte gave a languid blink worthy of Ello, or indeed o Elisabeth Bergner herself. It was followed by a very pretty smile. 'He *said* he was going to Switzerland ...'

'Bit sudden, isn't it?'

She shrugged. 'That's how he is.'

'Why would he leave via the office?'

'Last-minute work. He can't keep away.'

By now Forster had radioed for more men. They were searching the Bachhuber residence, although the Chief Inspector did not really expect to find anything.

'Magda, come with me a moment, please,' Forster said 'There's nothing to worry about.'

Magda, in smock-style navy-blue dress over a white blouse did not look worried. She followed Forster into a smal lounge, decked out in yellow silk wallpaper, with black lacquer screens dotted about, in the Chinese style. Forster waved away two SS who were turning out a Chinese black bureau, inlaid with mother-of-pearl. The Chief Inspector and the schoolgirl sat down side by side on Empire chairs.

Forster's mouth turned up at the corners. 'Magda, my daughter is your age,' he lied.

Magda nodded encouragingly.

'I'm proud of her, my Helga. She is a good National Socialist. And I think you are, too.'

'I hope so,' Magda said. 'I'm in the BdM, where I learn to

erve our Führer in any way I can, small or … big or small.'

Forster nodded. 'Good girl. So you understand that the needs of the Party come before all other loyalties, don't you? Even before loyalty to the family.'

Magda nodded vigorously, wide-eyed. 'Oh yes. I too belong to the Führer.' It was the slogan from a BdM poster

'Quite so. And today', Forster said, 'your opportunity is indeed to serve the Führer himself. An honour that is not given to many. In fact, Magda, I envy you the chance this day presents to you. Will you take your chance? Will you help the Führer?'

Magda nodded again.

'Magda, your papa is by no means a bad man. But he is misguided. We wish to make that clear to him. That is all. We won't hurt him. You follow?'

'Oh, yes.'

'Good girl. Where is he at the moment?'

'In Lucerne. Pension Walther. That's Walther with an *h*. W-A-L-T-H-E-R. He goes there every year, in September.'

'Really?'

'Mmmm. Yes.'

When Forster and the SS had gone, Magda put her arms round her mother. 'I suppose Papa's gone to Grandma's,' she said.

Lotte hesitated, but only for a second. 'Yes,' she said. 'Yes, I think he has.'

'That Forster man laughed at my diary,' Magda said. 'And he talks to me as if I'm a half-wit. I hate him.'

9

It was the first time Glaser had been back to his childhood home since his father's funeral three years ago. He telephoned his mother from Stuttgart train station, while waiting for the local train. It was a flying visit, he explained; he had no luggage. There were no questions in reply. The old lady faced life with grim acceptance.

As the branch line carried him home, he hungrily took in the vineyard-laden slopes. They soothed him. The taxi from the station took him past the frontage of Ludwigsburg's yellow baroque eighteenth-century palace. As a boy, Glaser had woken up to it every morning. He could see it across the extensive, sculptured formal grounds from his bedroom window. He wanted to touch it for reassurance, like a child.

The taxi drew up in Mömpelgardstrasse, at a solid, red-painted patrician townhouse, opposite the side-entrance to the grounds of the palace. Glaser was anticipating what specialties his mother would have ready for him to eat. The old lady did not disappoint. The first damsons of autumn were just coming into season.

'*Zwetschgenkucha!*' Glaser cried blissfully, in Swabian dialect, as he bit into his mother's damson flan. It was the month of new wine, and onion tart. And soon it would be time for the Martinsgans – the goose eaten in November. He felt, once again, in tune with the seasons.

Nature was still there, underlying life. There was a force of the spirit safe from the Nazis.

312

Even though it was only mid-afternoon, Glaser asked for
wine. Old Frau Glaser joined him in a *Viertle* of Goldberg,
the purest gold, tasting like sunshine. The Swabians
consume the entire harvest themselves, so Glaser could
never have got hold of it in Munich. He shut his eyes as he
drank it; it took him back, not to any one moment or part
of the past, but back into some generic better time which
blotted out the present. He was grateful for that; it was a
balm to his soul.

'You look ill,' his old mother said. 'Thin. Like when your
leg was amputated.'

Glaser ignored that. 'How's things?' he said.

'Things?'

'Yes. How's things?' He loaded the phrase with bitterness.
He meant: 'How much more have the Nazis taken over?' He
meant: 'What has happened to the Jews lately?'

Glaser had absorbed a Jewish presence, as he was growing
up. Just along the street there was a graceful house, with
elegant sash windows and bottle-green doors, each with red-
and-white painted panels. Glaser used to gaze in, longingly,
every time he passed it, with his satchel on his back, on his
way to school.

It was in this house that Joseph Süsskind Oppenheimer –
now known as 'Jew Süss' – had lived. Oppenheimer, osten-
sibly Finance Minister, had been Count Carl Alexander of
Württemberg's de facto regent. He had masterminded
Württemberg's prosperity; starting Ludwigsburg's porcelain
industry.

But as soon as Carl Alexander died, Joseph Oppenheimer
was taken up the hill to the local prison, in Asperg, and
tortured. He confessed to all manner of crimes he hadn't
committed. After due process of the law, he was executed.
Glaser had always hated the injustice of it.

Old Frau Glaser turned the full force of her clear, still

beautiful, china-blue eyes on her son. She wrote long but infrequent letters, and would receive but not make telephone calls. So there was news – about the town's Jewish population. Rather too much news, in the old lady's view.

'I wrote to you about Max Elsas,' she said.

Glaser nodded. Max, the patriarch of the Elsas family had started Elsas and Sons, the textile factory, the biggest in Ludwigsburg. He was a city councillor. On his seventieth birthday, he had been honoured by a civic reception at the enchanting Monrepos Castle by the lake. The entire town turned out for it. The photographs of the Glaser parents at the reception, smiling next to Max and Ida Elsas, faced Glaser on the hundred-year-old Kerner dresser.

At the beginning of last year, Herr Elsas had been elected to Stuttgart Chamber of Commerce. In April of this year, he had been deprived of all civic offices, was forced to sell his factory for a pittance, had his bank account seized by the bank, and was banned from the local inn, where he had been a regular at his *Stammtisch* for fifty years.

'I went to call on him,' Frau Glaser said. 'He's seventy-five now. He said they might as well wall him up in his home. He doesn't go out any more.'

Glaser nodded, his face a mask. 'And Dr Pintus?'

'Why do you ask?' said his mother.

'Because I want to know.'

'Yes. You always wanted to know. Curiosity. It cost you dearly.' She nodded at his leg, stretched out in front of him in the rocking chair.

'So tell me.'

The old lady sipped her wine: Along with the two other Jewish general practitioners in Ludwigsburg, Dr Pintus' practice, in Mathildenstrasse, in the centre of town, had been picketed in April. This followed a Nazi advertisement in the local newspaper, demanding a boycott of Jewish doctors, lawyers and businesses – Ludwigsburg's four Jewish horse-traders had also been singled out.

'He's still practising,' Frau Glaser finished up. 'Just about. I still go. There are only a few patients left, though.'

Glaser pictured the dreamy, short-sighted doctor – whose own health was fragile. He used to visit the farmers in the outlying villages in the depths of winter. Glaser saw him, in his mind's eye, as he had seen him then, with red bowtie peeping out above his scarf and coat, as children attached ropes to his home-made sled and pulled him along over metre-high snow. The kiddies took it in turns to jump up on the sled behind him, then off again to do a bit more pulling.

The homespun Swabian farmers were protective of their bookish doctor. He used the *du* form to them, as he did with everybody he spoke to. They treated him with kid gloves, while he took on some of their coarse bluntness:

'Will I get better, doctor?'

'No. You've lived off the fat of the land; now the fat of the land will live off you.'

Glaser changed the subject. 'Have there been any messages for me?'

'Here? No.'

'Very well. Tomorrow I shall go to the exhibition.'

His mother stared at him. 'The art exhibition? In Stuttgart?'

'Yes.'

'You're crazy!'

'I want to see it for myself,' Glaser said.

'Curiosity,' Old Frau Glaser murmured. 'You think you can do anything. You think you can fly. You mark my words. It'll finish you yet.'

10

Stuttgart City Gallery, in Kronprinzen Palais, was a place Glaser had always loved. His first pocket money had been spent on train fare from Ludwigsburg to look at the paintings. Sometimes he went alone; sometimes with a classmate.

Later, he took girlfriends there. He insisted they separate, to look at the art, and meet up afterwards, at the exit. They then crossed the road, arm in arm, to the Gartenhaus Café.

Over coffee and cakes, they discussed the paintings, the artists, compared their likes and dislikes, and what had moved them and what had not. The young Glaser had not minded if his companion had different tastes to him. He liked a good argument. But if the girl had no opinions at all, he quickly lost interest in her.

In those early days, Glaser's father – Alois Glaser, the distinguished lawyer and jurist – was on the Supervisory Board of the gallery. The curator, Count Claus von Baudissin, was a frequent visitor to the Glaser home. At least, he was until he joined the Nazi Party and embraced Jew-hatred. Then the Glaser parents cut him off. Baudissin had recently been seconded to an SS-brigade; Himmler was appointing art experts to every SS combat group. Just before he left, he had set up this exhibition.

There was a banner across the gallery's grimy neoclassical facade, proclaiming the 'Exhibition of Shame'. Glaser shook his head in weary disbelief at the title: *The Spirit of November: Art in the Service of Decay*. 'November' referred to

316

the 'November Criminals' – Hitler's recombinable con-
spiracy of Jews, Marxists and Social Democrats, who were
supposed to have lost Germany the war, in November 1918.

The man who had actually lost Germany the war – even
more so than Hindenburg, his commanding officer, who
was now President – was General Ludendorff. Ludendorff
had sued for peace too early, calling for the November
Armistice. Uniquely in the history of warfare, thousands
of undefeated soldiers, bewildered at the surrender, had
marched back home in formation, with their weapons intact. Many of them went straight into the various Freikorps
units.

Glaser imagined himself buttonholing Hitler, and telling
him this: 'Herr Hitler, the man responsible for losing
Germany the war was marching right next to you, at the
Beer Hall Putsch – Erich Ludendorff. It wasn't the Jews.
It wasn't the Marxists. It wasn't the Social Democrats. To
avenge Germany's defeat, all you had to do was turn round
and shoot him.'

Would it have made any difference? Probably not.

Entrance to the exhibition was free, though only those over
twenty-one were allowed in, presumably because of the
corrupting effect of what was on show. Glaser joined a
lengthy queue of visitors, stretching to the end of the block.

Having reached the entrance, he eased his way through
the crush to read the exhibition's aims, set out in hand-
painted black Gothic script on a wooden panel, just inside
the door:

The exhibition means to give, at the outset of a new age
for the German people, a first-hand survey of the grue-
some last chapter of those decades of cultural decadence
that preceded the great change.

The spacious exhibition rooms, so familiar from his youth, had been reduced by trelliswork structures, creating cramped rooms within rooms. The visitor was crowded right up against the paintings, which had been hung close together, crooked, and at odd heights, on rough burlap stretched over the trelliswork. They were poorly lit, by light from distant windows. Comments about them were painted on notices pinned to the burlap, in large red or black lettering, with plenty of exclamation marks.

The first comment Glaser read was next to Oskar Schlemmer's portrait, *Paracelsus: The Lawgiver*. It said 'Your taxpayers' money has been wasted on this daub.' It quoted a huge amount paid by the gallery for the painting. The price had been converted to the old Reichsmark value, before the mid-1920s currency reform, to make it look extortionate.

As Glaser knew well, *Paracelsus: The Lawgiver* had been bought for the gallery by Baudissin five years ago. It had not excited any comment then, either about the work itself or the price paid for it. Glaser rather liked it.

But as he stood, admiring the stylised, rounded, white face of Paracelsus, pointing at himself, in that intriguingly self-referential, individualised way, a middle-aged couple read the scrawled comments about it, and started complaining about this 'swindle' by 'Jew art dealers'.

Glaser walked on, along trelliswork fencing which corralled him and the crowd around him into the next area. A small space had been dedicated to the work of Jewish artists.

One of the many myths Hitler had managed to establish in the public mind was that there were not many Jewish painters. Jankel Adler, Marc Chagall and Lasar Segall were represented, and vilified, here, but the Nazis had missed, or did not know about, Chaim Soutine, David Bomberg or, closer to home, Katz, Ludwig and Else Meidner, Haizmann,

Freundlich and many others.

Max Liebermann, formerly President of the Prussian Academy of Arts, was a Jew, but not really an Expressionist. Would he be represented? Glaser looked round the ghastly little fenced cubicle. He wasn't, but that might have been an oversight, not policy.

Glaser looked at Philipp Bauknecht's *Three Herdsmen*. The bright colours of its Expressionist treatment, and perhaps the shepherds being pictured in earnest discussion, provoked the commentary in red capital letters next to it: 'German sons of the soil, the Yid view.' Glaser shook his head.

The next room was dedicated to 'the progressive collapse of sensitivity to form and colour.' Glaser joined a knot of visitors, to see what it was they were talking about, with such evident derision. It was Lovis Corinth's *Ecce Homo*. Corinth had taught August Macke in his early days. Glaser was heavy-hearted at seeing him represented here.

'He's making fun of us,' Glaser heard someone say. The handwritten information told the public that *Ecce Homo* had been painted after Corinth had had a stroke. Glaser knew that some of his paintings, done before the stroke, had been accepted and approved of by the Nazis.

Political paintings were featured in the next area – not a subject which moved Glaser, particularly. There was a quotation from the communist Georg Grosz on a daubed notice: 'How does the artist rise in the bourgeoisie? By cheating.' Grosz's sketch *Blood is the Best Sauce* showed soldiers bayoneting workers, while two square-headed bourgeois tucked into a huge meal with wine, in the foreground.

Out of sheer bloody-mindedness, toward Grosz, not the Nazis, Glaser wondered what the wine was, and whether it was a good vintage. The Nazi-scrawled legend above the drawing read 'Grosz's satires on the family and society are intended to whip up hatred.'

319

Grosz probably would not have disagreed with that.

The crowds were a little thinner, further on into the exhibition. They were quiet at the sight of 'moral degeneracy, harlots and pimps.' Labelled 'Deriding German Womanhood', nudes by Karl Hofer, Kirchner, Paul Kleinschmidt and Otto Muller were bunched up in two uneven rows. Glaser felt that German womanhood was better served by them than by the empty, though equally explicit, nudes of Hitler's pet artist, Adolf Ziegler – affectionately known as The Prince Of Pubic Hair.

Glaser looked round for a favourite of his, Dix's brothel scene, *The Salon*. He had mixed feelings about not finding it here. He thought it showed tenderness and compassion for women. Dix painted breasts, in their manifold variety and beauty, as well as anyone Glaser had ever seen. But Dix appeared further on. His powerful anti-war paintings were condemned as unpatriotic and treasonable.

Glaser had a soft spot for Otto Dix, an artist of great creativity and originality, fundamentally incapable of painting a boring line or colour. Dix often painted artificial limbs – piles of them sometimes – and amputees. This actually amused Glaser. Here, the biting *War Cripples* was held up for condemnation. It showed four stylised beings made grotesque by war. One had two pegs for feet, one one peg, one was in a wheel-chair and one, pushing the wheelchair, was displaying the card showing him registered as war-wounded.

Glaser hoped Dix was safe, and surviving. He had been dismissed from his teaching post – as had Oskar Schlemmer, Käthe Kollwitz; the local artist, Willi Baumeister; and Beckmann and Hofer and Max Liebermann and Pechstein. Some – like Beckmann – had got out. Many of them, Glaser knew, were surviving in the Third Reich by what was being called 'inner emigration' They stayed in their homes as much as possible, relying on relatives for food, hardly moving, hardly daring to breathe.

In the next room, Glaser thought of Schultze-Naumburg's work of breaking down the distinction between image-making and art – which in effect was the abolition of art. All the scrawled captions here used the vocabulary of biology, parasitology and illness to attack Expressionist painting. Glaser read one of them:

It is not the mission of art to wallow in filth for filth's sake, to paint the human being only in a state of putrefaction, to draw cretins as symbols of motherhood, or to present deformed idiots as representatives of manly strength.

The crowd were noticeably quieter here. Was there a sense of regret? Glaser could only hope so. He looked at Otto Mueller's *Gypsy Woman,* who was a negress. Enough, on its own, to make the work an object of vilification.

Glaser was growing weary; thinking of heading for the exit. Then he saw a picture by Edvard Munch. Munch's *The Sick Child* was regarded as the first Expressionist masterpiece. 'It's not the chair that should be painted,' Munch had written, 'but what the artist has felt at the sight of it.' Expressionists paint from the inside, out. In the translation from Norwegian Glaser had read, Munch called this '*Seelemalerei* – soul art.'

But even so, Glaser had not expected to find his work here. Munch really *was* Nordic. He was not only blond, blue-eyed and tall, but considerably better-looking than anybody in the Nazi hierarchy – not a particularly high bar to reach, admittedly. He had also been presented with the Goethe Medal for Science and Art, just last year, by President Hindenburg.

But then Glaser remembered: Adolf Ziegler – in his capacity as head of the Munich Academy – had pronounced that the work, not the acceptability of the artist, was paramount in assessing racial deviance.

So, high up on the wall, tilted at an angle, was *The Kiss* – a study in the cobalt blue Munch favoured. A couple were merged in passion, kissing behind a blue curtain, while tiny figures of passers-by went about their lives in a blue street.

Glaser loved the clandestine element in the couple's love. They were right to hide their love. All great love, he believed, must be hidden, to protect it. Lotte often rebuked him for being too closed in on himself – too secretive. But, in the deepest matters, this secrecy was essential. And never more so than in these terrible times, when the very goodness of life itself was being seized, tossed in mockery, and smashed.

Glaser had had enough and made his way through the crowds to the exit. He almost missed it. He saw it on his way out, when he wasn't even looking at the paintings any more. He stopped in front of *Blue Horses*, suddenly happy. Here was the soul of Franz Marc, fused with the soul of animals and landscape. It was moving and beautiful. Truly beautiful. For the first time in a long time Glaser felt there was hope. As long as there were horses, blue horses, there was hope.

Glaser left the exhibition and took a taxi to Poppenweiler. Was it curiosity, as his mother kept saying? Maybe. That or defiance. The smell of manure all over the single street assailed him. He was glad he had brought his silver-topped black cane, Lotte's present to him, as he made his way gingerly over to the barn. There was nobody about.

Even the horses in the fields didn't look up at him.

He went into the huge, dark Dutch barn. The last time he had been here, he was eighteen, the same age Kaspar was now. He looked up. There was a lower hayloft and a higher one, up where the roof narrowed. For a second he felt sick and giddy. He waited until it cleared.

Emmi Raschke had been in his class at school in Ludwigs-burg. She was the most beautiful girl he or anybody else had ever seen. She was so beautiful it burdened her; it made her sad. He never understood why she chose him – not until now. Now, with the intensity of coming doom, he felt he had only to open his mind, and the very universe itself would give up its secrets for him to understand.

Emmi Raschke was not only beautiful, she was also witty. She was always making jokes; it came naturally to her. Nobody laughed much, because nobody ever listened to her. She was the Beautiful One; she was not allowed to be anything else. But Gerhard Glaser had listened. He had laughed at her jokes – he had always appreciated humour.

So he had won Emmi, the beauty. And when he had been sent to Munich for treatment, as a partial amputee, he had won another beauty. The schoolgirl Lotte Bachhuber had been visiting her father, in the same hospital ward. Who would have thought it? They had kept in touch until he finished his law studies. They wrote; they visited each other. Then he had come to Munich to practise law and marry her.

Glaser leaned on his cane and looked up, overcoming the dizziness this time. He had just made love to Emmi, on a blazing August day, after the harvest. It was his first time and hers, and it had been wonderful. A triumph. She had screamed her love and pleasure at his possession of her. All the world lay at his feet. He had forgotten, that was all, that they had gone up to the top loft, not the lower one, to be more secret. He had roared his love for life, and star-jumped through the air. All the way down. And landed with his entire weight on his left leg.

11

When Glaser returned home from Poppenweiler, a note was waiting for him on the Kerner dresser.

'Who is it from?' he asked his mother, before he opened it.

'I don't know. I found it on the mat in the hall. It's addressed to you.'

The note said. 'See you at the Station Restaurant at two o'clock tomorrow. I'll bring everything you need for the journey. Your friend, Kurt.'

There was an afternoon train from Stuttgart to Munich. He was clearly intended to be on it. 'I shall be leaving tomorrow, Mama,' Glaser said.

'Yes,' old Frau Glaser replied. 'I thought you might be.'

Just as Glaser was leaving next day, his mother presented him with a heavily wrapped parcel. Glaser was irritated. The note from Sepp Kunde hinted that he should bring nothing with him, as the dynamite, presumably in a case of some sort, would be given to him.

'Open it,' Frau Glaser said.

'What here? Now?' They were standing in the hallway. The taxi was waiting outside.

'Yes.'

Glaser was about to protest. Then he understood. His mother thought she might never see him again. He tore impatiently at the paper, sealed round the gift. Inside, was an exquisite Seraphia de Becké faience dish; Ludwigsburg

324

pottery, flower pattern, centred on an open red rose. The choice had been carefully made. Since boyhood, Glaser had preferred the lower-fired, cheaper, pottery-ware to the refined cobalt-blue patterned porcelain.

'Thank you, Mama,' he said. He clumsily rewrapped his gift and went out to the taxi. As it drove off, he realised he had forgotten to say goodbye.

The station restaurant occupied more than half of the area of Ludwigsburg station. It was a ponderous portal to travel, with a high-arched ceiling and massive dusty windows. Glaser nursed a glass of opaque new wine and a slice of onion tart, as he waited for Sepp Kunde. His present from his mother lay awkwardly in his lap, its brown paper coming undone. There were more waiters and waitresses than customers, but even so Kunde's appearance out of nowhere, at his table, startled him. He was carrying a large workers' case.

'Gerhard, how nice to see you again, after so long.'

A wave of irritation swamped Glaser at Kunde's easy manner. He had held the power of life and death over this man at their first meeting, at the Dachau camp, and now he was presuming to treat him like one of his comrades. They were using the *du* form with each other, but Kunde had rather forced that at the meeting with the communists.

He nodded and said, '*Grüss Gott*, Kunde' curtly.

Sepp Kunde sat, pushing the case under the table, next to Glaser. He ordered a Dinkelacker beer. They sat in silence until it appeared, in a grey half-litre clay mug. Kunde eyed its mass of foam approvingly, then took a huge swig, tilting his head back. His Adam's apple moved spasmodically as he swallowed.

Finally, he banged the mug down. 'So. How's things, Gerhard?' he said.

'Fine.'

'If I give you an address in Munich, can you remember it without writing it down?'

'I think I can manage that. Yes.'

'Türkenstrasse. Number ninety-four. The name on the doorbell is Limmer.'

Glaser nodded. He badly wanted Kunde to go. He had never carried a suitcase the size of the one now nestling against his artificial leg. After a lot of thought, he had brought the ebony cane with him, mainly because he was reluctant to abandon it in Ludwigsburg. But he was unsure if it would be a help or a hindrance. He wanted to use the walk to the ticket office to experiment with case and cane. He was apprehensive and wanted to get on with it.

Kunde, however, was in no hurry, or so it seemed. 'The dynamite is in a false-bottom of the suitcase,' he said. 'There's some space at the top, though not much.' He nodded at Glaser's parcel. 'Hey – give me that. I'll put it in the case for you now.'

Glaser nodded. He handed the dish in its flapping brown paper to the communist, feeling the familiar mix of anger and helplessness when people undertook routine tasks for him. Kunde put the dish on top of the high false bottom of the case, relocked it, then pushed it back under the table.

'Here's the key to the case,' he said. 'You might get away with a superficial search, if they don't suspect you.' As they both knew, the Nazis had been checking all but the most local of trains, looking for couriers and subversive material, since the summer. 'Bringing that parcel was maybe not such a bad idea,' Kunde added.

Glaser, the tyro conspirator, accepted his undeserved praise with a nod. He doubted he would remain undetected after even a superficial search, with or without his parcel. To his relief, Kunde's next few massive swallows emptied his mug, which he left upside-down on the table. He banged the table with his knuckles.

'Gerhard, my fellow Swabian, you will understand what I mean when I say I hope we never see each other again?'

Glaser was getting really fed up, not only with the diminutive communist, but with this cloying Swabian brotherhood stuff. He thought of himself as a lawyer first, a family man second, and a German third. Being Swabian meant little to him, apart, maybe, from the outstanding food and wine. It occurred him that he loathed communists not only intellectually, but aesthetically. They got hold of one simple idea and hammered it into the ground, over and over and over again. It was amazing how ugly and one-dimensional that made them.

'I, too, hope we never meet again,' Glaser said, with complete sincerity.

Kunde stood, gave Glaser a long firm handshake, man to man, or Swabian to Swabian, and struck one final blow in the class war by making no attempt to pay for his beer when he left.

Glaser called the waitress over. He paid for Kunde's beer and for his own food and drink. She did not give him a glance, as he walked out with a case he had not come in with.

But even before he reached the heavy double-doors at the exit, he realised he just could not balance himself with both case and cane. The cane stopped him leaning to the left, to compensate for the weight of the case in his right hand. He was constantly nearly toppling over to the right. He detoured to the toilets and abandoned the cane in a cubicle.

The unhindered walk to the ticket office was more successful, as he learned to rebalance himself. He was dreading the steps to the platform. In the event, he stopped at the foot of the stone stairs, simultaneously inviting and dreading assistance. Sure enough, a concerned elderly woman in black, in an elaborate brimmed hat, ordered her husband to carry the case up for him. The husband had a gold Party pin at his lapel. He huffed and puffed, banging the case down at the top of the stairs, to show his resentment at the task. Glaser managed a suitable expression of gratitude.

Trains on the branch line to Stuttgart were frequent. When the next one came, he half threw the case up the iron platform-step and followed it. He kept it next to him for this much shorter part of the journey. The vineyards at the Ludwigsburg end of the route reminded him of the Trollinger the von Hesserts had served, that first time he was a guest in Ello's room.

At Stuttgart Hauptbahnhof, Glaser coped with disembarking from the local train, and the walk, and the steps to another platform, to await the Munich long-distance. But the platform was packed solid with travellers. The train was due in twenty minutes. He found a place on a bench and sat down.

The train was late. As it stopped, and the first passengers disembarked, everyone on the platform swarmed forward, pushing and shoving, barging past the disembarkers. Glaser was swept along in the crowd, to the steep steps, then up into a carriage, just about keeping his balance.

Inside, as he had planned, he put the case up on the luggage rack and sat two or three seats up from it, where he could still see it. The case was quickly surrounded by other peoples' luggage. An enormous rucksack belonging to a middle-aged man in hiking clothes was half on top of it. The hiker must be on the way to join a hiking group or club of some sort – all hikes now had to be authorised; hiking alone was illegal.

Glaser leaned back, exhausted, in his seat. He was sweating, but dry mouthed. At least the weather was reasonable. He did not think he could have coped with the slippery surfaces rain brought.

He was lucky to have found a place. Not only was every seat in the train quickly occupied, travellers were jammed up against each other, standing in every available inch of floor-space.

This, Glaser felt, was either very good or very bad: Nazis doing a document check might give up quickly, from sheer discomfort. On the other hand, if they had suspicions, they were likely to order everybody off the train, while they conducted a search. Glaser knew this happened regularly. The delays and cancellations it caused were one reason the trains were always so crowded, and always late.

Glaser noticed how many travellers around him were in uniform, of one sort or another: SA, soldiers, Hitler Youth, a few SS or SD, even a group of BdM girls about Magda's age. It was like a troop mobilisation. People often compared these times with August 1914. That sense of excitement. The war was not over, after all. The new Germany, under Adolf Hitler, would continue it, and the last battle would be our victory. Glaser groaned aloud at the thought.

The first names the train passed through were typically Swabian: Esslingen, Plochingen, Göppingen. Glaser did not wish to leave them behind. He felt as if he were being taken from his past into an unwelcome present. He thought of Lotte, not as she is now, but as the tall, graceful, Titian-headed teenager; Lotte Bachhuber, as he had first known her.

The train headed south before it turned east. There was a check at Memmingen station. Glaser saw them on the platform, out of the window, through hissing white steam from the train. Gestapo. He was in a middle carriage. Two of them boarded from each end. At a major check like this, he knew they would be searching luggage, as well as checking identity cards.

Now what? He could fetch his case and disembark – a

MICHAEL DEAN

traveller heading for Memmingen. But he must do it quickly, or it would be obvious he was evading the check. He had not found out if there was another train after this one. He cursed himself for his carelessness.

He glanced down the platform. Passengers and their luggage were being taken off the train; cases were being opened, travellers interrogated, lists checked. He had slipped his followers in Munich, outside the Ministry of Justice. Surely his name was on the wanted list?

At that moment, the middle-aged hiker claimed his rucksack from the overhead luggage rack, straining past fellow passengers.

'Excuse me,' Glaser called out. 'Can you give me my case? It's next to your rucksack.'

The hiker, hectic and bad-tempered from being buffeted by his fellow passengers, glared at him. But by now Glaser had stood and was making his way through the crush. His handicap was evident. Most people assumed he was a wounded war veteran, like so many others. The hiker's expression softened.

With a show of strength, he swung the case through the air. Its balance was clearly not what he had expected. Glaser failed to take it from him cleanly. It fell on the floor, banging against a woman, who dutifully screamed. A young man in a Hitler Youth Leader uniform picked the case up and returned it to Glaser with a smile.

Glaser followed the hiker, who barged a way through to the carriage door, bellowing 'Excuse me!' non-stop, although there was clearly no hurry. People were still being taken off the train. It would be detained for a long time – perhaps for hours. The platform was already crowded, a scene of chaos. Each pair of Gestapo men was engulfed by a growing circle of travellers, most with luggage, waiting to be checked.

Glaser made his way along the platform toward the

330

station exit. He was expecting a challenging shout every
step of the way, but none came.

Outside Memmingen station there were, to Glaser's relief,
three black taxis. He commandeered the first, calculating
how far he could ask to go. The driver stowed the case in
the boot. Glaser sat in the front.

'*Heil Hitler!*' he said, as the driver took his place again
behind the wheel.

'*Heil Hitler!* Where to?'

'Landsberg-am-Lech,' Glaser said. He realised it would be
safer to have a cover story, so he started chatting. 'Take me
to the fortress,' he said. 'I'm a lawyer, prosecuting some of
the scum we've put away in there.'

'They don't need lawyers,' said the driver, as he pulled
out of the station. 'Straight to the executioner's axe with
the lot of them. That's what I say.'

'Hey!' Glaser said. 'You'll put me out of a job, my good
man.'

The taxi driver laughed. Glaser made patriotic chit-chat
for the rest of the drive. He was surprised how easy it was:
Hitler is like a sculptor, Glaser told the driver. He pulverises
the figurines of tiny warring factions into their constituent
raw clay, then reconstitutes one huge noble Aryan figure
from that clay. The driver hadn't heard that one. He
nodded approvingly.

He himself, Glaser said, was from Stuttgart. 'Not a
single shop in Stuttgart,' he went on, 'is now Jewish owned.
Everything is cleaned up – *Judenrein*.' The driver nodded
approvingly.

Eventually, they stopped outside a high-walled building
which looked like a sanatorium. Glaser had never seen
Landsberg Fortress before. He glanced curiously at the
stone archway leading to the prison, as the taxi driver
hauled his case from the boot.

He could be standing right where the Party photographer, Hoffmann, had taken his photograph of Hitler on his release from Landsberg: a saturnine Hitler stood sideways on to the photographer's car, in belted mackintosh and plus-fours, hand hovering – as so often – over his groin.

Stranded outside the fortress-prison, with his case, Glaser had no idea what to do next.

He was reluctant to ask for help at the gatehouse, next to the archway. After a few minutes, another taxi appeared, bringing visitors. He thankfully hailed it on its way out, telling the driver he was heading for Munich. The driver took him to Landsberg-Nord station. He caught the next local evening train.

It was half empty. Glaser looked for travellers who might be workers. He found a couple, in blue overalls, and got into conversation. Feeling more of a heel than he had with the taxi driver from Memmingen station, he invented a colourful story about his war wound, and how he had been awarded an Iron Cross first class for his bravery. When the train arrived at Munich Hauptbahnhof, he asked them if they would carry his case to a taxi. It was the first time he had ever asked for help in this way. They were happy to oblige.

Walking slowly, Glaser let the one carrying the case get ahead, talking fast to the other one. With his suitcase loaded, he told the driver to go to the top of Türkenstrasse.

He watched the taxi out of sight before he rang the Limmers' bell. An old man opened the door and wordlessly let him in. When he unlocked the suitcase, in the Limmers' tiny main room, the dish his mother had given him was smashed to tiny pieces. As far as he could tell, the dynamite was fine.

12

When Sepp Kunde reached Munich, tired, hungry and footsore after walking by night and sleeping in woods and hedgerows by day, the elderly Limmer parents welcomed him as a hero. They installed him in their now absent son's bedroom.

That same night, at midnight, Kunde walked to the site of the future House of German Art, at the top end of Prinzregentenstrasse. A construction resembling an open-air theatre was being built for the opening ceremony. As Ello had said in her telephone call to him at the Linde, the white granite block was in place, and it was unguarded. It was on a shallow black stone platform, large enough to take the Party Bonzen and eminent guests.

Kunde stepped onto the platform. Even a small man like him could bend comfortably over the granite block. He looked into it. It had already been hollowed out at the top, to accommodate the scroll in its steel tube, which Ello had told him Hitler would place in it.

After it had been placed, plaster would no doubt be poured on top of it. Kunde quickly measured the block with a tape-measure, memorising the dimensions.

Back at the Limmer place, Kunde slept like a dog for twelve hours, then sat motionless for a while, before starting work.

Georg Limmer's old bedroom was bedecked with pennants from a former Red Football Club and Red Cycling

Club. There were also some Reemtsma cigarette cards of footballers, on the dresser. As a boy, Kunde had collected sets of Reemtsma cigarette cards himself. He had sent up for the album and meticulously pasted them all in, on the kitchen table of the cottage in Poppenweiler.

But he regretted it now. Ello had told him the owner of the cigarette company, Philipp F. Reemtsma, was a Nazi capitalist of the worst sort. He had put up a sizeable chunk of the twelve million Reichsmarks for the House of German Art. An industrialist called Flick and her own father had put up most of the rest, Ello had said. Reemtsma, Flick and Ello's father, Cajetan von Hessert, would all be guests of honour at the ceremony.

Happy and absorbed, Kunde sat cross-legged, tailor-fashion, on the floor. He was surrounded by his tools: an assortment of wood planes, hammers, set-squares, tin shears, graving tools, a pad saw, a precision ruler, scissors, pliers, wood clamps, rasps and fine wood files. As well as the dynamite, he also had clock movements, insulated wire and a six-volt storage battery.

The battery was to supply electricity, as a hissing fuse was out of the question. A pistol shot would have been possible, but would have been his death warrant as well as Hitler's. He had the precise time of Hitler's speech from Ello. It was to begin at two-thirty on October 15th.

The primary mechanical action of the bomb was a fifteen-day Westminster alarm clock. A series of cog-wheels and levers, soldered to the back of the movement, would activate the timing device, set to three o'clock. At that time, it would move a lever. This in turn triggered a system of springs and weights to launch a steel-tipped shuttle, which would strike the percussion cap of a rifle round, minus its bullet, embedded in the dynamite. By the time the dynamite blew, Kunde intended to be safely in Austria.

As he worked, he entered a familiar world where the

soothing necessity of precision excluded all else. It was a world free of people, whose unremitting evil and venality never ceased to disgust him. But after a few hours, for the first time in his life, his concentration wavered.

He was making the plaster to paste over the top of the bomb. It was a finicky non-technical job, not one he particularly enjoyed. He had to blend the plaster to the exact colour of the granite. And while he was doing this, he had carnal thoughts of Ello. They made him tumescent at once. Then he became aware of a strange inner warmth which until now he had felt only as a result of precision working. He was plagued by a restlessness entirely alien to him. It was accompanied by a yearning to see her, to be in her company. He fought it down, but it scared him.

He hoped to install everything in one night. Carrying the bomb to the site was, he reckoned, the most dangerous part of the operation. In a battered rucksack, he packed some clothes and toiletries on top of the various components of the bomb. Wearing a worn dark-blue suit, a brown pullover and black shoes, he bade the Limmers goodbye and set off.

It was a moonless night. He had chosen his route through the streets with care, walking in a huge circle almost as far as the Victory Gate, so he could approach the site from the north, through the Englischer Garten. He arrived just after midnight. He was fresh, having taken plenty of sleep during the day, and content and at peace with himself.

He deepened the existing hollow in the granite block patiently, using steel hand-drills of different diameters. To save space, he had abandoned plans to have a back-up clock. They would just have to hope Hitler's phenomenal luck finally deserted him. Working by the light of a torch wrapped in a blue handkerchief, he started to place the mechanism in the granite block. The explosion could be timed up to fifteen days after starting the clock.

He packed the clockwork mechanism, sealed with insulating material, inside a wooden box lined with cork. It was completely sealed except for two holes, through which he fed the ignition wires attached to the detonator. Then he attached the detonator to the dynamite.

A piece of plywood, cut to the dimensions of the block, was placed over the bomb and a layer of plaster applied over it. The colour was a perfect match. At the end of it all, a faint ticking from the Westminster clock was audible, even through the box lined with cork, but only if you put your ear next to the granite block.

Kunde admired his handiwork. There was enough dynamite to blast the granite block to pieces, killing everyone on the raised stone platform. Fortunately, Hitler could not be seen in public with Ello. She would therefore be in the wooden grandstands, twenty metres away. Anybody back there would be safe. So even Glaser's bourgeois squeamishness was being catered for: No paintings damaged, only Nazis and Nazi sympathisers killed.

To minimise the risk to the Limmer parents, Kunde had arranged to stay away from their flat overnight. He spent the rest of the night, and the next day, hiding out under the trees in the Englischer Garten.

At midnight on the following night, he set off – trudging towards the Austrian border. He reached it five nights later, and crossed into Austrian territory over a remote mountain path. Once there, he kept on walking, so miserable he could have howled, because he would never see Ello again.

And all that time, the bomb in the granite block ticked quietly away toward its explosion date – fifteen days from the day he had set it, which was on October 1st.

13

The evening that, as Christa Forster put it, her husband abandoned the children at the cinema, the Forsters quarrelled. Christa accused Karl-Heinz of being obsessed with Glaser. Not only that, the obsession was changing his character. Once easy-going and smiling, he was increasingly morose and uncommunicative.

Karl-Heinz Forster's response was complex, far-reaching and permanent: he withdrew from Christa, and to an extent from the children. He clammed up about his work. And he became a fervent Nazi. So when he wangled himself a secondment to the SD, big news he would once have trumpeted with grins, hugs and celebrations, he did not tell Christa or the children about it at all.

Forster had assumed that the Reich Security Service – SD – would take command of Hitler's security for the Day of German Art, as the ceremony on October 15th was known. The day when Glaser and his gang would attempt to assassinate the Führer. Forster was consumed by the need to foil the plot and finally arrest Glaser.

The Chief Inspector contemptuously dismissed the part of von Hessert's statement, as reported by Elsperger, which attempted to exonerate Glaser. He referred to the plot at all times as the Glaser – Kunde plot. He had yet again requested Glaser's arrest and interrogation under torture, but Heydrich had again overruled him. Glaser, Heydrich had instructed, could not be touched, as long as von

337

Hessert said he was innocent.

So Forster had to content himself with personally placing Glaser in the October 15th A-File – listing enemies of the Reich living in the vicinity of an event to be protected.

The feebleness of this routine measure had left him fuming with rage. To make himself feel better, he had ordered another detailed search of Glaser's flat, on the suspect's return to Munich, and another search of the Bachhuber place.

Forster had also checked the Pension Walther in Lucerne, the name Magda had given him. It did not exist. Glaser had not been in Lucerne, or anywhere else in Switzerland. He had been staying with his mother. This was confirmed by the Gestapo in Ludwigsburg, but unfortunately only after his return.

Glaser had been spotted arriving back at Munich Hauptbahnhof, with no luggage. But as he had left with no luggage, all that signified was that he had clothing at the family home. There was no trace of Kunde, despite the massive effort put into the search for him, both in Munich and in the area around Poppenweiler.

Heydrich briefed Forster on security for the Day of German Art: Hess had issued a directive that there was to be co-operation between the various organisations involved: the SD, SS, SA, Leibstandarte Adolf Hitler (LSAH), Reichsarbeitsdienst, Gestapo, Political Police and the Führer Begleit-Kommando.

Preliminary security measures had reflected this co-operation: A-Files had been pooled. Security checks on the workmen building the site had been circulated. All organisations were issued with the same 1:25,000 map of the area around the site, with possible sniper vantage points marked in black or red. A second map, showing the sewerage system in the area, had also been issued to all organisations. The work of interviewing local explosives experts and watch and clockmakers had been shared.

The security measures were started three weeks ahead of the event. Forster had wanted them started earlier, in view of the proven threat to the Führer. Heydrich had, for once, supported him on this, but they had both been overruled by Hess. The reason given was that boredom set in if security measures were started too early, and boredom and over-familiarity led to mistakes. Forster regarded that as pathetic.

Then there had been an unexpected development, which had caused more delay: A conciliatory Heydrich told Forster about it, over coffee in his office. Out of the blue, Himmler had been told by Hess that the Old Fighters were to be put in overall charge of security for October 15th. This was a *Führerbefehl* – a personal command from Hitler.

It was unusual, Heydrich told Forster, unparalleled even, for Hitler to intervene in such details, but Heydrich said he was not surprised. The laying of the First Stone of the New Reich, in the Führer's beloved Munich, should surely be overseen by the men who had been with him longest – the Old Fighters. It was more surprising, to Heydrich at any rate, that of all the Old Fighters Hitler had chosen Julius Schreck for the honour of supervising security.

Forster said nothing, but he made the connection: When Sauer had sold Hitler's drawings of Geli to Ascher Weintraub, the Sauers' maid had reported it to Forster, as she had been well paid to do.

Forster, as Hess had instructed, had informed Georg Winter. The house servant had no doubt taken the tougher Julius Schreck with him to see Weintraub. They had recovered the drawings (murdering the Jew art dealer in the process). As a reward, no doubt, the chauffeur had asked to be put in charge of security for the Day of German Art. It would be a public sign of the Führer's esteem, putting one over on the Party newcomers and Party Bonzen he so resented.

Forster became even more sure of his supposition as the meeting to plan security for October 15th began, in Heydrich's office. Although Heydrich was in the chair, Schreck was immediately on his right, dressed not as a chauffeur, but as an SS-brigade leader.

Altogether, Forster noted with a touch of his old sardonic amusement, there were twelve men each side of the rectangular table stretching the length of Heydrich's office. One of the few – along with Forster – in mufti was Ernst Buchner, Director of Bavarian Art Galleries. Heydrich had invited him as an afterthought, in his capacity of organiser of the pageant.

When nominated by Heydrich, Buchner began describing the Objects of Homage, as they were known, sent by twenty-seven cities and eight provinces of the Reich, to mark their allegiance, on the significant coming day. Many were certificates, offering expressions of devotion to the Führer in beautiful calligraphy, usually combined with a hand-drawn rendering of the city's coat of arms.

There were also photographs and drawings of the various cities, or landscapes of the surrounding countryside. A woodcut portrait of Martin Luther, by Lucas Cranach the Younger, was among the works of art sent in homage, as were Adolph von Menzel lithographs, illustrating the History of Frederick the Great.

This litany was received in heavy, bored silence by the uniformed soldiers and police along the table. Forster hadn't grinned as widely for months. Buchner, mopping his brow with his red-spotted handkerchief, proceeded to details of the street decorations for the day, starting with those along the route of the Führer's cavalcade.

Speaking in a monotone, he told the meeting that Prinzregentenstrasse was to be lined with 160 pylons, each nearly forty feet high, crowned with the eagle and swastika. From the Hauptbahnhof to the city centre, there would be two hundred and thirty-four Blood Flags, at intervals of twenty-five feet, flying from flagpoles nearly thirty-five feet high.

Buchner then launched into a description of the pageant, on the theme of the Glorious History of German Culture, that was to follow the Führer's speech. He started to describe each float, in its order in the procession. This, however, was judged irrelevant to security. To the relief of the meeting, Heydrich held up a hand, commanding a halt to the droning monologue.

They proceeded to draw up three zones of concentrically tightening security around the site. Arrangements were made for patrols and guards; directives were drafted for the cessation of all releases from prisons and concentration camps; passes and codewords were agreed; the search both of sewers, and the flats of suspects was planned.

They drew up the usual Special Regulations for specific events. Forster had a suggestion ready. He put it forward authoritatively. It should be forbidden to throw flowers at the Führer's cavalcade, he said, in case a bunch of flowers concealed a bomb. This was well received.

The personal security of the Führer was then discussed. Hitler had forbidden a Reichswehr guard of honour, Heydrich told the meeting. Nobody, naturally, commented on the reason for this, but they all knew what it was: the Führer still had to appear to defer to the ancient and crumbling President Hindenburg. He had declared army honour guards as reserved for him.

Mindful of Hess's directive about co-operation, Heydrich continued, Hitler's security at the site would devolve on all the organisations represented in the room. As the Führer often declared that security should not come between him and his people, and should therefore be unobtrusive, security officers would be in plain clothes and would wear no insignia at all. Each man, therefore, would be trained to recognise the officer on his right and left by sight. Heydrich looked at all the representatives at the meeting in turn. Forster approved. He gave his chief a couple of crisp nods to signify as much.

At the end of all this, Heydrich handed over to Schreck, who announced which duties would be undertaken by the Old Fighters – after the *Führerbefehl*, they naturally had first option.

Schreck informed the meeting that the Old Fighters would mount a four-man honour guard, day and night, at the corners of the granite block, now always referred to as the First Stone of the New Reich. Every Munich Old Fighter would proudly serve his turn, Schreck said. He, Julius Schreck, as founder of the SS, proud bearer of the SS number one, would lead the first group of four.

There was a swelling murmur of *Richtig! Prima!* and a thunderous banging of knuckles on the table, as representatives of all the other organisations fell over themselves to signal agreement at the justice and rectitude of this arrangement, commanded by the Führer. Schreck smiled.

'The guard mounted by the Old Fighters will commence this evening,' Heydrich said, nodding at the Official Minute Taker, signalling the closure of the meeting. 'I give to the Minutes that the Honour Guard on the First Stone of the New Reich will commence at 6p.m., on October 2nd, 1933.'

14

Ello was back at the family villa, partly to get away from the block warden at the university, but also to take personal charge of the nursing arrangements made for Rudi. On the Day of German Art, she was woken by a dreadful noise of hammering and drilling from outside. She looked out of her bedroom window. Karolinenplatz was being decked out in black by a small army of workmen.

Over a late breakfast, her father told her the reason: Nazi dead, fallen for the revolution, were not to be forgotten, even on a day of celebration – *especially* on a day of celebration: men like Leo Schlageter, and the martyrs killed at the Beer Hall Putsch. Cajetan von Hessert, sipping thin breakfast coffee, was all for the idea.

A ring at the doorbell announced the chauffeur Schreck, come to drive her to the Prinzregentenplatz apartment. Ello was to travel in the Führer cavalcade, a signal honour which had been skilfully placed in Hitler's mind by Anni Winter.

She left Schreck waiting in the hallway while she changed and did her hair. Then she went back into the breakfast-room to say goodbye to her father. Cajetan was going directly to the ceremony. As there was plenty of time, he was reading the financial pages of the newspaper. Ello planted a pecking kiss on his forehead; the first time she had kissed him since she was seven.

'What's up with you?' he said. 'Ello? Look at me. Have you been crying?'

'No, I just slept badly. Rudi had a bad night.'

'I have no sympathy, Ello. If Rüdiger keeps bad company, he must expect to be beaten up and robbed in some low dive.'

'Quite. Goodbye, Papa.'

'Goodbye. How many more times?' Cajetan von Hessert disappeared back into the broadsheet folds of the *Münchner Neueste Nachrichten*.

Outside it was chilly, with drizzle stopping and starting. Ello shivered in the back seat of the Mercedes, and not only because she was in the company of the creepy Schreck.

The chauffeur had difficulty getting the Mercedes through the crush of workmen. Ello did not arrive at Hitler's apartment until they had finished lunch.

At a loose end until they left for the ceremony, she was passing Geli's room when she heard yelling from inside. She listened at the closed door. Hitler was shouting at Schreck and Hess. She feared the worst and sent a maid to fetch Anni Winter. The housekeeper appeared quickly, in one of her inevitable floral dresses.

'I heard the Führer shouting in Geli's room,' Ello said bluntly. 'What's going on?'

Anni's eyes shone. 'Well, madam. I'm sure Herr Hitler will tell you himself in due course. But he has just decided that Fräulein Raubal's earthly remains, together with his drawings of her, are to be placed in the foundation-stone.'

Ello shut her eyes: the First Stone of the New Reich was to be Geli's tomb. The entire Third Reich was to be Geli's bedroom – a specially designed mausoleum. Ello was swamped with dread. 'So, what will …?'

'I think there may be a short delay, madam,' Anni said. 'The stone will have to be hollowed out further to make room. I believe that is why Schreck is getting excited.'

'Thank you, Anni.'

The housekeeper gave a bobbing curtsey, a yellow-toothed smile, and was gone. Ello then made a snap decision – a decision which haunted her for the rest of her life. In fact, as she lay on her deathbed, at the age of eighty, in a handsome old brownstone in Brooklyn, with her loving children and grandchildren around her, calling that decision to mind was her last conscious act on earth.

She decided to tell Gerhard Glaser the bomb had been discovered.

Schreck, in SS uniform, summoned an SD motorcycle escort, drove the Mercedes full- tilt out of the square, and hurled it along Prinzregentenstrasse. The wide boulevard was already lined with cheering crowds, six or seven deep, waving triangular swastika flags on sticks. Oblivious to them, Schreck raced the heavy car to the site of the ceremony, at the top of the street.

Screens were hastily thrown up around the stone, while Schreck and two SD attacked the hollow with drills. In the noise, they did not hear the ticking of Kunde's Westminster clock. They penetrated the plaster easily, then splintered the unexpected plywood underneath.

In doing so, Schreck drilled through the insulated wires leading from the clock to the detonators. One wire was exposed to view. Oblivious of the danger, Schreck seized a rifle from one of the SD and furiously smashed away with the stock, destroying the clock. The bomb mechanism and the dynamite were uncovered and removed.

Masons were already on hand, ready to cover the scroll with plaster, when it had been laid in the stone. They made good the damage, then deepened the hollow, as the Führer had commanded. The screens were removed round the block of granite.

Schreck contacted Hess by radio. Hess decided to go ahead, as if nothing had happened. On his authority, the

Führer was not to be told of the bomb plot until after the ceremony. The cavalcade was about to leave the apartment. The ceremony was running on time.

As the procession of three Mercedes cars arrived at the site, an orchestra in traditional Bavarian costume, under a black Baldachin, struck up the Prelude from *Die Meistersinger von Nürnberg*. Ranks of SA, SS, Bavarian Police – all unarmed – and Hitler Youth stood at attention, as the dignitaries left their cars. Bunting covered bleachers surrounded the site. The area around the block of granite was planted with a thicket of Blood Flags, and strewn with carpets and streamers in red.

Ello, in a Grecian-style white dress, left the third car, tripped across the carpet and took her seat next to the photographer Hoffmann in the front row of the grand-stand. Hitler and Hess walked to the stone platform, followed by an adjutant carrying a canvas workers' bag, grabbed at the Prinzregentenplatz apartment at the last minute. It contained an urn, inside which were Geli's ashes and Hitler's drawings of her.

At the stone platform, the Führer was greeted by a figure dressed as Hans Sachs, the sixteenth-century cobbler, who was also a *Meistersinger* and writer of plays to be performed during Carnival. Already lined up on the stone platform were Nazi luminaries, and other guests of honour; including the Papal Nuncio, Vasallo di Torregrossa, and the financiers Philipp Reemtsma, Friedrich Flick and Cajetan von Hessert.

Heydrich, who had hosted a grand, musical opening ceremony at the Wittelsbach Palace the previous evening, was chattering away to the lanky, bespectacled mayor, Karl Fiehler, and the bullet-headed Gauleiter, Adolf Wagner, who was standing with his weight on his wooden right leg, hands on hips, roaring with laughter.

Standing alone and aside from them, von Epp was staring blankly into the middle distance. One day before his sixty-fifth birthday, he had been sidelined politically – his newly invented title of *Reichstatthalter* of Bavaria had turned out to be meaningless – and he was steadfastly refusing to contemplate the whirlwind he had helped whistle up.

The Nuncio, however, met Hitler's gaze with a look of admiration. 'For a long time I did not understand you,' di Torregrossa said, 'but now I do.'

Hitler looked through him. He no longer required the Nuncio's understanding, if he ever had. All that stood between him and total power was the fast-decaying body of President Hindenburg. He was looking beyond even power, to ultimate victory. And a longed-for death.

Ello stood, and left her seat. Hoffmann left his place at the same time, Rolleiflex camera at the ready, so her departure was not especially noticeable. She made her way through the crowds, across Prinz-Carl-Palais, the short distance to Galeriestrasse.

As the music stopped, Hitler laid a black metal tube into the hollowed granite block. It contained a handwritten scroll:

This Temple of Art is the First Building of the New Reich. It owes its existence to the will and the wishes of the renewer of the German Reich, Chancellor Adolf Hitler.

At a sign from Hess, the UFA film unit recording the event suspended filming. Hitler then took the urn containing Geli's ashes and his drawings of her – the drawings that had cost Ascher Weintraub his life – and placed it into the hollow, next to the tube with the scroll. One of the masons took a white bucket and poured a plaster and powdered-granite mixture into the block, filling it to the top. The

347

mixture would be hardened dry by the time Hitler finished his speech. After a pause of no more than a few seconds, the UFA film unit resumed filming.

Ello did not know how much danger Sepp was in, as a result of the bomb having been discovered. She had no idea where he was. He said he would leave for Austria, after he planted the bomb, but she did not know if he had. Part of her longed for him to still be in Munich. Did she think Sepp could possibly be with Glaser? However unlikely that was, logically, her heart raced and her body glowed as she half ran to Galeriestrasse, now swathed in billowing white and red from every building. She hardly cared any more that Hitler had survived, and their plans had come to nothing.

Two Political Police in plain clothes in a car outside Glaser's block of flats saw her go in. They recognised her, and radioed Forster. Forster told them to follow Glaser, if he left the flat, but on no account to enter it while Fräulein von Hessert was there.

Glaser took Ello's news with a wooden face. He said nothing at all. Kaspar was far more animated, vividly cursing Hitler and his luck – Germany's misfortune. Ello hurried back across the road to her place at the opening ceremony. Hitler, standing over the white granite block, was just beginning his speech:

'A race has fallen apart and is to be rebuilt. Today we do not want to dwell on the misfortune which befell us; the catastrophe which overcame us. We wish only to recognise that that which was broken must be built anew, so that decay can be transformed to something new and alive ...'

With the collar of his mackintosh turned up, Glaser made

his way down to the stone cellar of the block of flats. Like every resident, he had a key to the cellar door, which leads out to the alleyway. They were not watching the alleyway. They never did. He made his way out to the main Ludwigstrasse and headed south along Theatinerstrasse.

It had started to drizzle again. It made the pavement slippery.

Even though he was walking away from the ceremony, the streets were thronged with people. There were no cars or trams; traffic had been banned. He saw some floats from the pageant, coming toward him along the road. They were making their way to their starting position. It seemed fitting to Glaser that he was witnessing a Carnival procession – or part of one – going the wrong way, at the wrong time of year. The world had been perversely twisted; the world was out of joint.

The first float contained a twenty-metre-high plaster model of the House of German Art, as it would one day be – all neoclassical columns and mock-Greek porticos. The float rolled forward at walking pace, surrounded by men dressed as Charlemagne, Henry the Lion, Friedrich Barbarossa, Arminius – the full panoply of Germanic heroism.

The next float contained a huge golden eagle, symbolising a thousand-year Reich. It was surrounded by sitting and kneeling votive Valkyries, some with iron pieces around their breasts, some bare-breasted. Glaser found it impossible not to look – to desire them. A third float offered a giant papier-mâché Goethe, already a little the worse for wear in the rain.

As he walked, striding as fast as he could, Glaser thought of James Ensor. The Belgian pre-Expressionist was a flute player, like Kaspar. There was a photograph of him on a rooftop, sitting next to the chimney pot, playing his flute in his best suit. Ensor grew up above his parents' shop in Ostend, which sold Carnival masks. He saw Carnival not as a spectacle seen by the people, but as something they act out.

Glaser thought the Nazi twist of Carnival went even further. All the people must take part, there are no on-lookers. People are subsumed, they are changed into carnivalesque figures, with no souls, like the vestals and vassals on the floats he had just seen. They were part of a stylishly garish costumed procession to war and death, in the name of fabricated history, inside-out justice, gibberish science and lies.

In Ensor's *Entry of Christ into Brussels*, a mad farouche crowd of death-heads and masks welcomes Ensor as the phoney Christ at the head of a Carnival parade. But Ensor was harmless. This crowd was welcoming Adolf Hitler.

Glaser walked on.

Hitler continued his speech:

'Want and misery came upon our race with a terrible force. The foundations of our society are crumbling, and the fists of those bringing still further destruction are pounding at the very gates of the temples of our faith. Turmoil and conflict at every turn.'

As he passed the Cathedral, Glaser began to tire. His stump ached. He longingly pictured the quadrupled windows and clock tower of the Main Police Station. He hoped the Material Evidence Room, in the basement, would not be locked. He started to compose a tale to get somebody to unlock it, in case it was. The Mauser pistol used to kill Weintraub would still be there. It would have been unloaded, of course, but unspent cartridges are kept near the gun, in case they need to be fired for further forensic tests.

15

As the Main Police Station finally came into view, Glaser realised he had not thought of how he was going to get into the building itself. The door might be locked, on this great public holiday. He hoped a caretaker would have been left on duty.

But the doors were wide open. The vestibule desk was empty. He was assailed by a boom of gramophone music and a roar of revelry from offices on his right. Some female screams of delight broke into the bass notes of the music. As he paused on the threshold, there came the sound of breaking glass. It was so heavy Glaser thought a bottle, rather than a glass, had been smashed. A Green Police officer with his uniform dishevelled staggered out of a room at the end of the corridor. He swayed past Glaser and out into the street, without a glance.

Glaser thankfully remembered that the Main Police Station had a lift. Breathing heavily, he made his way to it, past a pool of evidently fresh vomit. The lift stank of vomit, too. The Material Evidence Room was three floors down, in the cellar. It was locked.

'Man shall not live by bread alone. When we regard the rebuilding of our race as the task of our age and our lives, we see not only an ailing economy, but an endangered culture. We can only envision that the German race will rise anew if German culture and above all German art emerge once more.'

Glaser stood there, nonplussed. The journey back up to the ground floor was a complete impossibility. He did not know why that should be, but he knew it with great certainty. There could be no plausible excuse for getting the Material Evidence Room opened in the middle of a festive celebration. He had come as far as he could. He would have slumped down on the floor, had such a manoeuvre been physically possible for him. He tried to weep, but no tears came. Then he heard sounds from inside the Material Evidence Room. It sounded like one couple, at least, having sexual intercourse.

Glaser thundered on the heavy wooden door with both fists. 'Open!' he cried out. 'Open in the name of the Political Police. Open or it will be the worse for you.' There was a muttered stream of swear words from the other side of the door.

'*Schon gut! Schon gut!*'

Glaser hit the door again with his fists. Eventually, it opened and a man wearing only a pair of SA trousers stood there, struggling to button his fly. Glaser pushed past him, into the Material Evidence Room. The man's love-partner was trying to hide behind one of room's many gunmetal cabinets. He was struggling into the uniform of an SA lieutenant.

'Get out!' Glaser yelled. 'Get out now, and return to duty, before I report you.'

Whey-faced, the two men fled, completing their dressing as they ran. Glaser stared at the array of huge metal cabinets, placed in chevrons. Each deep drawer of each cabinet was labelled with the name and date of the case. After a few minutes search, Glaser found the drawer with material evidence from the Weintraub case. He pulled it, and it opened smoothly on oiled runners.

In a linen bag, he found Ascher Weintraub's black jacket, folded and encrusted with dried blood. Also in the bag was the gun used to kill him. As he had surmised, the cartridges, five of them, three spent, two unspent, were in an envelope by the gun.

'Today we are consummating a symbolic deed. In painfully parting with what has been lost, we confidently begin to build the new, with our sights set on the future.'

After a few minutes fumbling, he loaded the gun. He put it in his mac pocket, then took the lift back up to the ground floor. An SS-man had passed out, measuring his length in the corridor. The screams from the revellers were even louder, as was the dance-band music from the gramophone. He left the Main Police Station and walked back the way he had come.

'A House of German Art shall rise up. Young Germany is constructing a special building to house its art.'

He made his way back toward the Cathedral. It had stopped raining.

'We are one race; we want to be one Reich. Just as we are fanatical in our commitment to the greatness of this Reich, to its peace, and to its honour as well; so, too, will we be adamant in not tolerating any arbitrary spirit of discord that may threaten the unity of our nation, or that an ignorant eccentricity weaken the political will.'

The walk back was easier. He had found a rhythm and was able to ignore the pain.

Reaching his goal began to seem inevitable to him. He had two cartridges in the gun, but whatever happened he would surely have time for only one shot. One shot. One shot and Germany's agony would be over.

353

When he reached the site of the laying of the foundation-stone, he could hardly believe his luck. There were no guards at all. He made his way through the crowd. He could see Hitler clearly.

'If today I have the proud fortune to be able to lay this cornerstone, then I hope that in doing so, I am showing this city and this country the way to the future.'

16

Two SD in plain clothes had spotted Glaser as he passed the cathedral, on the way back. He had been tracked ever since. 'Leave him to me,' Forster had radioed to all officers. The Chief Inspector began to make his way through the crowd.

'Since Berlin is the capital of the Reich; Hamburg and Bremen are the German shipping capitals; Leipzig and Cologne the capitals of German trade; and Essen and Chemnitz the capitals of German industry, so should Munich once more become the capital of German art.'

The crowds were thick, but Glaser was patiently making his way through them. The two SD following him radioed Forster for new instructions, but Forster again told all officers to leave Glaser to him. The Chief Inspector furiously shouldered his way through the crowd, toward where Glaser had last been reported. 'Police!' he bellowed. 'Stand aside there. Police!'

Glaser drew the pistol from the pocket of his mac. He had Hitler in his sights, somebody in the crowd saw him and there was a scream.

'May this city recall to mind its real mission of being a shrine to the sublime and the beautiful. It is in this spirit that we wish to lay this cornerstone for the First Building of the New Reich, dedicated to German Art.'

The figure costumed as Hans Sachs passed Hitler a silver hammer, just as Hoffmann crept close to him, Rolleiflex at the ready. The picture Hoffmann took went round the world; one of his best-known studies of the Führer. But it was a fake. The delicate silver hammer broke when Hitler hit it against a corner of the granite. Hoffmann's photograph, however, was skilfully doctored. It shows a whole hammer striking home. So that is what the German people saw. And that is what they were told.

Just as the hammer broke, Forster's fist smashed into the side of Glaser's head. He dropped the pistol as he fell. He was surrounded on the ground by plain-clothes security men. One of them picked up the pistol. Forster's boots were thudding into Glaser. The Chief Inspector had to be pulled off by his own men.

Part IX
Autumn 1933

1

Rudolf Hess was most satisfied with Chief Inspector Forster: his police work had led to the recovery of the Führer's drawings, with no scandal. He had uncovered and dealt with a plot to assassinate the Führer, and arrested the ringleader. Again, his work had been so competent and tactful that nothing of the plot was known to the outside world. This was important, at this delicate time of consolidation of the Third Reich's power.

Forster was summoned to Hess's office. 'I have a message for you from the Führer himself,' Hess said. 'He believes that the failure of this bomb plot against him is yet more evidence that he has been chosen by fate to complete his mission. He has instructed me to offer you any reward you wish.'

Forster replied that his only wish was to serve the Führer. That could be achieved more directly, he suggested, if he left police work for service in the SS.

Hess appointed him to lead the newly formed SS-brigade attached to the Political Police, at the SS rank of *Brigadeführer*, to which Heydrich had also just been promoted. As a further accolade, the brigade was to be named for him – *Standarte Karl-Heinz Forster*. Forster requested Elsperger as his second-in-command, in recognition of his outstanding work for the Reich.

Next day, the new *Brigadeführer* collected his uniform. He looked at himself in the mirror in his empty flat – Christa had taken the children away to her mother's. The uniform, crisp and fresh from the Hugo Boss factory over at Metzingen, was the deepest black. There was a swastika armband over the left sleeve, yellow braid on both shoulders, an oak leaf cluster on the lapel. On the index finger of his right hand, Forster wore a Death's Head Ring, a gift from Heydrich, identical to the one Heydrich's own chief, Himmler, had given him.

A car collected him and took him to the SS Headquarters in Karlstrasse, where he swore an Oath of Honour to serve Adolf Hitler unto death. He then undertook his first task in a life of direct service of the Führer: He interviewed Gerhard Glaser.

2

Glaser had been hustled away from the minor disturbance he had created at the laying of the First Stone of the New Reich. He was taken to Stadelheim, like a common criminal. There, his wounds were bathed and he was patched up. To his surprise, he was searched at the prison hospital by a trusty – none other than Sepp Kunde's twin, August.

'Do they think I'll tell you where Sepp is? I really don't know, you know.'

August gave a leery grin. His physical resemblance to Sepp was astonishing, but his manner was completely different. A sly, shifty quality pervaded everything he did.

'I've been told to make sure you don't commit suicide,' August said. 'That's what they're worried about.'

'I shan't do that.'

'Good. Take everything out of your pockets, please. If you've got anything you don't want them to see, you can give it to me. I'll get rid of it.'

Glaser stared at him. August was evidently sincere.

'There isn't anything,' Glaser said. 'I've got nothing to hide.'

When Glaser had handed everything over, August summoned a guard. Glaser's possessions were itemised; he signed for their removal. To his relief, no attempt was made to take his artificial leg.

He was taken to the cell he was to share with August. It

361

was brightly lit. He lowered himself onto his steel bed with a straw mattress over it, and lay with his hands behind his head. August chattered for a while, blithering on about the prison food, and what you were allowed to have sent in. His mindless small-talk, again, was so different from his twin, who spoke only when he had something to say. Before long Glaser fell asleep, while August was still talking – his exhaustion overcoming both the chatter and the light in his eyes.

There was a jangling of keys and the door banged open. A man in a badly cut grey suit entered the cell. He had a Hitler moustache and hair shaved high up the back of his head, like Himmler: 'Messner!' – he introduced himself. 'Glaser! Come! Interrogation!'

Messner handcuffed Glaser behind his back and pushed him outside. He tried to take his prisoner under the arm, as they walked along a corridor. Glaser fell twice. Messner was finally persuaded to let him walk unhandcuffed, at his own speed.

Forster had commandeered the Prison Director's office. He was alone in it, in his new SS uniform. He dismissed Messner to the outer office. Glaser wondered if Forster would gloat or become violent. He did neither.

'Sit down, Glaser. Where is Kunde?'

'I have no idea.'

'When did you last see him?'

'Three weeks ago.'

'Where?'

'At Ludwigsburg railway station. He gave me a suitcase full of dynamite to bring back to Munich.'

'Where did he get the dynamite?'

'I have no idea.'

'How did he arrange the meeting?'

'He left a note at my mother's house.'

'Where is the note now?'

'I destroyed it.'

'I will have that checked.'

'I'm sure you will.'

'Where was Kunde staying?'

'I have no idea.'

'Where did he go after he left you?'

'I have no idea.'

'How many people were involved in the plot to assassinate the Führer?'

'Two. Myself and Sepp.'

'And Rüdiger von Hessert?'

'He had nothing to do with it.'

'Did he know about it?'

'No.'

'That's odd. The information about it came from him. It was he who betrayed you.'

'I don't believe you.'

Forster gave a passable imitation of his old smile. 'I think you do. He was to pick up the dynamite in his father's car, but got cold feet.'

'Sepp and I discussed using von Hessert, but he is too unreliable. He is an iconoclast, but at heart a loyal Nazi. We never told him a thing.'

'Rubbish. And Ello von Hessert?'

'What about her?'

'She visited you just before you tried to kill the Führer.'

'Ello knows how I feel about Hitler. She knew nothing about the plot, but she had her suspicions. She was making sure I was in the flat, so Hitler was safe.'

'If Fräulein von Hessert knew of your traitorous feelings about the Führer, why did she not report them?'

'She did. Both she and Rüdiger warned Hitler about us.'

'Warned Hitler personally?'

'Yes.'

'How do you know?'

'Ello told me. She wanted us to mend our ways and become good National Socialists. She is Hitler's girlfriend after all.'

Forster shot him a look of reluctant admiration. He would not dare check this with Hitler personally, as Glaser knew perfectly well. In fact, not only was the Führer out of his league, so was Ello von Hessert. He would have to leave her to Hess.

'Why did you leave it so late to get the gun?' Forster asked, with genuine curiosity.

'I couldn't keep a gun in the flat in case you searched it again. I intended to get the Weintraub murder weapon earlier, but I had to wait until Ello left the flat.'

'Why get a gun at all if there was a bomb? You can't have known the bomb had been discovered – unless Fräulein von Hessert told you.'

'My task was to fire the pistol both at Hitler and the bomb – to detonate it.'

'There was a clock to detonate it.'

'Clocks don't always work. Hitler has been very lucky in the past.'

'I don't believe you. The plan you are outlining would mean your certain capture.'

'It was worth it. It ... would have been worth it.'

'Only someone not concerned about his family would act in the way you are describing. You know what could happen to them. Are you not concerned about your family?'

'I'm very concerned. But killing Hitler was more important than any other consideration.'

'Even your family?'

'Yes.'

'Glaser, I shall give you one minute to tell me the truth. If you do not, I shall be visiting your family. You are aware of the policy of *Sippenhaft*, I'm sure.'

Glaser was only too aware of *Sippenhaft* – the arrest and

punishment of the suspect's entire family. He went pale but said nothing.

There was a heavy silence. 'Very well,' Forster said eventually. 'On your own head be it.'

3

Brigadeführer Forster, resplendent in his new uniform, had Katya Bachhuber's home searched again. The front door was broken down, even though no resistance was offered. Bedding, covers, books, files, clothes and dirty washing were ripped apart, then thrown on the floor. The furniture and cushions were slashed with bayonets. Anything made of leather, as well as every piece of jewellery, and silver cutlery, was taken. The crockery was either taken or smashed. All documents were removed, even school reports. The radio was stolen. Purses, including the maids' purses, were ransacked for cash. Katya Bachuber was not, however, charged with any offence.

Forster and his men then went to the Glaser flat. Lotte, Kaspar and Magda were made to stand in the middle of the drawing room and watch. Forster turned all the lights on, then fetched the vacuum cleaner, plugged it in and left it running so that, as he put it, 'You'll have a nice high electricity bill.'

To the background sound of a roaring vacuum cleaner, Lotte's harmonium was smashed to pieces. All the paintings – known to be reproductions and therefore not saleable – were slashed. The family's personal possessions were destroyed, one by one, as was the children's school work. The wine was either guzzled during the search, from the bottle, or taken away. The Persian rug was rolled up by a trooper and taken as booty.

At the end of it, amid the wreck of the Glaser home, Forster read to Lotte and Kaspar the statements they had made when Glaser had slipped his followers, to go to Ludwigsburg.

'Lotte Glaser and Kaspar Glaser,' Forster said. 'You are hereby charged with non-cooperation with a Political Police investigation.'

Kaspar shot his mother a look of support. Both were silent. Magda was crying. Forster turned to her. 'Magda Glaser. You gave false information to the Political Police.' Forster meant the non-existent Pension Walther. 'You are hereby charged with obstructing an investigation, not merely non-cooperation.'

To laughter from the SS-troopers, Magda's sobs redoubled. Lotte put her arm round her. Kaspar wanted to comfort her too, but found no way.

'What will happen to my husband?' Lotte said, still with her arm around Magda.

'He will be put on trial.'

Lotte looked Forster in the eye. 'I would like to see him.'

'So would I,' Kaspar said.

Forster nodded. 'I'll make the necessary arrangements'

At a trial at a Special Court the same day, Lotte Glaser was sentenced to one month's detention at a former monastery at Breitenau, south of Kassel, newly converted by the Gestapo to a concentration camp for women. Her request to visit her husband before her sentence began was granted, as it was in the case of Kaspar.

But it went worse for the youth. His teasing had got under Forster's skin, as it was meant to. Because of his 'un-National Socialist mentality and behaviour', as the *Brigade-führer* put it in his report, the Special Court sentenced Kaspar to two years under punishment regime in Dachau.

Magda was charged and tried separately. In his report to

the judges, Forster implied that she may have been involved in the assassination attempt itself. He felt he had been made a fool of by a slip of a girl – and he did not like it. He could see Glaser's face, in his mind's eye, as he drew up the charges. Magda's term in Dachau was to begin with immediate effect. She was sentenced to five years.

4

Forster had performed excellently, thought Rudolf Hess, but there were still loose ends. Hess was the man for loose ends. He fussily made sure he was ready, pulling his uniform jacket straight, combing his hair. Then he told his secretary to send Ello von Hessert in.

As soon as the young woman entered and began to walk toward him, Hess flicked the intercom to the outer office to 'ON', jumped up and waved her to a chair.

'Thank you for coming, Fräulein von Hessert.' Hess sat down again, curling his leg twice round the leg of his chair.

'Not at all,' said Ello. She gave him a brief, though sweet, smile.

'Fräulein von Hessert ...'

'Yes?'

There was a long pause. 'Please understand, *gnädiges Fräulein*, I need to establish one or two facts. To make sure there have been no errors, or misunderstandings. Over certain events. May I put one or two routine questions to you?'

'Go ahead.'

'Fräulein von Hessert, cast your mind back, if you will, to the night of your dear mother's birthday party. An occasion I much enjoyed, by the way.'

'Oh, good-o! I was so hoping you had.'

'Yes. Earlier that evening, were you at Dr Glaser's flat, in Galeriestrasse?'

'Yes.'

'And … at seven o'clock that evening, from the flat, did you dial …' Hess consulted the papers in front of him, although he knew the number perfectly well. 'Did you dial 45385? And hold a conversation?'

Ello's mouth was dry. 'I think you know I did.'

Hess nodded. He unwound his leg from the chair. 'Yes, indeed. That is … um … the telephone number of the Führer's residence.' Hess paused. 'You told Frau Winter you had left something personal at the apartment.' Hess looked at the papers. 'You wanted to collect it, in the Führer's absence. What was that … that you wanted …?'

'I really can't remember.'

Hess nodded. 'Yes, I see. Frau Winter says …' He consulted his papers again. 'She says that you later told her there was nothing you wanted to collect, but you wished to spend some time alone in Fräulein Raubal's old room. Is that correct?'

'Yes.'

'Why?'

'I can't remember.'

'I see. The plans for the House of German Art were in the apartment at that time, were they not?'

Ello shut her eyes. 'I have no idea.'

'You had seen them earlier that day?'

'Yes.'

'Did you have a suitcase with you?'

'I believe I did.'

'Why?'

'It had my dress in it. I changed for the evening in Geli's room.'

'Why change there?'

Ello shrugged. There was silence for a minute.

'Moving on to more recent events, Fräulein von Hessert. Did you leave your place of honour at the laying of the foundation-stone of the House of German Art, to visit Dr Glaser?'

'Yes.'

'Why did you do that?'

'I wanted to see how he was.'

'Had he been unwell?'

'No.'

'Immediately after your visit, Dr Glaser slipped out by the back way to evade detection, collected a gun and attempted to assassinate the Führer, did he not?'

'Stop playing with me, Herr Hess. If you are going to arrest me, please get on with it.'

Hess stared at her for a second, then blinked rapidly. 'Fräulein von Hessert, you are applying, I believe, for posts as a psychologist in America? New York? Now that you have graduated.'

'How did you know that? Are you opening my letters?'

A voice boomed from behind her. 'No, I told him.'

Ello wheeled round in her chair. Her father, his face black with anger, stood in the doorway to Hess's outer office. Hess fussily waved past him, through the open door, to his secretary, telling her to turn the intercom off. Cajetan von Hessert covered the massive office in long strides, seized a chair and sat next to Hess, ostentatiously on the interrogator's side, not his daughter's.

'What's going on?' Ello asked him.

'I think it is *I* who should be asking *you* that question, missy!' The father spoke softly, but he was shaking with rage.

'Fräulein von Hessert …' Hess resumed.

Cajetan von Hessert held up his right hand. 'Ello, we expect your applications to New York to be successful,' he said. 'You will leave Germany tomorrow, with a large sum of money. You will not come back. You may write bread-and-butter letters to your mother, who, thank God, knows

371

nothing about any of this. It would break her heart. How could you do this to us?'

'I'm sorry,' Ello said. She licked her lips.

Hess spoke again. 'Fräulein von Hessert, you have had a certain amount of ... access to the Führer,' he said. 'This must at all costs remain confidential.' Hess glanced at Cajetan von Hessert, with an apologetic shrug, but went on. 'We have a network of agents in America, you see. And ...'

'Ello,' Cajetan von Hessert interrupted. 'If you breathe a word about the Führer in America, anything at all, Hess will have you killed. And I want you to know, it will be with my blessing. We have a long reach, my girl. Someone will be watching you, and you will not know who it is. You never met the Führer. Clear?'

Ello nodded. 'Clear.'

There was silence for a moment, father and daughter looking at each other. When Cajetan von Hessert spoke, his voice was breaking. 'You knew I would be on the platform, next to Hitler, didn't you?'

'Yes.'

There was another long silence, then Hess spoke. 'We have drawn up a document, outlining an agreement.' Hess pressed a button on the intercom. 'Frau Schrödel, please.'

Hess's secretary appeared with a piece of paper. She gave it to Ello, along with a pen.

The document was one paragraph long. Ello read it, put it on Hess's desk, signed it, and handed it to him. 'What about Rudi?' she asked her father.

'Rüdiger will be given another chance. Not that he deserves it. As soon as he recovers from his illness, he will resume his law training. He will become a useful National Socialist lawyer. You may write to him, too. But your letters will be read, so keep it bland. No telephone calls.'

Ello nodded. Frau Schrödel wordlessly handed her a travel-wallet. It contained ten thousand United States dollars. There was also a first-class train ticket to Bremer-haven, and a ticket for a first-class suite on the steamship *Europa*, where Paul Troost-designed luxury would carry her to New York.

Both tickets were one-way.

5

The cell door was flung wide open. A tall young man in a black lawyer's gown stood there, blinking behind thick spectacles. He motioned the guards to stay, and leave the door open – he was clearly not intending to be there long. Glaser recalled having seen him at Prielmayerstrasse, but could not put a name to the face.

'My name is Klein,' the tall lawyer supplied. 'I am your court-appointed defence lawyer. Do you have any questions?'

'How are my family?'

'I deal only with the matter before the court. Do you have any questions about that?'

'What is our line of defence?'

Klein's eyes widened, behind the thick glasses. 'We have none. You were caught with a gun in your hand, about to shoot our beloved Führer, Adolf Hitler, as the culmination of a wicked planned plot. You are a traitor to the Revolution, to the Third Reich and to the German people.'

'Thank you.'

'I suppose you could plead insanity. But the court would see through it.'

'And that is your idea of being a defence lawyer, is it?'

'Don't use that tone to me! As if your predicament were my fault. I will see you tomorrow, in court.'

Klein stalked out. As the door was locked behind him,

August Kunde was shaking with laughter, on his bunk. Glaser joined in.

At ten next morning, Glaser's hands were handcuffed in front of him, by Green Police guards. He was taken to the Ministry of Justice, in a police van, and led to Court One.

There, he sat on the accused bench, with the guards either side of him. His handcuffs were removed. The public benches filled with uniformed observers from various organisations of the Reich. The courtroom was full, though virtually silent. There was no sign of Forster.

Three judges in red robes and red biretta-style hats appeared from a side door, and sat at the desk, on the dais, at the front. One of them was carrying the papers from the case. They removed their hats. Then they stood again.

'*Heil Hitler!*' called out the judge in the middle, giving a fully extended Hitler salute.

The room stood and chorused '*Heil Hitler*' back again. Glaser was hauled to his feet by the guards: '*Heil Hitler.*'

The presiding judge, the one in the middle, was in his early forties, dark-haired, quite small, with an aquiline face. Glaser had never seen him before. 'The prisoner will approach the bench. Hearing of evidence,' he bawled out, in an unexpectedly high voice.

Glaser was brought between the two guards to face the presiding judge, looking up at him.

'You were caught with a gun, attempting to assassinate the Führer,' the Presiding Judge yelled down to him. 'This was a planned and premeditated crime based on your mad idea that the Führer was responsible for the death of his beloved niece.' The judge picked up the report Glaser had written about Geli's death, the report which had disappeared from the files. He waved it in the air. 'What have you got to say for yourself?'

Glaser said what he had prepared to say: 'Our country is

in the grip of a man with the moral compass of a toddler,'
he said. 'Germany is now his toy, and he will smash it
against the wall.'

'What mad raving is this?' screamed the judge. 'Do you
want to plead insanity, is that it? He continues to disgrace
the court he is supposed to serve, spewing out a stream of
traitorous claptrap!' The judge's scream grew even louder.
'Glaser, do you deny you conspired with a criminal to
commit murder? A criminal whose case you investigated,
and whose release from protective custody you fraudulently
obtained.'

'It wasn't fraudulent. He …'

'Is Kunde a criminal or not?' screamed the judge.

'No.'

'Does he have a criminal record?'

Glaser was silent.

'Are you hard of hearing? If he has a criminal record,
that's what I asked you.'

'Yes. He does.'

'Then he is a criminal. You fool! You dolt! You poltroon!
Kunde is also a parasite and a communist. What sort of a
lawyer is he, this Glaser?' The judge looked round the room
at the silent ranks of uniformed men. 'I'll tell you. This
Glaser is a lawyer who pisses on the law. Pisses on the law he
is supposed to uphold. If it were not for the vigilance of
those protecting the Führer, he would be a murderer now,
like his friend, Kunde.'

'I wish I was! I wish I had killed Hitler!'

This drew a roar from the seven or eight packed rows of
watchers.

'Shut your gob!' The judge screamed at Glaser, pointing
an accusing finger at him. 'You are hereby disbarred from
the profession you have disgraced. You are no longer a
lawyer. We proceed to sentencing. Defence!' The judge
shot a look at Klein, on the lawyers' bench, staring at

the floor. 'Any questions?'

Klein nodded 'no'.

The judge turned back to Glaser. 'You honourless lump!' he screamed. 'Miserable piece of shit! You have betrayed the trust placed in you by the Reich, in the person of the Führer.' He put the red hat back on. 'Sentenced to death. Anything to say?'

Glaser looked at him. 'Yes,' he said. 'I have. One day you will stand where I stand now. And may the souls of the coming dead forgive you.'

'Take him away!'

Glaser was led out and driven back to Stadelheim in the police van. There, he was taken to a small ante-room. A dread came over him.

'What's this?' he asked a guard. 'When is the sentence?'

'In half an hour's time.'

Glaser gasped. He retched, but stopped himself from vomiting. He sat heavily on a hard wooden chair. The guard left but quickly returned. 'Visitors,' he said.

'Visitors?'

Glaser was led out, to a bare, whitewashed room containing only a table and chairs. Seated at the table were Lotte and Kaspar. They stood as he came in. Glaser embraced Lotte. She buried her face in his shoulder. Then she disengaged, to let Kaspar hug his father. The youth was red in the face with the effort of not crying, but suddenly the dam burst. He broke his hug with Glaser, to wipe away his tears, furious with himself. Then he spoke, blurting out what was in his heart:

'I am so proud of you. I am proud to have you as my father. No man ever had a better.'

'I wish that were true,' Glaser muttered. 'Lotte …'

'I love you, Gerhard,' Lotte said, 'until I too leave this earth. They cannot take my soul, Gerhard. And they cannot take my love. And if my soul and my love is all I have left, then so be it.'

Glaser had tears in his eyes. 'Magda …?'

'She's … with Katya.'

'Tell Magda I sent my love.'

The guards gently but firmly led Glaser away. His pipe had been brought to the ante-room, along with his tobacco and matches. He packed and smoked a pipe. The prison chaplain entered. Glaser unprotestingly let him give blessing. The chaplain was still there when three men in black, with black top hats, came for him

They handcuffed him again, and led him outside, to an executioner's block in a small stone courtyard. He was lifted bodily, then lowered into position, lying with his neck on the block. A wooden yoke was lowered, fitting above his neck, stretching it. The executioner, with a sharpened axe, appeared behind him.

Glaser had planned, over the last pipe he smoked, to cry out 'Freedom lives' as his last words on earth. In the event, he tried to say 'I love you, Lotte, Kaspar, Magda.' But the first swing of the axe caught him at an angle, smashing his throat. He said only 'I love', before he choked to death in his own blood.

Because of the visit, he died believing his family were safe.

Afterword – November 1988

The Ceremony of Remembrance, on the fiftieth anniversary of the destruction of the town's synagogue, was led by the Mayor of Ludwigsburg, Hans-Jochen Henke. Lotte Glaser was a guest of honour. As she sat watching the ceremony, she conjured images of her long-dead family. Kaspar's face floated in front of her eyes.

As she had always feared, Kaspar's defiance had cost him dear. Six months into his sentence at Dachau, the guards had been making him hop from foot to foot, shouting 'I am the shit-head Glaser, and my father was a traitor.' The youth had stood it for nearly an hour, then smashed one of them in the face. They whipped and beat him to death, over five days, rubbing salt in his wounds overnight.

Now in her early nineties, and frail, Lotte was muffled against the November cold. She was sitting in the front row of a temporary stand, erected in what was now called Synagogenplatz. Beno Elsas, old Max Elsas's son, was next to her. Beno had marched into Ludwigsburg as part of the American army freeing the town at the end of World War II. He was ferociously attentive to Lotte's needs – bristling combatively if anyone else tried to take care of her.

Lotte Glaser watched through rheumy eyes as the handsome figure of Herr Henke placed flowers on the memorial stone on the site of the destroyed synagogue, and bowed his head. There was a moment's silence, broken only by Beno fiercely whispering in Lotte's ear every detail of the wide-ranging Programme of Restitution, and the links established between the town's teacher training college and equivalent institutions in Israel. To Beno, and to Lotte, every word was a hammer blow at the Nazis, and their twelve-year Reich.

There followed a talk on the history of Ludwigsburg's Jews by Dr Albert Sting. Lotte, with Beno's arm tightly round her, began to cry when Max Elsas and Dr Pintus were remembered. She heard Gerhard's voice again, telling her about them. Old Max had been murdered in Theresienstadt. Dr Pintus had died as he approached Dachau, either from a heart attack or suicide. Dr Sting was announcing that streets in Ludwigsburg were to be named in honour of Max Elsas and Walter Pintus.

After the ceremony, there was a civic lunch at Ludwigsburg's *Ratskeller*, at which Lotte ate Gerhard's favourite Swabian specialties and drank a small glass of the Goldberg wine he loved so much.

In the afternoon, she was again a guest of honour, this time at Ludwigsburg's famous Centre for the Investigation of Nazi War Crimes. Beno told her that the Centre, on the main Schorndorferstrasse, had once been a women's prison, which the Nazis had built using smashed gravestones from the Jewish cemetery.

Lotte met many of the lawyers involved in gathering evidence of Nazi crimes, which they then handed to the prosecuting authorities. She marvelled at how young they all seemed, and how many of them were not from Swabia. One lawyer, a bright-as-a-button young lady, smilingly told her that the incomers liked Ludwigsburg, as a place to live, and found the work worthwhile and fulfilling.

Lotte said she was pleased. 'What's your name?' she asked.

'Weisshaupt, Frau Glaser. Magda Weisshaupt. I'm originally from North Rhine-Westphalia.'

'Magda! That was my daughter's name.'

Lotte told her about her Magda: Even in Dachau, she refused to acknowledge her brother – a fellow prisoner. After he was killed, she retreated into a secret place in her mind. Lotte visited her in a sanatorium after the war, every week for twenty years, until she died. But Magda never knew who she was.

'Oh, that's so sad,' Magda Weisshaupt said.

'Yes,' said Lotte. 'But I'm glad I told you.'

'I'm glad, too. We must face sad events. And overcome them.'

'Yes.'

Lotte unveiled a plaque at the opening of the Gerhard Glaser Room, at the Centre. This room was to be the base of a small team of lawyers, led by Magda Weisshaupt. They would find and document German acts of opposition and resistance during the Nazi period – so these brave men and women were not forgotten.

Lotte had been asked to make a speech, after she unveiled the plaque bearing Gerhard's name. She told the assembled lawyers that Gerhard would have been among their number, working here, had he lived.

'My husband,' she said, 'lived for the law, and died fighting criminals. He would have been delighted to see the law triumphant, here today. He would have been happy to see West Germany become what it has become – a country to be proud of, a state under the law. He would love to have seen the return of at least a few of the Jews to his beloved Ludwigsburg. On his behalf, I hope that one day as many Jews will return as once lived here. That will be, if I may take the Nazi phrase from them, the Final Solution. Our Final Solution. Then we will have won. And then my Gerhard can rest in peace.'

On her way out, escorted by Magda Weisshaupt, and on the arm of Beno Elsas, she noticed a small room, full of paintings, and asked to be shown it. The paintings were by Fritz Ketz, an artist who had made Ludwigsburg his home.

Lotte stopped in front of Ketz's drawing of Ahaseurus – the Eternal Jew. It showed an old rabbinical figure below Christ on the cross. He was being tormented, beaten and abused by the crowd. Ketz's compassion for the Jew shone through the brutal drawing.

'Gerhard would have liked that,' Lotte said.

The last painting she saw, before she left, was Ketz's *Spring Landscape Near Erlenhof.* In a simple composition, its Expressionist treatment showed the yellow of spring rising, as wind bent the trees.

'He would have liked that, too,' she said. 'What happened to the artist, Fritz Ketz? Did he survive the Nazis?'

'He had to destroy a lot of his paintings,' said Magda. 'At one point, he kept all his drawings packed in a bag, in case he had to flee. But, yes, he survived.'

'I'm glad,' Lotte said. 'I'm glad he survived.'

Author's Note

Some chapters of this novel originally appeared in *The Crooked Cross* (Quaestor 2000), sometimes in a different form and in a different order.

Because this is a work of fiction, the demands of drama have sometimes taken precedence over the reflection of real events.

The following characters are fictional: Katya Bachuber, Anton Elsperger, Christa Forster, Erwin Forster, Helga Forster, Lotte Glaser, Kaspar Glaser, Magda Glaser, Old Frau Glaser, Cajetan von Hessert, Carola von Hessert, Ello von Hessert, Rüdiger von Hessert, Herr Klein, Sepp Kunde, August Kunde, Mrs Luckacsckova, Martina (typist), Emmi Raschke, Frau Sauer, Herr Vollmer, Ascher Weintraub, Magda Weisshaupt, Herr and Frau Weitig.

All other characters, and people named, have their origin in non-fiction sources, although in some cases everything about them, including their first names, has been invented. Among the main characters, this applies to Gerhard Glaser and Karl-Heinz Forster.

Thanks to Katherine Taylor, for research help in Munich. My wife accompanied me on research trips, where she noticed more than I did, and made several helpful suggestions. This book is dedicated to her, and so is the author.

Michael Dean, January 2012

BC	6/13
BP	6/14